The Crimson Inkwell

D1398531

The Crimson Inkwell

A Gaslamps Trinkets Novel

By Kenneth A. Baldwin

EBURNEAN
BOOKS

For Desmond. May you find the moondust trail.

Chapter One

Et tu, Brutus

Critics are evil monsters. On a closer read of Dante, it isn't difficult to find a remote, special place for their breed among the lower levels of hell. They're somewhere right between fraudsters and heretics. It's worth noting that Eve, when taking a bite of that forbidden fruit, did so only at the annoying, incessant insistence of a critic.

Thus, I feel my disappointment justified when, on reaching the bright red door of Langley's Miscellany for my morning debrief with Byron Livingston, I happened across one of these vile creatures. On the outside steps, he tipped his hat to me as if to say "good-day." But if he considered the day good, he must have already, at nine in the morning, gutted at least one poor journalist. And, seeing as Langley's was the publication for which I wrote, I was nearly certain that journalist was me.

I shuffled through the door and shivered. Inside, I could feel the autumn chill that possesses those buildings too frugal to burn coal in September. Sure enough, Byron, my betrothed and editor, had not yet taken off his coat. He stood near his office, staring pensively at his prized skylark, which rested quietly on a wooden perch in its wire cage. I could tell he was troubled. The wrinkles in his eyebrows, already deep set for a man in his forties, still held their crease from the morning's vexations. No doubt, he had been stewing over whatever Brutus, the loving name I'd lended to our most regular critic, had to say.

Byron rarely showed me his troubles. In fact, I treasured the moments when I happened upon him like this. It reminded me that he, like me, might not always be the picture of polite happiness. The moment vanished as he noticed me enter, and he gave me a broad smile under his large mustache.

"Luella, good morning," he said, standing to grasp my hands. The coat fell to the floor, revealing a herringbone waistcoat. "You look radiant. I love the way you've done your hair."

That had to be a lie. I looked perturbed, and my hair, somewhere between dark brown and red, had hardly seen a brush that morning.

"What did Brutus want?" I asked.

"Brutus? I haven't the foggiest—oh right! I forgot your pet name for our friend—"

"He's not our friend," I cut in. "Is he?"

"Why not sit down for some tea? Mrs. Barker just brought over some biscuits from down the street," he said, motioning to the cramped editing table. The two same tired teacups sat there waiting to go through their same old routine. In fact, everything about the office looked about the same as it always did. The small, spent fireplace sat in a corner across from Byron's small office, which was nearly tucked out of sight. Old, weathered, wood wainscoting came waist-high on the walls. The windows, though dirty, let in an abundant portion of the morning light. Pages were strewn on chairs, tables, windowsills and the floor, which didn't enjoy nearly enough rug.

"Why must you always draw out bad news?" I asked.

"I don't intend to. I just believe the world is far more pleasant when viewed over the rim of a teacup," he replied, pulling out a chair with an encouraging grin. The scraping of the chair woke up the bird, which eased into a few attempts of its practiced song.

I took off my gloves and sat down, pursing my lips as he slowly poured the tea. Byron Livingston. The man who took a chance on me, a twenty-five-year-old woman. When I met him, he was full of life and energy, even for a man past forty. He had a passion for journalism and economy and, by the way he had talked, would soon become the very wealthy owner of a popular weekly magazine. However, the intricacies of the publishing business weren't as favorable as he anticipated, and now he seemed to grow older every day as he toiled to publish his weekly. *Langley's Miscellany*. He made out alright, but I wasn't expecting an estate of our own after the wedding. In fact, I wouldn't be surprised if we moved into the rundown flat above the publishing house where he lived now. "Until business improves, as it surely will!" he always tittered on whenever I expressed concern about his finances and their future.

Until business improved, indeed. Brutus had our jugular in a vice grip.

"Well?" I spat out, breaking the tea-time tranquility.

"Well, how is your sister?" he asked, taking a sip.

"She has a bit of a cough. Who doesn't? It's midway through autumn."

"The poor dear. What a lovely blouse you're wearing. Is that the one I bought for you?"

It wasn't, and I hardly looked any different than I did any other day. I wasn't big on fashion. I liked my clothes to be attractive but practical. My sister on, the other hand, made herself presentable even when on her sickbed.

"Of course. It goes so well with my grey vest and skirt. Now will you tell me what Brutus said or not?"

He stiffly replaced his teacup. "Well, if it's all business then. Mr. Blakely," I winced as he used my pseudonym, "you're right. It wasn't a friendly call."

"How bad?"

"It wasn't all bad. In fact, he didn't hate it. What was the word he used? He said he was... indifferent."

The word knocked the wind right out of me. "Indifferent?"

"Neither here nor there," Byron said. "Not good and not bad."

"You said it wasn't bad," I stammered. "Indifferent is the worst type of bad. All our hard work might as well just be letters and words printed on a paper napkin. Neither here nor there? That someone might pass it in the street and walk on, or worse! That someone might actually take the time to read my piece but then go on and never think of it again?"

"You're getting yourself riled up, my dear," he said. "Have a biscuit."

I did not want a biscuit, but I took one.

"Byron, do you agree with him?"

He set down the biscuits and stood up. He leaned against the window and lit his pipe, taking a deep drag on it. The smell of the tobacco reminded me of my father. My father had sacrificed much so that I might be educated. The first time I published an article, I took the printed edition to Papa's sickbed. I helped him read it, and when we finished, tears streamed on his cheeks into his whiskers. I'd only seen my father cry once. He died a week later.

"I'm so very fond of you," Byron started. "I continually try to check this sentiment so that it doesn't seep into our relationship as author and editor."

"And you know I appreciate that," I said.

"Sometimes I fear that my, well, my feelings for you sway my objectivity. But, I'll be damned if the man that came in here this morning was right. You are a fantastic writer. If there is fault, it must be found elsewhere. I am to blame."

Inside of me, I felt Byron was speaking absolute nonsense, but I'm not one to stop a man from spouting out his own crude type of love poem. Even if it is ill-timed.

"You report on the stories I suggest," he continued. "And, since *Langley's Miscellany* is a smaller publication, we don't get the same tips and leads as the bigger papers. I'm ashamed to say it. I'm failing you, my darling."

Personally, I find this type of humility not a little grating and disingenuous. Perhaps Byron spoke the words honestly, but I suspected their sincerity sprung, not from their veracity, but his desire to spare me pain. I thought this in spite of his brazen disclaimer to the contrary. Seized by this conclusion, I found myself at an emotional crossroads, unsure of whether to take strength from his devotion or languish in his confirmation of Brutus' critique.

Men are never so unmanly as when swept up by an insecure infatuation.

All the same, I know not to bite an outstretched hand. Langley's had given me a rare opportunity to test my mettle. He was not the first editor to whom I had submitted my work. I had applied at a dozen other publications before, and they, pen name or no, were convinced that, as a woman from a station like mine, I didn't have the snuff to compete in the pressing world of journalism and authorship. Byron saved me.

We met at a dinner party arranged by my sister. I forget the precise occasion, but Byron could tell you all the details. To this day, I'm thankful we did not start our relationship on business footing.

In fact, it wasn't until many meetings and a proposal later that I learned he managed Langley's, and he only told me after learning that I was an aspiring writer. Before that, our relationship had been all about "Do you know so and so?" and "Have you ever read such and such?" But, after revealing his true identity as editor and publisher, he said he was always looking for good stories and would be happy to give me an audition. After all, sooner or later, our finances would conjoin, and what would be better than to have a dual threat from the hearth? Naturally, he had reminded me, this wouldn't relieve me of my wifely chores and duties, especially once children came about, but I still counted it a measure ahead of any other. Not just to be led by a husband but yoked to his enterprise, it felt modern, progressive, and exciting.

But as time went on, the illustrious nature of our arrangement had faded. When I first began writing for him, I naively eyed our city's top literary prize, The Golden Inkwell, reserved each year for Dawnhurst-on-Severn's most esteemed columnist. With a backer like Byron Livingston, I would at least qualify for consideration of the award. I had a platform. I just had to write more prolific stories than any of my colleagues or competitors. There could be no sweeter realization of my father's hopes for my future than having the Golden Inkwell on my mantle.

Once, I thought I had come close. Soon after I started writing for Langley's, one of my stories titled "*At Home with a Woman*" caused quite the stir in our little city. The story detailed the benefits of aspiring to the type of gentlemanly conduct, be it in business, social or domestic responsibilities, that inspires women to affection. The story was widely read, and since I published it under the pen name Travis Blakely, even men even took it seriously.

A reporter who chronicled literary achievement in Dawnhurst came to our door one workday and asked to speak with Mr. Blakely. I was tempted to give away my identity in exchange for the interview, but Byron scooped up the reporter and claimed no small amount of credit for my work. As he had explained where the idea came from and its lasting importance for our society, I felt the bitter dredges of resentment in my throat.

Afterward, he had explained it was important for my career that I retain my pen name for now, and I couldn't argue with his reasoning, but I couldn't help but notice the arrogant gleam in his eye, the residual high of being interviewed by a reporter and anticipation of public praise.

Much to our mutual disappointment, I had never been able to replicate that initial success, and Travis Blakely lost whatever momentum he had toward the Golden Inkwell.

Now, with my professional prestige neatly departmentalized in Byron's mind, when my stories performed poorly, I failed doubly, once as a writer and again as a wife-to-be. I recognized in Byron's management style no progressive, pro-feminist temperament but a fear that I might decide to break our engagement should he now choose to cut me off.

Did he fear for nothing? The question scared me. Perhaps because it held a mirror up to my criticism of him. I was afraid to think about what I might do if he decided to let me go. I wanted to believe that I could happily live out my life as Mrs. Livingston, giving my opinion here or there on the publication when asked. Another part of me whispered that my gift of literacy was too dear to me, too central to my identity, just to spectate the print business as an onlooker. So, we had melted into a cocktail of love and business, unable to distinguish one relationship from another, ambition from security, or my love of writing from my love for the man who so clearly would give the world for me.

"What do you think about that?" Byron asked, puffing thoughtfully on his pipe. I snapped to attention.

"I'm sorry. I'm afraid I must have missed your last point."

"Are you well, my dear?" he asked, the skylark singing merrily and energetically by now.

"Fine, just lost in my head for a moment."

"I was asking whether or not you think we could afford to bring on a lad to dig up leads for us. *Harold's Weekly* has at least three or four on staff for that. It's no wonder we're behind on the big stories when the editor and publisher are also trying to sniff out where the action is. You know me. I'm independent to a fault, but I think I'm beginning to understand that I have only so many hands."

"Nonsense," I responded. "You're stretched thin as it is. How could we afford to hire on a lad if you won't even put the fire on?"

"I'm terribly sorry! Look at me forgetting!" he said through a large puff of smoke and starting toward the fireplace.

"I don't bring it up for my sake. I can't imagine our competitors sit there editing stories without taking their coats off. If there is more work to be done, allow me to do it."

"Oh, no! Luella, please. I can manage to hire a lad. It's no trouble."

"Neither for me," I quipped, but I could tell by the way he left his mouth slightly agape that there was something about my proposal that made him feel a little uneasy. "Don't you think I can do the job?"

"It's just—well, I'm not sure if it's a woman's place. To find these stories, you might find yourself in some rough areas of town."

"Excellent. Then they will never see me coming," I said, rising before he could protest again. I gathered my gloves and thanked him for the tea and biscuits, but he crossed from the hearth and barred my way.

"Luella, I won't allow it. You're not to go sniffing out any leads. Do you understand? I forbid it. What if something happened to you?"

I chewed on my lip. What did he expect me to do? If I needed leads and he couldn't spare the time or money to get them, then I could only see one way forward.

"Promise me," he insisted.

I fingered the wire cage and listened to the bird sing sweetly inside of it.

"Are you asking me as my editor or my fiancé?" I asked.

"Both," he replied without a moment's hesitation.

I sighed but nodded dutifully.

"Please don't worry too much about the critics," he said, taking my hand firmly in his. "I'm certain we will still sell plenty of copies. Our savings will be on schedule for our pending marriage, my dear. This I promise. I think that most people will truly be interested in your piece on proper street etiquette for rainy days."

His summary of my most recent article made me blush a deep fuchsia. I was grateful he had already bent to kiss my hand. I walked away from the shop bitterly aware that Brutus was doing us a favor by even reading me at all.

Chapter Two

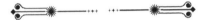

The Dawnhurst Police

When I got home, I found my sister lying on her bed, feigning illness. We had a humble flat that felt warm and spacious when she was in a good mood and like a miserable dump when she was in a humor such as this. She was prostrated across the old mattress, a hand to her head, but fully dressed as though to go out walking. I suspected her illness had more to do with a certain Jacob Rigby than with the fever, but to suggest such was blasphemy.

She was six years my younger, and I adored her. The tendrils that threatened old maidenhood were just starting to tighten their grip on her. She had just passed through the uncomfortable stages of teenage vanity and human mortality. One moment, she believed herself to be the catch of all London, let alone Dawnhurst. The next, she was convinced no one would ever marry her.

I feared the latter, though I wasn't without hope. After all, she was blessed with the family beauty. Where I struggled to tame my hair into a messy bun or remember whether a crinoline was on its way in or out of fashion, she could have lectured at length on the subject. She didn't profess vain knowledge either. One of my father's parting gifts to her was a dress he spent way too much money on that she didn't yet fit into. It hung in her bedroom. I believed myself capable of saying, objectively, Anna was beautiful.

I had heard rumors, though, that some men found her boisterous and unseemly. Though she was now twenty, one might be convinced she was still sixteen after talking with her at a party, and though many men might turn a blind eye in exchange for a pretty face, Anna sought out courtiers less shallow than that.

She had settled on Jacob Rigby, a gentleman of eighteen years, apprenticed to his father as a barrister. He was a respectable man, though a less respectable match. The difference in their ages might not matter in twenty years, but now it hinted at scandal. Fortunately, her social immaturity saved her from disclosing that she was his senior to all but those who asked directly. It hardly seemed fair for her. After all, Byron was much older than I was, but society didn't seem to care if it went the other way.

Still, things were promising between the two of them. But whether it was the disparity in their ages or her rumored immaturity, something about the way Jacob treated my sister gave off a fickle impression.

Perhaps this explained her unapologetic flop on our bed. I gave her some water and helped her change into a nightgown, while biting back comments about it not being called a mid-morning gown. I loved her dearly, my sister, but could not fathom why she bothered getting dressed to go out if she was just going to lament in bed.

"You don't understand fashion and beauty like I do," she said to me, her voice heavy with drama. "Feeling beauty on the outside is enough to change how you feel on the inside."

"I see it's worked marvelously in your case," I replied.

"Oh, you're right! I've wasted the entire morning!"

She was pretending to be asleep by the time I left.

As engrossing as it was, I couldn't spare much more time fretting over my sister. We had agreed that her interests were best served trying to find a husband, and the burden of the daily bills would be left to me. I couldn't imagine Anna lasting long working in a factory or hawking wares on the street. She was no good at cooking or mending, and she often lost her train of thought in daydreaming. One day long ago, as I tried to share my passion for the classics with her, she threw up her hands and exclaimed she had no interest in writing or reading. She was literate—I made sure of that— but she could not stand reading as a pastime or even to improve her education.

You might say she was born to be a wife. If I were my sister, I don't know how I'd survive. Some children were a solid mix of their two parents. The rest of us take after one or the other. She was my mother. I was my father.

We had a paltry inheritance left to us by our hard-working father. We tried to stretch it out as thin as cheesecloth, but in the end, without getting married myself, I knew I'd be responsible for Anna. I worked odd jobs where I could, once as a delivery girl, once as a factory girl, once in a kitchen. I even had a stroke of luck working as a governess for a wealthier family that lived near the river. It was a wonderful job, except that the child was a spoiled demon. I was let go promptly when the mistress of the house discovered I was the daughter of a factory worker. Something about impropriety and her child learning improper morals.

Then I met Byron, and he actually gave my writing a shot. My first wage at Langley's felt like fresh water. We weren't starving by any stretch, but it was a signal of different times. Ironic. When I finally found a job writing, I also finally found a man.

I left our humble home and stewed over possible solutions to speed along Anna's not-so-scandalous affair with Jacob until I was well on my way to the old precinct, located on the very edge of my promise to my editor.

If Byron wanted better leads and better stories, why not start where the trouble ends? The Dawnhurst Police Force.

I had strong memories of the station. My father had occasionally run with a troublesome lot. Before he turned ill, he would often come down to talk friends out of arrests for public drunkenness and other such unforgivable crimes. There was one stodgy police lieutenant, by now made sergeant, who might remember me as a girl. That became less likely each passing year.

I had promised Byron I wouldn't go in search of leads. He was worried about me heading into seedy areas of Dawnhurst. But, what harm was there in a woman going to visit an old family friend at the local police station in the mid-morning? And if a story came out of it, so be it.

I walked through the town. We were undeniably into autumn now.

The cobblestone streets were littered with dead or dying leaves from the trees that lined the walks. The station was just on the west side of the river, not a far walk from Langley's, actually. The city likely could have used its presence more in the east, but the wealthy wanted to feel secure, and after all, they paid the greater part of the taxes. So they said.

I knew the city well, now having lived on both sides of the river. In fact, the boundaries of the city were the boundaries of my life. I had never traveled beyond them. My everyday life was wrapped up inside of it, and I liked it that way. Familiar monuments called to me from all corners. A large clock tower stood tall to the north—it hadn't rung in many years, but it still felt like a herald. On the southeast strip, close to the river was the church in which my parents married. I hadn't been there in years. In fact, my last time there had been around when the tower stopped chiming. My parents were buried in the attached graveyard.

But, what made Dawnhurst exciting to me was that, everywhere you went, there were peddlers or newsstands hawking the city's most recent publications in a great contest over pocket change and the Golden Inkwell. You could often find stray papers, discarded a day or week before, lining the gutters. The city hadn't always been like this. When I was a girl, I don't remember so many people reading, but something in the last twenty years had set the city on fire with journalism and literature.

I walked into the police station, past its blue, brightly painted, and sturdy front door. Inside, the hard-working daylight coming through the barred front and back windows of the building mingled with illumination from the occasional, gas lamp on the wall or desks in the darker areas of the station. A stringy looking fellow with bright red hair sat at the front counter. Behind him, I could see the commotion of a city police station. If I closed my eyes, it sounded almost like a buzzing beehive. Rows of desks sat in haphazard lines toward the back of the large room. Officers bustled in and out, brandishing batons and donning their hats while roughly barking familiar jabs at their compatriots on the way out the door. I received not a few sidelong glances. Some made me feel violated, others belittled, all of them out of place.

The red-haired fellow was hard at work on an impossibly large stack of papers and didn't seem to notice any of the commotion around him.

"Excuse me," I said, after clearing my throat.

"Who's missing?" The clerk didn't look up.

"I beg your pardon?"

"Missing persons will file with Ms. Turner down the hall."

"I'm not here to report a missing person," I replied. This was enough to give the clerk at least a moment's pause. He glanced his terrier of a face up at me and squinted one eye in the lamplight.

"Has your husband beat you?"

"I'm not married. I'm looking for Sergeant George Cooper."

"Sarge, you've got a visitor!" he bellowed down the hallway behind him before turning back to me. "Right down the hallway, Miss. He'll be happy to have a visitor that isn't a felon. I guess, assuming you're not here to turn yourself in... You aren't uh, you know, soliciting wares and suddenly discovered religion if you catch my meaning?"

This I did not grace with a verbal response. Instead, I leveled my eyes at him the way I used to as governess of an impish child, took off my gloves menacingly, and started down the hall.

"Please have a seat," said whom I presumed to be the Ms. Turner the clerk had mentioned. She wore a tweed skirt and vest, and her hair was done up into what was once a bun. She too was busy in paperwork, pounding away furiously at a typewriter. I brushed off a filthy chair and waited. I watched Ms. Turner for some time, wondering what pathway may have brought her to this desk. She appeared older than me. It's difficult to guess the age of women around the middle of their lives, but the gentle lines around her eyes hinted to me that she was now closer to forty than thirty. I noticed no wedding ring.

I felt an almost immediate kinship to Ms. Turner. It wasn't a large stretch to imagine that I was looking at myself in ten years, pounding away at a typewriter, perhaps trying to publish works of my own in my spare time outside of my professional duties.

I have Byron now. I had to remind myself about my fiancé so often. How silly. Even when I was here on his bidding, for his publication no less.

"I wasn't drinking on the job, sir!" I heard a man's raised voice through the sergeant's door.

Ms. Turner slowly looked up at me. "They all say that."

The door swung wide open, and I was struck by what I could only assume was the model for a police force figurine. The man had an acutely trim waistline that stretched up into a broad chest and shoulders. His hair was combed impeccably, as if each strand dared not stray from its assigned position. His eyes, alert and lively, were peculiarly warm for being steely grey. His brow furrowed, and his neatly trimmed policeman's mustache curved downward into a disconcerting frown.

He swept through the office door and stood erect, as though he was at a self-called attention. Behind him, the large Sergeant George Cooper, a man whom I could only describe as a younger, meaner looking Father Christmas, filled the doorway.

"I don't want outlandish stories, Lieutenant. I want arrests. I want brigands behind bars. I want young do-it-alls like you to stop trying to turn every little case into the next apocalypse," Sergeant Cooper stammered. He was only mostly red in the face.

The young lieutenant stood and, though he looked thoroughly unamused, took the tongue lashing admirably.

"You've got a visitor," butted in Ms. Turner. Sergeant Cooper looked at me, and his expression instantly melted into a rehearsed sympathy.

"Ma'am, my deepest apologies," he said, putting his hand on his heart. "Do you have a missing person to report?"

"No," I stuttered. "I'm here… do you get a lot of missing persons?"

"Most of the women we see in here are reporting a missing husband or, regrettably, a missing child," he replied.

"I'm sorry to hear that. But, and, well, I'm not sure how to put this exactly. I'm here from *Langley's Miscellany*, and I—"

Before I could finish my sentence, the warm expression on Sergeant Cooper's face melted away.

"You're a reporter. Thank you, Miss, but the door's over there." He turned and retreated back into his office. I stuck my foot in the door, which was more painful than I thought it might be.

"I don't want to be a bother. I'm just curious about the latest. I don't mean to fabricate anything or inflate your efforts. I just—"

"You just want to be first to know about the dreadful muck the police force deals with each day."

"Well, yes," I replied.

"Like I said, Miss, the door is over there. I have a lot to do." He put on a pair of spectacles and sat down at his desk. I felt a burn creep up my cheeks. It was one thing to be denied, another to be rejected right in front of a woman I had suddenly come to admire and a deeply handsome police lieutenant. The propriety!

"Please, you knew my father," I said. He looked up at me over his spectacles. They were comically small for his large face. "Gerald

Winthrop."

"Jerry Winthrop?" the sergeant said with a laugh. "Devils blind me. You were the scrap of a thing always hiding in the corner, thinking we couldn't see you."

I nodded. He barked out a triumphant laugh.

"Your father was a hell of a man! Always sticking his nose in places it didn't belong. Any mate of his in trouble, he'd be here before a spit trying to talk their way out it." He stared into the air as if he could see my father in the office presently. "How is Jerry doing? I got into more arguments with him. He could take a yelling and deal it out in turn. If only my lieutenants had half the backbone. We exchanged words like lads in a fistfight.

"Well, I hope you got the last word in then," I said. His countenance dropped sharply.

"You don't mean—how'd it happen?"

"Fever. Or something like that. I never did get a straight answer from the doctors." I hated doctors. A fair majority of them might as well be bunkmates with critics.

"Doctors are thieves," the sergeant said.

"I'm very sorry for your loss, Miss," said a clear voice behind me. They were the first words the lieutenant said to me. The purity in his voice took me off guard. After losing my father, I'd heard "I'm sorry for your loss" time and time again. In nearly every case, it was mere etiquette, obligation, and passing fancy, as though someone might check a box of a tidy little list somewhere by saying the appropriate thing. This man, whom I barely knew, sounded arrestingly sincere.

I turned toward him, and he bowed slightly. Behind him, Ms. Turner slid into focus with two very inquisitive eyebrows.

"Yes, well, this is Lieutenant Edward Thomas. He's our resident... bleeding heart and imaginist," Sergeant Cooper said. Edward extended a hand.

"It's a pleasure to make your acquaintance," I said. His eyes were smothering. I couldn't seem to escape them. He had no shyness about looking a stranger squarely in the face, that's for certain.

"The pleasure is mine," I managed. "Imaginist?" I inquired of the sergeant.

"No doubt in it. In fact, Lieutenant Thomas may be exactly what you're looking for," he said with a coy smile.

"I'm engaged," I spit out.

Sergeant Cooper erupted into an ungraciously loud belly laugh. I noticed Ms. Turner turn her face down to suppress a giggle as well. Edward flushed.

"I'm sure you are. I meant for the stories you've been looking for," Cooper said. I immediately felt feverish as itchy perspiration appeared on the small of my back. Luella Winthrop. Gift with words, I have.

"He has a story for me then?" I muttered, eager to move on.

"Aye. Lieutenant Thomas here claims to have seen a ghost!"

Chapter Three

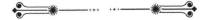

Domestic Comforts

My walk home was caught up in a furious brainstorm, interrupted only by a quick stop by a seamstress to pick up a scarf I had ordered for Anna. We had gone walking recently, and she had gawked over it, insisting that it brought out the color of her eyes. I loved surprising Anna with little gifts. She rewarded me with the best reactions whenever I gave her a present, but I was so distracted I almost purchased the scarf in black! That black would not bring out the color of her eyes; even I could understand that.

By the time I arrived on Harbor Street where we lived, I could hardly have recounted how I got there or how many times cabs or hansoms had barked at me to get out of the road. I was too busy going over the details of Lieutenant Thomas' story. Sergeant Cooper was right—he may have been exactly what I was looking for.

In that professional sort of way.

I wrangled Anna's parcel under my arm and clutched my leather-bound notebook, checking that it had not sprouted wings and escaped my grip. It felt almost like lightning, knowing that my scribbled notes might be the genesis of my first real, attention-grabbing story since "*At Home with a Woman*."

A real police officer convinced he had seen a supernatural phenomenon! And, he was so convinced he was willing to risk his name on it, even when challenged by his superiors. He and Sergeant Cooper had requested that the name Edward Thomas not be included in any story, but there were plenty of ways around that. *The Handsome Constable* might not do the trick, as it would at once appear too womanly and likely tip off readers that a woman, or perhaps a man of a different nature, stood behind my pen name, Travis Blakely. The effect would be the same in either scenario: lost readers. No, this story wanted something objective but vague, something concrete enough to give readers the confidence he was a real member of the force, yet ambiguous enough so as not to betray his identity.

Maybe it was the gas street lights just now heralding in the first of night, but it suddenly seemed that writing was just an exercise in shadow dancing.

Steely Grey, perhaps, or *Officer Steely Grey*?

I could almost see Brutus's face now. He'd pucker his chubby little face and squint hard at the writing, scrutinizing it over and over again, but even he would have to admit the story was compelling. It was hard not to run away with my imagination, seeing leafy boughs where only a bit of seed lay. Still, this could be my chance to rise above the din of Dawnhurst's obsession with the printed page. Every week, it seemed another weekly or monthly magazine was circulating the city. The readers were voracious, especially on the west side of the river. At dinner parties or out on the town, if you hadn't the most recent such and such from Mr. So and So, you had just about nothing to talk about with anyone. To be a Mr. So and So! It could be a ticket to the top. The possibilities made me delirious.

I was so distracted, I practically ran into the carriage parked out front of my flat. I laughed at myself for a moment, happy to be so engaged in a story that reality had slipped from me. Work of this kind brings such euphoria, such a departure from the elements, gravity even.

But now, reconditioning myself to notice my surroundings, something felt wrong. Through our small kitchen window, I noticed the silhouette of a man. Explanations have a funny way of arriving at once and being quarrelsome houseguests.

A man in Anna's room? Terror seized me. What if it were a burglar or a brigand? Greater terror still if that gentleman caller, Jacob Rigby, had grown so bold!

I bounded up the steps, flung open the door, and burst down the dark hallway. I was practically thrusting my key into the lock when I discovered the door stood ajar. I pushed it open, ready to fight someone or yell or both.

In the kitchen sat Mrs. Crow, the old widow who lived across the hall, knitting a tangled mess of a scarf with shaky hands. Anna sat rigidly next to her, a shawl loosely draped over the nightgown I had left her in that morning.

"Luella," Mrs. Crow said. "Not to worry, I've been here making sure there's no funny business going about."

Before I could press her further, I noticed our landlord, Charles Stringham, sipping a cup of a tea from our mother's china. Tenants are never happy to see their landlord, but I will confess this was less dreadful than discovering my baby sister in the depths of passion or being stabbed to death. Then again, by the feel of the room, a stabbing might be forthcoming.

Charles Stringham was a remarkably ordinary looking man. At forty-five, he was near Byron's age, with an ever-growing friar bald patch and a receding hairline, but otherwise had nothing to recommend himself as special. He was not quite striking, nor quite ugly. He was not assertive and confident, nor shy and reclusive. He was just the type of man that made you feel like everything he said could have been said slightly faster, so you hadn't wasted quite as much time.

"Luella," Mr. Stringham said, performing a little half-stand and bow. "Always a pleasure."

"Mr. Stringham, to what do we owe this surprise evening visit?" I asked, setting my things on the counter. Anna's face was quite pale. "I have to insist you speak quickly, sir. My sister is unwell."

"She's white as a ghost!" said Mrs. Crow, dramatically. "And here she is, making tea for her landlord, who already sucks her dry! You ought to be ashamed of yourself, Mr. Stringham."

Mr. Stringham stumbled over himself, dribbling tea down the front of his waistcoat. "Why I—I never meant to. Forgive the intrusion. I just —"

"Thank you, Mrs. Crow, but I'm sure Mr. Stringham meant no harm. Though, sir, there's a look about you that makes me uneasy."

"I'm here on business," he said, clearing his throat.

"You're only ever here on business. Years as a landlord, not once a social call," Mrs. Crow continued. She needed no invitation, or special occasion for that matter, to verbally eviscerate landlords and everything they stood for.

"Why not take Anna back to her room, Mrs. Crow. I can entertain Mr. Stringham here," I said. She reluctantly nodded her head and ushered Anna through the kitchen door, ensuring to throw one last evil eye at our landlord for good measure.

"I'm right in here if he gets any funny ideas," she croaked.

"Thank you, Mrs. Crow!" I shouted. Funny ideas please, he was so much older than I. Then again, I supposed so was my fiancé.

"Poor Mrs. Crow. I think she is starting to go fuzzy at the edges," he said.

"Now, now. Be nice. Why not tell me why you're here?" I eased into a chair and poured myself a well-needed cup of tea. The kettle was still warm, thankfully. A business conversation with a landlord could not be pleasant news. Has history ever surrendered an account of a landlord swinging by a tenant for naught but good news? The only example I could conjure up was Dickens' Ebenezer Scrooge, and it took three ghosts to change his mind. The way Mr. Stringham was massaging his temples suggested no break in this rich tradition.

"I'm afraid it's not good news," he said. Surprise. "In fact, if there were any other way about it, I wouldn't be here. Well, here it is. I have to increase the leasehold fees."

This was worse than I had expected. "An increase? How much of an increase?" Talking about it was clearly making him uncomfortable. He shifted in his chair and avoided eye contact.

"Another twenty shillings."

"Twenty shillings!" I sputtered. "That's nearly double."

"It's my mother, I'm afraid," he began. "She's taken ill and has to move to the countryside. I'm her only son. I need to support her. I don't want to do it."

"We've been tenants for many years. If you could give us a few months to see if we could scrape it all together."

"I can't allow it. It's all happened suddenly for me as well, and now for you as well, I know. But life isn't all easy and pudding, is it? Her expenses are already rolling in."

"Another twenty shillings might put us on the streets," I said, leveling my eyes at him.

"I would hate to turn you out. Is there anyone that might be able to help you?" he asked.

His question immediately conjured up my betrothed. Byron would bend over backwards to help if I would let him. How could I, though? After all the risk he was already undertaking on my behalf. My failed stories. His poor reviews. He was already living out of his print shop. Could I live, in good conscience, watching him skip meals so that I could pay rent for my sister and me?

"Could you give me at least a week to sort myself out? Then I could give you a clearer answer." The truth was, I could hardly think about the raise in rent. I was still too excited about Lieutenant Thomas. Besides, who knows what minds would be like in a week's time? Maybe Mr. Stringham would feel too guilty to go through with it.

"I think I can manage that," he said, picking up his jacket. "But no more than a week. I'm sorry it has to be this way."

"Not as sorry as I am," I said. "I would see you out, but I think you know the way. This is your property, after all." It was a dart, and I saw that it hit its mark. He left without another word.

As soon as the door latched, Mrs. Crow came tiptoeing into the kitchen.

"What did he want, dear?" she asked.

"He's raising the rent."

"Typical. Just typical! How can he dare do such a thing?"

"Something about his mother needing a holiday."

"You hear it all the time. Male landholder this. Male landholder that. You show me a man with a bit of property, and I'll show you a man with half a soul."

I envied Mrs. Crow. I don't know what age magically loosens the tongue, but I personally can't wait to arrive there. Truthfully, I was furious with Mr. Stringham. Sure, he had every right to increase the rent. In fact, I suspected that he raised rent for other tenants without disturbing our rate in the past, but he surely must have known such an egregious increase would put us out. Where else were we supposed to go? I didn't believe Anna capable of developing the callous attitude needed to live in the slums. Two young women living in the cheapest, most neglected area of the city? Could there be any salvation from such a station?

I thanked Mrs. Crow, and after several vows that all men would meet their end one day (prophecies I assured her were bound to come true), she left us alone with our troubles. I gathered my things and made my way to my sister's room. Her complexion was improving. By morning, I suspected she'd be feeling much better. I hoped I'd feel better too—relieved of the guilt I carried for disbelieving her earlier. Younger siblings never grow up, do they? I suspected that, even when she reached sixty years, I would still consider her a child.

"Is everyone gone then?" she asked, sitting up in bed.

"They are. I'm assuming you listened at the door?"

"As much as I was able. Mrs. Crow was thoroughly forcing me to bed, though. She had me busy washing for the third time to distract me while she listened at the door herself!"

"I think Mr. Stringham is serious about this," I said. "The timing is just awful."

"Luella, what will we do? I'll be ruined if we have to find cheaper lodgings. It's hard enough getting Jacob's family's approval as it is. If they hear we've been put out on the street—"

"I'll come up with something," I replied.

"Will I have to find a position? I don't think the future Mrs. Rigby could be a factory girl, but perhaps I could find a job at a more respectable profession. A governess, perhaps. You were a governess once. Do you think I could do it?"

I tried to imagine Anna juggling children's schedules and teaching them their lessons. Even if she could find a position, she wouldn't last a week.

"Let's not panic just yet. Aren't you expecting a proposal sometime soon?"

"Of course, you're right," she said with a practiced exhale. "It's just a matter of time before Jacob proposes. And besides, you have an engagement already. Why not just marry Byron now? I'm sure he would be willing."

I stared at the blanket. Why not just marry Byron? Moving into the print shop would be better than moving to the poor house, and I was certain he'd have open arms for Anna until she was wed. So why not just marry Byron?

"How is it so warm in here?"

"Mrs. Crow wouldn't rest until it was a tropical jungle. She said it was better for my health."

"You couldn't just bundle up?" I teased.

"Do you want me to catch ill?"

"Don't be so dramatic."

"Me? Dramatic? You're the one avoiding my question. Why not marry Byron? He's a good man, and he obviously cares about you. Sure, you may not be truly wealthy, but he'll be sure you're never in need, at least."

My sister was never afraid to force my back against a wall. Why not just marry Byron? What elusive grandeur did I maintain of a life more noble and rich, full of passion? Admittedly, sometimes I dreamed of living in a world more saturated with color than the gray of the city or the average busywork of the day to day. Could Byron ever remind me of more than words and articles desperate to be read, loved, and hated by the masses?

Was it wrong of me to hold out for a life that felt like more than a stepping stone?

My mother would have scolded me for these feelings. I could almost hear her voice now. A respectable, domestic life should be the dream of every little girl. That's what she would say. She would have sided with Anna in a moment. Byron was a sensible match, and I wasn't getting any younger. But, I always had been a daddy's girl. How many times I had run into his arms as she hollered after me?

"In any respect, I don't believe that you or I should go about marrying anybody just to solve an immediate financial strait," I said, tucking her in.

"I'll find work," she said, without hearing me. "I can work as a secretary. Henrietta Grieg got a position just last week as a secretary for a banker downtown."

"You're doing nothing until you feel better," I replied. "And besides, you wouldn't want anything to cut into your time with Jacob. You and I can both sense that he's close to finding his courage. It may be a moot point, anyway. I think I have a story that could set us on the right foot."

"Something better than the history of drapes?" Her question was sincere, but I couldn't help but feel a little defensive.

"It was just a bad title," I protested. "If someone had taken the time to read it—"

My sister yawned. She was tired and ill. I was wrong to worry her like this. Our threatened eviction could have waited until morning. I could only hope the infatuation of young love could dampen the impact of bad news. I hear it always has. I imagine it always will.

"Just promise me," she said, nestling into her blankets, "you'll let me know before we're evicted from our home. In the meantime, I'll turn up the charm with Jacob. See if I can convince him to… buy the cow, if you catch my meaning."

"Anna!" I gasped. She giggled and feigned shock. I grabbed her parcel and hit her with it. "Maybe you don't deserve this after all."

"Deserve what? Anna! Luella, what is this? Is it for me?"

"Just something I noticed you staring at during one of our recent walks."

She ripped into the package and squealed with delight. She went on embracing me and jumping up to try it on, laughing all the time. I admired her from the bed as she posed in the looking glass next to the dress Father gave her, feeling warm despite Mr. Stringham's ultimatum. For tonight, at least, I had my family and the glow of hope that comes with a promising story.

Moments like this are to be treasured.

Chapter Four

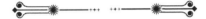

Romancing the Editor

It took me ages to fall asleep that night. I kept tossing and turning, perusing the sequence of events that Lieutenant Thomas had relayed to me. His story had all the wonderful tidbits that might keep a reader enthralled. I wanted to get to work writing it, turning my notes into something solid. I guess it's hardly any surprise that, when I did fall asleep, the lieutenant's story lived out in my dreams.

I stood on a walk next to a grimy street in darkness, just as he had described it. I could faintly see the woman dressed in working clothes, as he had mentioned, across from me, walking at a reckless pace over the cobblestones. Behind her, an imposing man in a black coat quickened his stride and followed behind her. Even in the dream, a ghastly sense of unease settled over me, and I could not help but try to intervene.

Before I could cross the street to warn her about the man, she turned down an alleyway. He disappeared around the corner right behind her. Then, in a flash, as is often the case in dreams, I wasn't in the street—I was in the dark alleyway. I looked for the woman, but I only saw the dim outline of crates and barrels—she was nowhere to be found. I looked down at myself and was surprised to find the woman's clothes adorning my own body. I felt more afraid, younger, more petite.

I turned around and saw the man with the dark coat coming directly toward me. My instinct was to turn and run, but my feet were glued to the spot. Fear held my lungs in a vice grip. Perspiration formed at the base of my skull in a hot wave. I willed myself to move, flee, cry for help, attack, anything, when I saw my assailant's face. My breath caught in my throat. He looked just like my father.

I woke with a start next to my sister, heaving breaths in and out. I looked around the room, trying to shed off the lingering distrust a nightmare injects into its victims. I watched the dust particles gently float in early morning light. It had been years since I had experienced a nightmare. I felt so wonderfully childish, afraid of every shadow in the morning light, afraid to get out of bed and check for monsters.

Anna groaned and pulled over an ample share of the blankets. I was grateful for the wakeup call of cold air on my feet.

The story was going to be a hit. I could hardly wait to get to Langley's and tell Byron.

As soon as the seven o'clock hour struck, I hurried to ready myself. Byron would be at the print shop by eight at the latest. I couldn't help but put on one of his favorite dresses, a deep purple sort of thing that I always considered a bit gaudy, especially for daytime wear, but the weather was beginning its march into the cold and overcast mood typical of Dawnhurst during autumn, and for some reason, darker colors have always found favor with the cold.

Truthfully, I felt a little out of place when it came to choosing dresses and frilling myself up. If I could dress like Rebecca Turner at the police station every day, I think that would be more practical than all the hoops, bustles, and dramatic folds that preoccupied the minds of other women. Fashion was expensive. It was time consuming. And, worst of all, it was always changing. Still, I wasn't someone to carry this argument to its bitter end. If I had news to share with Byron, and I wanted him to be excited about it, why not wrap it up in that purple dress he liked? Besides, my sister would be proud of me.

As I walked from my house to Langley's, my mind had time to settle, as it often does with crisp morning exercise. I realized exactly how much was on my mind. I wrestled with a cocktail of emotions. How could Stringham be kicking us out? How could *Langley's Miscellany* be selling so poorly? How could Brutus be so audacious toward my previous article? I felt nervous about my upcoming story pitch. There was no telling how Byron might react to such a radical departure from my usual work. Ever since I had faded from the excitement of my one success, he had become more and more conservative on the topics he let me write on.

All this anxiety mixed bitterly with the awkward emotions left over from my nightmare, in which I was convinced my father was about to attack me in a dark alley. My gentle, loving father—I had dreamed about him in the past but never as much as I wished. I could remember vividly the beautiful, albeit melancholy, feeling of waking up after dreams in which I was a little girl again and he spun me around or somehow found the funds to take me to the theater. To see such unbridled aggression in his eyes, like I did last night, left me feeling like I hadn't slept at all.

Was my father angry with me somehow? I didn't know if I believed in ghosts or spirits, but at times, I could almost swear that I felt him near. My nightmare might have been a manifestation that he was displeased with my current life, perhaps with what I'd done with his gift of literacy or with my choice of husband-to-be.

More uncomfortable still was the sudden realization that these thoughts inexplicably led me to a similar resting place: a strange sense of longing and the mental portrait of a policeman with steely grey eyes. I tried to shake my head. Girlish thoughts for girlish feelings.

"Is something the matter?" Byron asked, looking over his spectacles and this morning's edition of the *Times*. He sat cross-legged at the table, as was his custom. I had hardly even noticed him pouring the tea in front of me, let alone remembered entering the shop.

"Everything is quite well," I said. "Excuse me. I guess I'm just a bit distracted this morning."

"Wouldn't be a good writer if you weren't distracted," he said smiling. He took another half teaspoon of sugar and dumped it into his cup. "Have you tried the scones? Mrs. Barker tried to infuse them with some lavender, and I think they're a delight."

"I have, and they're quite good. Listen," I began, "I went down to the Dawnhurst Police Station yesterday." He lowered his paper.

"Luella, say you didn't. You promised me."

"Well, I didn't just go to stir up trouble. My father used to be friends with a police sergeant there. I went to check in."

"Just went to check in? Do you go there often?" he asked. I shook my head sheepishly. I hadn't been since before my father died.

"I'm no fool, Luella. Went to check in, rubbish! The police station! Who knows what rough lot you ran into down there?"

"It was time to rekindle an old relationship. One that might benefit my safety. It's never a bad thing to be friendly with the police force. And, if I might also prevail on him to provide some interesting news of what's been happening about the city, that's just the nature of the conversation. I can't help that, can I?"

"I'm sorry that you had to go about this business. I should have hired someone," he said, rising to his feet. He folded his newspaper and threw it on the table, looking unequivocally guilty.

"It wasn't bad. There's no need to overreact," I insisted. "In fact, as luck would have it, he did have an interesting story to share."

He braced himself. I could see the tension in his muscles make his back go rigid. He clearly did not feel comfortable with the image of me out there getting into the mud and grit he imagined came with investigating a crime thriller.

"I'm excited to hear it," he managed through pursed lips.

I took a deep breath. "Well, at the station yesterday, I met a man named Lieutenant Edward Thomas. He was in the middle of being berated by his superior officer, Sergeant Cooper (my late father's friend), because of a report Edward had filed the previous day." I felt his first name on my tongue like honey. Edward. How exotic to be on a first name basis with a police lieutenant—a young one, not a stodgy sergeant that looked at me like a little girl.

"It turns out, the evening before, he was on patrol in a darker area in Southside Dawnhurst. It was a cold evening, and the fog was settling in. Soon, it was nearly so thick that he could hardly see between one lamp and the next. He thought he might try to find some higher ground or go get an extra lantern, when he thought he saw a woman walking alone at a tremendous pace through the night on the other side of the street. He thought it uncommon for a woman to be out at this time of night by herself in such a rough part of town. So, he set off to follow her."

Recalling the story out loud, in my own words, made me feel as if I had been there, which after my dream last night, I suppose in some ways I had. Living it through retelling made me breathe in the fear and wonder Edward must have felt on the job. He must have been possessed by an outlandish courage. How formidable and daunting to be a policeman in this day and age.

"Did he find the poor woman?" Byron asked, curiosity getting the better of him.

"That's just it. As he stepped into the street, he saw a shadowy figure pass in the fog, under the same lamp where he had seen the woman. The man, or so he assumed it was a man, followed exactly in her wake at an even more furious pace. Edward recognized at once the gait of an assailant, and he gave chase."

"Good gracious," Byron exclaimed, leaning back in his chair. "This in our own city? And you walked home alone last night, I imagine, as well."

"Don't get too excited about all that, Byron! Just hear the story out," I said. "He ran through the fog after the assailant and, consequently, after the woman. The three of them continued at length down the street. Through the fog, he could see a vague silhouette of the woman when she passed under a gas lamp ahead and a much more distinct silhouette of the man, until finally the woman ahead tucked behind a corner into an alleyway. The man followed right after her."

"Then, Edward heard an ear-piercing scream. He ran to catch up, dreading that he was too late to save the woman, but when he arrived, he saw her, braced up against the alley's brick wall, looking like fear itself. On the ground in front of her lay the assailant, dead, garbed all in black. And, standing next to the assailant was what Edward described as a fog man."

"A fog man?" Byron said, eyes alternating between wide disbelief and narrow suspicion.

"The fog man looked directly at him with a mostly transparent, gaseous face. Instead of eyes, it simply had indentations in the fog, much like you might see if you impressed a divot into mashed potatoes with a spoon. The fog man turned, took a few steps at an astounding speed, and jumped into the night, pulling into himself all the dense fog that had moments before blanketed the street. The night was now clear as still water. Edward ran out of the alley to get a better look at the thing, but he found nothing. When he returned to the alley, the woman was gone. The body remained."

Byron sat in silence for a good while at the end of my story. He took out his pipe in that fatherly way of his and stood by the window, puffing and thinking. The silence gave me a moment to reflect on the eeriness of the tale and the very concrete dream I had the night before.

A dream where my father was a masked assailant, and I was detective and victim all at once. I shuddered and pulled my shawl closer around my shoulders. Why didn't Byron ever stoke the fire? Not even his bird felt like singing on a cold, overcast day like this.

"So, what do you think? Should we publish it?" I asked, finally.

"You mean as a piece of fiction?" he replied, with an overtly stoic gaze. Fiction?

"As an article in the *Miscellany*," I said, "like my other articles."

"Would we be purporting that this article was a factual police incident?"

"It was a police report! That's why Edward took such heat from his superior," I insisted. "Don't you see? The credibility of the police officer is what makes the whole story worthwhile at all."

"So, you want to set the city into an uproar. What would people do if they actually believed a murderous fog creature was roaming about?" He tapped his foot.

"Well, at least we'd be making ripples again. Heaven's sakes, Byron, I feel like I've been eating table scraps since *"At Home with a Woman."* This could be a chance to be talked about again. Maybe even, heaven forbid, a story that could put me at least in the running for the Golden Inkwell this year."

He scoffed and quickly recovered but not before it hurt. A scoff? He didn't think I'd ever be in the running for the Golden Inkwell. I shut my eyes. I hadn't said I had a chance at winning. I just wanted to be in the running. It's not like I said I wanted to win the whole thing. My betrothed's disdainful expression seared into my memory like a hot iron.

Perhaps he was right. It was just like me to let my dreams outrun my feet. Byron would know.

"Don't you worry that we'd be slandering a poor man's reputation as a fanciful lunatic?" Byron asked in a gently apologetic tone. "I made a promise to myself, Luella, that I wouldn't get into that type of journalism."

"Sergeant Cooper brought that up, but I've worked it all out already. We can give him a pen name, The Steely-Eyed Detective," I said with a flourish of the hands.

"Steely-Eyed Detective?" he echoed. I saw his brain masticate the words, tasting a bitter flavor. In his eyes, I saw the briefest flash of mistrust, betrayal, even pain.

"Or some other title that will keep the ladies buying at the newsstands," I said. "You were worried about my sensitive nature being offended by digging up these stories, but you still have much to learn about women. Not only do we hope for this type of story, but we live for it. They'll be chattering in groups on the streets, banding together. Our story, whether it be true or not, will follow them home at night, keep them scared of mysterious shadows. They'll jump at sudden noises and giggle about it with their friends."

"That would be quite the spectacle. You're sure the police are willing to stand by it?" The warmth and color in his face returned gradually as he took the bait. Steely-Eyed Detective was just a moniker to sell a publication. *Our* publication. I crossed the room to him and grasped his hands.

"I'd bet my life on it." He stared down at our locked hands and smiled deeply. I don't know why I felt dishonest, but I didn't have much time to think about it. Before I knew what was happening, he planted a big kiss on my lips.

"Byron!" I cried, pulling away.

"Apologies, apologies!" he stammered through a masked grin. He didn't do a good job hiding how pleased he was with himself. "That was forward of me and improper."

"Hardly," I justified to him and myself. "We are engaged after all. I was just—well, just surprised. And we're standing right in front of this window where everyone could see."

He laughed. He rarely laughed, but it was my favorite of his characteristics. His laugh was infectious and oafish, and I couldn't help but smile with him. "The devil with all of them," he said. "We're about to publish '*The Steely-Eyed Detective and the Fog Man Caper*'!"

I almost felt an urge him to kiss him right back.

Chapter Five

The Carnival

The story went over better than we could have hoped. I wrote it up in a fury, filled with renewed exhilaration for the work after Byron's endorsement. It felt so much easier getting through production when I wasn't going on and on about table napkins or the intricacies of lapels. The words came out as if on their own. It felt like the story wanted to be told and was just waiting for me to put a pen to paper. Later that week, when I saw "*The Steely-Eyed Detective*" printed in capital letters on the front page of *Langley's Miscellany*, I felt an absurd rush go to my head.

I'll never be able to repay Byron for the gamble he took on me. Rather than just appease my bold story idea, he fully invested his time, attention, and resources as if it were his own passion project. He printed double his usual stock and called in favors he had been stockpiling with colleagues in the printing business. He ordered a no-holds-barred assault on a total rebrand.

The whole business was exhilarating and terrifying. When our delivery man showed up to haul them off, I felt my stomach do backflips as if it were a trapeze artist. I kept staring out the window to look at the people on the streets. How could I not? At any moment, I might see someone pass by with one of our papers! These were the true critics. The lady pushing a pram. The chimney sweep between shifts. The vendors hawking their merchandise. The businessmen. The factory girls. The working girls. The policemen. Brutus had words to cut us with, but these people wielded indifference and purse strings. With the investment we had put in, their apathy could ruin more than my ego.

The first day after publication, we noted nothing extraordinary. We met our usual figures in sales, and with the double order weight on my shoulders, I was just about ready to call it quits with the writing business. Guilt swept over me like a rogue wave. I didn't think a gamble like this would ruin my betrothed, but even if he could absorb the loss, could I ever repay a debt like that? It was hardly a way to begin a marriage. I could tell Byron was nervous as well, less by his reactions to the boy who brought tidings from the newsstands and more by his inherent excitement each time that boy rang the door.

At home, I couldn't eat a thing, despite Anna's insistence. I was a right fool to think a petty ghost story was going to turn the publishing business on its head. To think my head had been filled with thoughts of smashing success, and the Golden Inkwell no less. What was more common and banal than a ghost story? I'd turned Langley's into a mere drunkard spouting tales at a pub!

That night, after finally falling asleep, I found myself sitting in the church where my father was buried. Tall stone columns held up its high ceiling, just the way I remembered it from his funeral, but fog spread heavily in the church like a visible blanket, as if the guilt of its Sunday attendees settled like smoke. It felt unsettling and cold; I recognized it at once as the fog from my previous nightmare. I sat in the middle of the pews, seats stretching out in each direction. I could hardly see three benches away from me, what with the fog, though pinpricks of candlelight from the front of the chapel called through the haze like beacons of another life.

"My darling Luella," I heard a voice say, and there sat my father like a phantom, his face creased in deep smile-carved wrinkles around his mouth and eyes. They shone brightly at me, as blue as though he were still living and enjoying the coursing blood of mortality.

"Papa!" I cried, wrapping him in an embrace. I knew it was a dream —it had to be—but I felt the coarse, wool jacket he used to wear on my arms and the scratch of his whiskers on my cheek. It had been so long since I'd seen him, even in the unearthly realm of sleep. I missed even the dream of my father. "Is this real?"

"What say we avoid answering as long as we can, eh?" He brushed a stray hair from my face.

"Papa, I miss you so much. Tell me this isn't just a dream. Tell me it's a visit. Tell me you're still out there somewhere." He put a finger to my lips to quiet me and suggest the topic was as taboo as complaining about one of my mother's meals.

"By George, the church looks queer though, doesn't it? Did it always look like this?"

"I had the most terrible dream about you. You—you killed someone! It shook me so deeply."

"Well, I hope the bloke deserved it," he said with a playful smile. I hit him in the arm.

"I'm serious! It's not a joke. The man was chasing a woman, and you came from the fog to kill him."

"My darling, didn't I tell you when you were younger, if you dabble in ghost stories, nightmares are inevitable. And if you write ghost stories for the papers, you might as well invite demons to dinner." He put an arm around me and laughed. The laugh was contagious and warm, just as I remembered. I leaned my head on his shoulder. There were a million questions I wanted to ask him, dream or not.

"Are you proud of me, Papa?" I spat out ungracefully. "Of how I've cared for Anna? Of my writing?"

He turned a thought over in his head and popped his jaw before answering.

"I'm glad you're finally getting a chance to write and not one of those rubbish stories meant just to keep you busy."

"Byron means well," I said. "He's given me a job and a wage."

"Me thinks you pay a steep price for your salary," he said. I didn't want to talk about Byron. I shook my head.

"Do you think 'The Steely-Eyed Detective' will be a success?" I traced an old tattered patch on the arm of his coat. He took me by the shoulders and turned to face me.

"You're more than a single story. I know there's more in you."

Tears welled in my eyes as I guessed at his meaning.

"The Golden Inkwell. . . But, how could I? I'm trying, Papa, but I'm just a young girl from the east side," I said. He smiled conspiratorially before standing and kissing my hand.

"In that case, show 'em what a poor girl from the east side can do." He backed away from me until the fog swallowed him. I tried to follow but lost my way in the downy white until I surfaced, blinking in the morning light.

It was still early, and I laid in bed stewing over my dream. Apart from my recent nightmare, I hadn't dreamed of my father in years. He felt so real that the pain of his loss renewed afresh. I missed his guiding hand, the way he always seemed to know what he was about. I had tried my best for Anna since he died, but half the time, I felt I was guessing, and the other half I was making it up.

My father's words both encouraged and beleaguered me, but the more I thought on it, the more fanciful it all seemed to be. He was gone. It was just a dream, a silly dream for a silly girl who missed her father. I had more practical things to worry about. After all, I still had a hanging story that could sink my fiancé!

After forcing down a quick breakfast of jam on half a piece of bread, I nearly ran to the print shop. When I opened the door, there was a ferocious spirit going on inside. Byron was abuzz with such an energy that I was afraid to approach him. A few men, whom I did not recognize, swept past me and out the door, and Mr. Storm and Mr. Jacob sat scribbling furiously at whatever flat surface they could manage.

"Byron?" I interrupted, approaching him as he worked away at the office typewriter under the watchful eyes of Gerald Storm.

"Everything's a mess," he said without pause. "I've got so much to put in place. So much to set straight. I don't even know how I'll manage!"

"Is it that bad then? Is Langley's ruined?" His words hit me like sledgehammers. I knew it. This was the end of me.

"Ruined me? My darling, they've sold out completely. There's not a copy of *Langley's Miscellany* to be found anywhere!"

Not one to be found? Anywhere?

My knees buckled. Was this just a cruel prank?

"You can't be serious." I gasped.

"Serious? Why do you think I'm running around like this? I got in this morning, and there were requests for more batches! It seems our little print shop has taken on significantly more than I think we can muster! It's absolutely glorious!"

"Oh Byron! It's wonderful!" I ran and enveloped him in a full embrace, hiding my tears over his shoulder. I did it. I actually wrote a success! My father's smiling, clever face from the night before flashed through my mind, mingled with every happy memory of him. The whole journey of learning to read and write flushed over me until I was left gripping my father tightly. I did it, Papa! I did it.

I was lost in a mixed state of my euphoria and reality. I couldn't have expressed who I was embracing or who else was in the room, but I was embracing someone, not in supplication, but in victory.

The rest of the morning was a busy rush. Who knew success would mean so much work! We scrambled to get another batch of *Langley's* out the door to be published, and we paid our delivery man extra for his increased time, a bonus if he could get it to all our distributors before two pm. Then, exhausted from our work, we set back and waited, toasting ourselves with glasses of wine, despite the early hour.

I left the print shop later that evening, tipsy from the cordial and the sense of triumph from the day. I couldn't wait to share my good news with my dear Anna. Perhaps we could go out to a late dinner, but when I got home, her practiced handwriting informed me that she was out with Jacob. I frowned. It was probably best that she was out with Mr. Rigby, but I couldn't deny my disappointment. I was too full of life and excitement to sit home alone and wait for her to get back. I could try Mrs. Crow, but she wouldn't understand, not fully anyway, not the way a sister could.

I was convinced, however, not to let this night go to waste. It was still early enough for a woman to walk about unescorted. Surely, there was something to see or enjoy. What was it? Thursday? I was a hit writer. What was I doing cooped up by myself?

My thoughts lingered to an advertisement I had seen the other day for a traveling carnival show down by the old empty lot on the east side of the river bank. It'd be a bit daring to attend by myself, but who knew what type of fun, or even inspiration, awaited there? In any respect, I hadn't treated myself like this in ages.

Decided, I set off at once after scribbling a quick note for Anna should she return before I did. It was unlikely.

I had spent my entire life in Dawnhurst, and we had lived in a smattering of different flats. After my father died, we did a brief turn in the darkest, seediest area of the city, sandwiched between the east side of the river and the factories. I had tried to forget our time there. The only memories that remained were frigid winds blowing through my blanket during the winter and the nauseating smell of unwashed drunkards in the summer.

The city had developed on either side of the Severn. We had done nearly everything we could to be on the west side. The city's more prominent families lived on the west, as well as the more pleasant industries. The florists. The bakers. The cobblers. It wasn't uncommon to run into well-dressed couples on strolls around the small and scattered parks around the west. The printers and publishers were on the west as well, at least the reputable ones. Byron would have dropped dead before seeing Langley's headquarters on the east.

The carnival had been set up in a large clearing on a vacant acre or so almost hugging the east shore. A similar lot faced it across the river on the west. That the carnival had set up on the east side said a great deal about who the proprietors must have assumed would come. That wasn't to say anything of the carnival's financial situation but more of the quality and nature of their headlining exhibits. Certainly, they would lean toward the macabre and mystic. After Edward's account of the fog man, I couldn't help but feel that a carnival on the vacant lot on the east side was the perfect place to celebrate "The Steely-Eyed Detective." I owed some type of gratitude to my readers, and at least a good representation of them would be attracted to a carnival such as this one.

From some ways off, I could see the alien, eerie glow of electric lights. The sight quickened my pulse and made me feel dangerous. What could be more fitting than for me to prod confidently across Thompson's South Bridge into the unknown, ever-darkening evening?

I crested a small hill, and the carnival's grandiose tents came into view. I was prepared to see typically bright colored bunting and banners, in red and white or yellow and blue, but the tents emanated an eerie green color, almost as if there was an unsettling haze over the whole area. It mingled with the electric lights and cast funny shadows. Perhaps it was just my imagination or the celebration cordial, but even the tent poles seemed crooked and stuck into the ground at funny angles. I pinched myself. The sight reminded me of my recent dreams.

The carnival was well attended. There were costumed men and women dancing about, fire breathers, carts hawking exotic foods and gifts. I found small crowds in front of fortune tellers and magicians. I saw gypsies and giants from the far east. My nostrils were assailed with pungent aromatics, spices and smells from different, unknown lands. It created an intoxicating atmosphere. I tried to orient myself to decide what I should do first. I was celebrating, after all. Everywhere I turned, there was something new to look at. Here, a woman beckoning me in to browse her magical tonics. There, a man inviting me to investigate his taxidermy faerie collection.

I smiled as I waded deeper into the foray, noting an eclectic mix of different kinds of people. Surely, my readers roamed among them. How sweet it was to write for both the east and west sides of the river. Humans are, in spite of social status, united in an interest in the mysterious and unknown. We stood together, intrigued by the curiously disproportionate Frenchman swinging around a magic rope that changed colors or the exotic reptile exhibit with creatures, the keeper claimed, that could speak plain English. Deep down, didn't everyone believe in some kind of magic?

An old hag with gnarled fingers beckoned me toward a shadowy yurt promising me to see into the future. I stood for a moment watching a man move what his handler claimed to be a solid ton of granite, but I got distracted by wandering acrobats, competing for attention with two red-headed twins that must have been over two meters tall. They tossed knives dangerously back and forth between each other.

I wandered still deeper, by now pinching myself to ensure I wasn't dreaming. Had the whole day been the imaginations of my sleeping mind? Would I wake any moment to receive the news that my story had been a colossal failure and Byron was second-guessing our engagement?

I purchased a cone of honey-roasted nuts, the perfect complement to watching a woman hypnotize a young man and turn him into a crudely, self-deprecating spectacle. I laughed along with what looked like the largest gathering of spectators I had seen yet. His belt fell to the floor and tripped him as he tried to pursue the beautiful hypnotist around in a grand circle.

This was freedom: standing among strangers, observing the world without fear. I knew I could write and produce stories that could contend with the others. Brutus, and whatever he was to write as a critique in the coming days, be damned. I could survive. I had the mind to create stories others would read. Even without Byron, I could survive if need be.

I bit into a bitter nut. There's always one in every bunch, after all. Its rancid flavor fought with the gentle notes of honey and smoke. Despite its generous sweet coating, the bad came through. It reminded me immediately of a Christmas from many years before, when I had saved up to bring Anna home some honey-roasted nuts. I had been so excited to give them to her, but the entire bunch had gone bad. I'd been had by the peddler and should have known the reduced price he offered me was indicative of some defect.

Somehow, tasting the rancid flavor caused the excitement of the day to catch up with me. The exhaustion set in, and my legs and torso felt hollow. Under my skirts and bodice, I felt like a barrel perched on two bamboo canes. I looked for a seat and found a log bench near a tent. I stumbled my way over and plopped myself down ungracefully.

"Too much excitement for one evening?" A husky, baritone voice floated from behind me, cutting through the din. I turned halfway in my seat and saw the silhouette of a man standing behind the open flap of a yurt. His question hung in the air. I could feel his gaze rest on me. I should have been alarmed, being all alone in a bizarre carnival, out of strength, and now confronted by a strange man in the dark. Instead, my senses were slipping from me. I was tired. I had just settled myself on the log, and I wasn't inclined to move.

"I just need to sit for a moment, thank you," I replied.

"Mind if I join you?" he asked.

"You can do what you like," I said. I could feel my reservations melting into the evening. It must have been the side effects of the emotional journey I'd been on that morning. Still, I was determined to hold on to the dignity and pride I'd won that day. Tonight, I wasn't just a member of the masses. I wasn't just a woman to be scared of strangers or shadows. I didn't need to move if a stranger wanted to share a log bench.

The man sat down with a sigh. I heard him take a crisp bite out of an apple. Out of the corner of my eye, I saw a beautiful Burgos pointer follow behind him and sit erect and obedient at his flank. I kept my head forward, feigning interest in the hypnotist, who now had another woman hypnotized. Her two thralls danced together at her command.

"That used to be me," he said, gesturing to the center of the ring with a half-eaten apple.

"I beg your pardon?"

"There in the center. Used to have my own show. They had me on the advertisements," he said, taking a bite. "Times change."

"You used to be a hypnotist?" My curiosity was getting the better of me. I inclined my head ever so slightly and darted my eyes, catching a glimpse of his features. The electric lights across the crowd lit up the stubble on his face, brown, red, and black. Perhaps a Scotsman? Though I didn't detect the unmistakable northern accent. I was tempted to look at him openly to assess his features more fully, but I held back. Not yet. Let him feel my disinterest.

"Not a hypnotist, no." I heard a smile in his voice. It was congenial. "Tried that once; it didn't end well. Hypnotized myself by accident. Couldn't snap out of it for a week."

This absurd account did me in. I shifted in my seat and gave him my full attention. "Is that meant to be a joke?" I asked.

"Depends. Do you like to laugh?" he replied, giving me a boyish grin. I puzzled on his question. I laughed with Anna occasionally. Something about this man made me feel nineteen. I don't know whether it was the playful expression on his face or the absolute mess of brown hair on his head. His eyes were a deep, honey color, though that might have just been tricks by the lights. He had a peculiar talent of looking very comfortable sitting anywhere, and this effect permeated into my demeanor. Girlish feelings swelled in my bosom.

He wore a ratty old robe made of what once may have been velvet, patched over in faded groupings of foreign silk and tapestry. Underneath, his linen shirt, collarless, was largely unbuttoned down to his slim fitting waistcoat. His question, and his appearance, took me off-guard.

"Do I know you, sir?" I asked.

"She called me sir," he said to the pointer. It sniffed the apple in his hand in response. I could not place his face, but something must account for this feeling of familiarity. I was not accustomed to feeling swept up by the charms of strange men, but I caught myself leaning toward him.

What was I thinking? My thoughts flew to Byron like a lifeline. Me, an engaged woman! It wasn't right to be here alone. The propriety of it! The very appearance of evil! I had made him a promise. What if someone saw me? How would he react if reports of this got back to his ears?

This man was so unlike Byron, too. He felt young. He felt vibrant. He felt unreasonable. How did he feel all these things by slinking onto a bench and eating an apple? I stood.

"No, not a hypnotist," he continued, seemingly disregarding my imminent departure. "I had a show of a very different kind. A better show. But, I guess you're only as good as your last performance."

I should have walked away. My head told me to walk away, but I felt like he was chiding me. As good as your last performance? My thoughts flew unbidden to the face of my father in a fog-filled church. You're more than a single story. Isn't that what he'd said?

I needed water. I wanted something to take the bitter nut taste out of my mouth. Meandering aromas in the air smothered me, aromas that were free and intoxicating only moments before. All around, people clapped and marveled at the many facades of the carnival. They consumed the entertainment like a drug then wandered on to the next amusement.

Only as good as your last performance. I watched the hypnotist in the center ring. The two strangers who had danced only minutes prior were now put into attack mode, being held at bay by another two volunteers, so they wouldn't tear each other limb from limb. It was terrifying. I reflected on my first sip of success. Was I hypnotized? Was I the hypnotist?

I stewed over what I wanted for myself. My recent story should have made me so happy, but the day had not yet expired, and I already felt empty. It was, after all, a single success. Soon, my story would be just another bit of ink on scrap paper lying in the mud. My father had wanted more for me, sacrificed so that I could accomplish more than this, perhaps, with time, something as illustrious as our city's most prestigious literary award.

I suddenly realized why I came to the carnival in the first place. I wasn't after celebration. I had celebrated all day with Byron. In my mind, the success had lit something dark and desperate inside of me, something that a strange man breathed life into with an offhand comment. Maybe what I found so familiar in him was the wisdom of my father.

Inside of me, lurking behind the drunken dizziness and puffed up pride, crouched a looming, fanged question.

What next?

I needed more stories, and Edward wasn't going to see a ghost every day.

"Why aren't you still in the center ring?" I asked.

"A dangerous accident. A paying customer met an unfortunate end," he said grimly. The hair on my neck prickled.

"What kind of show did you say performed, Mister…"

"I'm Bram," he said, standing. He walked to the entrance of his yurt and lifted the flap. "Would you care to see?"

Chapter Six

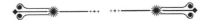

The Retired Magician

The yurt's canvas closed behind me, leaving my eyes to adjust to the darkness. The yurt's interior was stretched out in a simple large circle, lit by a large fire in the center and accented by a series of well-used candles. A hole in the top of the ceiling let the smoke escape and prevented an overwhelming campfire smell from seeping into the living space. In its place, more of the carnival's foreign perfume permeated the air.

The pointer gaited over to a ratty blanket next to a dirty, though intricately designed, rug. A small desk stood next to a surprisingly sturdy bed. I imagined it would be difficult for a transient to lug around. The walls (if you could call them walls) were adorned with tapestries fastened to the wood structural beams and paper advertisements from what I could only assume was Bram's show before it was shut down. I squinted to make out the images. The fire gave them an eerie mood. I also noticed a small dining table with an odd-looking tea kettle and an oversized kettle bottomed mug.

"It's not much, but it's homey," Bram said with a sweeping gesture of his arm. He picked a dead leaf off a potted dwarf tree near the entrance. "A good host would offer you something to drink."

My heart pulsated in my throat. Entering the yurt crossed some line in my mind. In here, I was this man's guest or prisoner. Anything could happen, and I doubted I could get out or to help in time. What was I doing? My mother's voice sounded in my head about dangerous men with dangerous wants.

I could still leave now. If I just turned around right now, I could get out and to safety. I could run home or to Byron's and pretend this was all a dream.

"That won't be necessary," I said, my nose in the air. Run. I could still leave. I shouldn't risk throwing away my life.

But Bram's words wouldn't go away. You're only as good as your last performance. How could I return empty-handed? Overnight, *Langley's Miscellany* had become a huge success. Byron would be expecting more stories. If I couldn't replicate success like this, what was I to him? Just a wife? He would never admit to it, but deep down, he would know I was a one trick pony or that I was lazy.

Worse still, my father's challenge stuck to me. I had to be more than one story if I was to win the Golden Inkwell.

"So how about this show you were talking about?" I asked.

"You're sure you don't want anything?" Bram had opened a little cupboard and fingered through a set of bottles. They clinked in different musical tones.

"Quite sure," I spit out. "You promised to show me something quite remarkable."

"Funny, I don't remember saying that exactly," he said, sinking into a chair near the tea table with one of the bottles. He reached into a sack and pulled out another apple. He cut out a wedge and ate it off his knife. A knife? My pulse quickened again. Suddenly, everything looked like a weapon. The bottle. The knife. The Burgos Pointer.

Get out of here. Get the story. The two thoughts waged war inside of me.

"You promised a story. You told me your headline act was cut short when someone died, and you invited me to see what the show was. Looking around now, I see you were lying and that there was no show. You're wasting my time."

He peered at me, head tilted, from his seat. I felt like he was looking right inside of me. I eyed the knife.

"What do you think is going on here?" he asked. "Are you—are you afraid?"

"I beg your pardon?"

"You look like a spitting cat, hair on end."

"I do not," I stammered. "I just—" I forced my shoulders to relax and tried to look natural.

"Do you think I'm going to...attack you or something?" The pointer yawned and curled up for an evening nap.

"Well," I said, gathering my courage, "you are gesturing with a knife."

He laughed, stuck the knife into the table with an overly dramatic flourish, and stood up. "Let's just work this out really quick." He crossed to the yurt opening and drew back the canvas. "You are discriminating against me because I'm a carnival performer, and I don't appreciate it."

"I'm discriminating?" I echoed, gaping.

"This meeting is over," he continued and started out the door.

Before I knew what I was doing, I had him by the hand, yanking him back into his own living space. "No, no, wait!" I cried. "Please, I need to hear what happened." As the words came out, they sounded like an excuse even to me. I was grasping. My father's words were driving me crazy. You're only as good as your last story. Or were those Bram's words? What was it about this man?

"You apologize?" he asked, leveling his eyes at me. The fire glowed off the honey color in them, giving the illusion that they were ablaze.

"Apologize for what?" I demanded.

"You're a writer, am I correct?" he asked.

"How did you know that?" I asked, letting go of his hand. He sauntered over to his bed and plopped down.

"Something about you. A strand of hair, a way of holding yourself... an obsessive drive to uncover a sensationalist story."

"Am I that obvious?"

"I don't know if my story can help you," he said. "When the accident happened, every newspaper in the city was crawling over it. I think it'd be old news." He sauntered across the room and plopped onto his humble bed as though it were a chaise.

"I think that depends on what the accident was like," I said. I was determined to get something from him. A lead. A connection. I couldn't leave empty-handed. I needed something to validate my recent article, a thread of anything promising I had more. "Please, I need this. I've just had a breakthrough hit, and I'm afraid I don't have anything else left in me." I was shocked by my own honesty.

"You seem to be in quite a hurry. What are you running from?" he asked.

I wanted to tell him nothing, to ask what he was talking about, but it was as though he knew my thoughts. What was I running from? The east side of the river? The life my parents led? Troubles with the landlord? No. There was more.

"I just want a story," I said evenly. He sighed and scratched his head before beckoning over.

"I'm not telling you anything unless I feel I can trust you," he said, beckoning me over. "Come take a seat here, and we'll talk." He patted a spot next to him on the bed and picked up a book from a small side table.

I hesitated.

"Look, I already had my reputation upended once by reporters who used and abused me. You want a story? You're going to have to convince me that you're not just another scandalmonger." He nonchalantly flipped his book open as if he had no preference as to whether I stayed or went.

I crossed to him. Maybe he was a hypnotist, but I sat down next to him on the bed. I was tense. My head was dizzy, but here I was, sitting on a bed next to a man I met minutes ago, because I wanted another insane story to write about.

For some reason, it felt wonderful.

We sat in silence together for a long moment, neither of us saying anything. He kept reading to himself. I felt my heartbeat slow down. My muscles began their long journey back to a relaxed state. We looked at each other, and he smiled warmly.

"Do you believe in magic?" he whispered. At the moment, I wasn't sure what I believed in. I had always tried to live a prudent life. My father raised me as a Christian, in his own way. He couldn't read well, and I later discovered that the Bible verses he quoted to me growing up said something slightly different in the actual text.

"I met a man the other day who did," I responded, thinking of Edward. "He was willing to stake his professional reputation on it."

"And you are still unconvinced," he prodded.

"I've never experienced magic," I confessed. "I'd feel foolish confessing to believe in something I'd never experienced."

"But you have no reservations writing about magic," he accused. How did he know what I wrote about?

"I can write about other people believing in magic."

"What if I told you I made a career on magic?" He raised his eyebrows at me, daring me to ask him more.

"You were an illusionist," I said. He let out a deep chuckle, one of those laughs that never break past the diaphragm.

"Let me show you something." He leaned across me and reached under the bed, pulling out a small puzzle box. Small, intricate wood panels rotated as he manipulated their facets until they locked into a cube doubled in size. He slid the lid off to extract an old key. I watched intently, soaking in his movements as if I might, by memory, catch the puzzle box's secret.

He took the key across the room to an old chest in a shadowy corner. I hadn't noticed it before. It was cloaked by a queer shadow. He turned his back to me as he unlocked it, obscuring my view. I craned my neck, trying to catch a glimpse of the chest's contents, but witnessed nothing.

"There's something in here that I think you may take a particular interest in," he murmured. He turned to face me, cradling something in his hand before motioning for me to follow him to the writing desk. I followed, trying to glimpse what he was holding. "You've never had an experience with magic? Or so you say. In my experience, we encounter magic every day. It's just not what people expect. There aren't sparks or glowing orbs... well, at least not most of the time. The majority of magic goes unnoticed because it looks painfully ordinary. It's a self-defense, you see. As magic is discovered and exploited, it loses power, so it camouflages itself masterfully. It makes locating magic very difficult. Magic exists where we cannot see."

He sat me down in a chair at the writing desk, moved aside the tea kettle, and placed a blank piece of paper before me. I stared at it, stupidly, waiting for something to happen.

"What should I be looking at?" I asked after several moments.

"You're a writer, aren't you?" he said, placing a pen in my hand. He slid over a glass inkwell, dyed crimson, made almost black by the ink inside it. "You tell me."

The pen was remarkably heavy for its size. It was fashioned in the steel barrel style that had all but wiped out the quill, but it was intricately carved and etched with symbols I didn't recognize. It glinted different shades in the light between green and blue, reminding me of gemstone exhibits of alexandrite I had seen once one at a museum I had taken Anna to for her birthday. The writing point made a small elegant curve, finishing in a sharp end. It looked unlikely to hold much ink, and again, the weight of the pen would make it thoroughly uncomfortable as a writing instrument.

The inkwell was encased in a web of ornate metalwork that spiraled in peculiar designs. Perhaps Egyptian? Celtic? Gaelic?

"You want me to write? And with this?" I scoffed. "You really had me going there with your swooshy voice and mysterious words. Magic this, magic that."

"Three of my comrades died locating that pen," he replied, a smile on his lips equal parts smug and grim. I wasn't sure whether to believe him.

"Well, if that's true, I'm very sorry. I'm just not sure what you want me to do with it," I stammered.

"Write."

"My whole purpose here was to find a story. Once I've found it, I can write it at home."

"Write whatever you like. Fact. Fiction. Write whatever story you think would push your publication to the top. Write what you feel."

"It doesn't work like that!" I cried. "We aren't a fiction magazine. I find stories; I report them." He leaned in over me, putting his face very close to mine. I could feel his breath on my cheek. He smelled like apples and something else dangerous I couldn't place.

"There. You've finally stumbled on the magic," he whispered into my ear. "This pen has a funny way of turning fiction into fact."

I gaped at the pen, not sure whether to take him seriously. My heart was racing again with disbelief and nerves. He remained uncomfortably close to me, and it suddenly felt very warm in the tent. I looked up at him, and he did not retreat. We just sat there, staring at one another, sizing the other up. For a moment, I was convinced he was going to kiss me, a prospect that should have sent me running. Instead, I was glued to the seat. But no kiss came, and that was enough to spur me to action.

I dropped the pen on the desk. "I'm such a fool," I muttered. "I have to go."

"You don't believe me?"

"I believe," I said, turning on him, "that you are an expert con. How many women have you led in here with vague promises and your little act? If you can pull that one over, I guess that's its own type of magic, isn't it?"

I looked around as if to gather my things, but I hadn't brought anything with me.

"Consider, before you leave, what you might be walking away from," he taunted with an infuriating smile. "Your circumstance is no different. You still need a story. You wanted to write about a washed-up carnival man who lost his spot in the center ring because of a circus accident years ago. Instead, I'm offering you something more."

"You are offering me nonsense. I need real stories. I need stories like the one Edward Thomas provided me," I said.

"And because Edward Thomas is a policeman, the fact that he saw a fogman was good enough for Travis Blakely?" His gaze was steady, piercing, like a bluffing card shark. My breath caught. I had never mentioned details from the fog man encounter, and I certainly hadn't mentioned my pen name.

"How do you know about that?"

"A writer like you can't hide behind a pen name," he said. "The Steely-Eyed Detective. It was a very gripping tale."

"Who have you been talking to?"

"If you are so convinced the pen is a hoax, prove me wrong," he said, holding it up toward me. I bit my lip. I felt tired, exhausted even. I felt guilty, like I betrayed Byron by coming here, conversing with this stranger, touching his hand, and sitting on his bed. Yet, his words made me feel something wild inside. I wanted this to work.

I was fighting it because I wanted a reason to believe him. I liked the idea of such an exotic friend. I liked the idea of such an exotic story.

"If the pen can turn fact into fiction, why aren't you in the center ring?" I asked.

"Like I said, magic knows to camouflage itself. There are certain rules." His hand was still outstretched, inviting. Hesitantly, I plucked the pen from it and slowly sat down at the desk again. He crouched on the other side of it to face me. "Write anything that comes to your mind, so long as it isn't about someone you know."

"Someone I know?"

"The pen won't work to benefit your life directly," he said, smiling. "But for a writer, even news about strangers can be beneficial. If it helps, think of something outlandish then replace the names with anonymous pronouns."

The pen felt like it was moving on its own, wriggling in my hand. I put it to the paper and scribbled something. He wanted outlandish? I'd give him outlandish.

"Perfect," he said, whipping the paper up and throwing it into the fire. We watched it burn together. I felt like a child, pretending at witches and wizards. The more the flames consumed the piece of paper, the more foolish I felt. How did I, in the course of twenty-four hours, go from a newly celebrated writer to playing pretend and magic in a desperate attempt to get my next story? This could not have been what my father had in mind.

"What now?" I stammered impatiently.

"I'll see you tomorrow," Bram said, his eyes fixed on the fire.

His complacent indifference toward me made me furious. For some reason, I felt like I had given him a part of myself that night.

"You most certainly will not," I said. I stormed out of the yurt and broke into a run for home.

Chapter Seven

Hangover

My head reeled the next morning. My hair was still slightly damp from the washing I gave myself before bed. I had tried to expunge the smells of the carnival from myself and, to no avail, scrub off some of the guilt I felt at my infidelity. I felt dirty. Many women would say I hadn't been unfaithful, but I knew that, if Byron ever learned about my night's interactions with Bram... I shuddered to think what it might do to him.

Was it right for me to keep it a secret? I had planned on telling him about my trip to the carnival if it had yielded a story. I may have left out some important details, but I would have at least told him that I went there alone. With a story in hand, surely, it could be believed, justified even. I simply was story sleuthing, as he called it. But now, what did I have to show for my indecency?

When I got home the night before, my sister was still out. I was asleep by the time she got in. Usually, I would have scolded her, but I wasn't even sure what time I got home. It could have been eight pm or midnight. I could have slept three hours or ten. I felt unusually sore inside and out.

I skipped my usual breakfast with Byron, instead heading down the street to pick up some pastry items from Barker's Bakery. I was there early enough to have my pick of the shop. I walked inside.

"Luella!" Mrs. Barker cried. "Haven't stopped by the shop for a good while. And with such dreadful bags under your eyes. Are you well, dear?"

Mrs. Barker didn't mince words. She and Mrs. Crow played cards together on the weekend. I could only imagine the conversations they had there. What must the glamor of being aged and having abandoned concerns about others' opinions be like? I imagined they knew everything about everybody between the two of them. Mrs. Barker noticing my haggard, tired face meant Mrs. Crow later asking me about problems with my engagement.

"I didn't sleep well," I replied, blushing. "Do you have any filled buns this morning?"

"They're what I'm known for, dear. Wouldn't be Barker's without our signature filled buns," she said. Mr. Barker burst from a small door behind the baker's counter with a large crate full of bread loaves.

"Another dozen," he barked, bumping into his wife. "The rye was temperamental this morning. Oh! Hello, Luella! Tired? You look like the Severn spit you right out."

"Don't tell her that, George!" Mrs. Barker said, swatting her husband with a hand towel.

"I only mean that I hope she's well!"

"She looks beautiful, like a spring flower! You wouldn't know anything about it, would you?"

"Must be my eyes then. Forgive me, Luella. I must have been staring at the oven fires too long. You do look lovely."

I purchased the buns quickly and walked out, secure and validated in my decision not to go to Byron's. Even the bakers noticed the effects of my little night haunt. Byron would take one look at me and send for the doctor. I hated doctors.

I hurried home to find Anna at the breakfast table, nursing a cup of tea. She looked positively euphoric.

"Luella!" She sighed as I walked in. "You were asleep when I got home, but I simply must tell you about my evening with Jacob!" She whispered the last word, savoring the sound of it as if it were a fine wine. I forced a smile and used my sisterly compassion to swallow my own problems for the time being. I hadn't decided whether I would divulge my secret to Anna. In so many ways, I betrayed her trust as much as I had Byron's. After all, what would Jacob's family think if her sister was wrapped up in a scandal? Plus, assuming things with Jacob didn't pan out, as I suspected they may not, she relied on me for her welfare. Byron was our ticket off the tightrope we were walking. One step out of place and we'd be back to the gutter. With Byron, we could be more. He wasn't elite or absurdly wealthy, but at least we'd be taken care of. We wouldn't have to worry about Mr. Stringham any longer.

Mr. Stringham! I'd nearly forgotten about him. I wanted to hear about Anna's evening, but I had to get to work. One hit story was nice, but we had increased rent to worry about. "You're more than your last story." My father's words rang in my memory, drawing me back to the strange aromas and sensations from Bram's yurt the night before.

"The evening began with a walk near the docks," she said. "Jacob picked me up here, and he looked so handsome. He wore that navy jacket. You know? The one I like so much?"

I nodded, trying to listen. Anxiety was creeping into the back of my brain. So many questions combatted for space in there. At the base of all of it was the pressure to discover another story. Why journalism? Why couldn't I have written a novel or painted a painting that would produce significant figures and give me a moment's rest? I was a slave now, a slave to the hunt.

"That was when he showed me these earrings he got me. You didn't even notice!"

I smiled as she displayed her earrings, but I couldn't concentrate. I kept coming in and out of what she said. I thought about Byron. I thought about Bram. I thought about Edward. I thought about Anna, even though she sat right in front of me and I couldn't focus on what she was saying.

"Luella, your eyes keep darting back and forth. Is something wrong?"

I pinched the skin on the back of my hand to snap myself out of my episode. "Everything is just fine," I said. "I haven't even told you my own news."

"You have news! Well, of course, you must share but please don't spoil my fun. After I finish my story, I'll be all ears for yours." Poor

Anna. If she had anything to say, she would just about burst until she could let it out. She was guileless like that. I saw a future Mrs. Crow or Mrs. Barker in her. Then again, maybe she lacked the interest in others' misfortunes like they had, and she didn't observe things as shrewdly as those two gossips. Mrs. Barker could tell something was wrong just by looking at me. Why couldn't Anna? She was on her third bun.

"That's when we turned a corner, and he revealed his big surprise," she continued. "It was enchanting, sister. He took me to the queerest carnival on the east shore."

"Carnival?" I echoed.

"Yes! It was the most curious little carnival, too!"

I couldn't believe it. Could it be possible that my hazy inclination brought me to the same outing my sister attended?

"It had these electric lights that gave everything an eerie glow. I don't know if I could ever grow accustomed to electric lights. But, for a date with Jacob, it was wonderfully mysterious," she said.

The coincidence was too jarring. I needed to make sense of things. My mind gripped reality like a hand taking hold of a spinning wheel. There couldn't have been more than one carnival by the docks. While I was consorting with a strange man in a tent, my dear sister could have been mere meters away. I sat on his bed with him! If something had happened. If he had forced his way with me, or I lost my faculties and. . .

I couldn't finish the thought. I was supposed to be raising my sister —to be an example! What state of mind had I been in last night? What madness! I risked everything. Why? Thirst for a new story was a poor excuse, and I couldn't fully invest my conviction in it. There had to be another way to realize my father's vision.

"I have to go," I interrupted. Anna's mouth locked in its open position.

"Go?" she stammered. "But I hardly saw you at all yesterday! You haven't told me your news. Heavens, I haven't even finished mine!"

"I have an appointment I forgot about," I lied.

"I won't let you just go off like this," she protested. "At least give me a hint, or I'll be devastated all day. Did you set a date with Byron at last?"

I wiped my hands on a napkin and gathered my gloves.

"The story took. It turns out, I'm a hit writer," I said with a curt nod. She shouted and applauded me as I walked out the door.

Chapter Eight

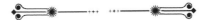

From the Ashes

I didn't know where I was going. I couldn't go to Byron. I couldn't face him yet. Instead, I wandered the streets, investigating cobblestone byways I had passed all my life without notice. There were dead flowers in the little green patches here and there tucked behind brick quarter walls. Occasionally along the way, dormant trees grew stark and gnarled from holes in the sidewalk. Their crooked tendrils beckoned at me accusingly.

It was a typically overcast day in late September. I just needed to walk. The autumn air nipped at my cheeks. The mid-morning had the streets alive in activity. Horses trotted by under the whip of their drivers. Clean men in dark waistcoats and gloves carried parcels down the street, burying their chin in their collars to guard against the breeze off the river not far away. Nowhere could I escape the call of salesmen shouting out recent headlines.

"City police causing panic with story about Fog Men!" one man called to me as I passed. I wasn't sure which had me more frightened: the fogman or the specter of my recent success. How could I possibly replicate it? I wandered by a poor woman on her knees, begging for alms, and thought I saw my own face under the bonnet, sickly coughing. I dug in my purse for a few coins, wishing I could spare more. As usual, my reserves were shallower than I'd wish, but I tossed in a few just the same.

Soon, I'd have the rent to worry about. One story wouldn't deal with Mr. Stringham. Not for the long term by any rate. Perhaps soon, I too was destined for the street. No. I had choices. I could marry Byron, even if I didn't tell him about going to the carnival. I had to find another story.

The city looked so much like itself. One street after another presenting houses, storefronts, building facades. Here a butcher, there a thatcher. The scent of bread from the bakeries beckoned to me through open doors or windows. I passed more newsstands and tried to shake off my surprise at seeing Langley's in a prominent showing nearest the road. "The Steely-Eyed Detective: Case of the Fog Man" by Travis Blakely. In my head, the pen name rang with Bram's voice. I couldn't shake the curious tone of his voice while divulging my secret. How did he know? Had he been stalking me? Spying on me?

Could it really be magic?

I wound up at Barker's Bakeshop, where Mrs. Barker rung up my order without asking what I wanted. Apparently, I had become quite a regular. I walked out with a parcel of their iced buns and went on my way.

My mother had taught Anna and me often when we were children, when in doubt, find something to do for someone else. It was a good Christian approach to life. I hadn't yet expressed my due gratitude to Edward. Perhaps these iced buns would be just the thing. Now there was some magic I could get behind. The magical effect of a superb baked good.

Maybe life could stay simple. I didn't actually do anything inappropriate with Bram. I grabbed his hand, but that was just to prevent him from walking out on me. I'd have done the same with a brother. Sitting on the bed could also be considered familial. With time, the guilt would be swept into reasonable explanation, and I might not feel anything at all. Life could still go on. If I walked into the station now, I could dig up more leads, and I could keep writing on the police force. Maybe Edward would see another ghost. Even if it wasn't a ghost, I was sure the coppers uncovered enough oddities to keep Langley's afloat. I didn't need to be the best-selling writer in the country, simply a respectable one.

But, there was still that lingering moment when Bram had almost kissed me. More importantly, I was afraid in that moment I had wanted him to.

I brushed these thoughts aside with a few quick steps up and into the station.

"I'm here looking for Lieutenant Edward Thomas," I said to the same red-headed clerk behind the desk.

He bent over his copy of *The Dawnhurst Happenings* and looked up at me. "Are you here to file a missing persons report?"

"What? No! For the last time," I said, "I'm not here to file a missing person. I just want to talk with somebody."

"Talk with someone, mum? Are you experiencing some type of trauma? Need to get it off your mind? You don't look well." I was furious that this dimwitted man wouldn't just treat me like a normal human being. But, I was even more furious that his question was completely merited.

"Edward Thomas," I repeated through gritted teeth.

"Right, right. I think he is down the hall near the holding cell," the man said, turning back to his papers. "Just brought in a proper brigand, he did. Don't usually let women back there. Why don't you have a seat down the hall?"

I was growing accustomed to glowering at this man over a resentful nose, but I thanked him nonetheless, made my way down, and took a seat again, across from Ms. Turner. She was, as before, flying her fingers over a typewriter, her hair pulled back haphazardly, with a stray lock falling in front of her face. I spied a copy of *Langley's* sticking out from under her stack of papers. She looked at me and blew the hair out of the way.

"You're back," she said. "Here to see Sergeant Cooper? Or are you here to see the *Steely-Eyed Detective*." She glanced for a split second toward the hidden weekly.

I blushed, clutching my pack of pastries.

"I just—I wanted to see if Edward—Lieutenant Thomas—had any other stories I could—"

"Darling, we all read the piece. I, frankly, loved it," she said.

"You did?" For the very first time, I allowed myself to feel flattered and relieved. I couldn't explain why, but Ms. Turner's opinion meant a great deal to me.

"Certainly. And you could do much worse than Lieutenant Thomas."

The shade in my face deepened. "It's not like that. I'm engaged," I stammered.

"You mentioned that the other day, too. Relax, dear, it's all just fiction anyway, isn't it?" she winked. I was speechless. Nothing in my story suggested that Edward and I were anything more than acquaintances. I wasn't even mentioned in the story at all. I wrote under a pen name, for heaven's sake. My thoughts drifted back to Byron's reaction when I unveiled the story's title. He was immediately jealous. I pretended not to notice, but only a fool would think otherwise.

How many times in a week was I going to break Byron's heart?

I sat in silence, brooding over Ms. Turner's insinuations. I could sweep the comments of old nosey geese like Mrs. Crow and Mrs. Barker under the rug. My sister was my baby sister. She was obsessed with Jacob. I expected nothing less from her. But, if Ms. Turner told me I had written a love story, then I guess I had written a love story.

But this was nonsense. I hardly knew her at all. I'd spoken with her two times, briefly. What did it matter if she thought my writing was girlish? What did I care if all the women in my life were hollow? Can't a woman talk about a man without raising eyebrows all over the world?

The clerk from the front promptly brought Edward to me and dismissed himself. The poor man stood alert and erect, which by now I considered his usual demeanor, but he was also soaking wet under a scratchy looking blanket. I could see into his chest, where he wore a dry, unbuttoned henley shirt, patched with transparent damp spots. His hair was neatly combed, still shiny as if he had recently gone swimming. His eyes took me in, brows relaxed into an amiable expression.

"And what happened to you?" Ms. Turner asked, not getting up from her desk.

"Fool of a man tried to escape across to the east bank of the river," he responded, without taking his eyes from me. He added a warm smile and tilted his head to Ms. Turner. "Got him, though."

My imagination bore me to the scene where Edward, brave and bold, chased some criminal to the bridge. It must have been a scene, seeing the iron-eyed wolf dive into the water and wrestle his foe to the shoreline. I stared.

"Your story was a success, Ms. Winthrop," he said with a courteous bow. "Every officer we have is now calling me the Steely-Eyed Detective. The actual detectives are furious about it."

"But I never mentioned your name. How did they know it was you?"

"I'm afraid my story of seeing a phantom in the fog had already circulated among the ranks by the time your story published," he replied, drawing in a deep breath that filled out his chest under the blanket.

"I'm sorry. I didn't mean any harm," I said. How stupid of me to think I could really keep this man's identity a secret. It was a pipe dream, especially around his colleagues.

"I saw what I saw, Ms. Winthrop," he said plainly. "I don't feel ashamed about it. If the other men don't believe me, they can fight me if they want, but truth is truth, and I'll stick by my story."

There was something about him standing there spouting off his conviction that shook me. Truth was truth. This police lieutenant, I was confident, would go through just about anything before breaking his word or retreating. His integrity filled the room. In comparison, I reflected on my own position. I had always imagined writers as paladins of truth and right. Writers brought knowledge to light, elaborated on points that may be unforeseen to others, and unveiled valid emotional context. I, after the pressure of one hot sale, fell apart at the seams and was driven to great lengths to extend my success.

Are you a woman that likes to laugh? Bram's words kept burrowing their way back to the surface of my memory.

"Your courage inspires me, Lieutenant Thomas," I finally managed to say.

"You are the inspiration, Ms. Winthrop. I admire your gumption to write the way you do. Given your use of a male pen name, I can only imagine you fought quite hard to be where you are now."

I blushed. "Well, it's nothing like fighting criminals."

"No. It's far more courageous," he said with a soft smile. He looked like a Greek statue. How could a Greek statue smile so softly?

"These are for you," I said, clumsily presenting my parcel, hearing Ms. Turner's eyebrows pique in curiosity.

"For me?"

"I just wanted to say thank you," I replied, finding it very hard to meet his gaze. "Your account has made no small impact on my career."

"I was just doing my job, Ms. Winthrop. It's hardly worth rewarding me for."

"Take it as a token of friendship then," I insisted. He looked at me tenderly before accepting and peeking inside the parcel. He laughed.

"Well, if only all friendships started on such a delicious and wonderful footing. Thank you very much." He bowed his head. I blushed. Ms. Turner breathed heavily.

"What story are you working on next?" he asked.

"That's exactly why I'm here," I answered after clearing my throat. "You haven't happened to see any more ghosts recently, have you?"

Ms. Turner snorted. I forgot she was there. It was a small hallway, after all. We both looked at her.

"I'm sorry," she said. "If you wanted a private conversation, you really should have had it somewhere other than, you know, my desk." Edward looked amused and unfazed. What must it be like to go through life without fearing God or man?

"I'm afraid I haven't," he said, turning back to me.

"I hoped as much, for your sake," I said, touching his arm, which, unsurprisingly, was quite firm. "Perhaps you wouldn't mind me writing about this episode that has you soaking wet."

"Not much to tell, really."

He was cut off by an absolute racket near the front of the station. I recognized Sergeant Cooper's voice booming orders at his subordinates clear as crystal through the wall. We turned, and I saw him coming our way, practically filling the hallway. A clerk followed, desperately trying to keep up and take his jacket.

"Just take the ruddy thing!" he bellowed. "We're going to be hit with a storm of reporters. Just our lucky day. If it weren't so funny, I'd just be livid about the whole thing!" He stopped at Ms. Turner's desk and noticed me. "And the first one is already here! Good ruddy afternoon!"

"What is it Sergeant?" Edward asked.

"How did you know to be here already? I should have known you would be. You had the smell of ink from the get-go. But go on, fill us in! What is the secret reporter magic that alerts them to things that aren't their business?" he asked, pointing a big, fat finger at me. With his other hand, he fished an iced bun out of the package in Edward's hands and took a big bite.

"I beg your pardon," I responded. The nerve of this man to point at me like that, my father's friend or no.

"You're here for the skinny," he insisted through a mouthful of food.

"I don't know what you're talking about. I was just here trying to a drum up a story from Lieutenant Thomas."

"Well, whatever you got from him, let me do you a favor. This one's better," he said, heading through his door, plopping into his chair, and swinging two dirty shoes on to his desk.

Edward, Ms. Turner, and I all gaped at him.

"It's been a bank robbery," he said, "except not just a usual bank robbery. Two gents rode in on horseback, dressed in *shining ruddy armor*, as if they were King Arthur's lot, waved their swords around, grabbed the money, and rode off."

"Odd's fish!" cried Edward.

I felt my knees weaken. I put a hand on the door frame to steady myself.

"Gets better, though," Cooper continued. "We caught up to them and managed to talk them down off the horses and to hand over their tools of medieval warfare. We get their helmets off, and it's none other than Mr. Bradford and his manservant! They couldn't even remember how they got there."

"Mr. Bradford?" Ms. Turner echoed. "The president of the railway station?"

I couldn't breathe. The world got fuzzy, and my eyes rolled back. Muffled voices and someone's arms ushered me into a chair.

"Ms. Winthrop, are you alright?" I think it was Edward talking, but I couldn't concentrate. This had to be a trick, or else I was dreaming. They were pulling one over on me.

How did Sergeant Cooper know what I had scribbled with that pen?

Chapter Nine

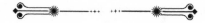

Fit of Jealousy

It took the Sergeant nearly an hour to convince me that what he was saying was true. I didn't believe him until he had me examine what could only be a slash wound from a broadsword on one of his men.

It took even longer for me to convince them that I was well after my faint. "I was just overheated," I repeated again and again. After drinking a substantial amount of water and elevating my feet against my will, I finally won the day and was allowed to leave for the very urgent business I promised to have.

Edward seemed particularly hesitant to let me go. His eyes lingered on me under deeply furrowed brows. He urged me to allow him to get me a hansom, but I refused. "I prefer to walk," I said. "It'll be good for me after such a spell." To this, he could not but acquiesce.

After turning the corner and escaping what I knew were watchful eyes through windows, I doubled my pace. I had questions, and I wanted answers.

First, though, I felt vindicated. I had gone to that carnival with the intent to get a story, and I came away with a story well enough. Given the lengths I went to uncover it, I owed it to Byron to write the story and launch his publication into greater success. Justification was such sweet relief! My outing was a celebration of the freedom that came with being a successful writer. I could go anywhere and transform my experience into something tangible for my sister and me.

While I was there, I did what all good writers do. I observed, sniffed out something odd, and investigated. My intuition led me to another story. Was it magic? I doubted it. It was more likely that Bram had somehow worked out some type of con to get Mr. Bradford to behave in such a way. Perhaps he drugged him. Perhaps he drugged me last night. Who could say? Maybe it was hypnotism. I had watched ordinary people behave in bizarre ways at the carnival in the hypnotist's ring. Dressing up silly and performing an act like this had the stench of that hypnotist's act all over it.

Most importantly, I now had a sturdy reason to hold up my choices from the night before, sturdier than being tipsy from celebration cordials. Did that mean I would tell Byron about the carnival? I doubted he would understand. What difference should it make to him where the story came from anyway. The poor wreck got insecure enough when I talked about Edward. I couldn't imagine how he would manage hearing about my encounter with Bram. He'd worry himself sick for no reason at all. After all, nothing really happened between us. He just showed me a bizarre trinket that he claimed was magic.

I just never thought he'd go to such lengths to elaborate on his claims.

It didn't matter. The story was genuine, and it shouldn't go to waste. Then I could put it all out of my mind and never see Bram again.

I flung open the door of *Langley's Miscellany* and discovered from Mr. Storm that Byron was out. This was all the better, as it gave me time to write up a draft. I set to work at a typewriter on a little desk in the rear of the shop and attacked the keys with a fury, accompanied by the lovely song of Byron's skylark.

An hour passed without my knowing, and I only paused then to take a quick stretch. The article was coming along wonderfully. I smiled at my, dare I say, colorful description of two knights on horseback taking Victoria's Bank by storm and laying siege to the place. Only to be hunted down by a valiant band of our very own police force.

I thought it made for great reading, perhaps not quite as compelling as a ghost in the alleys but compelling all the same. I glanced around the shop. Mr. Storm had left at some point during my writing frenzy. My stomach groaned, and I realized that I had hardly touched the filled buns I brought home for breakfast with Anna. Now, it was nearly two o'clock. Maybe Byron had left some biscuits around from our intended breakfast this morning. I began my search.

On what usually served as our breakfast table by the window were several copies of our publication of the "Steely-Eyed Detective," as well as loose life versions of publications from our competitors. But, pushed to the side of the table was an empty plate and covered basket. The basket looked promising.

I found my prey inside the basket: some of Mrs. Barker's finest cheese biscuits with pepper. I snatched one up hungrily and absentmindedly started reading whatever happened to be in front of me.

Some bills hid behind a few copies of the latest *Manfield's Happenings*, one hastily torn. Byron was often quiet with me about the paper's expenses. This report, presumably from the past month, looked adequately dire. Up until our most recent publication, the magazine hadn't been performing the way we had hoped. Poor Byron must have been dipping into some personal reserves to keep things afloat. He would call that an investment. I would call it gambling on writers. Fortunately, for him, things were changing now. I was confident I could help bring up the numbers. If the past week had anything to do with it, finances would be the least of our worries.

Under the bill, I saw another letter, this one delicately preserved. The return address listed its sender as Carolina Drake. I had never heard that name before. The handwriting looped gracefully across the envelope unhurried and unapologetic.

I felt a knot turn in my stomach. I turned over the envelope in my hand and saw the seal was unbroken. A temptation rose up inside of me to tear into it, a desire uncharacteristic of me. I was not the jealous type. There had been occasions before when Byron had received the attentions of another woman at social gatherings, and I had hardly cared at all. But now, the feeling seized me like stumbling on a hornet's nest. Anxiety gripped me, wrapped up in a peculiar type of anger and suspicion. Who was Carolina Drake?

Jealousy was strange and sickly sweet. I felt it chase out my other needs. My appetite was gone, and an overwhelming wave of anger slowly crept up my body. If this were treachery, Byron would pay.

I dropped my biscuit and the letter with a start as Byron swung the door open. I tried to shuffle the papers in which I'd been snooping casually and quickly.

"Luella! You're here! I was afraid something had happened to you this morning or last night," he said. "Your sister said you ran out for an appointment."

"You went to my flat?" I asked, more edge in my voice than I cared to let on. He usually never dared, unless invited. Intrusive man. Foolish man.

Why did I feel so angry?

"I was worried," he replied. "After saying our goodnights, I was struck to the bone with a chilling feeling that I might not see you again."

"Might not see me again? What rubbish are you going on about?"

"It's all well and good for us to publish hair-raising tales, but you're a good writer," he said with a sigh.

"You were worried the fog man was going to attack me?" I asked. I clenched my hand. He had some cheek feigning worry while a letter lay on our table from another woman. If he was scared of anything, it shouldn't have been the phantom.

"Well, not the fog man necessarily. I don't know what that Lieutenant really saw, but the streets can be dangerous. I should have walked you home." He sat down across from me and put his hat on the table.

"This is nonsense, Byron," I said. "I've taken care of myself for a long time, and I'm quite capable of getting home in the early evening on my own."

"So, nothing happened to you last night? My reservations were for nothing?" he asked, sincerity dripping from the worry lines in his forehead. Nothing happened to me last night? I tried not to feel defensive, not to imagine an accusatory tone. I bit my tongue and set my jawline firm.

"Oh, would you stop it? I already told you. Nothing happened. I just went home," I lied. He heaved a sigh of relief and leaned back into his chair. I only felt a little guilt pinch at my cheeks, but it would pass.

"Well, thank goodness for that," he said with a sigh. "It's bad enough you go to that police station. Can you just promise me you won't get carried away with all of this?"

"Carried away?" Yes, perhaps I got carried away. A part of me wished I had. No. No, I did not. That was my temper talking. I shook my head. Something felt off, like dissonant piano keys. I couldn't ever remember having a bad temper.

"I mean to say a lot of writers will go investigate leads all over the city. Can't we just both agree right here that you won't go chasing a story deep into the east side?" He grabbed my hand firmly.

"And you'd just have me let the story go instead?" I asked. I didn't like accepting limitations. I had grown up in part of the east side, after all. I knew it better than he did. He should have been thanking me. He didn't know how lucky he had it.

"There are plenty of other stories, or at least less dangerous ways to research them. I don't want something happening to you."

"Byron, do you intend to lock me up like your prized bird?" I wasn't sure if he registered the sarcasm.

"Can you blame me?" he said with a pitiable frown. "What would happen to me if something happened to you?"

He'd go out of business, at least if these statements were any indication, and if the letter on the table was what I suspected, he deserved worse than that.

My head felt sensitive, as though I had a migraine but without the pain. I didn't like feeling like this. This wasn't like me. I need something. A release. Anything. . .

"Who is Carolina Drake?" I blurted out. He stared and blinked blankly.

"Carolina who?"

"Carolina Drake," I blushed but maintained my indignance. Merely giving the question voice was enough to begin venting my frustration. "You have a letter from her on the table."

"Do I?" He crossed to the table excitedly, found the letter, and tore it open. "Marvelous!"

I knit my brow, feeling more sheepish as the knot in my stomach began to unravel.

"I wrote Ms. Drake inquiring more details about how Travis Blakely might go about getting noticed by the Golden Inkwell committee."

"The Golden Inkwell committee?" I asked, feeling more embarrassed every second.

"Yes, you know how these things go. The Golden Inkwell goes to the best writer, but it never hurts to make sure the committee doesn't forget to look everywhere."

It was stupid of me to jump to conclusions, and my apathy toward his effort gave me away. Here I had been accusing him of infidelity when he was working to bolster my career.

"Why, who did you think Ms. Drake was?" he asked. I buried my eyes in the floor trying to invent an answer. "My dear Luella, you couldn't possibly think—" He burst into a laugh, which I did not appreciate at all.

"What is so funny?"

"Just the thought that you might be jealous. You! Honestly, it comes as quite a relief. Jealously is a sure mark of affection, after all."

I rolled my eyes, eager to put the incident behind me. I wasn't sure I agreed that jealously was a healthy symptom of love. If anything, it might signal insecurity or a crack along the foundation somewhere. Still, if his little triumph made him overlook my little episode, then let him have it. After all, he was right. It wasn't like me to be jealous, and I didn't like how the accompanying anger tasted in my mouth. Feeling my emotions steer me like cab driver was not a welcome experience.

It took me a moment to realize, though, that Byron had changed his mind on my potential to win the Golden Inkwell. That was encouraging. Writing a letter to the committee was a sure change from his bit of scoffing he made at the idea the other day. He was proving to be an even more important ally than I originally thought. Maybe I didn't need to chase down criminals into the east side after all. Edward could do that for me. And, maybe I shouldn't wander into strange tents at strange carnivals. My acquiescence to his requests was a small price to pay for his devotion.

"Oh Byron, if you're done acting the ninny, I have something to tell you."

"Another story?" he asked, noticing my pile of paper at the typewriter in the back of the room.

"Another story."

Chapter Ten

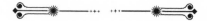

Bunbury's Restaurant

I knew Byron was going to love it. His eyes shone brightly as he read over my draft and took in painted visuals of a bygone era rearing its way into modern life. What man isn't interested in tales of swordplay and cops and robbers? He finished it, lavished a healthy dose of praise on me, and decided it would take the headline feature in this week's printing. He asked about another edition of the "Steely-Eyed Detective" as well, which I thought was good of him, considering Edward struck him as a rival not long before. By the time I left in the evening, we had *"Knights of the Wrong Table: A Bank Robbery in Full Armor"* and *"The Steely-Eyed Detective and The Water Thief"* done.

As Byron read over them both time and again, getting giddier with each read-through, I thought I could see the glint of copper in his eyes, as though he was counting the profits already. I was happy to make him so excited. After all, this is why we both got into the business, to compete, get to the very top of all the thousands of sheets of paper swirling around the city.

But, I didn't feel as giddy as Byron. If anything, I felt a pang of impatience, like I had an itch I couldn't scratch. Behind our new headlining story was another, deeper riddle. How did Bram convince Mr. Bradford to don a suit of armor and rob a bank? Earlier in the afternoon, I had swept that under the proverbial rug. Hypnotization. How difficult could it be, especially if he got the carnival's hypnotist in on the gag? But, it didn't answer some important questions. How did they get access to Mr. Bradford? It wasn't as if the hypnotist last night had snuck her subjects a potion. Being hypnotized, at least as I understood it, was a deliberate two-way interaction. It wasn't a poison that could be stealthily administered.

I shook my head, feeling foolish. It was certainly possible for Bram to get a meeting with Mr. Bradford. Why shouldn't he be able to? Maybe he knew him personally. Maybe Bram lied to Bradford's secretary and pretended to be an important patron.

On the other hand, why would the hypnotist agree to go to such great lengths in order to pull a prank on me? Surely, convincing Mr. Bradford to rob a bank would have put her at great personal risk.

It couldn't have been the story I wrote. It couldn't have been magic.

We encounter magic every day. It's just not what people expect. Those were Bram's words, and they stuck like a bad typewriter key.

Byron put down his spectacles and let out a satisfied hum. "Please, allow me to take you to dinner." I must have looked surprised. "Oh, come on! We should celebrate!"

"But, my sister is expecting me," I protested, searching for an excuse.

"Invite her along—and that boyfriend of hers as well," he carried on. "And don't look like I'm being unreasonably charitable. You're the one buying!" He gestured toward my draft. He looked positively stupid with his toothy grin. I don't know why I felt like hitting him. I should have been happy that my work made my editor feel financially secure.

"I'm not sure they will be able to make it," I replied.

"Nonsense! It's about time that we four had a night together. I've been curious about Jacob for a good time now, and I almost never get to talk with Anna."

His cavalier attitude toward our newfound financial success, combined with his assertive attempt at uniting the four of us for what he considered some type of family dinner, was off-putting. Who did he think he was? He wasn't the head of my family, at least not yet.

I managed a stiff smile. "I believe Jacob already has plans," I lied.

"Well, then he should cancel them. We're all going out." And that was that.

Before I knew it, the stories were off to the printer, and he had escorted me home. This was not his custom, and Anna was quite alarmed that the two of us showed up there. As luck would have it, she was getting ready to meet Jacob for an evening out. Their plans? Nondescript. It took Byron all of ten seconds to convince Anna that the four of us would make merry company at Bunbury's Restaurant. Her eyes grew wide as saucers, and in her excitement, she could not see the subtle, sisterly signals I tried to convey indicating my reluctance toward this appointment.

Anna told us Jacob would be at the house presently then disappeared to finish preparing herself. Byron sat himself down at the table to wait, taking out a copy of *Mansfield's Weekly* and laughing to himself at their articles.

"They won't be able to compete," he muttered to himself, grinning.

Meanwhile, my anxiety over the bank robbers settled more heavily. I became increasingly convinced that hypnotizing Mr. Bradford would be immensely difficult, if not impossible. And, if it were impossible, I had no explanation for his bizarre behavior. What was worse, Mr. Bradford had no explanation either, according to Sergeant Cooper.

I couldn't stop thinking about the intricate, heavy pen Bram handed to me. Did he even read what I wrote before tossing the paper into the fire? I didn't think he had. If he hadn't, then how could he have orchestrated it?

And, if he hadn't orchestrated it, how? How?

An hour later, we were all sitting at a table at Bunbury's, enjoying a fine champagne, roast beef, and whatever else my fiancé told us we wanted. Had I not been so preoccupied with my own agenda, I might have marveled at the intricate woodwork and fine curtains framing the restaurant. Anna did enough marveling for the both of us, though. The carpets were a deep green, the floor to ceiling drapes a bright gold and cream, and the chandeliers of fine crystal. In the center of the main dining room sat a large group of tables, with a generous space between them for servers to pass. A lesser restaurant would have packed in twice the tables to increase profits. Surrounding the center dining area were carved, secluded booths of mahogany, each with their own curtain, some drawn for privacy, others open to see out, and others open still to let others see in.

The first course crawled by. The waiter tried to suggest to us a series of French dishes. Anna ended up ordering something she couldn't pronounce. Jacob ordered a fine whiskey to go with our escargot and butter. By the time the main course arrived, Jacob and Byron were thick as thieves, deeply engrossed in a conversation about horse races.

"My good man, I'm afraid you're showing your inexperience," Byron said, chuckling.

"And you, sir, are showing your failure to adapt to new times. Breeding isn't the same as it used to be!"

By dessert, they had made a small wager, thus cementing what could only be considered the beginning of what they claimed to be a beautiful friendship. I couldn't help but notice the glass glazing both of their eyes, though. I thought their friendship implausible.

I did everything in my power to keep the meal going at a skipping pace without betraying my womanly duties toward good etiquette. Byron was in a peculiar mood, made even more strange by the combination of bourbon and champagne. He giggled, red-faced, at his own witticisms and refused to back down to trivial points of his argument with Jacob, which by now, I would deem less amiable than before. I wanted desperately to slip away and go track down the scoundrel behind Mr. Bradford's heist, if such a scoundrel existed. The food at Bunbury's was lavish and rich, but none of it tasted as spirited as the roasted nuts at the carnival the night before. Besides, I craved answers, not sweets.

Still, dessert came, accompanied by coffee. Byron insisted we try some of the walnut cake, which, in all fairness, was actually quite delicious, despite my humor. Swelling relief lightened my mood as I watched the napkins wadded and placed on the table. The more I sat brooding, the more I had decided that I was angry with Byron. The dinner was doubly distasteful to me. I had something that felt ultimately more pressing than eating at a nice restaurant, and Byron had taken it upon himself to legitimize a relationship between Anna and Jacob. I didn't feel that he had a right to do so. What connection did he have to Anna apart from one through me?

"But enough about horses," he said, leaning back to press his shoulders firmly against his chair. "Let's get on to a more pressing matter."

I inhaled in preparation to protest. Another round of conversation would put me firmly past any reasonable time of night to go find Bram and confront him.

"I don't catch your meaning, sir," said Jacob. Byron took out his pipe and fixed a businesslike curved grimace onto his face.

"You've been courting Miss Anna for some time now. I, for one, would like to know your intentions," he said. The table fell quiet. My mouth froze open, unsure of what to say.

"Byron, your concern is very kind, but—" Anna began.

"I think we're all interested in some answers," he continued. "She is a young woman, but she's not getting any younger, and you are taking a considerable portion of her time with whatever it is you're after. Don't you think it's time to man up?"

"Byron!" I hissed. "Do you really think it's your place to ask such a question?" I could feel the temperature of my blood rising at his bourbon-tinged audacity.

"Well, if not my place, then whose? The girl's father isn't here, and I don't know if I could stomach it to see a young lad take advantage of that kind of situation." I bristled at the word father.

"What exactly are you insinuating?" Jacob asked, red in the face.

"You're very young," Byron went on. "And everyone at this table knows that Anna is your senior. I just want to make sure you are taking this seriously, and before long, if you are to continue seeing her, we might see a proposal on its way."

I felt itches creep all up my spin and into my scalp. Perspiration beaded my forehead and clammed my palms. I looked around, wishing we were anywhere but in the middle of Bunbury's. Jacob scooted his chair back and rose, leaning over the table.

"Now wait just one minute, here!" Jacob seethed, unsteady from the alcohol. "You forget your place shop keep. Do you know who you're talking to?"

"Don't you flounce your family name around me. Your father may be rich, but you're not nobility," Byron said, rising from his own seat. I put my hand firmly on his arm.

"Byron, do not do this," I whispered through clenched teeth.

"If I were afraid of fancy upstarts like you, I'd still be in the gutter. But, I've grown long enough to know that a pedigree is not enough to save a bad egg."

"Is that what you consider me sir?" Jacob's question sounded like a threat.

"I demand you tell me your intentions with this girl, or you will not see her anymore!" Byron shouted. The restaurant had silenced.

"And what do you intend to do about it?" Jacob sneered.

Before I knew what happened, Jacob was on the floor with a red handprint across his face and a hint of blood on his lip. Byron breathed heavily. A gentleman from a neighboring table instantly went to Jacob to help him up.

"Anna, we're leaving," I said, glaring at Byron. "If these two gentlemen want to continue dueling on your behalf, we'll leave them to it."

I grabbed my sister's hand and led her from her seat, ignoring Byron's protests. Anna kept her face to the floor to hide the inevitable onslaught of hot tears I knew were coming. I felt all eyes in the dining room watch us as we made our exit, tracing our steps. I retrieved our coats from the maître d and ordered him to bring around a hansom. "Please, put the cost on Mr. Livingston's check," I demanded. I saw a vase of flowers. It looked relatively expensive, expensive enough at least. "Put these flowers on his check as well."

When the hansom came, I helped Anna in and clambered up after her. Byron trailed out of the restaurant after us.

"Luella, please, be sensible!" he said. I responded to him with a fierce look I had learned from reading about the Medusa. It was enough to shut him up as we drove off. I put an arm around my sister, and to this day, I remain impressed at how well she kept it together on the ride home. It was not a girl's response. It was a woman's.

As soon as we were indoors, however, the emotions burst out of her. I followed her to the bed and cradled her in my arms, rocking her back and forth.

"He's ruined everything!" she sobbed, taking deep, hiccupping gulps of air between her breaths. I didn't know what to tell her. I was surprised to feel tears on my own cheeks. I wanted to say that it would be alright, or that Jacob was a strong young man that wouldn't be deterred by such a slight to his character, but I had no idea what might come of such a public incident. Instead, we just cried together.

"We'll make it through this," I whispered as her cries slackened their furious pace.

"You can't marry him." She sat up out of my arms and grabbed both of my hands. "If he costs me Jacob, you just can't. I could never forgive him."

"Anna, let's not think of that—"

"If you marry him, I'll leave you." And she meant it. I'd never seen her so resolute. I didn't know what to do but nod dumbly. A brand-new fear, one I had never felt before, seeped into my bones. If I lost Anna, how would I live?

She burrowed her face back into my lap, allowing me to stroke her hair to soothe her. I knew she was right. If I could forgive Byron, he had to know it would become his sole objective to smooth things over between Jacob and my sister.

Otherwise, how could I marry him? He would drive a wedge between my sister and me. As far as I was concerned, if it came down to choosing between the two of them, I had decided long before I met Mr. Livingston.

Chapter Eleven

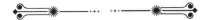

Muddy Old Stories

The next morning felt like a funeral. Anna ducked in and out of consciousness, lounging in the bed for hours, growling at me whenever I attempted to open the curtains to let in some light. Could I blame her? Last night had felt like a nightmare, but sleep had helped to clear my head at least, and knowing the best thing for heartache is iced buns and a cup of tea, I set out to Mrs. Barker's at once. Mrs. Crow was waiting for me on the steps outside.

"Lovely to see you, dear," she said, a whole basket of flowers in her hands. "Would you like a daisy? Last blooms of the year. Only a few pence."

"Good morning, Mrs. Crow. I didn't know you got into flower selling," I said.

"Oh, just a hobby mostly," she said, looking down at her bushel. I suspected she was downplaying her financial situation. "Have to keep busy with something." I smiled and started past her, but she stepped in my way. "I was wondering, Luella, if everything isn't well with poor Ms. Anna."

Of course. Somehow, she knew. Perhaps Mrs. Crow had been hiding out in disguise at the restaurant. One day, I would sit this woman down and learn her information gathering ways.

"It's just," she continued, "I heard her crying last night. I hope everything is faring well with her gentleman prospect."

I cursed our thin walls. Do the poor possess no privacy?

"There's just been a hiccup," I said. "I expect things will smooth out. Young love, you know?" I nodded curtly and tried to make my way off the step, when again she butted in.

"And how are things going with Mr. Livingston?" she continued. "I don't get to hear much about that since you accepted his proposal. Any word on a date for the wedding?"

Her bold question caught me off-guard and started my blood boiling. I tried to respond but managed only to get out a pensive hum. I swallowed hard.

Why did I have to answer Mrs. Crow? It wasn't her place to ask such a thing, and it wasn't something I much wanted to talk about either. Annoyance and frustration flared inside of me. I put a steadied hand on her shoulder. I just wanted to get back to Bram to learn more about the pen. Was that too much to ask?

"I'm afraid I really must be going." I dropped some of the few coins left in my purse in her hand and took a small bunch of dianthuses from her. "For the flower," I said and left her open-mouthed on the steps.

As I walked away, my temper simmered down again. My patience had been so short lately. It wasn't like me to get angry at little things. My mother had a temper. I never liked her for it. The stress and pressure of the writing must have been getting to me. Perhaps I judged my mother too harshly. She must have been stressed as well, what with our economic condition and her two children to raise.

When I got to the Barkers' Bake Shop, I encountered similar questions. I evaded them artfully, if I do say so myself, with vague responses of, "Anna isn't feeling well" and "Byron is as Byron does." I threw in a cocked eyebrow to seal the deal. If I know anything about people, they prefer to feel like they're in the know over knowing precisely what they're in the know about.

Back at home, Anna still had not roused from bed.

"Sister, are you planning on getting up today?"

"I'm not well," she said. I put the back of my hand on her forehead.

"You feel fine to me."

"I tell you! I'm not well. I think I may have cholera," she said, flopping another direction on the bed. I worried over her, but there wasn't much for me to do for her in this state. Heartbreak is dealt with in stages. The utter devastation of the first movement must be ridden out like a section of disagreeable road on horseback.

"There are iced buns on the table. I'm going out," I told her, fastening my shawl.

"Not to see that despicable man!" she said, face fresh with energy, shaking off her bout of cholera. Now, she was lucid as a fox. Was there any hope for Byron?

"If you mean Byron, then no," I said. "I won't be seeing him today. You get some rest."

I left the house to a chorus of grumbly, backhanded remarks about my betrothed. I didn't feel like defending him. I had my own reasons for being upset with him, and I feared that he didn't possess the character required to make it up to me. How can a man apologize for being overassertive and violent? To grovel would be uncomely; to snivel would make things even worse. I would accept only one form of currency for his forgiveness, a solid, well-backboned apology without any self-deprecation. Yes, that would be the only way to convince me even to think about standing up for him to my sister.

Byron, on many occasions, had proved he adored me. He worshipped the ground I walked on in many respects. If I had asked to holiday in Paris, I would fear he might break his back moving the channel, so I wouldn't have to cross it. I could not have that in a husband. I needed someone to look up to, an equal, who treated me with respect and himself with equal respect. How could I ever be happy with a man that, on committing human error, created a serf of himself. Was that a genuine apology? How could it be?

I found myself wondering about what Edward Thomas might do to apologize to a woman. He was so firm in his ideals, unmovable in his honor. I wondered if he ever found himself in a position to apologize for anything in the first place. If so, I imagined him shaking heaven and earth to right his wrong in the least ostentatious way possible.

"Dearest Luella," I imagined him saying, "my behavior was inexcusable at dinner last night. Please accept my apology. I've spoken with the two affected parties, and they've agreed to be married, happily, but both desire your blessing, something I concur is wholeheartedly necessary. Forgive me if you can. In the meantime, I will continue to catch criminals."

I smiled just thinking about.

I wasn't on my way to Edward, though. I had been distracted the evening before from my purpose of confronting Bram, and now I wouldn't wait until the evening. I was marching right to the fairgrounds, secrecy be damned. If someone saw me, let the news trickle back to Byron. If he were concerned about me inquiring after another man, he could chew on that a while for all I cared.

I crested a hill and crossed the river to the east side. The fairgrounds lost a considerable portion of their magic in the sunlight. The electric lights had no effect, and the eerie blue glow I had seen on my first visit dissipated in the sunlight, if it existed at all. The crooked and gnarled poles holding up tents and bunting, peculiar and strange in the evening, just looked like shoddy workmanship in disrepair.

It was still before noon, and the carnival's personnel were busy at work around cooking pots or else debating the appropriate way to hang new banners and flags to attract more onlookers to less frequented side shows. The fair, clearly, didn't open to the public until late afternoon when the sun set.

As I walked to the entry gate at the edge of the grounds, a giant, burly man in a bowler hat dropped his mirror and razor and rushed to block my entrance.

"Fair is closed until four, mum," he said, with a deep, gravelly voice.

"I'm not here to see the fair. I was just looking for—for a friend of mine," I replied. I cleared my throat and tried to sound confident.

"A friend of yours, eh?" he replied, working at a bit of something between his teeth with his tongue. "Name?"

"Bram."

"Surname?"

"I don't know his surname," I said.

"It doesn't sound like you really know the bloke. You're his friend you say?"

"Yes! He has a messy crop of brown hair and eyes the color of honey." On hearing this, the big brute folded his arms across his chest and buried his chin into his neck, looking at me under his bushy eyebrows.

"It sounds like you might have a thing for this guy," he suggested.

"Oh, that's original," I quipped. I was quickly losing my patience with this behemoth. "If you won't let me in, just go ask him yourself! I'm sure you know him. Tell him the woman from the other night is here to see him." This last request did nothing to help my case.

"The woman from the other night?" He raised both eyebrows and smiled toothily. "Oh. I'll tell him. You, uh, just make yourself comfortable."

He left me at the front, fuming. As he walked off, I looked for something to throw after him. The best I could find was a paper advertisement, which I feared wouldn't deliver my desired effect. The girl from the other night. Please. I plopped myself onto a rather primitive wood bench, more of a plank set across two stumps really, and hoped this wouldn't take long. I was tired of too much time to myself to stew and mull things over. Tired of thinking about Byron. Tired of dealing with Jacob Rigby and my sister.

I was drawing circles in the dirt when the man returned.

"He says he will receive you in his tent." The big buffoon grinned. "Have a nice time. I believe you know the way."

"I don't actually," I said as a quick reprimand, and I forced him to direct me to the very doorstep—if there was a door or a step. He left me there, grumbling about more important things he had to do than waste time chauffeuring Bram's women around.

The tent looked so plain and unassuming. Bram's dog lay in the dirt, gnawing on a girthy shoulder bone from what I imagined was an elk. The pointer didn't even look up at me.

"Mr. Bram," I called.

"Come on in," he replied from the dark interior.

"I think I would prefer not to," I said. This time would be different. I would maintain control of the situation.

"Suit yourself." I waited but saw no movement.

"Well, aren't you going to come out?"

"I think I prefer not to," he replied. Insufferable man! "Excellent story today, by the way. Though I think you may have missed some of the finer details." Curse him and his little games.

"How did you do it?" I shouted into the tent.

"Do what?"

"Convince Mr. Bradford to rob a bank," I said, trying to peer in. It was useless, though. The morning sun blinded me, and I couldn't make out any details inside the dark interior, though I could faintly smell the exotic perfumes from the night before clinging to the canvas of his yurt.

"That's a conversation best had over a cup of tea," he called back. "I'd love to tell you whenever you feel like you have the time to join me." The dog yawned.

So, this is how it would be. I evaluated my options. I could walk away without any explanation, any hope of writing another big story, and without getting answers about my bizarre connection to this man, or I could walk inside.

I folded my arms and stamped back toward the entrance. How did I even fit in that tent the other night with his ego? I walked through the fair, seeing the empty stalls that, in a few hours, would be filled with illusion and spectacle. Did I really doubt that man was capable of finding some underhanded way of forcing Mr. Bradford into a robbery? Flyers and discarded pages from publications lay dirtied in the mud.

Familiar words caught my eye. "The Steely-Eyed Detective." The page lay there ripped and splattered with grime. I bent down to pick it up. It was almost unreadable.

I glanced across the river at the west side of Dawnhurst on Severn, where somewhere my little flat and grieving sister waited for me, a fiancé who inspired little affection, the expectation of the next great story.

At this point, what did I have to lose really? I felt the crushing indifference of the world, the short lived, muddy echo of my words. No one would care if I went in. No one would care much what happened inside the tent either.

I rolled my eyes, grit my teeth, and turned back around. The pointer perked up its ears.

Chapter Twelve

Magic

The yurt was almost exactly as I remembered it, though now, being better lit from a generous portion of sunlight coming in from the hole on top, it seemed considerably smaller and less foreboding. I saw the bed, neatly made, the writing desk where and I scribbled down that silly little story, and even got a better glimpse at the chest from which he collected his so-called magic pen.

The chest was painted a weathered seafoam color, and every edge was decorated with appliques and wooden panels in what looked like a type of otherworldly hieroglyphic. Its hinges and metal components were a pale pewter.

Bram sat at the little table, a plate of half-eaten scones in front of him. He looked very comfortable, his face hidden behind an edition of my very own *Langley's Miscellany*.

"All in all, I'd say it should sell quite well." He started reading aloud. "*Steel and mettle* (clever play on words there) *clashed as iron-clad bandits unsheathed an historic plot. Equal parts awe and fear kept bank employees glued to the floor as one of King Arthur's own emptied the vaults at Victoria's National and tried to make his escape. Our own police force gave chase in nothing less than a pseudo dream state. If by chance, you happened to see two knights, clad in full armor on horseback chased by our city police, know that you were not dreaming or drunk. These are just the type of ruffians the Dawnhurst coppers must deal with: the president of the railway station, Mr. Bradford, and his manservant.*" He lowered the paper. "Between this and the fogman, it's a wonder anyone left their house this morning. What kind of city is this, anyway?"

"How did you do it?"

"How'd I do what? Scone?" he asked, pouring me some tea. Why was everyone always trying to make me eat?

"How did you convince Mr. Bradford to dress up like a knight and rob a bank? What tremendous risk! He was the President of the railway station. He's lost everything." I sat down, but I didn't take a scone.

"You mean to ask, how did you get Mr. Bradford to rob a bank?" he said, putting down the magazine.

"Oh, come on. Knock it off already. Was it the hypnotist? Or perhaps it was a type of drug? Or was it something darker, like blackmail?"

"I've never met Mr. Bradford in my life," he insisted.

"Then how did he know what I scribbled down on that little piece of paper?" Bram was testing my patience. I didn't believe his excuses for a second, yet I answered my own question with a second. How did Bram know what I wrote down on that piece of paper? I took a breath and collected myself. "I understand. I'm grateful for the story, and I wouldn't want you to feel like I would rat you out. If it is blackmail, and I were you, I doubt I would go blabbing about it either."

"It wasn't blackmail," he replied, coyly taking a sip from his teacup.

"It's just, well, I never meant for you to do such a thing. I wanted a story, I know, but I never thought that you might go so far as to commit a crime to ensure I had one," I said.

"I didn't think this first episode would convince you," he responded. "In fact, I was quite sure. You are sucked so far into the brick and mortar of this city that you could be, and indeed are, a foot away from magic and you still don't recognize it."

"There is no such thing as magic!" I cried more loudly than I intended. I sounded like a child throwing a tantrum. There couldn't be magic. I wouldn't believe it, not in a world where a simple fever could take my father from me.

"Said the woman who has experienced one of the most bizarre coincidences of the century, perhaps the millennium. How do you explain the bank robbery, then?"

"Would you drop the mystical act already? I know that you had something to do with it, and I'm grateful. I just wanted to tell you that type of thing won't be necessary."

"Don't be blind, Luella!"

My mouth dropped open, and I felt the uncomfortable, eerie feeling I had experienced when he revealed my pen name from the night before. "How did you know my name?" The nerve of this man! How dare he collect bits of my private life in such a way. "Have you been stalking me? I have friends in the police force, and I have half a mind to—"

"The police force, there! Wake up! Admit that this type of thing is possible. Admit that, in the absence of a logical solution, your writing last night might just be creating an extralogical one. You wrote an insane story with the pen, ink, and paper. The story turned to life, just as I've seen it do before."

I stood up. It was a mistake coming here. I wasn't sure what I was hoping to gain. An explanation? Closure? "You and I are alike, aren't we?" I said. "We both peddle outlandish stories. I just write mine down, and you try to take in whatever sap will listen. I can't believe I fell for such a thing." I turned to make my way out.

"Heavens above, woman! You are a writer with no explanations. You just report and don't digest! Is that all you want from your career? Explain to me the Steely-Eyed Detective and his Fog Man then."

I froze.

"I imagine this man to be of a certain integrity," he went on. "After all, you insisted it was an official police report from which you derived your information. So, he must have been either a drunk or a man of unshakable conviction to report something he could not explain and risk the ridicule that came with it."

"How do you know that?" I asked facing him.

"Because years ago, I also saw something I couldn't explain," he said with a grim smile. "So, consider your detective, and not in that womanly, admiring way I'm afraid you've already been swept up in. Haven't you paused to ask yourself what he really saw in that alleyway?"

My limbs were losing their weight. I could feel my head begin to spin. "It was a man in the fog."

"No. It wasn't. This was a sober, resolute policeman. He's seen men in the fog before. This was different."

Why hadn't I bothered to consider this before? What had I been writing on? I slumped back into my chair.

"A trick in the lamp light," I offered.

"Wrong again. That doesn't explain the woman screaming, and it doesn't explain the fog vanishing in a matter of seconds."

"A gust of wind... maybe the woman was the murderer trying to throw him off the scent..."

"It's much more disappointing than that, Luella. It was a phantom," he said, clutching both sides of the table to lean over toward me and drive his point home.

Magic? I could not doubt Edward. The more I knew him, the more I was convinced nothing could persuade me that he was dishonest, fanciful, or vain. Bram might make up stories to get his way. Edward, though, I could rely on for the truth and truth only. If he saw a fogman, then how could I discredit him?

"Can you honestly tell me you haven't felt the magic since you used it the other night? Has the pen not called to you?" he continued, leaning toward me, closing in.

My heart quickened. My thoughts slowed down, and I felt like my mind was racing through a vacuum, working a mile a minute but with nothing to show for it. I tried going down a hundred different branches, pushing logic for another explanation, only to end up back at the awesome, terrifying word: magic. I thought about Edward and the dream I had where my father was an assailant. His question conjured up, for some reason I couldn't explain, my recent outbreak of jealousy and even my flare of annoyance toward Mrs. Crow for asking simple questions. These feelings had been so unlike me. Was I just losing my temper, or was it something more?

"Even if the fogman was a real phantom," I stuttered, "that doesn't prove anything about your pen."

"And it never will prove anything. But that's the point of magic," he said, settling back into his chair. "If the phantom is real, you can conclude that there are other phenomena out there for which there is no real explanation. Many of these can be explained away by our own ignorance, and someone with a true scientific background could illuminate their methods. But, there are still whole categories of irregularities that can't be explained by the scientists either. One example might be writing something down on a piece of paper and burning it, only to see those very words come to pass on an unwitting stranger."

"But how am I supposed to differentiate?" It was a sweet nectar to drink, and I thought it was all too easy to get caught up in something like this. Soon, I'd jump at every shadow, and everything I couldn't explain would be magic to me. That was no fit way to live.

"Like I told you," he responded, "magic has all kinds of camouflage. But it is at least somewhat replicable." He looked so honest standing there between the shafts of light coming from outside. He had this attractive, contagious smile on his lips. "You haven't touched your scone."

My mind was still spinning. I wanted to scream, or faint, or something. Magic? Real? If it was true, I was sitting with the owner of a pen that could make any story come true, any of *my* stories come true.

"You said there were limitations on the pen?" I asked.

"Oh yes," he replied. "Remember, magic is in a war of self-preservation. It works so as not to arouse suspicion. From what I've been able to uncover, it won't respond to attempts to influence your personal life directly. One man tried to use it once to meld his wife and his mistress into one person, poor sap."

"What happened?"

"Nothing or maybe something. His wife met the mistress by chance while chatting in a cafe. She left him the next morning."

"A chance encounter," I said.

"Possibly." He smiled like a scientist explaining a discovery. Camouflage.

"Well, what other limitations then?"

"I've only been able to deduce a few for this specific artifact. It follows that the pen is very unlikely to create things that would be out of place for our time, at least in bringing things from a different reality or from the future. Your knights in shining armor, for example, worked I think because our era is still familiar with those stories. After all, horses are very commonplace, and most have us have seen a suit of armor on display somewhere. It'd be unlikely, though, for us to convince the magic to conjure up a fire breathing dragon. It'd be too ostentatious, draw too much attention."

"But you think that, so long as we are writing surprising, albeit possible events, they just happen to materialize?"

"Think of it this way," he suggested. "Maybe the pen is a little window to the future and just guides your hand to write whatever is just about to happen."

Thinking of magic like this, scientifically, well-studied, made it feel so much tidier and more comfortable. It was also a major relief to consider maybe the world didn't react to the magic of the pen, and rather the pen foresaw details about the future. If the magic were real, I couldn't help but feel a little guilty about the policeman who got cut by a sword taking down the knight robbers. How was I supposed to know they'd actually materialize?

"That seems unlikely," I replied. "You mean to suggest that Mr. Bradford may have been planning on robbing a bank in full armor even on his own accord?"

He picked up a glass of water and a scone and sauntered over to the nearly dead potted plant by the entry flap. "I'd be inclined to agree with you, except that I've been noticing not a few strange things happening lately. Your detective's fogman is only a small example. Have you had any strange dreams lately? I know I have." He buried a scone somewhere in the pot and gazed intently at the plant's branches. I did not feel comfortable discussing my dreams with him. Even if he was right.

"But if the pen can't directly influence your own world, it's practically useless," I said.

"Except to someone like a writer of incredible non-fiction." He smiled and came back to the table. "Would you like a cup of tea?"

If he was right, this pen could be my ticket to something so much more than writing whatever stories I could glean from the police department. It could be my ticket to the Golden Inkwell. On any miraculous story, we'd be first to print while other publications scrambled to get their reporters mobilized.

The freedom swelled inside of me. I could write for anyone. I could leave Byron's little magazine and go somewhere much larger. I could grant my sister's desire and not marry him. I didn't have to marry anybody if I didn't want to. I looked across the table. Bram, uniquely handsome as always, looked at me intently with his honey-tinted eyes. He looked manly and dangerous sitting there. What must he have sacrificed to find this artifact? He said his comrades had died in its pursuit. What else had he gone through?

There was more to this nomadic carnival worker than met the eye. I thought I could see something deeper in his face, a strange, enchanted depth in his very movements.

"I'd love a cup of tea," I said, unable to hide the wide smile forming on my face. "We have work to do."

Chapter Thirteen

By the River

Bram insisted we take a walk to talk it over. Both of us were convinced that just improvising and writing whatever came to mind was likely not the best course of action, just in case the pen did dictate reality and not vice versa. After all, Mr. Bradford was a ruined man. I'm sure he would insist that he was under some type of trance or experiencing the effects of a drug or fever, but even if he managed to escape a significant prison sentence, he'd never escape the reputation of being the armor-clad bank robber.

I felt no small measure of guilt knowing this. But, as I had conceded before, it was like tossing an apple from a second story window, believing no one was below. How could I have known the pen would work? What's more, I never named Mr. Bradford in my description. I just wrote words down on a piece of paper using nondescript pronouns. Mr. Bradford surely still had his agency.

It also helped that Mr. Bradford had already earned himself a reputation for being a menace. Women were never eager to be alone with him, and men thought he had a funny way of conducting his affairs. There was never any type of formal accusation made against him, but he managed to find himself in the middle of more than one suddenly disrupted engagement and a couple of full-fledged marriages.

No matter. Our quest was straightforward. I simply had to come up with another story to use as an experiment. If I could find a way to produce stories consistently that enthralled readers without creating situations that made people go to jail, then I'd be in business, likely as the most widely read writer in England.

Bram didn't seem as enthused as I was.

"You're telling me that you wield an immense power like this and you want to make trifling stories that don't make any difference?" he asked. He peered at me over his shoulder. We sat side by side near the river, under a wide linden tree. His pointer jogged along the riverbank chasing ducks.

"Well, I can't very well go about ruining people's lives in good conscience, now can I?" I retorted.

"You don't know them," he continued. "Why should you care what happens to them?"

"Bram, you are being entirely immoral and unethical!"

"I'm just thinking in your best interest. Take this proposed one here," he said, holding up a scrap we had scribbled on with a less magical pen. "It's all well and good for this man's house to be invaded by hundreds of frogs, but if another paper prints about an actually gripping murder, there's no way you'll outsell them."

"I disagree," I said haughtily. "Would you really rather read about boring old murder more than such a peculiar circumstance as a house filled with frogs?"

"The French will take it as a slight," he said. I burst out in a fit of laughter. My cheeks hurt from smiling so widely, and my diaphragm, out of practice, ached. Bram looked at me and rolled his eyes, trying to suppress a smile of his own. His comment started something inside of me. I couldn't remember the last time I laughed like this. Bram's dog sauntered over, wet from the river, and shook out its coat. The water sprayed all over me.

I laid back on the grass and tried to slow down my breathing, looking up at the many branches, mostly bare. The day was uncommonly warm for the time of year. The grass, turning yellow now, felt cool under me.

The laughter slowly subsided, replaced with a euphoric glow. I felt a strong connection to the man sitting next to me, though we had only met once before. He offered me so much without thought of return. He had yet to give me any reason to fear harm from him, except for one thing.

"How did you know my name?" I asked, pulling myself up onto an elbow. He watched the water in the river for some time before responding.

"I don't know if I want to tell you," he said.

"Don't you think it's a breach of trust? If you have some means of gathering information about me, I feel that I deserve to know it. If we're going to embark on this... well, whatever this is... together."

"You're going to have to accept that there are things you can't know about me." He tossed a bit of grass he'd been tying into a knot away from him and picked at another. "Besides, I'm not sure you'll believe me."

"More magic?" I asked, eyes bright with wonder, ready to believe almost anything fantastical.

"Not magic. At least, not the magic you're thinking about," he said, with a smile to himself. His smile was charming in an interesting, unique way.

"Well then?"

"I didn't know your name the first time we met."

"So, you learned it, but how?"

He drew a breath in. "After seeing you write something the other night, I was determined to see how the pen responded. I assumed you wrote something adequately bizarre, and I was, in no small way, curious. After your Steely Detective story, which I found deeply entertaining, I wanted to see what you would whip up, creativity unleashed."

"Why thank you," I chimed with a gracious and theatrical bow. What was I? Drunk?

"I wasn't quite sure how it would work, so I headed down to the police station to laze about and see if I could pick up any news about it there. By the time I got there, the Sergeant and a man I could only describe as steely-eyed," here, he gave me a playful wink, "were standing over a very groggy version of you, sitting collapsed on a chair. They continued to call your name to get you to come to, muttering something about the shock being too great. Well, seeing you like that, I have to confess I felt a twang of worry, so I grabbed a neglected coat and hat, donned them, and stuck around, posing as a copper to ensure you hadn't died of shock."

"How very chivalrous of you!" I jabbed. "Watching from afar to see if a woman sees her way through an episode."

"Oh, come off it. There was enough chivalry over by you to last you a lifetime over. Once you came to, you kept going on in this dazed sort of way about armored knights and bank robbers. I dropped off my coat and hat at the front desk, told the chap not to work too hard, and made my merry way out the door."

"So, you were spying on me," I said.

"I just went to the police station to hear a story, same as you," he replied. "I knew you wouldn't believe me."

"It's just very convenient, don't you think, that you happen to be at the right time and place to learn so much about me." I was baiting him. I was acting like a teenager.

"And how else do you propose I get such information?"

"The old-fashioned way. You ask me. We can spend time together, and you get to know me."

"And how would your fiancé feel about that?"

Bram might as well have a grabbed a bucket of the cold river water and soaked me with it. Mention of Byron had an immediate chilling effect on my mood, bringing back to my mind all the troubles of reality, troubles the pen could not help me with.

This afternoon was one of the best I'd spent in a very long time, not as the victorious high that comes after hard work and accomplishment, but in a casual, comfortable sort of way. I felt so at home with Bram. The very mention of Byron, and his attached entanglement with my sister, felt like work in a world to which I wasn't eager to return. I wanted my time here with Bram to continue.

"Can you keep a secret?" I asked him. He barked out a laugh.

"You're asking the loner carnival worker that has a trunk full of magic items if he can keep a secret?"

"Ah ha!" I cried victoriously. "I thought that trunk might have some more oddities in it. How very trusting of you, especially to a fanciful, successful writer."

"You're crazy now, like me. No one will believe something like that, even if you were to win the Golden Inkwell."

"I don't want to marry my fiancé," I said after a deep breath. He looked at me with increased interest, wrinkles around his eyes forming as his brain decoded what I told him here, alone, under a linden tree next to a river. I think I was about as surprised as he was. I had never said it out loud before, and I wasn't sure why I said it now. Perhaps I was just angry with him about his spectacle of a dinner. But, maybe it went deeper than that. Maybe Byron had always represented safety for my sister and me.

I had spent years building calluses over the scars I had from previous courtships. There had been several, but something about me had driven them away.

By the time I was twenty-four, I was convinced that was it for me, that I was destined to be a widow without a deceased husband. This conclusion placed immense stress on my mind to get Anna successfully, and happily, married off. I became her mother. When Byron expressed his interest, I was cautious. I never experienced the obnoxious obsession Anna felt for Jacob. I wasn't sure I'd felt any infatuation at all, just the comfort of a smart match. Byron was a net, breaking my imminent fall to years of hard work, appreciated by no one, and loved by no one but a sister.

"Does he treat you poorly?" Bram asked.

"Nothing like that," I replied. "I mean, he's not perfect by any means, and he sure misstepped recently, but I believe he adores me."

"Then I don't understand," he continued. "What more could you look for in a spouse than earnest devotion and adoration?"

I could not answer his question directly, not with my true feelings. He would think I was a shallow woman, marrying Byron only for his money. I snickered. Byron wasn't rich. If I was shallow, I was certainly stupid.

Still, hadn't my blood set to boiling when I saw Byron's correspondence with another woman? He had said that jealousy was a sure sign of affection. I had never felt such a surge of jealousy in my life. Maybe he was right. I could have just been taking our relationship for granted. Older women had always told me that love was a learned skill.

On the other hand, I looked at Bram. How could I tell him that I'd never had with my betrothed a moment like the one we were experiencing now.

"If you try to kiss me, I'll run away," he said. My eyes went wide.

"Kiss you? What on earth are you talking about?"

"I don't know! You have this look on your face like you're drinking summer wine in autumn. I just thought I would put my foot down here and now." I blushed, searching for words.

"You've misunderstood me," I stammered. "I'm not disinterested in my fiancé because of you."

"I never said you were," he protested.

"Well, good, then. We understand each other."

"You're disinterested in your fiancé because of the Steely-Eyed Detective," he said slyly, eyes fixed on the river, the words sliding out of the side of his mouth. Bram had a gift for rendering me speechless. He said what he thought without regard of the consequence. I was also becoming increasingly aware of his intelligence. I couldn't honestly deny his accusation.

It wasn't Edward specifically, but the very fact that the first time I spoke with him, I couldn't seem to escape his gray eyes or concentrate on my conversation with Sergeant Cooper. That attraction wedged doubt into my relationship with Byron. When I was with either Bram or Edward, Byron was far from my mind, until I used him as a type of backstop when I felt socially uncomfortable. Byron was older than me, and so often I looked at him as I might have my father. Was that the basis for a good lifelong match? Or would I be plagued by encountering men like Bram and Edward the rest of my days? I had felt jealousy, yes, but Byron would never make me feel a sense of passion and adventure.

Pursuing this line of thinking dragged me down quickly into my current situation. I was betrothed to Byron. That arrangement was still intact. If I did break it off, I didn't know how confident I was that he would continue to run my stories. Could I, in good faith, ask him to?

Most importantly, if this was my greatest concern, did I have a duty to end the engagement anyway?

"Should we go back and write the story or not?" I said as the afternoon soured thinking about the distance between a life that could be and my own circumstances. Bram's magic pen could still act as a doorway to a new, bright future full of wonder and opportunity.

"What, the frogs?" He groaned.

"The frogs have my vote. I'll let you choose next time." I stood, getting up off the grass. "Within reason, that is."

I helped him up, and he patted himself off.

"Then I'd be an accomplice to whatever madness you come up with," he complained.

"You're the one with the magic pen! I'm just an idea girl."

He laughed, whistled for his dog to follow, and started back toward the uneven grouping of canopies. What must his life have been like? The fair had been in our town for only a couple of weeks. Before that?

"Why are you doing this for me?" I asked. He stopped but didn't turn around. He seemed to be looking at the fairgrounds. I saw a weight settle over his shoulders. A surge of empathy connected us. I, with my mess to return to, he with his.

"I must be bored," he called back to me. "Are you coming, Mr. Blakely?"

Chapter Fourteen

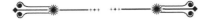

Dueling

I wrote up the story in his tent. I didn't want to go write it at the print shop with Byron there. Besides, I found myself deeply enjoying Bram's company. As I worked away on a peculiar typewriter he had collected from whom he described as a mad tinker (the letters weren't in the spaces I was familiar with), he told me stories, tried to convince me to eat fruits and cakes, made me tea, and even demonstrated some of the sleight of hand he used in his old act.

"I had to dress up the real magic with the fake stuff," he said, vanishing an egg under a handkerchief. "It was the only way I could get people to pay attention." The dog, who I learned was named Cyrus, yawned and curled up for a nap. Apparently, he had seen the trick before.

The story took me three times as long as it usually would, and by the time I was done, he had learned an awful lot about me, including the working relationship I had with Byron and that I had a dear sister. With his incessant questions, it was a marvel he didn't know the name of my perfume.

"I thought you might have a sister."

"How on earth could you guess that?"

"There's a way about you. Women with sisters sometimes take in information or hear something, and they store it away to tell their sister later. There's a distinct 'wait 'til sister hears of this' expression."

He was a keen observer like that. He also volunteered to run my story to the print shop, so I didn't have to show my face there, an offer I turned down, knowing what a scene it might cause if Byron started receiving my stories from a handsome man closer to my age than he was.

He brought up a troubling point, though. I didn't feel prepared to face my betrothed yet, and I couldn't send my stories with my sister either. They might kill each other, or else she might try some public form of humiliation against him. I couldn't trust Mrs. Crow—she would open and read anything I gave to her, and then she would learn my secret pen name. Mrs. Barker was the same, and besides she was busy running a bakery. Iced buns wait for no one.

Going through my options made me depressed. I didn't have many friends, a fact I tried to ignore by keeping myself busy. This was my lot for clinging to my independence so ardently.

With my story done, I bid Bram a farewell, agreeing that we would write again later during the week. In the meantime, we'd both brainstorm ideas on our own. I advised him not to keep his brainstorm lighthearted. I didn't want to ruin lives. He bowed politely, and I offered him my hand, which he shook curtly.

I cleared my throat.

"Yes?" he asked. I held out my hand longer, emulating a queenly grace.

"A curt handshake?" I raised an eyebrow.

"What else are you expecting?" he asked.

"I think we're both aware of the tradition. It's customary to grace a lady's hand with a kiss."

"A lady's hand?" He crouched down and lifted Cyrus to my hand. The pointer smothered it with a slobbery tongue. "There you are, my lady."

I wiped my hand on his sleeve, despite his protests, and made my way from the tent back toward the west side.

When I got home, I found Anna frozen in the middle of some needlework, a vacant stare out the window. I knew that any attempts to console her would be fruitless. Evidently, Jacob had not yet contacted her, which I took to be a bad sign.

"I'm worthless to him!" she lamented. I took the needlework from her and set it on the table. I guiltily rubbed her back, hiding my cheerfulness. It seemed wrong that my lot was looking up as Anna's was in such a state, but I couldn't help my levity. I had a delicious secret. A fantastical secret! Even if things between Anna and Jacob didn't work out, I'd found a gold mine.

We dined solemnly on a stew that Mrs. Crow was kind enough to share with us. We contributed some bread rolls and willing ears to hear the latest gossip about town, news that we couldn't focus on for more than a moment. It was in one ear and out the other. We were both too distracted, Anna concerned with Jacob and I ruminating over all my new possibilities. I found myself smiling at potatoes and holding back giggles when spreading butter over bread as I remembered some of Bram's absurd retellings of the carnival lifestyle, some of the failed illusions he tried to demonstrate to me, or the indignant attitude Cyrus had toward him.

Anna retired early, and I stayed up puzzling over how I was going to deliver my stories to my employer.

The next morning, I left Anna still asleep and set out to the police station with an idea in mind. It was an unusually sunny day, and I thought I heard birds chirping in the trees as if it were springtime. The path to the police station felt more familiar now, and along the way, I passed by the usual herd of print stands, stealing glances at the headlines. They all seemed so trivial, almost amateur, now. Just a couple of weeks ago, I had coveted positions at these publications. They were untouchable summits, almost sacred. Now, it just felt like they were about to be second fiddle. The feeling made my head swim.

If, of course, Bram was right, and the pen really worked as he said. But, I'd seen it work once already, and for some reason, I found myself trusting him. He felt real, genuine.

I skipped up the steps of the station and bound through the door, feeling comfortable in the space; things felt familiar. The old windows, the musty smell, and the usual red-headed lamppost leaning back in his chair, reading a copy of the *Dawnhurst Happenings*. He noticed me over his paper and, at once, settled into his practiced, professional demeanor. He looked up at me sympathetically.

"Here to report a missin-"

"Do you not recognize me?" I interrupted, gesturing to my face. "You have a compulsion about missing people, do you realize?"

"Sure, I recognize you, miss, with a pretty face like yours. I'm just always nervous that this time will be the time you're here to report a missing per—"

"I'll show myself down the hall," I said, dismissing him. He was hopeless. I made my way toward Sergeant Cooper's office and was happy to see his door closed. It would make my present business simpler without his typical bah humbug mentality toward journalists. I turned and saw Ms. Turner, busy as usual on a typewriter, noting warmly the half-hidden copy of *Langley's Miscellany* under a stack of her work papers.

"Ms. Turner," I said, breaking her concentration. She looked up at me, somehow bright and beautiful despite the messy, frazzled do on her head held together by a pen.

"Mrs. Steely Detective," she chided. "Back again for another story? I'm not sure we can keep up with the demand."

"Actually, no I was just—"

"Who am I kidding? Of course, we can. You'll never believe what Lieutenant Thomas did this time." I couldn't deny my curiosity when it came to Edward Thomas.

"What?"

"A duel. He had a duel with sabers."

"Is he alright?" My heart leapt into my throat. A duel? The idiot man! I immediately saw him in my mind, dead on a lawn or bleeding in a hospital bed. What would I do if Edward was hurt? It was astonishing how quickly my elated mood vacated my breast. What was he thinking? What could possibly persuade him to act so foolishly?

My mind darted to the pen, to Mr. Bradford's odd villainous behavior, and couldn't help but wonder what other magic trinkets were out there in the world. Was some otherworldly force at work on Edward? I felt a deep fear spring up from within me, and with it, helplessness, anger.

"Your poor glove will never be the same if you keep wringing it like that," Ms. Turner went on, noting the death grip I had on my pair of walking gloves. Her smug expression made me feel childish. If she were so calm, Edward couldn't be that hurt. Then again, Ms. Turner had a strong mind, and maybe she had become desensitized to the trauma of police work. I wrestled with my sudden emotions, trying to understand what to make of them. I was not usually this unhinged.

"He's doing fine," she continued. "Got a nasty slash across his right shoulder, but apart from that, he's in good spirits." Sweet relief flooded my bosom. Thank heavens. I sat down in what was now my usual chair, tasting something sour in my mouth.

"What on earth did he get himself into a duel for?" I asked, slapping my gloves down on the table, not caring to hide my irritation.

"That's just it," she said. "He had been sniffing out a feud between a devil of a man who had taken in some highborn lad on a gambling debt. From what I gather, the lad couldn't pay, and the man demanded the 'honorable exchange.' Lieutenant Thomas arrived just in time to see the poor boy of seventeen hefting the weight of a sword for likely the first time in his life, facing off against the brute. He called for a stop to it, but the man insisted he would be satisfied. That's when Thomas grabbed the blade from the lad, proclaimed the boy was under his protection, and the man would have to be satisfied by a fight with a police officer."

"And they fought? Did Edward kill him?" I gulped. I could imagine Edward valiantly defending the boy to his opponent's bitter end if it was necessary. The man never shirked from what he saw as his duty, I knew. His honor both inspired and terrified me.

"Killed him? Absolutely not! They fought for nearly an hour, at which point the man was so exhausted he had a breathing attack. More uniforms had arrived by then. Lieutenant Thomas kicked the man's sword to his partners, bandaged his shoulder, and escorted the boy home without so much as a sweat. At least, that's the way the other lads on the force are telling it. How's that for a story?"

It was warm in the room; I started fanning myself with a loose police report. "Where is he now?"

"Back out on duty." He was a formidable man, more of a man than most that I knew—perhaps all I knew. I saw in him the qualities of a pack leader, high breasted and fearless. I couldn't help but compare him to Bram. The two were strikingly different. Edward was noble and heroic. Bram was, well, unique.

"I will certainly have to write it up after getting his account of what happened," I said, shaking off my imagination. I sat down and smoothed out my skirts, allowing my heart rate to slow.

"Ms. Winthrop, it appears your non-romantic feelings toward the

Lieutenant have you in a fix." Ms. Turner grinned deviously. I tried my very best not to blush.

"If you're done playing at a teenage girl, I actually came here to talk to you."

"Me? Whatever for?"

"I was wondering if I might interest you in a side job for about an hour or two a week."

"I see. Well, I have a job," she said with cold resolution.

"Oh, I know that. In fact, I've admired you these times we've spoken. You represent much of what I aspire to be."

"Plus, I am quite busy. My days occupied here, my evenings jam packed, spent occupied by Misters Dickens, Hardy, Keats. I could go on, but why bore you?"

"I'm sorry. I didn't realize," I said.

"Well, it's true. I'm simply quite busy with lots of things. Many different kinds of things, too. You wouldn't believe them if I told you. Though, I appreciate the compliment, and out of curiosity, what is it exactly that you had in mind?"

"What I really need is a favor, and I'm willing to pay you for it if necessary."

"What kind of favor?" She studied me with an inquisitive, raised eyebrow.

"I'm just getting very busy tracking down some of the stories I've been working on, and I need someone to deliver my work to my publisher, as well as collect any paycheck he may have for me."

"Alright..." Her voice carried a leading tone, prompting further explanation. Was it that easy to tell I was lying? I never had been good at it.

"I just figured, since I'm here finding stories, it'd be easier for me. Save me a trip, you know?" I was trying my best to be convincing, awkward smiles and all. She paused before standing up and making her way to the front of the desk. She leaned against it casually, folding her arms and staring down at me in my chair, only air between us. She studied me for a good minute before speaking.

"I'll do it," she said, "if you will tell me the truth about why." She waited stonily for my reply. I should have known I couldn't pull one over on her. She was basically a wiser, more mature version of myself, and I wouldn't have believed me either. I searched for words in every part of my brain but found none. How sweet that a writer find herself betrayed by her own words.

Maybe it was the sheer range of emotions I'd been through in the past forty-eight hours, but everything came to the surface all at once: my situation with Byron, my sister's predicament with Jacob, my secret rendezvous with Bram, Mr. Stringham's eviction threat, my insecurity as a writer, the death of my father, my curious yearning to keep feeling the magic from the pen, everything. Something begged me to say it all aloud to a woman who might just be willing to be a friend. Tears bubbled to my eyes and flowed freely as if I were a child. I just shook at my head at her.

"Well, now we're getting somewhere," she said.

Chapter Fifteen

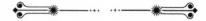

Doug's Fish and Chips

"I can't say I blame you," Rebecca Turner told me. She sat across a table from me, sipping on small cup of coffee after a large lunch. We had just finished eating in a local fish and chips pub on several blocks into the east side. The place was rough and tumble, what I would usually expect from an east side pub. The floors were run down, and the thick set wood beams, like those of an old ship's interior, held up a low ceiling. There was a framed, tattered union jack near the entrance alongside a small, modest portrait of a woman. The air smelled strongly of hot oil and fried potatoes, and it was generously warm for the season, despite the sizeable, though old, windows along the opposite wall.

Rebecca, as she insisted I now call her, was practically a celebrity with the owner. When we had walked in, a rowdy man with a full beard and hard-working suspenders barked at her like a seal, complaining that she didn't care a lick about him. I was shocked at how brusquely he yelled at a woman, but she gave back as brutally as she received, queuing a chorus of laughter from all the serving boys and, fortunately, from the bear of a man himself.

"I credit Doug for my uncanny knack at keeping a handle on ol' Sergeant Cooper," she wryly said. As she explained this to me, Doug came around from the kitchen and put a heavy arm over her shoulders.

"Becca, who's your friend?" he asked, turning to me.

"Be nice," she replied.

"Did she warn you that this is a grubby type of place?" he said, trying to bait her. Or perhaps he was trying to bait Rebecca.

"She didn't really mention where we were going at all," I replied.

"Best to keep it a surprise. Otherwise, she wouldn't have come," Rebecca countered with a gentle and affectionate slap on Doug's beard where his cheek might have been. His face had to be in there somewhere. He laughed heartily and with enough rasp to sand down a hatchet.

"Who are you, my wife?" he teased. He certainly was a good-humored fellow, the type of good-humored man I would never want to find on the opposite side of an argument. He went over to an occupied table by the window, which had a surprisingly good view down an open street with a glimpse of the river and, with a few words, had scared away its inhabitants. They hurriedly pushed by us to exit the pub, full of slurred grumblings about the nerve of the establishment and that their friends would hear about this brazen inexcusable rudeness, by jove.

He waved them away nonchalantly and motioned his big hand toward the table. "Your usual spot is open, Becca."

"Thank you, Doug. Better bring out three orders and make sure you give the lady an extra helping of your secret sauce. It'll be her first time."

The beard shifted into what I could only assume was a smile.

"You'll never guess what's in it," he said, the words sliding out deviously. His face beamed with pride though, and I determined that a man who cared this much about his humble work had to be honest and good. I wished there were more people like him on the east side, in fact. Perhaps, if there were, I wouldn't have been so eager to get away from it.

What followed was a veritable culinary pageant. Three troughs were brought out, each with six pieces of dark, golden-brown fried fish, chips cut up into thin matchsticks, and a bowl filled with a creamy, pink-orange mixture. Becca had jumped in without delay, and before long, I followed suit, abandoning all pretext of knife and forking. There weren't any knives or forks on our table anyway.

The fish was absolutely incredible, tangy with malt vinegar, and the secret sauce was worthy of Doug's fierce pride. It tasted familiar, like I could almost count off the spices, but their names stuck on the tip of my tongue, like old forgotten acquaintances.

As I dove deeper into the meal, Rebecca probed me with questions. Start from the top. What's going on? How long had we been engaged? Where'd we meet? When's the wedding? How did we manage to get into an editor/writer relationship? What's happened to disrupt everything? How does my sister feel about him? How do I feel about him? Why not can the whole thing? Was this love or convenience? What did I mean I couldn't distinguish? How did I feel when talking to Edward? Did I ever feel the same when talking with Byron? Would I leave Byron for Edward if it came down to it?

"What kind of question is that?" I stammered, deeply drunk on the rich food.

"An honest one," she replied, wiping her hands with a napkin.

"So how was it?" boomed the bear, towering over me and eclipsing the light. Doug's beard was wet around the mouth from a good pint of something. Something strong by the smell of it. Regarding his size, I wondered how much alcohol he could hold. A keg? A barrel? He plopped down next to Becca across the table.

"It was delicious, thank you," I said, honestly.

"The secret's in the sauce," he touted, touching the side of his nose with his index finger. Becca elbowed him.

"Doug, we have a question for you," she began. "You were married once. Love or convenience?"

"You mean why I married?" he grunted.

"I mean which is more important?"

He let out a deep breath that seemed to go on for at least a minute. I watched him stroke his beard, thoughtfully, rolling the question over behind his deep-set eyes.

"Who's asking?"

"My friend here finds herself in a love quandary," Rebecca explained. "Having some experience yourself, what would you tell her? She is engaged to a man whom she clearly does not love—"

"Rebecca!"

"And there might be someone else."

She spoke about Edward, but I thought about Bram. I thought about how free I felt around him. Wasn't that something to aspire to in marriage, the weightless, fearless feeling of being yourself? At the same time, now that Rebecca brought it up, had Edward not taken my breath at our first meeting? Did he not inspire me to be something more than I thought I believed possible? That was something to desire in a partner. He was a rock on which I could build motivation to improve myself continually.

"I didn't inherit this palace," Doug said, gesturing to his pub. "You should have seen it when we first started out. It was a dump. Piss stains in the corners, pardon my language, miss. Broken benches, counter was falling off. It wasn't much at all, but it was mine." He paused to take a drink from his mug.

"When I met Melinda, she was a dream in a dress. Her family wasn't wealthy by any real lot, but they was wealthier than me. Her parents had her fixed with this cobbler, who at least ran a respectable trade, they said. Truth be told, I can't fault the man. He was a good man. Still is. I walk by his shop every now and again. He's handsome as hell, too, in that classic sort of way. Back then, I wasn't the gallant stallion you see before you now. Her parents were right. He could have provided a very nice life for her. She'd have had a respectable house, kids, a right nice life. He would have treated her right."

"So, what happened?" I asked.

"Well, one day, he proposed to her. Poor thing, she said yes. Her family was in the other room at the time; they were all about to go out to dinner. Everyone was happy as could be. She came over to me the next morning in a fit. I could tell something was wrong right away. She sat me down on a chair, folded her arms in this way that made her look like she could take on a pit bull, and said, 'You're gonna lose me, Doug, unless you can whip something up really good right now. And I mean really good, because there's not a lot wrong with him.'"

Rebecca put a hand on his back, urging him on.

"And I spit out this crazy idea. Right there on the spot. I told her I was going to open a pub, sell my fish and chips. I'd made 'em for my mates and they liked 'em. So, why not? Completely hair-brained, but she looked at me in such a way and said, 'You promise our children won't go hungry?' 'Not if they like fish and chips,' I told her. She threw her arms around me, bathed my face in kisses, and promised me her heart forever. I'll never know why she believed in the idea of this pub so much."

His eyes glistened in the lamplight as he stared into the air. I imagined he saw Melinda between the tables, from his memory, polishing glasses or talking warmly with customers. His beard curled inward near the side of his mouth. I felt a little ashamed at my assessment of the place from when I walked in.

"What happened to her?" I asked. I knew it was a bold question, and maybe I should have asked Rebecca another time, but the reporter in me had learned not to shy away from tough questions.

"She died," he said, flatly. "Her and the baby."

Instinctively, I reached out my hand and clasped his gently over the table. We sat in silence for a long moment, he not even acknowledging our presence, until he finally turned to me and patted my hand congenially.

"Love or convenience?" he said. "I can't decide for you, now can I? I've got this pub to run."

He stood, gingerly grabbed our finished food trays, and whisked them off to the kitchen, patting some patrons on the back or straightening a painting along his way. I stared after him as long as I could before turning and studying the pub's interior with new eyes. It was meticulously kept in a man's type of way. Everything in its proper place, each table well cleaned and cared for. The pub was impressive, not because the decor was lavish (in fact, if anything, the tables and chairs were quite plain), but because it gave off a sense of immortality. The table beneath our drinks was made of sturdy oak. If it were up to Doug, I think the table would have stood there until the end of the world. It certainly would until the end of his.

"So, am I going to be turning in those stories for you? Or will you be making amends with the fiancé and turning them in yourself?" Rebecca asked, with a know-it-all smile. I smirked at the real question she was asking, and I knew no answer I could give would be the right one. Making up with Byron wasn't an option right now, and that also demonstrated my detachment. But, having Rebecca deliver my stories wasn't any better. Both roads led me away from Byron. It was an unfair question to ask. As far as I was concerned, it wasn't quite that simple.

"I'll be happy to have you turn them in for me," I replied. She nodded.

"As you wish it," she said, taking another sip of her drink. We both laughed. I felt as though I knew Rebecca much better than I should have. And, what was more surprising, she seemed to like me—not as a business acquaintance or as a participant in the social choreography where women support each other as they pursue domesticity.

"Why are you being so kind to me?" I asked. She swilled her cup.

"Come, now. You speak like kindness is so rare."

"Really, Rebecca, I don't know what I did to—" She cut me off with a wave of the hand.

"Something about you, I guess." She looked at me. No. She looked past me as if someone sat right in the same air I occupied, but in a moment, it was gone. She shook her head and finished her drink with a big draught. "What are we doing here? I have deliveries to make."

Chapter Sixteen

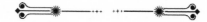

Fatherly Wisdom

I was happy to have a friend. I couldn't remember the last time I had a peer to talk with, apart from my sister. I had had co-workers at the factory years ago, but I wouldn't say we had been friends. There was always an undercurrent of mistrust between us that I couldn't explain. Then there was Mrs. Crow, but I don't think I'd call her a friend, a caring neighbor perhaps, but not a friend.

As the days went on, Rebecca proved herself to be a sister of circumstance, even if not by blood. She regularly made time to turn in stories to Byron on my behalf. When I tried to pay her, she simply smirked and said, "You're buying." Then we would head over to Doug's and enjoy fish, chips, and wonderful stories told by the owner and some of his regulars.

If Byron had an issue with my courier, he didn't bring it up. Mrs. Crow said that he had come by the house a couple of times with a despondent look in his eye, but she had explained that women need time to breathe and heal sometimes. I was happy to know that he was stewing in the consequences of his behavior. Men are like puppies in that way, best to rub their nose in it a little.

Besides, it's not like I was pretending not to be home. I really was out of the house, enjoying a blissful few weeks. I spent a good deal of time with Bram, conjuring up more incredible stories we could write with our magical pen. My creativity had burst to life in ways I never could have dreamed. Bram said it was the magic waking up inside of me, and maybe he was right. After accepting that magic was real, the magic I had always heard about in storybooks, I began to see it more and more in my daily life. I recognized it in the dormant trees, in the constant flow of the river, in the hundreds of tinctured clouds and thousands of distant stars. The more I saw it, the more I realized that I longed for magic my entire life. Now, while Bram and I experimented with it, it became an indispensable part of my life.

I woke up with twitching fingers, my mind racing after dreams I couldn't remember and unbound emotional experiences. Where my jealous outbreak at Byron or my impatience with Mrs. Crow once scared me, now I felt a longing to let my true unbridled self be free more often. The hard and fast social rules of society were limitations. It felt like having some type of beautiful withdrawal. I couldn't wait to dive back in, to feel the rush of my raw, true self.

In my most private thoughts, I considered Bram to be the most magical and increasingly indispensable of it all.

The pen kept working just as he had said it would. The House of Frogs story sold incredibly well. Not only was *Langley's* the first paper to report on a story, but we were literally writing the events before they happened. After the House of Frogs, as promised, Bram insisted that he write the next article, mentioning something about too much magical exposure.

He responded in true style by coming up with a story about an art heist at an estate in the country. The twist? The art was stolen by a well-trained herd of dogs that were let loose on the estate. An ode to Cyrus, he told me, scratching his dog behind the ears.

The owners didn't even realize the piece had been stolen until after they managed to shoo all the mongrels out of the house. Only then did they look out the second story window to see three hounds carrying the painting gently in their mouths to an unmarked carriage. Naturally, they gave chase, but they found only an empty carriage in the wood; all traces of the horses, driver, passengers, and painting were gone.

If the House of Frogs and the bank robbery story had been successful, this Mongrel Art Thieves story set the city ablaze. I saw it everywhere around town and completely sold out at newsstands. To my delight, *Langley's* competitors had plenty of copies of their dull headlines available for sale. *The Intricacies of Choosing a Pet Bird. Parliaments' Big Fumble. Salisbury and Gladstone At It Again.* Where was the magic in any of that?

Dawnhurst on Severn's paper business had transformed, and I could see a sparkle in the eyes of passersby. Under their hats, they looked about the city, as though the lampposts may come to life or any stray pup they saw might be involved in organized crime. A feeling of magic was spreading, and it felt wonderful.

Then it was my turn again, but I wanted to dive deeper. I wanted to innovate, find ways to add details and bring the stories to life even more. I thought this could be done with the addition of little non-sequiturs that might be related to the principle incident but only to an adventurous mind. My story was about a wife who went missing for three days, only to return to her husband convinced she was a cat. It was a mildly peculiar story but started to jump off the page when rumors of witchcraft in the neighborhood circulated, and neighbors reported bizarre lights in the wood a mile from their home.

I continued to dream about my father. Sometimes, I saw him in the church like I had before; other times, we sat in the police station or even at our old home in the east side. In every dream, the curious fog blanketed our environment in abundance, giving off a bizarre feeling of unreality. I told him about my stories and their public success. He laughed and slapped his leg.

"Now that's the ticket," he said. "What marvelous tales! You'll revolutionize the community. Where do you find stories like that?"

"I've fallen in with some interesting sources," I said. Even in my dream, I didn't tell him about the pen. I wasn't sure what he might think of it.

"I bet old Livingston is chuffed."

"I don't know. I haven't spoken with him for weeks," and I explained the outbreak at the restaurant. "Anna might dismember me if I were to marry him now."

"And what about that detective fellow? You get a look in your eyes about him I'd recognize anywhere. Your mother looked like that once about me, you know."

"I'm engaged," I said, blushing.

"You're not married," he replied. "And if you're in love with someone else, you don't have much an excuse to stay engaged."

"Even if it'd break his heart?" I asked.

"He's not a child, Luella. He's a grown man. He'll be alright," he said.

I wasn't sure I agreed. Byron was so deeply invested in me. At his age, I might be his last hope for a family.

"Don't underestimate a man's ability to fall in love anew."

"How did you know I was thinking that?" I asked. He stood up to go. "You're leaving already?"

"It's nearly morning. Keep up the stories, Luella. Whatever is working now, don't stop. Lean in. Writing can be so magical, can't it?"

Meanwhile, *Langley's Miscellany* enjoyed wild success for several weeks in a row. Rebecca brought back tidings of significant earnings at Langley's, although I was still waiting to see this reflected in my paycheck. I had nearly forgotten about Mr. Stringham's eviction threat. He hadn't come back to bother us about though, and I had just paid what little more I could for the month. Hopefully that was enough. I dreamed of moving with Anna to a better flat or even a house of our own. If I kept this up, I'd certainly merit the income. But, to increase my wages, I had a feeling I would need to speak with Byron, something I was not yet prepared to do, especially since Anna had not relented her grudge one iota toward him.

Perhaps a house of our own would be unnecessary anyway. Who knew? Maybe she could effect a miraculous turn with her suitor. There was no point in upgrading our housing if we would be changing our living arrangement anyway.

Which led me back to the heavy weight that was home life. Anna's condition had not improved, although she had met with Jacob on a few occasions. I took her mood after these meetings as a poor indicator of any progress. Whenever I asked her about him, she simply broke down and cried. I quickly decided that no news was bad news, and knowing my sister, I would get an earful once something positive developed. Sadly, I wasn't optimistic. I hoped they would smooth things over on their first meeting after that dinner. If they couldn't... it wasn't promising.

It didn't help that Anna had used this occasion to dive headlong into an increased measure of affection for him. She begged forgiveness when they were together. She plead with him to forget the incident, promising she would make him happy. She started spending what little allowance she had on gifts for him. It was heartbreaking. His family came from wealth. What did a poor-quality vest or watch mean to him?

Meanwhile, in a similarly pathetic way, Byron berated me with apology letters, delivered through Rebecca. To be honest, I didn't even read them all the way through. After the first one, they seemed rather repetitive. He had been drinking. He wasn't thinking straight. It wasn't his place. If we could just talk in person, he could explain himself... He was groveling, and it made me embarrassed. Besides, he was just saying things I knew already. His apology letters tried to explain things away by stating the obvious, as if some illumination of the facts would inspire a change of heart. If this behavior was depressing from Anna, it was emasculating from Byron.

At the bottom of each of these letters were the words," Won't you come back to the shop?" By this, we both knew he meant, "Is the engagement still on?"

Naturally, I couldn't return to the shop until I knew my answer.

The more time I spent away from Byron, and the more time I spent with Bram, the more I became convinced that a life apart from Byron was not only possible but inevitable. How could I explain the boundaries that separated us? My sister would not have him a member of the family. I felt I could forgive him for his behavior at the restaurant, but the damage to my affection was irreparable. Prior to that evening, Byron had been an innocent supporter of everything I stood for. He was without blemish for which I could fault him. That reputation endeared me to him, but wasn't a slip up like the one at the restaurant inevitable? Now, I fell asleep thinking about jokes Bram had told me or hypothesizing what it would be like to be escorted by Edward to a party, putting my hand on his strong arm, the guest of a police lieutenant.

While Bram and I had been busy coming up with stories and playing with magic, Edward was hard at work fighting gallant battles against the hordes of dark villainy our city could throw his way. Rebecca was always ready to tell me his latest accomplishment, and often, as if on cue, he would walk into the room right as she finished. The effect was not lost on her listener. Whether I had just heard about him thwarting a robbery in-progress, catching a pickpocket, or being the perfect gentleman with a grieving widow, Edward seemed less and less mortal every day. What made matters worse, he dropped all his other tasks and paid such close attention to me whenever we were together. It made me feel like the only woman in the world.

I longed for a means of getting to know Edward outside the police station. How would he behave in more casual settings? How was he as a companion at dinner? Did he ever take a break, or was he always on duty, trying to unearth criminals from their dark hiding places?

"Why don't you just ask him to lunch?" Rebecca said as she flew through keys on her typewriter. I learned that she spent much of her time transcribing handwritten police reports. Our occupations weren't all that different in that regard.

"Just ask him?" I sputtered. "I won't even start on the lack of propriety you're suggesting."

"Please, just stop. The lady who hasn't spoken with her fiancé in weeks is suddenly concerned with proprietary."

"I can't just ask him."

"Ask who?" Sergeant Cooper's voice interrupted our girlish back and forth. "What are you two yammering on about?"

I stood, mouth open, searching for a good response. Rebecca, ever eager to push me into action, took it on herself to get him involved.

"Ms. Winthrop is trying to work up the courage to ask a young man to lunch," she said.

"Rebecca!" I blushed deeply.

"Rebecca?" Cooper said. "I should have known you two would fall in thick as thieves. You better not be sharing sensitive police information with this reporter, Ms. Turner."

"Sergeant, you insult my professional sensibility if you think I value friendship over truth and justice." She smiled at him, and I wasn't sure if she was mocking him or speaking honestly.

At that moment, Edward strode into the room, his jacket unbuttoned, hat underarm, pretty as a picture.

"Ms. Turner, Ms. Winthrop," he greeted us with a nod. "A pleasure to see you again."

For some reason, my awkward silence stretched on, and I couldn't seem to string together a "nice to see you, too." Instead, the four of us stood there for what seemed like a half hour, until Rebecca finally flashed a set of suggestive eyes to Sergeant Cooper.

"What? Oh. Oh! Really? Oh," he blurted out, trying his best to commit to an episode of throat clearing. "Lieutenant, it's a good thing you're here. Ms. Winthrop needs to, erm, interview you."

"I do?" I interjected with a pointed glare.

"Whatever she would like. Ms. Winthrop, you know that you have my most sincere candor," Edward said, with a concerned smile. I tried to shoot a venomous glare at Rebecca, but she just kept working her eyes at the Sergeant.

"No, no. Not here, I'm, uh, tired of reporters cluttering the station. The poor woman must be hungry. Why not... er... take her to lunch or something."

"That is completely unnecessary—"

"It would be an absolute pleasure," Edward said, putting his hat on with a laid-back tilt. Sergeant Cooper looked inexpressibly uncomfortable, fingering the brim of his hat like a nervous schoolboy and smiling as awkwardly as the first time he asked me if I was there to report a missing person. Rebecca was doing her very best not to burst out in a fit of laughter.

"She would make excellent company for a lunch break, if she is willing," Edward said. He offered me his arm, and before I could register what was happening, he was leading me out of the station, my hand on his strong arm. I turned back in time to see Rebecca peering around the hallway corner after us, a joyful scream exploding out of her eyes.

Chapter Seventeen

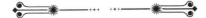

The Hound and the Bear

Edward insisted that I choose where to go for lunch, and blanking entirely, I spat out the only place that I could think of: Doug's Fish and Chip Pub. Immediately after it came out, I regretted it. Doug and I had worked up an amiable back and forth, but I had never gone there without Rebecca. For some reason, I wasn't sure that bringing a police officer with me on my first solo trip was the best idea.

"I didn't even know this pub was here," Edward commented with an air of admiration. "And I pride myself on knowing the city quite well." He smiled at me sweetly. His comment subtly illuminated the daily grind he must encounter. I heard about the story-worthy escapades, but he must go through a great deal of tedium between moments of excitement. That was a comforting thought. So long as I was more interesting than his daily tedium, then he couldn't consider the lunch a complete loss.

I was in my own moment of excitement just being out with him like this. I couldn't sort out how I felt. I wanted to smile and hide all at once. I didn't know how I was going to eat; my stomach was in all sorts of knots, and I was suddenly very conscious of my posture and figure. On top of it all, I was worried to be taking Edward to an establishment like Doug's. With any luck, Doug wouldn't be there today.

I knew it was a vain hope. Doug likely slept in that pub. In the past couple of weeks, Rebecca and I ate there a handful of times. I continued to fret about my personal dynamic with the proprietor. In the best scenario, I imagined my friendship with Doug would be similar to having an older brother. So, was this like taking a man to meet my older brother. To make matters worse, he was a police officer. Was I being unfair suspecting Doug wasn't exactly bosom buddies with many policemen?

What was I thinking? At least, I was being honest with myself. I was struck with him. Rebecca would be thrilled.

To make matters worse, I had told Bram I'd be meeting him that afternoon to work on another story. My lunch date with Edward was an absolute surprise. I was sure to miss that appointment with Bram, and there was no way to reach out to him to reschedule. I wasn't eager to explain to Bram that I had skipped out on him because I was at lunch with the Steely Detective. I was already hiding Bram from Byron. Now, I was hiding Edward from Bram. What a mess. Maybe I was more beautiful than I gave myself credit for.

I was also hiding Bram from Rebecca. I had never told her about him. My courage failed me when I related all of my other troubles, believing that my rendezvous with a strange man alone may have been too much for her good opinion of me. Now, we had such a good friendship blossoming, I didn't want to strain it by making her think I was crazy. How would I explain to her why I continued to go back to spend my afternoons with him? How could I explain the magic pen to her? She would never believe it. What would she believe in its stead?

"Is this the place?" Edward asked. We had just reached the pub, its old, well-kept wood sign swinging as usual on its post above the door. It read a generic "Fish and Chips" with an artful fish drawing.

"It is," I said. He led me in, confidently pushing the door open. Doug's waiting staff immediately recognized me and started toward me with friendly greetings, but when they saw Edward's uniform, they checked their warmth. They sat us at my usual table.

"They seem like a friendly wait staff. I'm curious though, Ms. Winthrop, how did you happen across a place like this?"

"Rebecca introduced me, actually."

"Ms. Turner? I should have known," he laughed. "What's good here?"

"The fish and chips," a deep voice behind him boomed. Doug towered over us, his usual imposing figure at work. He must have skipped combing his beard that morning because it looked more unruly than normal.

"Makes sense," Edward said, unfazed. "I'll take them. And whatever Ms. Winthrop would like as well."

"I thought it was you, Luella," Doug said. "You must be a witch."

"A witch?" I asked, my heart rate rising. Could Doug know about the magic? "What are you talking about?"

"You've transformed my lovely Rebecca into a pretty policeman," he said, gesturing to Edward. Hopefully, no one noticed my blank expression of relief. I was getting paranoid.

"You two know each other?" Edward asked.

"Doug owns the pub," I explained. "And, he's a good friend of Rebecca's."

"You own the pub?" Edward asked. "She's a beauty, sir."

"Don't call me sir. I'm Doug Tanner," he said. I was having a difficult time determining whether they were about to fight or join in a manly handshake.

"Mr. Tanner, then," Edward continued. "I'll withhold my handshake until after I've tried your fish and chips."

Doug belched out a menacing laugh. "Three orders coming up, then."

"There are only the two of us," Edward protested.

"I'm not sure you know who you're having lunch with," Doug replied as he turned and headed back to the kitchen. Edward shook his head.

"Seems like a rough character."

"I quite like him," I said. "He's a self-made man, raised this place back from the dead. I don't know many men with the same type of resolve."

"Don't get me wrong, Ms. Winthrop. I think men need to be a little rough. Not with their loved ones, mind you, but it's not a soft world, and I think a man should know how to set his feet and know how to lick it," Edward said, smiling. "I want to say the pub is great. But, it really comes down to his fish and chips."

"You're withholding judgment of a man until you taste his food?"

"Food comes from within," he countered. "Judging by the cleanliness and the style of the place, I think he's likely a good man, but you can't know until you've tasted a bit of his heart."

I grimaced. "Fish and chips and heart. Suddenly, I've lost my appetite."

We both laughed. Mine sounded ungraceful. His sounded like a good reading of Longfellow.

"Forgive me, Ms. Winthrop," he said. "I'm not the writer at the table. You could have said it more elegantly, I'm sure." I smiled at him.

"You're too kind. Please, if you would, call me Luella." He returned my smile.

"If you wish. It's a much more beautiful name than Travis Blakely." His comment caught me off-guard. I hadn't been giving my pen name much thought lately. With Rebecca turning in my stories for me, I hadn't even signed my stories now for a couple of weeks, trusting Byron would add those particulars. After all, he had suggested the pen name in the first place.

"How did you come up with your pen name?" he asked.

"Travis was my father's name," I said. "Blakely was the last name of the author of the first book I learned to read."

"Your father must have been a great man."

"He was a factory worker. Nothing grand." I could almost see his weary eyes after a day at work. I was so little. I never understood why he looked so tired, but he was never too tired for me.

"His daughter's character speaks on his behalf," he said. My character. Did I merit such a compliment?

"Well, what about your parents?" I asked. The conversation grew too much about me. I already knew that Edward was a polished gentleman. I wanted to know him more deeply. There had to be a human being under the Adonis statue.

"My father was deeply dissatisfied that I joined the police force," he said, eyeing his glass. "He wanted me to inherit the Thomas family business."

"Which is?"

"Banking," he said with a grim sigh.

"You sound ashamed."

"It's a fine business to be about. Many might consider it a dishonorable occupation, but I think that's unfair. It's just... I always thought my father could have been more. When have you ever heard of a banker changing the world for the better?"

"I suppose it depends on what the banker might finance."

"Even if a banker does finance a charitable cause, it's because the numbers are sound. It's a profession that encourages a cold-hearted logic."

"Is that why you became a policeman, to change the world?" I asked. He looked out the window toward the river.

"If you ask my father, I joined the police to spite him. If you ask my mother, I joined to send her to an early grave."

"I'm asking you, though." He turned to me. Was I picking up a shade of frustration. He looked as though he searched for words.

"Do you think the city needs the police," he asked finally.

"After the stories I've written about you, I'd say so."

"Then how could I sit back and let others bear the risk?"

He looked like a bright-eyed retriever, sitting there, erectly postured and filled with mastered energy. He was so pure, so valiant, I had a hard time believing he was sincere, but there was no trace of the liar's smile on the corners of his lips. He possessed the visage of a man who would die for his ideals or, more daringly, live from them.

"You are the bravest man I've ever met," I said, reaching out to squeeze his hand. I didn't think about it; my hand just seemed to move on its own before I could stop it. He looked at it and squeezed back, sending my heart into a mild hurricane.

"There are some things in this city worth defending," he replied, his eyes locking on mine like magnets. I could only hold his gaze for a few seconds before clearing my throat and pulling my hand back. He nodded with a smile that made me forget my name.

Doug broke our tranquility by plopping down three troughs of his famous fish and chips.

"Three orders," he said. "For the man with a delicate palette." I wasn't sure what I was watching here. Again, one moment, Doug looked like he was going to crush Edward. The next, I thought they may start a brotherly wrestling match. Doug took a seat next to me and put both elbows squarely on the table, folding his hands in front of his mouth.

"Thank you, sir."

"What did I just tell you about calling me sir?" Doug growled.

"What is this stuff?" Edward asked, picking up the small dish of Doug's secret sauce. I smiled, remembering my first taste of it. It seemed like a long time ago, but it hadn't even been a month. Doug eyed him warily.

"It's his secret sauce," I offered. Edward smiled slyly back at Doug.

"Now that's more like it." Edward took a large piece of fish, dipped it into a generous portion of the sauce, and popped it in his mouth. While he chewed, Doug continued staring him down, bull against matador.

"Heavens, man," Edward said. "That's a bit of alright."

Doug pounded a triumphant fist down on the table. "Best in the city! You can't find better!"

"You devil rascal, man! I wish I could disagree with you."

After that, it was all smiles, pats on the back, and sharing stories about scars. I was delighted. If I was looking for an experience to see the human side of Edward, I realized now, Doug was the perfect vessel to arrive at my goal. They showed each other battle wounds from bar fights or chasing down criminals. They bonded over cricket matches and swapped recipes they picked up from unsavory characters. I listened on, enthralled, happy to see that Edward wasn't all manners and protocol. In fact, he even lost track of the time and jumped at his pocket watch when he saw the hour.

"Doug, you fiend! You've kept me well past the hour. The Sergeant will have my hat."

"He'd better not. You've been accompanying this young lady; she simply required your attention."

"Is that true, Luella?" Edward asked. Truthfully, I would have loved his attention for the rest of the week. I drunk his stories in deeply and lost myself, admiring how his jawline looked in the tavern light. Something about sitting well after food with great company was enough to imitate the effects of alcohol. Remembering it was daytime was like a shocking revelation.

"I plan on telling Cooper that I fainted on the roadside," I said.

"Well, then my tardiness seems justified," he replied, jovially. Doug bellowed his hearty, raspy laugh.

"You've got a lively one here," Doug said. "I'd hold on to her."

To this, I didn't quite know what to say. My heart caught a little, and I had nothing with which to respond. Edward didn't seem to have a response either. He just smiled at me, sweetly. Did I dare to believe that he meant to agree? Did he want to hold on to me, whatever that meant?

"I'll let you two go, though. I have my own work to do," Doug said, standing, and grabbing our troughs. "You take care of yourself, Lieutenant."

"Likewise, Doug. Expect to see me again soon."

Edward went to grab our coats from the coat rack near the door, giving Doug ample opportunity to jab me. "So, this is that love quandary Becca went on about?"

I quickly shushed him and sent him chuckling back to the kitchen. Edward returned, helped me into my coat, and offered his arm. I took it happily and tried my best to disguise the foolish, giddy grin spreading across my face. This was a life I could get used to. Lunching with Edward, working with Bram, socializing with Rebecca and Doug. They were so new, yet they roused me from a sleep I didn't know I was in. How many of these people, my people, had I missed out on through the years?

The only thing that could distract me from a blissful state like this was the magazine on the table near the entrance.

"Would you fetch that publication for me, Edward?" I asked, pausing.

He obliged, and I flipped the pages, calmly at first, then with increasing intensity.

"Is anything the matter, Luella?" Edward asked. I shook my head absentmindedly, but I knew this magazine. I still don't know why I picked it up. There was no good to be had of it. Who knows what happiness I could have enjoyed if I had continued pretending it didn't exist?

Instead, I found myself reading against my will, settling on a page that I knew all too well. My hand shook.

It was Brutus' review of Travis Blakely's most recent publications.

Chapter Eighteen

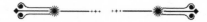

Fit of Fury

I arrived at Langley's just around closing time. It felt like months since I had last seen its red-painted wooden doorway. It was an apt color for my mood. The familiar sign swung gently in the breeze on the rod sticking out from the brick building. I had made the trek over at a furious pace, fuming the whole route, mulling over what I might say to Byron. There was an unnatural energy born inside of me, but this time, I didn't fight it. I let it sweep over me, and it felt good. I felt angry, on the war path, looking for someone to blame. My fingers twitched.

Brutus' review had rattled me. For a brief moment, I wished the past few weeks had never happened, that I could go back to writing articles on drapes and table manners, comfortably untouched by critique, success, and adventure. Was it wrong to wish for a world without magic?

I set my jaw and shook off the feeling. Byron was comfortable, but even if I could turn back time, I knew I couldn't live without more than domestic comfort. Besides, was not his true character revealed at Bunbury's Restaurant the other night? He struck Jacob across the face like a common brigand.

I banged on the big, red door. I had barged right in hundreds of times before, but things were different now. In any rate, I wanted to pound on something; why not the door?

"Let yourself in! We're not closed," Byron's muffled voice cried from inside.

"You might be if Brutus goes on any more like this!" I shouted back. The distinct sound of hurried movement announced my old fiancé even before the door swung open. He stood there, gaping at me, looking even older than I remembered him.

"Luella? You're here."

"How do you think I could stay away after a review like that? Are you going to let me in, or will I shrivel out here in the cold?"

"You don't need an invitation." He stepped aside, revealing the office with which I was too well familiar. It all lay in front of me almost exactly the way I'd left it. The only difference was a bit more clutter, and the place felt colder. I noticed no other reporters there. All the better, we could speak more openly.

"When were you going to tell me?" I asked, making my way briskly past him to my old chair at the back table. I didn't sit down.

"I haven't even seen you for weeks! Where have you been? Did you get my letters?"

"Let's not get into this now, Byron."

"Not get into this now?"

"Just all this." I shook my hands at him. They looked like claws with my clenched fingers in the air. I hadn't come to talk about his feelings. I wanted to know if Byron knew about the review in advance, how many times he'd met with Brutus since I last saw him, and if he was even complicit in the betrayal.

"Who's that woman you've been sending with your stories?" he asked. He leaned against the wall, seemingly unable to support his full weight. He must have known that our prospects for marriage were bleak. His whole body communicated it in every slouching bit of skin. Yet, I saw bright hope in his eyes, as if there was something inside ready to fight for this conversation if needs be.

"She's a friend. What business is it of yours?"

"Has she brought you my letters?" He fiddled with the chain of his pocket watch, like a nervous schoolboy.

"Yes, she brought me the letters."

"And?"

"Mysteriously absent in your letters was any mention about Brutus' review of my latest stories!"

"You're upset about that? How was I supposed to know what he was going to write?"

"When hasn't he shown up at that door to gloat and terrorize his victims? Did he not come here?" I advanced on him dangerously, and he retreated a step before catching himself.

"He did, but I could hardly think about him. I've been worried to death over you and your sister." He walked past me toward the desk in the back of the room. How this conversation was unlike our usual breakfast back and forth.

"What possible interest could you have in my sister?" I hissed.

"I have a deep interest in her welfare."

"Enough of an interest to embarrass her in front of her only prospect of marriage and an entire restaurant?" He was dragging me into the conversation I didn't want to have. I had promised myself the entire way here I wouldn't let this happen.

"I was just asking the lad what his intentions were! If they were truly so close to marriage, could such a trifle really disrupt his affection?"

I stood, fuming, partly because I knew he was right, partly because I imagined this last quip was directed at me. Fine. If he wanted to argue about personal business, so be it. "And this is the fatherly summation you've made of my sister's courtier?"

"Not a father but certainly a dear relative. She will be family to me, too, after all."

"Not if she has things her way." I caught myself breathing heavily.

"Surely you don't mean that," he said, looking up at me like a wounded animal. His facial features looked so heavy. I closed my eyes and clenched my fists, feeling the anger pool and swell. I was a writer, a voice within me seemed to say. Use your words to hurt him. He deserves it.

"You hit him, Byron! You struck him across the face. You were brutish and violent!" I swallowed. This wasn't me. My father had not taught me to use words to inflict harm. This was my temper. It was more than my temper. I felt like I was walking through a dark doorway somewhere in my mind.

I paused and took a deep breath. The anger did not dissipate, but I felt like I could resist it a little better at least.

"We can deal with this later. Right now, we have the weekly to think about. Brutus is calling me, your author, rubbish. He's recommending our work for the bin."

"My author?" he said, his eyes fixed on an invisible design he traced with his fingers on the table.

"Yes, your author," I said, bristling, after a minute of his silence. He was not making it easy for me to stay calm, not with these feelings raging inside of me. "And by the way, don't think I haven't noticed the figures on the paychecks coming back to me. You know as well as I do the financial boon my latest stories have brought, but it appears you've seen it fit to keep this success from me."

"Keep it from you? I've been paying your rent with it!"

I reeled, losing grasp of my self-control like a slippery rope. How dare he?

"You have control of my finances now, do you?" I fumed.

"You could have told me Mr. Stringham was going to put you out."

"It was none of your concern."

"How can my wife's welfare not be my concern?"

I slapped him squarely across the face.

"I'm not your wife yet," I seethed. "And I'd appreciate it if you were to keep our business relationship, my finances, and our domestic arrangement separated."

Through the doorway, dark and deep. I looked at my hand. This was not me. I had just done to him the very thing I condemned him for doing to Jacob. More than the slap, my words stung him. I knew they would. I had said them anyway.

"So, you're just here for business, then?" He cleared his throat.

"Business," I replied through a strained throat.

"Then, as your editor," Byron stood, "I'm afraid I have to inform you it's only your work Brutus is criticizing."

"What?" I felt my angry strength draining from my legs.

"As far as I've understood, Brutus didn't even mention *Langley's Miscellany* by name. He seemed only to take issue with author Travis Blakely."

I hadn't noticed that. I had been too distracted by seeing my own name smeared the way it was—or at least my pen name.

"Surely, the others must have drawn some criticism. Brutus always has issues with Mr. Storm's articles as well."

"None of them," he responded coolly.

"But readers will connect the dots. They'll match the writer to the publication. Don't think for a second his critique won't affect you. The stories have sold so well. You can't imagine your reputation will escape my rebuke."

"Don't you find it curious, though?" he asked. He had never spoken to me like this. He looked cold, devoid of feeling. He'd been constructive before, yes. Gently suggested, yes, but he'd never come out in a blatant attack this way.

"Brutus has never liked my work," I said. I turned away from him. I felt tears pooling behind my eyes.

"He's always had a lot to say about it," he said. "Reading his latest critique suggested only one thing to me: Brutus, as ever, is trying to convince me to drop you."

Drop me? As a writer? As a lover?

"But why?"

"My dear Mr. Blakely, it doesn't matter why. This is the life of a writer. Readers read, critics critique. Just a few weeks ago, you complained that Brutus called your work forgettable. Now that you've got his attention in full-page, black and white, you're complaining he doesn't like it."

I opened my mouth to protest, but he continued.

"Let's look at his critique and see if it's worth its weight, shall we?" He picked up a copy of the very magazine that started my spiraling anger. "Travis Blakely's recent string of stories, though sensational, provide very little substance to the commonwealth. While the unlearned laugh, to quote Shakespeare, the odd reporting of bizarre events probe into the believability of his sources and beg the question, am I reading a children's story or a professional publication? While he may continue to pilfer our pocketbooks with catchy titles that tingle our curiosity, at the end of the day, his writings will become nothing more than 'do you recall that one time.' This critic will spend his leisure reading time on things of more meat and encourages anyone else wishing to look respectable to do the same."

The tears were flowing now, silently and hot, down my cheeks. The words stung so much more now, hearing them from a man who loved me, than having read them printed in a stranger's voice.

"Do you agree with him?" I managed to say. I choked on the words.

"As an editor?" he asked. How badly I wanted to tell him no and retreat back into his sheltering embrace, publishing even my rubbish, insisting that I was worth the effort. At the same time, I looked on him with a fever dream, ready to rip him apart, daring him to give me any reason to storm out. I nodded. He sighed heavily.

"How can I dislike your recent efforts, considering what they've done for the accounts? We've never sold so many copies or been read more widely. But, when it comes to the substance of your stories, I cannot disagree with Brutus. I thought your old stories, though boring, were more sincere."

My old, boring stories. My new, shallow fluff. It was all too much. I sank back into the chair, a mess of a woman. I felt the weight of my unmarried years settle heavily on my shoulders, all those years I had gambled away, convinced that I could be different, convinced that I could make something of my father's sacrifice for my education. I had made it my business not to compromise my personality for another person. And where had it all led? Had I truly landed with nothing to show for my stubborn attitude but years of mediocrity and failure?

"Which brings us to Brutus' inevitable question. Should I drop you, Mr. Blakely?"

Who was this man? He was built of stone and not the fine chiseled marble that made up Edward. Byron looked at me like coarse, raw granite, casting a long, dark shadow over my outlook. Why should I give warmth when he gave none?

"What are you asking really, Byron? Are you punishing me for my absence?"

"You wanted to talk business. I'm simply acquiescing. "

Hot blood surged up my neck. "Do you have any idea what it's like for a woman like my sister? She wasn't raised as I was. My father sacrificed so much to instill virtues in me other than beauty. Anna was never so inclined. Without Jacob, what will become of her? You know all of this. Are you using this against me?"

"Whatever I did, I did it out of concern for whom I consider a sister as well. Weigh my perspective, Luella. You vanish for weeks, and in your place comes a strange woman to drop off your stories. I've been sick with worry, wondering where you are and with whom."

I found a grim smile on my face. If he only knew with whom I'd been keeping company, he'd be mortified. He'd cancel the engagement right here and now if he could see Bram's tent. A temptation to tell him bubbled to my lips. I could break him. Then the only boring story he'd have would be the same broken-hearted tale of a younger woman running off with a younger man.

"Was it worry that inspired you to speak such ugly, unguarded words just now?" I asked.

"You aren't yourself," Byron said. "Brutus' reviews have always bothered you but never like this. One might think your success at the print stands would provide you a shield against him. Why has he set you off so sharply?"

Curse Byron for knowing me well enough to see what I feared. I was not myself. Brutus' critique was nothing but words, yet seeing them had swept me into a frenetic fury. But, the fury was there, and I felt it burning, coming back stronger. Vicious words rattled in my head, begging for leave to fly like darts at their target. My fingers twitched. I thought about the pen. I wanted to use it to rectify whatever had done me wrong.

"I'm embarrassed to ask it, but my own conclusions lead me nowhere else," he continued. "Should I drop you? Or, rather, what is the state of our engagement? I—well—are you only interested in my magazine?"

"How dare you, Mr. Livingston," I managed to say. "Are you truly exploiting our business arrangement to produce effects in our romantic relationship?"

"I did not intend—"

"How could I ever trust a man who would stoop to such a level?"

"Is this your reply then? Why won't you answer me?"

"I will not because it is insulting to the core."

"Do you mean to leave me then?"

"I do not relieve you of your promises to me," I said. My rigid jawline dripped with righteous indignation. I gathered my things and strode out the door before he had time to reply.

Chapter Nineteen

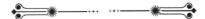

Bound by Fire

I got to the fairgrounds right as its queer electric lights reached out into the darkness. I nodded to the girl in the ticket booth-Sherry I think her name was-who waved me on through. A few weeks and I was already a regular. I wondered what the festival performers and workers thought of me. Bram's girl, perhaps. It hadn't bothered me until tonight. It was exciting before.

I still seethed from my encounter at Langley's. Byron's pitiful face burned in my memory like a hot coal. The evening air held a crisp chill, but between my elevated pulse and my brisk pace from Langley's door to the fair, I welcomed the cold breeze on my perspiration.

Bram had hinted to me that soon the fair would be closing, moving on. They usually packed up at the first snowfall. When I inquired what came next, he had just smiled vaguely. That memory infuriated me all the more now that his gimmick had made me the laughing stock of the writing world. I whizzed by the beginning of the night's crowds, all eager to see the oddities and illusions the macabre festival promised. They were eager to believe the world they lived in was a farce. These were my readers. I looked around and saw shallow expressions gaping stupidly at performers in costumes.

It only had taken weeks for the performers to educate me on the tricks of their trade. Where others saw magic, I saw only cheap sleights. Where some saw exotic monsters, I saw birds and house pets with dyed feathers and attached prosthetics. Only Bram knew real magic, and he used it for nothing.

Why had I not considered it before? What did it say about Bram's character that he stood alone with the keys to real magic only to pilfer it like a schoolboy? Where had he truly uncovered the pen? He had always evaded my questions about that. I only knew that a dangerous expedition had cost several men their lives. How did he plan such an expedition? Where did he find the men? The volunteers? Had there been other expeditions?

"Oiy, Luella!" Gerald, the giant buffoon in a permanent bowler cap shouted to me. He had a big, goofy grin on his face, carrying two large acrobat hoops. Many of the fair goers around him turned their heads toward me in response. I ignored them and pushed on to the familiar clearing where the hypnotists were hard at work bewitching their planted helpers in the audience.

Bram stood with a dark expression on his face, leaning against a tent pole, watching the performance. Though the audience around him burst into scattered applause and laughter, a storm cloud loomed over him. He saw me from afar and watched me cross the crowd toward him without interruption. Finally, we stood face to face, looking for words, I angry at him for no distinct reason, he playing aloof in the way he did when he felt wounded.

"We need to talk," I began.

"I waited for you all day. I'm a little busy watching my friend, Mona. She's hypnotized this man to believe the woman there cares about him."

"Don't be an idiot." I grabbed him by the wrist and swept into the tent.

"Please, stop, I need to see what happens to him," he complained in a monotone voice.

Inside, I whirled him into a chair to face me. He didn't seem alarmed the way I had expected. He didn't seem frightened of me, either. Why would he? What did I have to hold over him? Did I have a single measure of power in our relationship? In any relationship? No. He had held all of that for himself. Instead, I mustered up the strength to do the most Mrs. Crow-like thing I'd ever done. I whacked him with my purse. Then I hit him again and again, dropping the purse and turning to my balled-up fists instead.

"Violence now, is it?" he said, faintly trying to defend himself.

"This is all your fault!" I shouted. "You've ruined me! You've ruined every part of me!"

"I don't know what you're talking about," he replied. What a thing for a man to say! How many men have said that over the history of time?

"You—you—you lured me in here like a—like a fish!"

"Like a fish? Your words are failing you. What is it?"

"Yes, like a fish in a trap! There I was, swimming along happily, when you came along and just scooped me up like a big bucket of water."

The metaphor was breaking down, but then so was my life. He was stunned into silence all the same.

"I had everything!" I cried. "I had an engagement with a man who adored me and a budding career as an author and a loving relationship with a dear sister! But you don't care about any of that. You just wanted me in your web, like a nasty little spider."

He held up his hands in a display of surrender. Cyrus groaned from a blanket near the bed. "Something has clearly made you upset," Bram said.

"The hell it has! What else is in that chest?" I pointed directly at the locked chest on the side of his tent. It was the box from which he had first produced that ruddy pen, the same box he pretended didn't exist whenever I asked.

"I'm not telling you anything until you explain what happened." He calmly sat, studying me. A curious look spread over his features. "You seemed fine the other day. I should be cross with you. After all, you were supposed to come by earlier today, and you stiffed me. Do you want to know how I spent the day? Watching Gerald shave his own back with an axe. Yes. It was weird, but I had no excuse to turn him down."

"Do you think this is funny?" I asked, squinting at him in disbelief. "We can't continue this way. It always happens like this. I ask something or need a favor, and you set the terms."

"Do you think I've ever withheld anything from you?"

"It doesn't matter! It's the dynamic of power. I've spent my entire life avoiding this type of relationship with a man, and it took a magical trinket to lure me into one. Well, not anymore."

He stood and slowly crossed to the chest, weighing something in his mind.

"I was hoping to show you what was in this chest later this week," he said. I folded my arms.

"A likely story."

"Now, it appears I cannot." He shrugged and looked at me. I caught myself gaping.

"Why not?"

"It's a box of trinkets," he said. "Perhaps the least of which is the instrument of which you are so fond." He rolled his eyes on the word 'fond.'

"That doesn't explain anything."

"How do you expect me to show you new magic when you've gone completely into crisis over something as petty as that pen and ink?"

New magic? I had guessed as much but did not dare to think I may have been right. Like Edward's Fog Man, I pushed it off. So, what if there were more magic out there? What did it have to do with me? The pen alone had to do with me.

"I don't care what's in the box," I said. "But, the fact that you won't show me communicates volumes on what type of man you are."

"And you know so much, do you? I'm trying to protect you. If you knew what you were asking—just look at the effect your first magic experiment has had on you!"

My eyes swept the room, looking for the instrument he spoke of. It was lying on a fresh stack of paper near his bed. I crossed to it.

"Luella."

"Don't you dare say my name!"

I sensed him closing in on me, so I lunged for the pen. As I reached the bed stand, a heavy force from behind conclusively pinned me down on my back. I lay on the bed, the pen clenched in my fist, looking up directly into Bram's excited expression. My wrists were pinned to the mattress at the level of my eyes. My pulse sounded like a timpani drum.

"Unhand me!"

"You are not yourself."

"Says the man forcing his way on a woman. You brute! I'll scream!"

Why did everyone keep saying that to me? I struggled against him, beating him with my fists as hard as I was able. Inside, I felt the dark door open again. I was tired of fighting my temper. I was tired of letting things happen to me.

"More than you have already?" He released me but wrestled the pen from my grasp. I clutched at it, scratching at his arms, beating my fists at his torso.

"You can't keep lording that thing over me!" I shouted. He grabbed a sheet of paper and ran to his writing table. I stood. "What are you doing?"

He didn't respond. He just scribbled frantically on the sheet before crumpling it into a ball and throwing it into the coals at the center of his tent. The flames belched a small fireball in response.

"What did you write?" I demanded, but even as the words left my mouth, I felt the fury drain from me like rain from a rooftop. My legs suddenly grew weak, and I did not have the strength to stand. "Bram? What have you done?"

I collapsed heavily on his bed, landing on it askew.

"I can't move. What's happening to me?" I said. It was barely a whisper, and the world turned black.

When I woke, Bram sat next to the bed, holding my hand tenderly. "You'll be alright," he said. I felt like someone had knocked me out with a smart punch to the face. The room slowly stopped spinning, but I felt no power to move. Every part of me rested heavily, motionless, like it was made of lead.

"This is my fault," Bram said. "I should have known it would behave unpredictably."

"What would behave unpredictably?" My voice grew stronger now, but the fury that fueled me before had vacated my person. A strange calm came over me, accompanied only by an unconscious dread that it wouldn't last long.

"The pen. I've read that this has happened before but never this quickly or with such casual use. How do you feel?"

"Lighter," I said, "like a bay after a storm. What has happened before, Bram?"

"In the paltry records I've been able to gather that describe others' experiences with the pen—well, there are some stories of aggression."

I struggled to sit up. "You mean the pen is controlling the way I feel?" Fear rose in my bosom.

"Not exactly," he replied. "I'm not sure how it works." I withdrew my hand from him.

"You knew this could happen?"

"No. I just knew what I know about all magic. There are side effects if you get too involved. I tried to avoid this. I wrote every other story, for example. I insisted we didn't write as often as we could have."

"But, you knew something could have happened to me." My voice caught in my throat. So, this was the great answer. I had wondered why Bram took such interest in me. I was vain enough to think it was a typical man's interest. Instead, what was it? A scholarly fascination? A mystical hypothesis? I thought about my twitching fingers, my desire to use the pen again and again, and all the unnatural feelings I had experienced lately. My jealousy, annoyance, even my fury toward Byron yesterday. Brutus' review hadn't been his fault. What had I done? I blinked back tears.

"So, I'm just your experiment?" I asked, hoping for a reprieve. I studied his face, looking for any reason to believe I was wrong.

"Don't speak nonsense. It isn't like that."

"Then explain it to me," I insisted. "What am I to you?" It came tumbling out, edged with enough womanly emotion to make me despise myself. I had avoided asking and answering the same question since we'd met.

"I'm your friend," he said, himself emotional. I'd never seen him this way. He looked tired and wounded. I found no trace of the usual slyness adorning the corners of his mouth. His eyes saw past me to something, perhaps someone else, much the way Rebecca had done at Doug's ago. I felt invisible and couldn't shake the feeling that I didn't know this man. "A friend with whom I wanted to explore magic. I wanted to write with you."

A friend. He had ruined me just to see what might happen with his magical artifact.

"Write with me? Have you read the reviews?"

"Oh, don't listen to them. Reviewers can't write. That's why they review."

"They were right. You've lured me into drafting rubbish. Nothing we've created together is of any real worth. What do I have to show for it? My engagement is in pieces, and now I learn that I have some type of magical relationship with an inanimate object."

"What rubbish."

"I've done nothing but write sensational stories that don't mean anything. They're like sugar humbugs! And, even those stories are fake. None of the events I've been writing would have even happened if I hadn't written about them first."

Bram stood and tinkered with an old telescope from a nearby table.

"I think you're looking at it wrong," he said. "You think you're reporting on non-truths that happen because you make them."

"I can't see it another way."

"But you must see it another way. I believe you're reporting on events that will inevitably happen; it just so happens that the pen tells you first. I really do. The pen doesn't make anything happen. The pen is just a window."

"We've been over this, and I can't subscribe to it. I can't believe that a respectable member of society clad in full armor would have robbed a bank independent of my story. It's ridiculous!"

I stood, a little wobbly at first, and crossed the room to him.

"Magic is in the everyday," he said with a soft smile. "It just takes smoke and sparks to make people see it."

"It's all beside the point anyway. Even if you're right. They're still silly stories that don't make any difference." To think I had hoped to carve my way to the Golden Inkwell with this...

"Don't make any difference?" His voice was full and incredulous. "Can you be so blind?" He made a circuit of the tent, looking fixedly at different points, this way and that, like he could see hidden vistas and portraits, hanging invisible in the air. "What cause could be nobler than helping a city wake up and recognize what's in front of them? You've been breaking them out of their trances. You've been opening their eyes! There's something happening. I can feel it, and you're helping the world stand up and notice! The work we've done here. . ."

"The work we've done? So, this is your big crusade? You enlisted me without even asking. Am I a prisoner or a solider then?"

My hands were shaking now as the realization set in. I had acted so foolishly. I had fiddled with powers beyond God's natural laws. Flashbacks from my recent emotional outburst at Bram, Byron, even Mrs. Crow raced by my mind with horror. It was beyond the lengths of my character to talk to another human being in such a way. How could I have lashed out so viciously. I had spoken cruel words to a man who had only ever meant the best for me, and I had done it on purpose. And Bram had to pin me down and pull, well, whatever he did with that paper, to calm me down.

Great heavens! What demon had possessed my faculties? In some part, it was a welcome relief to know that my behavior could find blame outside my natural person. The relief was short-lived, though. I was sick. The anger. The dark door. It was all a part of me now.

I looked at Bram in terror. This man had tricked me into an enchantment, not against my will, but certainly without my informed consent. I didn't know which would have been worse: the deceit and this feeling of self-loathing or overwhelming force and its lasting echo of vulnerability.

The chest, which had inspired in me such curiosity these past weeks, now shot waves of dread through me. Who knew what other evils lurked beneath its lid? How could I have become so friendly with the monster who kept them?

"Bram, please." My voice shook as I reached a trembling hand out to him in supplication. "Release me from this. You can't hold me captive like this."

"You can't blame me, Luella. I didn't know. I tried to protect you."

"Please, I have to go back to my life. I have to erase these past weeks."

"You can't give up now! You're just learning the extent of the magic. The pen trusts you. It speaks to you so freely. The bizarre nature of these events stand witness that this encounter was destined to happen."

It was too much. I fell to my knees.

"I never asked for this."

"You wanted to be an extraordinary writer, did you not? Did you think you could achieve great things without great sacrifice?" He knelt down next to me. "There are ways to combat the effects you're experiencing. I can figure out how to help you."

"Oh, Bram," I said. I couldn't take this constant fluctuation. One moment, I was convinced Bram was a devil; the next, I thought he was my savior.

"This isn't about me. This is about you and your writing," Bram said. "You have to believe in this." He extended the pen toward me, inviting me to take it. "Your writing can change these people's lives. Your writing could wake them up. Show them that magic is right in front of them."

"It's not even my writing. If what you're saying is true, and if I can just intuit the future, I'm not writing. I'm just a slave to that instrument."

"Then what if your theory is true? What if your writing creates the future?"

"How could I live with that responsibility?"

"Writing is creating. You were born for that responsibility. Write the future. It's only for you."

I heard my father in his words, his belief in me. He had sacrificed so much for my education, more than I allowed myself to remember, especially toward the end of his life. I remembered overhearing his conversation with my mother. Her pleas for him to cover his doctor's bills. His insistence they could do nothing for him, and the money would be better spent elsewhere. Elsewhere.

I was elsewhere.

"I didn't want it this way. I just wanted to honor my father."

The fire flickered. What were only coals minutes ago were now sizeable flames. Their light played tricks in the tent. Their tips seemed to beckon to me in waves.

"Don't be afraid, Luella." He put a hand on my elbow and helped me up. "I'm with you. You can do something remarkable."

He walked me to the writing desk and put the pen there across a blank sheet of paper.

"If you are tired of writing silly stories, write something significant. Write something that Brutus can't call a trifle." He crossed to the tent door and held it open. "But, I've never intended to hold you prisoner. The choice must be yours."

I wasn't sure what I wanted. I wasn't sure how to think anymore. What was the future? What was my writing? I thought about my old reasons for using the pen. I was worried about the rent and the bills. It seemed so petty now.

The pen beckoned to me. Was it witchcraft, dark magic, or a benevolent gift?

Was it my only true tool to fulfill the life my father had wanted for me?

Bram looked so harmless with the flap of his yurt open like that. I wasn't sure whether to blame him or thank him. I felt like I had an escalating fever. Perhaps I was beginning to hallucinate. My vision was blurred, and I could hardly remember my name. But one thing rang through clear as crystal.

"His writing will become nothing more than 'do you remember that one time'." Brutus' critique was pounding in my brain. Drowning out all my other thoughts.

I held my breath and seized the pen as slowly as molasses,

scribbling furiously like a woman possessed. I didn't care what I was writing. I just reached out for details, any details my mind could summon. Bram came to the desk and began copying whatever came out of the pen as quickly as he could.

As I wrote, a wave of euphoria and dopamine shot through me, invigorating my senses and further clouding my mind. How could writing be anything but holy? Bram was right. I could wake up readers everywhere, and I would. All writers must sacrifice. I would sacrifice. The magic must come through. The fog was just the beginning.

My hand continued as though it had a mind of its own. I filled a page then a second. I jotted down names, details, things I would never have dared to write before.

Bram watched me as I put the pen to the paper. The flames called to me. The fire was so bright. Warm and welcoming, like the tickles of my father's whiskers on my cheek as a little girl. This was for him. This was for Anna. The flames danced, warm and welcoming, like an optimistic vision for the future.

Finally, the pen fell from my hand, and I collapsed to the floor. Bram folded his pages neatly and put them in a sealed envelope. Then he took my pages and tossed them into the flames.

The fire blazed a crimson red.

Chapter Twenty

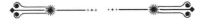

The Old Gossip

I stayed there well past midnight trying to recover from my episode, fueled by the feverous energy left in me by the pen's magical residue on my mood. Bram did not leave my side. I felt something odd and wholesome, as if the pen— or at least whatever nether worldly force that powered it—seemed satisfied. I tried to recall the details of the story, but I couldn't. I could see the paper I had written on in my mind, but in my memory, the pen wrote invisibly.

Whatever I had offered to my ailment, it caused the fire to behave in ways I'd never before seen. It blazed a bright red whenever I looked into it, flickering upward in strange shapes, more akin to bubbles and water than to natural flame. These shapes continued for hours, and the fireballs floated delicately around the tent. I didn't even marvel at them. They felt like old friends, discounting Brutus' critique and offering me support and praise with their warmth.

Bram's expression glowed with a mix of stupor and glee, whether caused by witnessing magic or by seeing me cause these effects I still cannot say. But, he hurried about the room, stoking the fire and reaching out his fingers, daring to touch the floating fireballs. They were, in a bizarre way, our children, as were these stories. He pushed me into the unknown, encouraged and dared me to defy the boundaries of a world I thought I knew. I, the writer, realized his aspirations. Together, we made the fireballs.

"What did I write?" I managed to ask Bram.

"Something Brutus won't be able to ignore."

"Tell me."

"It was a story about financial scandal. You wrote about a wealthy business owner who meets financial scandal when his dishonest book ledgers are discovered by a cutthroat competitor."

This latest story seemed to me the least fantastic and imaginative I had penned to date. It was simple. The details consisted of the type of rubbish I'd read time and time again in novels written by boring men and articles from the bigger papers from London. A career falls apart. A less than loveable maverick gets the dues he deserves. But, hopefully, its effects would grab Brutus by the lapels and make him pay attention. If he wanted stories of substance, it sounded like I'd given him one. After all, it was exactly the type of story that men in suits loved to read about. My father's daughter gagged at the thought.

Well, papa, you won't be gagging when I win the Golden Inkwell.

He handed me the sealed envelope. I accepted it with an upturned nose. I had no desire to read it. It almost broke my heart to see my name under such a dull, grimy bit of reporting.

After what felt like days, the flames finally died down, and my senses slowly returned to me, though my memory did not. Bram gave me some water, and I found I could get up and walk, despite my spinning head. Given the hour, Bram offered his bed to me, insisting he would sleep outside, but I settled by requesting that he escort me home. I wasn't sure I'd make it alone.

I must have tumbled in around three o'clock after a long, mostly silent walk together. I was too groggy and tired to process the day's events. My lunch with Edward seemed years ago. Instead, I allowed myself to be guided through the cold city streets by the man I didn't know if I should trust or detest. I could not, at my current state, unravel the arguments for and against our continued interaction. He had posed several to me, and common sense had insisted in its own right. For now, I had to take life one step at a time down dark, cobbled paths to Harbor Street.

I wanted nothing more than to fall asleep in my bed and wake up two months ago.

When I did arrive at home, I was shocked to see not only my dear sister waiting up for me but a very perturbed-looking Mrs. Crow.

"Oh Luella!" Anna cried, rushing forward to embrace me. "We feared the worst. But, what happened to you? You look ill. Are you hurt?"

"I'm just tired. I need to go to bed."

"Where have you been?" she asked.

"I was writing."

"Not at Langley's. We called on Mr. Livingston, and he said the two of you had a domestic," Mrs. Crow piped in like a ruffled owl on a perch. I was sure the woman's head could turn three hundred sixty degrees. Even in my current state of weariness, I couldn't help contesting her words for accuracy.

"You can hardly have a domestic with someone who doesn't live with you," I said.

"Well then, where were you?" asked Anna.

I took her hand, in part to steady myself, in part to reassure her. "I'll explain all tomorrow. Please, you must be exhausted, dear sister. I've kept you up waiting, and I'm sorry. But, I'm alright."

She nodded, but it took a good deal of time before she allowed me to persuade her to retire. First, she made me sit and drink some warm tea, while putting a hand to my forehead and helping me loosen my bodice. I insisted over and over again that everything was alright with me, but it was no use. When she finally left the kitchen to warm up the bed for me, I turned to our neighbor.

"Thank you, Mrs. Crow for staying up with her—"

"Your sister may be young and naive," Crow said, "but it's not my first late night waiting for a friend. I think it's time we have a talk."

A lecture from Mrs. Crow was the last thing I wanted.

"I have to beg your leave. I'm so very tired."

"Anna's ears are still tuned to her own concerns, but the ears of an old woman recognize a man's voice in the dark."

I froze. I had never before allowed Bram or Edward to walk me home. In fact, I seldom allowed Byron the occasion. I had considered it a sign of submission that I only wanted to yield after wedlock. For the others, it was a simple matter of discretion that I had blown directly out of the water tonight.

"I beg your pardon." My fingers started twitching.

"Don't play dumb with me," said Crow. "Your business is your business, but I can't let you bring ruin onto your family."

"Are you insinuating—"

"That you came home at three in the morning with a strange man? I'm not insinuating anything. I'm stating the facts! I don't care what happened; it's the image of the thing! Luella, I care about you, and it's hard for me to talk to you like this, but someone has to. Your behavior recently has been erratic, unsisterly, and irresponsible. Poor Anna has been going through one of the great episodes of her life."

"It's young love," I said, taken aback by Mrs. Crow's brash attack.

"It's love. Which, I'm now sure, is something you know less about than you let on."

Her words hit me like a cold-water slap on the face. Something inside of me, that dark unnatural heat, sprang up in response, chasing out my fatigue. But, now fear came with it. I was afraid of losing control.

"She is in love with that young man," she continued. "You may describe it as infatuation or frivolity, but you've been gone for weeks, and you don't know. While you've been away—doing whatever it is that you've been doing—I've tried my best to fill in the cracks. But, I'm not her sister, and I'm not your mother. It's time for you to gird up your petticoats and walk uprightly. I cannot allow you to waste away your sister's honest prospects at a happy and fruitful match because you're going through a mid-life crisis. Her relationship with Mr. Rigby is already in peril. How do you think his family would react to news that her sister is a philanderer?"

I didn't have the energy to fight the fire brewing, even though I knew she was right and that I could no longer trust my own emotions. I had been coerced, critiqued, and backed into too many corners for one day. My fists clenched. Enough was enough.

"Mrs. Crow, you are right. You're not my mother, nor are you a member of this family. If you are done pretending to know everything about our situation and how to fix it all, I must insist you leave."

"But, Luella—"

"Immediately!" I slammed my hands down hard on the table in an uncharacteristic display of force. She jerked backwards as my voice shook, and I pointed to the door. My jaw had gone rigid, and I felt powerful. It was a sweet, invigorating power, and it swam over me like warm water. I had had it with this old woman and her old-fashioned sense of what womanhood was about.

Mrs. Crow's old papery skin crinkled around her shocked frown. Her lip quivered, and she looked up at me with big, bright gray eyes welling with moisture. She looked ugly and wretched, and I saw in those eyes a deep pool of longing and loneliness. No fear. Just sadness. For a moment, I thought she was going to speak again, but instead she tenderly grabbed my hand, squeezed it, and made her way out the door.

I closed it firmly behind her. At the touch of her hand, the magic had fled right out of my system, leaving me empty again and even more tired than before. I shook. I had been so angry at one our dearest friends. I looked at the table and rubbed my fist where a bruise was forming. What if I had struck her?

I stumbled to our bedroom and fell asleep after hardly spending the energy to change out of my clothes.

I tumbled through a deep sleep full of odd dreams. Fireballs chased me around a shadowy and ash-filled park. A man in a fine suit stood in the middle of the park, knee-deep in a reflection pool, staring at me. No matter how I tried to call for his help, he just continued to stare.

I made my way toward him, but as I did so, he appeared to sink deeper into the pool. When I looked closer, I saw his hands and feet tied with strong cords. I rushed forward faster, ignoring fireballs, but the harder I pumped my legs, the further he appeared from me. A heavy fog settled in until the fireballs were all but embers in a dying campfire. With a terrible scream, the man plunged beneath the surface, and the fog completely obscured him from my view. When he was gone, the sound of my father laughing darkly echoed through the trees.

"Papa?" I cried, but the laugh just continued. "Papa, where are you? I need you!"

I woke up to the sound of a kettle and groggily checked my surroundings. I was at home in my room. The only relic from last night was Bram's sealed envelope on my nightstand. That's right. There was my sellout financial drudgery of a story. I rolled my eyes.

In the kitchen, Anna had set the table with a healthy breakfast of bread, cheese, and Barker's iced buns. I wrapped myself in a blanket and made my way gingerly to a seat. The world looked jarringly bright.

"Oh, you're up," Anna said. "You tossed and turned all night." I poured myself a large glass from a water jug on the table and gulped it down.

"I must have kept you up."

"Oh, I haven't been sleeping that well anyway," she said sheepishly.

She stood, bathed in the light that filtered through the drapes on the window. She nervously fiddled with a small kitchen towel and buried her eyes in the ground, a sad smile for me on her lips. Were those creases on her eyes, lines around her mouth? She looked older, worn, fatigued. I had stopped paying attention for a couple of weeks, and my baby sister grew up.

"Have you heard anything from Jacob?" I asked.

"We've spoken," she said. "It's not quite like it was before, but I'm working on it. I think it's improving. Mrs. Barker sent over some of the buns you love."

She produced a small basket from the counter.

"Anna, I'm sure you have a lot of questions," I said. She busied herself on the countertop with an apple.

"I just feel like I haven't seen you in a while," she said without looking at me. "I couldn't help but wonder if it was my fault."

"Your fault?" I echoed, my guilt multiplying.

"I know I've been difficult since that night at dinner. I even—" She turned and swallowed hard but still wouldn't meet my eyes. "I told you to choose between me and Byron. Oh, Luella, I've been so ungrateful."

I watched her realize the lessons I'd learned years ago, lessons that come from broken dreams. Be grateful because life owes you nothing. Hope for the possible, not the beautiful. A useful person still has worth. These were the distinctions that formed the haggard expressions of the loveless.

How could I explain to her that she was the jewel of my life? Her ultimatum against Byron had not been unwelcome, just an affirmation that my heart did not truly belong to him anymore than it belonged to the old, boring articles I wrote for him.

Anna was trying very hard to be strong in front of me. What demons she must have faced these past weeks. I had only compounded her difficulties with the heavy mantle of my withdrawal. The true weight of secrets is born by our loved ones.

I sprang up and embraced her with both of my arms. She was

surprised at first but, after just a moment, hugged me back tightly. I didn't want to let go. Her warmth swam through me. My sister loved me. What other magic could I need? I wanted to tell her everything, wished I could.

"There, there," she whispered, stroking my hair. "Everything's alright. I just missed you."

"I've missed you, too. Please, don't think that you have been the cause of any significant divide between Byron and me." I finally found the strength to separate from her and pulled her down into the seat adjacent to mine. "Oh, Anna, you're all grown up now."

"Grown up? I've been reeling from the fear of losing a man like a sixteen-year-old."

"But if you were sixteen, then you'd be foolish, because you were still so young. There is nothing girlish about fearing to lose a man with whom there was a true chance at forming a family."

"You don't seem afraid, though! I know that things aren't well with your fiancé, and it is all my fault!"

I took her hand in the way we used to do when telling secrets as younger girls.

"I'm not afraid, because I'm not in love with Byron," I said.

"Well, perhaps not in the way I was going on about Jacob, but I always thought that love changed when people got older."

"I believed that as well," I whispered. "Then, I met someone."

Anna's eyes went large as saucers.

"Tell me you haven't done anything rash. I couldn't help but overhear your conversation with Mrs. Crow last night."

"I'm afraid I've done enough to break an engagement, though, perhaps not so much as to scandalize the neighborhood. At least not if they heard the full story. Last night, for example, I was home late because I had been working on a story. The man who escorted me home was my writing partner."

"Writing stories with other men! Byron will be heartbroken. He'd have preferred if you kissed him. But, who is he? Is he the man to cause you to rethink your commitment?"

"In part," I said with a small smile. My resolve solidified as I spoke to her, such was the value of a sister. After yesterday's experience, I knew there would be no easy way to exit my career as a writer. The pen had a firm grip on me, and only Bram would know how to start breaking me free of it. At any rate, he seemed to know of a temporary solution, whatever it was that he threw in the fire last night. But, could this story propel me toward the Golden Inkwell? I could feel my father's sacrifice, like a debt on a ledger. The weight of it crushed me, and I couldn't tell how long the burden had been with me. If I could just win, my father's sacrifice would have been for something. The fact that he spent his money on my education instead of his medicine—I'd finally prove to him it was worth it. And yet, what price might it cost me?

After Bram's deception, I did not believe I could ever give my heart to him, if he ever even wanted that. At the same time, was there any way I could hold a meaningful marriage if I maintained Bram as my magical guide? I couldn't explain to another man that his attentions were platonic. I hadn't even been able to convince myself of that. These interrogatories led me to a single conclusion, one that had taunted me for several years. Marriage was a game for women with less unique situations, like Anna.

"Luella! What are you smiling about? You look years lighter than last night! What's happened to you? And what about Byron? Before you were so concerned about your practical future."

"That is true, dear sister. Honestly, your welfare was no small piece of that anxiety. But, with this new writing partner, I've become a success. Last night, I think we hit our stride, and I'm not sure we will need to worry about finances again. I'm considering even dropping my pen name."

"You're being so cryptic. Won't you plainly explain it to me?"

"I will in good time. I'm ready to make a big jump. I just have to wait and see how my latest story will perform."

"I was so convinced you had grown tired of me," Anna said.

"How could I grow tired of my muse?" I replied, touching her cheek gently before crossing to the counter to grab an iced bun. I was feeling better each passing minute, almost enough to convince myself that I had misinterpreted yesterday's events. Magical illness humbug. After all, I hadn't actually hurt anyone. Maybe these were all just mood swings. I felt fine now, and who knew how well last night's story would perform in the papers? I felt so good as I wrote it that I was convinced it had to be stunning.

I chose the stickiest bun I could find and was about to dive into it when I noticed a small parchment envelope on the counter, the seal unbroken.

"What's this?" I asked, scooping it up. A few small items rattled inside of it. "Medicine?"

Anna jumped from her seat to grab it from me.

"No, it's nothing," she said. "It's just something for Jacob. A present." She carefully placed the envelope in the cupboard. Poor Anna, reduced to desperate measures, buying little trinkets to earn Jacob's affection. She said it was getting better. That was something at least.

"You don't need to do all that, you know," I found myself telling her.

"I have to do whatever I can. Whatever it takes," she said solemnly. "I can't be like you, dear sister. I'm not clever or industrious. I'm getting older. Without Jacob, what will become of me?"

"I'll take care of you," I said. "I'll always take care of you."

She smiled, and we both knew that might not be enough for her.

Chapter Twenty-One

Nothing As It Should Be

It felt good having restored my sisterly bond with Anna. At least, in some part of my life, I could feel some order. I noticed it raised her spirits almost immediately. With some coaxing, she divulged all the latest details between her and Jacob, and the way she told it, I was actually encouraged that it might be headed toward a course correction.

She had managed to scrape from his mind the notion that she was expecting a proposal (which I considered ironic since that was exactly what she was expecting), leaving only her awkward objection to being anywhere around Byron. Until last night, Anna had viewed this as a great obstacle, finding it impossible to choose between the man she loved and her sister. Now her hopes were invested into my latest story as much as mine, though she did not know that I was planning to sacrifice domestic felicity for my writing. All writers must sacrifice. It was time I lived the principle I had considered a mere romantic turn of phrase.

All these plans were still wrapped up in the papers I had brought home with me the night before. There was still work to be done. I had to head over to the police station to verify that the events I had penned had indeed transpired. Then I'd have to call on Rebecca again to deliver my story to Langley's.

"I don't understand why you can't go drop off the story first," Anna complained. "I think I'll die from all this waiting."

"I can't face Byron after our argument last night," I said. "Rebecca has acted faithfully as my courier."

"Why not just let me take it?" she pleaded.

"You haven't seen Byron since the dinner. Are you sure you'd be up for it?"

"I'm not a child. I can put on a good face for a quarter of an hour. Besides, my heart has no room for rancor today. I'm filled with nerves and excitement. You really mean it? If this story is a success with your critics and the public, then you will break off your engagement? You don't know what that would do for Jacob's indecision."

I nodded. I shared more of her nerves than her excitement. I had never once written a story Brutus appreciated. Still, if he were ever to approve of my writing, it would be something like this: a financial scandal with reaching implications.

I scoffed. To me, the implications had a shorter reach than this type of story's readership. And if those men could reach their own toes, I'd be surprised.

Having Anna run the story to Langley's gave me pause for another reason, though. Having Rebecca deliver my stories served the dual purpose of verifying their accuracy before delivery. Usually, I would head to the station, casually hear the latest news, and once I heard my story had come true, Rebecca and I would go to lunch, and she would deliver the parcel right after. This also gave me an opportunity to furnish the story with the details I'd been missing when I wrote it the day before.

If Anna ran the story over first, I'd run the risk of having Byron publish a false account. We'd have to publish a retraction. It'd be damaging to the publication's credibility. Yet, had the magic ever failed me before? Surely, this was an over precaution.

"Please, sister. I'll die from sitting here idle," she pleaded. We both laughed at her mock immaturity. It was time to include my sister more fully in my life.

"Alright, but please don't talk politics," I said.

"I promise."

We left the flat at the same time. She headed to Langley's, I to the station.

The weather had grown significantly colder now. We still waited for our first snow of the season, but the clouds above threatened a drift ominously above. I didn't mind the cold. I was bundled up in a hood, and it felt fresh on my face. The cold had a salutary effect. It felt fresh and real, and I really felt I could use the rejuvenation.

The station was abuzz when I arrived. The bobbies swarmed around like a hive of worker bees. I often felt its comfortable bustle, but a peculiar spirit permeated the police force today.

"What's going on?" I asked Rebecca when I finally arrived at her office.

"What do you mean?" she asked, a large strand of hair dangling in front of her face.

"It's like a regular factory in here," I said.

"I guess you're right," she said. "I hadn't noticed. My nose has been in the books all morning. Seems like yesterday we had an abundance of new cases run in and—wait a minute. Full stop! How was lunch with Detective Thomas? The last I saw you, you were all blushes on his arm. Hardly proper for an engaged woman."

"It was a business lunch," I said.

"Business lunch? For whose business?"

"Not yours."

She smiled, knowingly, pausing from her type work. "Then, I'm sure you wouldn't be interested to know that he was practically skipping by the time he got back to the station yesterday."

Yesterday. We had that wonderful, wonderful lunch only a day ago. I felt as though I had aged a year.

"That wasn't the reaction I was expecting," Rebecca said.

"I beg your pardon?"

"If I had lit up a man's mood like you had, I'm sure I wouldn't look so despondent about it."

"Of course," I said, dodging an officer and his chained charge walking through the hallway. I ached inside. Rebecca looked like a character from a play, pen behind her ear, disheveled hair, gorgeous and witty. Her inquisitive eyebrow bored into me like it always did. I felt so lonely. I wish I had told her everything at our first lunch together instead of holding back my most sordid details. It was just me against the world, against Bram and Byron and a new magical malady I felt deep down inside of stomach.

"Can I ask you something?" I said, pulling a chair next to her.

"You look awfully serious. Did you do more than lunch with Edward yesterday?" She snickered but relented immediately when I didn't reciprocate.

"Do you remember the first story I wrote about the Steely-Eyed Detective?'

"The Fog Man? Of course, I was petrified of the dark for a week after."

"Do you believe it really happened?"

She laughed uneasily. She searched for something on her desk but did not find it. "Do you?"

"I asked first."

"I don't know," she said at last. "It doesn't seem that simple for some reason."

"Have you ever known Edward to lie about something like that?" I pressed.

"That's what makes it complicated, doesn't it? He doesn't lie. And, he doesn't drink on the job. I don't know why he would have invented a story like that. But, something inside of me says I can't believe it. Not really."

"Why not?"

"Because if I believed it, how could I ever walk home again? How could I trust anything?"

She spoke the words of my own heart. I had wandered far into dark brambles, eerie dreams, and chilling language to pursue petty fame. Now, they had me tangled, strangled me, and I could not escape. If the magic was real, was I lost? I wasn't an overly religious person, but the reality of supernatural powers was enough to make me consider the fate of my very soul.

"Luella, you're making me cross. Did you come here today just to unsettle me?"

"I'm caught up in something very dark," I said. Tears welled in my eyes. I could see her every faculty try to doubt me, but the intuition friends have for ferreting out lies took root in her. God bless woman's ability to recognize true, earnest cries for help. She gaped at me, open-mouthed, slow panic creeping into her brow. Her posture bristled with the current of a threatening unknown.

Before she could press further, the Steely-Eyed Detective strode into the room, himself a raincloud.

"Ms. Turner, do you have those reports typed up from yesterday?" he asked curtly. I was startled to see him and even more startled by his demeanor. The two of us craned our heads at him, as if we were stepping out of a dark room into sunlight.

"Oh, Lieutenant. Of course, they're right here," Rebecca said, handing him a folder.

"Thank you," he said with a formal nod. He took the folder and turned to go, with every intention of avoiding my eye contact or even acknowledging my presence. Rebecca turned to me with a helpless, open-mouthed expression. Edward had never behaved toward me this way before. His indifference could not be borne. For the final time in just twenty-four hours, I found myself gripping on to a precipice. It was too much.

"Edward," I loudly said. I stood. He could not ignore me now.

He stopped with heavy slumping shoulders and turned around to me. I saw written in his rigid jawline every intention to extend to me the same businesslike, formal attitude he had shown Rebecca. But, it vanished at once when he looked into my face.

"Luella! You've been crying. Is everything alright?"

"I might ask the same of you. Were you about to leave without so much as a hello?"

He looked trapped. How quickly men of integrity abandon their schemes. He searched for a reply but found only an embarrassed, boyish complexion.

"I'm sorry. Could I speak with you?"

"We are doing just that."

"Privately." He motioned to Sergeant Cooper's office.

"You mean privately with the Sergeant?"

"He's not here. He won't mind us using his office for a moment."

I wasn't sure if the request itself was awkward or if my discomfort stemmed from his delivery. I looked to Rebecca for help, but she just shrugged her shoulders, confusion sharpening on her brow. Instead, I simply followed Edward into the office. He closed the door behind us.

"Are you alright?" he asked. "Is there anything I can do?" He offered me his handkerchief to wipe my eyes.

"I'll be quite fine. You, on the other hand, look like you have a coal in your boot."

He smiled, sheepishly.

"You have such a way with words. I just—well, I wanted to apologize."

"Apologize? For what?"

"Yesterday, you came here looking for help with your stories."

"And you were very kind to assist me."

"Really? Which story did I provide you for your publication?"

I had no response. With all of the excitement, I hadn't even noticed that I failed to play my part in Cooper and Rebecca's farce. We were so happy at that lunch yesterday.

"You told me so many stories."

"You know as well I do that those were not the stories you were looking for. That's just it. Yesterday, I allowed myself to behave ungentlemanly."

I thought about his raucous back and forth with Doug. It was so charming, so endearing.

"I'm sure Doug could handle it. I don't know if he's used to treating with gentlemen."

"Must I come out and say it so plainly?" Edward asked, red in the face. His arms stretched out in exasperation. I could not help him. I didn't know what he meant.

"You are an engaged woman," he continued. "And I took advantage of your request for help as a way to get closer to you. That was not a work lunch, at least not to me. I'm so sorry, Luella! I sincerely hope I haven't interfered with your commitment. If I need to make it right, tell me how."

"You wanted to get closer to me?" My lungs were so full I felt they might burst through my chest. My heart pounded with youthful exuberance. We had used the same plan to get closer.

"Hearing you say it burns my conscience. I'm at your service. I will make this right if any wrong has come on your promised betrothal. I'll find a way."

My heart burst for him. I wanted him to sweep me up into his arms and stare deeply into my eyes fueled by the feelings for which he was so ashamed. As he stood there, I felt that he had bared his truest most vulnerable self to me. Even his guilt-ridden confession was an absolute treasure. I wanted to wipe away the guilt and the shame he felt, to validate these emotions with reciprocation.

I wanted to spend every lunch with him for the rest of my life. I would have loved nothing more than to meet his parents, to wait at home for him after his work, to stay up worried at night while he was on assignment. Most surprising of all, I wanted a chance to abandon my writing and just devote myself to his happiness. I wanted it all.

But, how could I?

After everything I'd done, I was not worthy of his companionship. I was not worthy to speak his name. This was my greatest secret and greatest shame, that I was unrelentingly drawn to the man in front of me but completely unredeemable. And now, as if to prove my point, I was bonded to Bram like a patient to a doctor. I was sick with something I could never burden Edward with. It was the purest agony to love someone and know my love could not cover my deficit.

He stood in front of me so nobly, defending the honor he believed I had.

"Oh Edward," I said, raising a hand to touch his cheek. "So often, I feel that you could save me if I'd only let you."

His face contorted into a puzzled expression, and he was about to speak when the door swung open.

"I don't remember granting you two leave to use my office as a personal hideaway," Sergeant Cooper barked as he pushed through us toward his desk.

"I apologize Sergeant," said Edward. "The station is bustling today, and I could hardly hear the lady speak."

"We need to talk, Edward." Cooper tossed his coat to the coat rack, missing it by a good two feet, and plopped down in his chair. He looked to be in a terrible humor, no sign of levity about him. "It's urgent. Ms. Winthrop, I'm afraid I have to ask you to leave."

I shook off my selfish concerns and thought to my task at hand. Anna would have arrived at Langley's by now. "What's the story?"

"Nothing that I think might interest you, Ms. Winthrop."

"Well, perhaps I can turn it into something," I suggested.

"No need to turn her away, surely," said Edward. Cooper eyed me with a queer expression. I'd never seen him in such a state of unease.

"Are you alright, Sergeant Cooper?" I asked.

"Perhaps it's for the best," he said, shifting his eyes between the two of us.

Edward stood at attention. "At your service, sir."

"It's not pretty, I'm afraid," Cooper said. "For heaven's sake, sit down, man."

We both sat. I cautiously eyed Edward in a state of confusion. There seemed to be a great deal of anxiety about the simple financial scandal I wrote about.

"One of the central bankers downtown has been discovered by his competitor to have been siphoning money from his clients' accounts," Cooper began. A small weight came off my shoulders. The pen had worked again. Anna's delivery would contain an accurate reporting.

"How much money?" Edward asked, his face beginning to twitch.

"A significant amount. There wasn't much hope for the man. His competitor has him pegged with proof, witnesses, everything. Edward, I'm sorry. It's your father."

The sound of a lion erupted from Edward's lungs, and he stood in a fury, knocking the chair behind him to the floor. "Damned man! Where do they have him? How could he have done this?"

I felt my body lose all weight. I was like an empty chrysalis, a flaky snakeskin, worth less than I ever considered possible. How could this have happened? Thomas was not the surname I had penned the night before. It couldn't have been. The pen didn't operate in this way. It wasn't supposed to generate events that might have a direct effect on my life. What had I done?

"You can't see him," Cooper said.

"And who the devil will stop me?" Edward demanded. Cooper took a deep, heavy breath.

"Your father hanged himself this morning."

Chapter Twenty-Two

Fool's Hope

"I've turned in your story!" Anna said. "Byron seemed happy to see me, but I kept to my word and didn't discuss anything but business. The poor old sap doesn't know what's coming, does he?"

Anna's voice was an echo, distant and indistinct. I stared out the small kitchen window at our little picture of the world. We never had much of a view, just of the brick wall across the street. For all the hours I had sat there, I could describe almost nothing about it.

I felt completely numb. I didn't know how I got home. I couldn't remember how long ago. All I could remember was the colossal pain and agony I saw take hold of Edward upon hearing his own flesh and blood had met financial scandal and suicide. Had I tried to console him? Had he rushed out? Sergeant Cooper had tried to mention something to me. I felt the memory of Rebecca's hand on my arm but had no thought or recollection to claim it as partner.

"Good heavens, Luella! You're white as a ghost, and you've been crying."

I turned to her. She looked wet. Her hat was still in her hand.

"You're damp."

"It's starting to rain, but what does that matter? What happened?"

I smiled. What a ridiculous question. I could not begin even the hint of an explanation. My poor baby sister. She was being cared for by a pathetic, narcissistic wretch. Even if I had the courage, she wouldn't believe me. And, if she did believe, she wouldn't forgive me. And, if she did forgive me, I couldn't allow her to.

The words I had spoken to her that morning and the night before stung like wasps on my scalp. I had filled her with false hopes, deposited counterfeit funds in our dream account. She was filled with a vision of the future, painted with scenes of her and Jacob, happily situated. I had insisted that I was about to hit pay dirt with my writing career, but now. . .

I couldn't continue with that devil pen! I couldn't continue writing at all! If anyone had ever abused the privilege, surely, I had. Could I continue to rely on the great Providence that inspires the minds of those who embark across the page after plunging myself into the darkness and filth of an infernal and evil shortcut? With every new article, I would shame Edward's name and family. I could not put my heart into a practice that cost the man I loved such pain and misfortune.

And I did love Edward! He was the stuff of my dreams. He could have provided me a life of modest means and immeasurable happiness. I would have happily broken my engagement with Byron. He was an open door to paradise, but now I had slammed it shut with such unequivocal force. I was the perfect fool, with love in my grasp, only to chase it off with unbridled ambition.

Now, I would never be the happiest of women because I could never make him the happiest of men. I was the wretched soul that cost him his father.

"Luella, please speak to me!" Anna shook me by the shoulders, dislodging fresh tears. I looked at her, and a thought struck me like a bolt of lightning.

The story.

The very least I could do was ensure that I did not contribute to Edward's shame by propagating the tale of his father's dishonor.

"Has Byron published my story?" I asked.

"I don't know. I doubt it. I only gave it to him a short while ago."

"Anna, I'm so sorry. I have to go," I got up, fueled by an intense eagerness to erase at least some minute portion of my blame in this nightmare.

"It's raining! Where are you going?"

"To Langley's." I searched desperately for my coat and hat.

"Whatever for?"

"I'll explain later!"

"You're going to retract the story, aren't you?"

"Anna, I have to. It will besmirch a good man's name."

"But you promised me this story was the beginning of our freedom. If you don't print it, what will we do?"

"That's not important right now." Where was that stupid coat?

"You're going to marry Byron." She sounded hollow.

"Anna, please—"

"You told me you wouldn't. You promised me. What about Jacob?"

"Anna!"

"Byron's almost ruined me once already! You can't do this. You just can't!"

"Enough about you and you and you!" I screamed. My fingers twitched. Dark, magical feelings swelled inside of me. Please, not now. Not against Anna. "That's all you think about! You and Jacob! Have you considered there's more to God's green earth than your fickle emotions and childish fantasies?"

Her mouth dropped open. I had never spoken to her like this. I wished I could have just walked away, but the magic spurned me on. I didn't have time to fight back. I needed to get to Langley's.

"Me? What about you?" I hadn't expected Anna to scream back. "You obsess with being a writer and throw away your future. I'd hardly blame you for it if you had the courage to actually follow through!"

"If you love Jacob then go be with him! Run away if you have to. Elope. Live in poverty. Do whatever it takes because that's what love is."

"What do you know about love?"

"I know more about it than you ever will!" I grasped the doorframe to steady myself. "Don't you see, Anna? I had it right in front of me. I had it, and I threw it away. Forever! Love is nothing more than sacrifice, like I'm doing for him now, and like I'm doing for you always."

"For whom?"

I rushed out the door, without a hat or coat, into the cold, icy rain.

The water battered down on me in terrible sheets. I ran down the road, coursing through puddles. I pushed my way through crowds of umbrellas and ignored the bewildered looks of passersby. Soon, I was soaked through, but I kept running, all of my attention on pushing myself to prevent the article's publication or to avoid slipping and falling on the cobblestone.

Please, if there was a God in heaven, please let the article still be there. I would trade anything.

I got to Langley's out of breath. My lungs were burning, and I must have looked a wreck, but I burst through the door.

"Byron, where are you?" I shouted. He emerged from inside his small back office with a cup of tea in his hand. He took one look at me before nearly dropping it to the floor.

"Luella! You're soaked through! What is the matter with you?" He grabbed a blanket and rushed to wrap me up in it. The heavy wool fabric pressed my wet clothes closer to my skin, giving me a chill. I hadn't realized how cold I was.

"Where's the story Anna brought you? Have you already published it?"

"It just went off to the printers twenty minutes ago. And what a bomb it was! If that's not going to win the Golden Inkwell, I don't know what will."

I collapsed into a chair, my last hope snuffed out. That was it then. My evil incantation was complete.

"Can we recall it?" I asked, knowing the answer already. I was too late. Not only did I have the blood of Edward's father on my hands, but I was complicit in spreading the news of his family's disgrace.

"Recall it? Didn't you hear what I just said?"

"Can we?"

"I doubt it," Byron replied, exasperated. "By the time we reach them, they will have already started setting the print. It would cost us a great deal to abandon the paper now. Why?"

"But it is possible?" A flicker of hope sparked from inside of me.

"Technically, but it would be madness. We'd miss tomorrow's edition. We'd lose a fortune."

I stood and grabbed his hands. "Please, Byron. I beg of you. We have to recall it."

"Is it inaccurate?"

"No, it's not that." I winced. I wished so badly it were inaccurate.

"Then what's the problem? I thought the story was riveting. One of your best! It will sell wonderfully."

How could I explain it without revealing my feelings for Edward? I was in no condition to invent excuses.

"Please, Byron, I can't explain it. I just need you to recall the paper."

"Don't talk nonsense! I will do no such thing."

"I'm begging you."

"I see what's happening here," he cast me a sidelong glance. "You're nervous about Brutus, but I'm telling you, not even Brutus will have words to discredit you this time. I was just about to mail this letter to Ms. Drake at the award committee."

"You're not hearing me," I said. My voice broke. Tears mingled with the water droplets falling from my hair and streaking down my face. "I need you to recall the story. Please."

"I can't do that to our other authors," he said. He was exasperated. He was looking for a reason to understand, but I could give him nothing. "With no explanation?"

"I can't tell you," I pleaded. "Byron, please, I've never asked you for something without reserve like this."

"Can't tell me?" he dropped my hands. "What game are you playing at? Why are you stringing me along like this? I don't know what mischief you're up to, but I can't support it. You're asking me to betray all the people who work on this paper and to do so at great personal loss. Why must I do this? You can't tell me. What kind of answer is that? It's rubbish. You've disrespected me now for weeks, but this is too much, Luella. It's simply too much."

My head was swimming. How could I make him understand? He was cold with me, angry even. I thought back to our last fight. Of course, he was angry. I had treated him so poorly the other day. Yesterday. It was only yesterday. He must have been so confused and frustrated. I had trampled on his feelings and our engagement callously.

I had gallivanted around with a mysterious and dangerous man I met less than month before at great risk to my future and any semblance of a future for my sister. Anna! I had played the absent sister to her as well. How she must have been suffering, with no one but Mrs. Crow to look after her, all while I behaved like a little girl, skipping from one fancy to another, excited over going out to lunch as if it was my first dinner party. I had lashed out at her. I had exalted her hopes and dashed them to pieces.

Was this why my father had sacrificed so much to teach me to read and write? What would he have said about my most recent stories? What would he have said about the dark workings of the pen? What good came of it? It produced nothing but silly nonsensical articles or else blood tales for the clink of some coin. I was splitting apart families to satisfy my own ego.

Now, I stood defenseless against the man whose promise and heart I had stamped on. I was mad to think Bram could truly provide the future that Byron had already offered. Bram was a rough, adventurous man, and I had wasted so much of my virtue even associating with him. And, I had betrayed Edward as no one else could have possibly done. I would never be worthy to look in his eyes again or to exchange even pleasantries in passing conversation.

"Oh, Byron. I've been such a fool."

He looked at me from across the room, and I saw the heavy mantle of understanding fall on his countenance.

"You're in some type of trouble, aren't you?"

"It's not what you think," I said. "One day, I hope I can explain, but now, I need your help. If that story gets published, I will be wounded forever. A recall can't put us out. Haven't my stories been selling?" He poured himself a drink from his desk drawer.

"They have, but I've spent the money paying off debts and reinvesting in broader circulation. I was relying on this next edition for—well, I was relying on it."

"Please Byron, I will cover the difference personally. I'll repay the debt somehow."

"It's not about the money, Luella. It's about loyalty to our colleagues. If we don't have an income tomorrow, they'll have to go without."

"You mean my loyalty to you."

"That isn't fair. It's not about loyalty between us. It's simply not. But, it's not a stretch to say that it is about trust."

"You don't trust me?"

"The last time we spoke, you railed at me. I'd been trying to apologize to you for weeks, and you wouldn't have it. You wouldn't even see me. Then you show up furious with me for something Brutus wrote about you. Now, you're asking for something very big from me, and you can't tell me any reason why."

He had me cornered. I couldn't blame him for turning me down.

Who knew what suspicions he had of my behavior? I had been busy burning this bridge. Who knew I was locking myself on the wrong side of it? I needed Byron now. I needed to make this right for Edward. I would never love Bram. I would never be worthy of Edward. Could I at least mitigate his misfortune? I'd give anything to do it.

"Please Byron," I said. "Do it for me as a wedding present."

No physician could have prescribed a more able remedy for his dreariness. His posture brightened, and he lost years off his life right before my eyes. Behind his cautious expression lurked the hope of an ecstatic smile.

"Luella, do you mean—I don't want to misunderstand."

I swallowed hard. "I think it's time we choose a date."

He let out a triumphant cry, like the horn of an elephant, and swept me up into his arms.

"Byron, I'm soaked!" I protested.

"I don't care. From now on, your burdens will be my burdens, and I will defend you until they lower me into the earth."

His arms felt full of life around me, more muscular than I ever remembered them. His eyes were full of youthful energy. He looked so handsome and comfortable. I closed my eyes, and he kissed me passionately on the mouth. I did not resist it. I took it in. I kissed him in return. It was time I committed to a sensible life.

He pulled back and looked me squarely in the eyes.

"You have my heart and my trust forever."

He grabbed his hat and coat and headed out the door into the rain, leaving me reeling from the days' events, my decision, and the kiss he gave me so sincerely.

A kiss for which I had closed my eyes and seen only Edward.

Chapter Twenty-Three

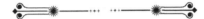

The Crimson Inkwell

From the window at Langley's, I watched Byron head down the street under his big black umbrella. The last of the day's light poked through the clouds and glistened off the black canvas that shielded him from the rain. The sight of it reminded me of shining armor, worn by my old, gallant knight, off to rescue me from one of my own mistakes.

He turned the corner, and I sat down, nestling myself deeper into the blanket he had wrapped around me. It was quiet. The last time I had been in the shop without Byron was when I wrote that first ridiculous story. Now I was trying to tie up the consequences of my last one. I was done as a writer. Travis Blakely was dead to me.

I walked over to the skylark and made sure it had enough seed. I wondered how many times the bird looked at the nearby window, through its wire cage, at the open sky.

I breathed in deeply and found myself searching for something to nibble on. I didn't realize how hungry I was. I hadn't eaten anything since the iced bun that morning, and it was catching up to me. My mouth felt dry. My heart felt like it was beating uncommonly slow, and my limbs lost their strength and doubled in weight.

I was exhausted, too tired to feel, too tired to think. I could only busy myself with staying awake, fighting off a beckoning, tempting sleep. I had to stay awake and wait for Byron to return with the news that we had successfully put a stop to printing our next edition. I couldn't fall asleep on Edward's chance at discretion.

But, I felt so sleepy. Or at least sluggish, lethargic, and uncomfortable. Deep down, next to the exhaustion and emptiness, I felt a nagging, gnawing feeling of dull anger. With all my other emotions so strongly weighing on me, I'd hoped the anger that had accompanied me since my outburst in this very room days ago had vacated my senses. Instead, it called to me like a familiar friend. It was a dull, red, constant power and burden, urging me forward to do something, anything.

I felt the pen.

This uncomfortable presence was enough to push my limbs off my chair and begin pacing. Waiting was torturous. I had to do something to get my mind off Byron and Edward. At the very least, I could change out of my wet clothes and make myself presentable for my fiancé on his return. I was sure there would be particulars to be sorted out. Who knew how much time was available to me? Yes. It was time to busy myself playing my role as the dutiful spouse. Could I fill a lifetime with to-do list items of this kind?

I left a note on his desk explaining I had gone home and would call on him later, found a spare umbrella, and made my way out the door.

When I arrived, I was chilled through all over again, and Anna was nowhere to be found. All the better, I didn't have the strength for another argument.

She had left the remains of a fire though, and I warmed myself before changing into a dry wool dress and heavy coat. We were well into a winter evening now, and though the rain had slowed, the air would still be crisp and frosty when I set back to Langley's.

Now to make myself look presentable for my rescuer and fiancé. I had no doubt my eyes were red and swollen from my day's tribulations, and although I was not blessed with the beauty of my younger sister, my mother told me as a girl that every case can be improved. I found the looking glass I had gifted to Anna years before and assessed the damage. I was surprised to see not only red, swollen eyes, but new wrinkles around my mouth and through my forehead. This ordeal with the pen had already added the burden of several, unlived years to my appearance. Those years had been stolen from me by stress, worry, fear, anger, and Bram.

Inside my eyes, next to the weariness, I saw the unnatural anger that had taken residence within me. It frightened me. The anger swelled. I did not choose this. Bram had thrust it on me without my consent or knowledge. He had made me prey to his magical experimentations. Curse the man! Who was he to take my freedom so casually? What right did he have to subject me to this condition?

It was clear to me now. I was addicted to experiencing the magic, as dependent on it as any laudanum addict or drunkard. These symptoms of anger were born from my dependency, and to break free would debase me to the ugly, sweaty, desperate walk of the recovering addict, if it was possible at all. And, I would have to bear the disease in silence, under the mask of domestic tranquility.

Bram, who I had considered a friend, and I thought cared deeply about me, had tricked and used me. In the looking glass, I saw a fool and imagined Bram in his yurt, laughing to himself with his smug, sly expression. The very thought made my blood boil.

He could not get away with this. A red, angry dragon inside of me breathed his fire up my throat and into the base of my skull. I felt such heat, such piercing heat, that I couldn't stay still. Someone would have to make him pay. Could I risk telling the police? No. It would implicate my infidelity. I would have to keep that a secret the rest of my life. My limbs acted of their own accord and moved me to retrieve the still wet umbrella.

I swung open my door and made my way to the fairgrounds under the strange electric lights across the river. At the very least, I would have satisfaction by informing him that his plan had fallen through, and I would not write another sentence with that damned pen.

The air was veiled with the full, looming darkness only approaching winter brings to the early hour. I was glad for my coat, as the chill of the air fought at the cracks between my clothes. It was good that I had traveled this road so often in the series of the past weeks because an unnatural fog seeped around corners and filled alleyways. I saw few other people on the streets.

The only warmth I found was from the exertion generated by my rapid pace and the dull burn of the anger somewhere deep inside me. Would I feel that dull burn always? I hadn't felt it so prominently even the day before, but I would be a fool to think it wasn't growing.

Soon, I crested the hill overlooking the fairgrounds and saw the glow of the electric lights, even more strange than their usual unearthly vibrancy, playing tricks on my eyes, turning their pinpricks into broad, blurry smears across my vision.

Days before, this vista would have brought me so much anxious excitement. Now, it filled me with a quiet fury and—confusion? What was there to be confused about? I had made my bed. I just had left to rub Bram's nose in it.

On closer inspection, something was not quite right. I heard no sounds of the crowds that swarmed the Exotic Creatures Tent and Hypnotist ring. I quickened my pace, and as I got closer, I saw some tents folded neatly on the ground, their tent poles slack in the mud beside them. The mud was littered in decomposing scraps of paper, the remnants of the fairgoers. I saw some of my own stories amongst advertisements for the fair and a gaggle of other publications.

Some small groups of carnival performers worked to collapse another tent in front of me. Horses were lapping at puddles from the recent rain; next to them lay half-prepared stacks of travel packs, bursting at the rope tying them closed.

This was it. They were preparing to leave. The conclusion dawned on me like the winter sunset. If the carnival was leaving, what would become of Bram?

I hurried through rows of packs, chests, and eclectic furniture stacked beside wagons. It pained me to see the people and environment of such a unique place being swept away. They were leaving me to my lot in the city, without so much as a goodbye. The carnival had transformed me just to abandon me.

I reached Bram's familiar yurt, relieved to see it still standing just the way I remembered. Cyrus chewed on a bone outside, his paws and haunches covered in mud. But, even the aloof dog couldn't rid me of my fear or my slow-growing anger.

I ducked inside and found Bram's belongings neatly and meticulously packed.

"You're leaving," I spat out without introduction.

"The fair has decided it's time for us to move along." He didn't stop making stacks of his belongings.

"Were you going to tell me?"

"I had a feeling you might find me before I left," he said, reassembling a wooden puzzle box.

"So that's it then? You're just packing up and going." I couldn't stand to see him packing so casually there like that, like he was getting away with a marvelous prank—pulling off the perfect crime.

"I don't have much of a choice." He sighed. "I don't choose when the fair stays or when it goes. I just follow."

"You don't think you have any unfinished business here?"

"Do I?"

"I would insist you do!" He couldn't play innocent with me. His play acting was infuriating. His riposte lingered in the air in front of his stupid grin. Was he pushing some flirtation? "Do you have any idea what you've done to me?"

"I wouldn't flatter myself by pretending to know your mind."

I couldn't help it. I walked up to him and shoved him hard. He stumbled backward on to the bed. I followed up quickly and slapped him across the face.

He looked up at me, and I down at him. The space between us filled to the brim with expectations and disappointment.

"Pretending to know my mind? Where was this humility for the past few weeks? I am a diseased woman. And, I know of no physician that can help me, no remedy to cure me. Only you, because you did this to me with half-truths and promises about your stupid pen."

He rubbed his cheek where I hit him but didn't look angry.

"Luella, please, will you stop hitting me?"

"What else is in that chest? Do you have something in there to bewitch women and hex away their senses? How did you persuade me to lower my guard? Why did you turn me into one of your dark experiments?"

"I never forced you to do anything. You're a grown woman."

"That's what you're telling yourself to feel good leaving me."

"We both knew that I was never going to stay forever," he said, exasperated.

"Forever no, but I thought a bit of warning perhaps, or some type of closure—"

"Come with me."

"I beg your pardon."

"Come *with* me."

He may as well have knocked me over with a cricket paddle. My breath seized in my throat.

"You don't have to accuse me of anything," he went on. "I know what I did, and I can't forgive myself for that. I was bold and arrogant. I thought I could control powers that were beyond my understanding, and now when I see you—" He motioned blankly with his hands, leaving his torso and midsection open. His gesture, combined with a painful expression I had never before seen on him, had an effect on me I cannot explain. In spite of everything, my instincts told me to reach out to him and close the gap between us. This feeling was enough to dull the swelled-up anger deep inside of me, making it doubly welcome. It would feel so warm to give in and let it go all at once.

"I have searched every note, every book, every account I have," he continued. "I swear to you, I thought your addiction would be impossible if you were only exposed to the magic in small, controlled doses. Come with me. I'll make it my life's mission to find a remedy for you. And, in the meantime, when the episodes of your fury overcome you, I'll sit with you, and I'll hold you, and I'll remind you of the magnificent woman that you are until those feelings subside."

I knew that he was guilty of my disease. I knew he had caused it, and that this was the very least he could have promised me to make up for his carelessness. But even knowing all of that, I could only describe the sincerity pouring out of his words and the genuine affection he now showed me in his peculiar way as romantic. Warm emotions filled my breast, and a sense of longing, deeper than even than my anger, sprang to life in an instant.

I look around his half-packed tent. It was by no means respectable, but the eclectic collection of furniture and rugs felt more welcoming than the walls at Langley's. Byron had always tried to decorate in ways that might please me. He often tried to surprise me with biscuits, tea, an occasional trinket, but no gifts or gestures could make up for what I knew would never be in our marriage. I always knew, deep down, that Byron would be a safe, old husband to make a young wife out of me. If I left with Bram, I could have more, and a hint of that possibility, even with a man whom I hated one day and clung to the next, would be better than a sure life of passionless and mildly pleasant domesticity.

If I left with Bram, maybe, there would be a chance for more than respect and friendship. Maybe one day, we could regenerate the spark that had been buried by this accusatory anger. I'm sure I would occasionally see Anna, and untethering myself from the old editor would free her to marry Jacob. If I left now, I would never have to face Edward again either. I'd never have to look into his eyes and know I killed his father. I'd never have to face up to the crushing guilt. To see him now, it would consume me body and soul. If I ran now. . .

"My attacks are going to get stronger, aren't they?" I asked.

He nodded grimly.

My heart begged me to go. It would be safer with Bram. He understood what I was. It would be unfair to Byron to trick him into marrying me. This was reasonable.

But, could I run? My father raised me to be a woman of integrity and industry. He taught me to face the world standing up. If I had even a shred of decency, could I run from the mess that I had brought to the people who cared about me? In my heart, I knew that, one day, despite the impossible difficulty and weight of it, I would have to see Edward again. I was chained to the positive outcome of his life as much as Bram might be to mine. Even if it meant a life void of true happiness, was it not on my ledger to see that Edward might find some peace? The calamity had set my feelings for him in stone. Yes, it took the greatest misfortune to recognize what love was, but such was my lot. Now that I knew it, I could not run from it. Marrying Byron meant loving Edward. That was what I had just decided at Langley's, and it was as true to me as the river running through Dawnhurst.

"I'm engaged," I said at last.

"I know that, but I can't help but feel that you may be engaged to someone out of convenience."

"We are setting a date for the wedding. Tonight. After I leave here."

Bram's chest deflated. He sunk into himself in spite of the clear effort he made to raise his chin.

"Why?" he asked. I searched for an answer. I couldn't tell him the truth of all of it.

"Because I love him," I lied.

He eyed me with his mouth ajar, hurt and suspicion mingling on his face. He studied me, waiting for me to revise what I said. When he saw I would not, he shook his head sadly.

"Then I wish you well," he replied. "And, as a friend, I must counsel you to remove yourself from my tent. It isn't proper for an engaged woman to treat with a bachelor this way."

He turned away from me to resume packing, spending an undue deal of attention to some letters in a small wooden box. That was it. The crack of reality's whip thundered down on the truth of our friendship.

We both had known this relationship could be not be discovered, and we had never mentioned it out loud before. It was a dark unspoken fact on which we based every moment together, a way for us both to know what was on the table in the first place. I knew from the beginning that this would end with him or me leaving or else him and me leaving.

Yet, how could I let him go? My hopes for salvation were with him and him alone. I didn't even know where to start looking for someone else to help rid me of my malady.

"Will you still find a way to heal me?" I asked.

He looked up at me across his shoulder.

"There is no contingency on what I said before. I will find a cure for this. I won't fail."

His severity both surprised and reassured me. Considering he had confessed to ignorance on my proposed cure, I felt an unsure degree of relief sweeping down my spine. He would venture into the unknown, but if someone in this world could find a cure, it would be Bram.

"Thank you," I said, my voice breaking. I turned to leave.

"One last thing," he said before I got to the door. "A wedding present."

He placed a small wrapped parcel in my hand.

"Should I open it now?"

"If you wish."

I gently unfolded the cloth wrapping. In my hand lay a small crimson inkwell.

"I'm sorry I couldn't get you a golden one. I wish you all the best, Luella Winthrop." He kissed me gently on the cheek, turned around, and got back to packing.

The feeling of his lips on my skin lasted my entire walk home.

Chapter Twenty-Four

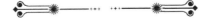

The Church in Milford Square

I woke the next morning to calm sunshine. The rainclouds from yesterday had cleared, and the city hosted its first light blanket of snow. It was a gentle snow, the variety that would melt by the noonday sun. Still, it made the air clear and clean, a hint that I was not dreaming. I lay in bed for a good while, wondering if everything I'd experienced over the past couple of days had been just that—a dream. In my memory, it all seemed hazy, boozy, and feverish. In the still quiet of a fresh snowfall, all of it was impossible. There was no magic. There was not even a carnival. I had never gone to the police looking to drum up stories. I hadn't played with fireballs or watched Byron blow up at my sister's fiancé. There was no magic, and I hadn't caused the death of Edward's father.

It was all a dream. Please, let it all have been a dream.

I turned on my side and pulled the blankets over me to indulge in a few more minutes of sleep, but as I did so, I saw a little glass inkwell, surrounded by ornate metal carvings and filled with a deep red ink, sitting on my nightstand. It sat there like a ghost, a bloody messenger from a time and place I wished to forget.

I wanted to fall back asleep. If I could just pass the threshold of consciousness, I could return to what was real. But, under the covers, I felt the unwelcome reminder of my constant companion, the bubbling anger in the pit of my stomach. This was life. This was the destination of my previous choices.

I rolled out of bed and enrobed myself with a long wrap before making my way to the kitchen to put a kettle on. Anna stayed in bed, and I was left to the reverence of the morning. The still in the air made me feel as though I was wading through it. Every motion was a swim stroke. The world was still sleeping, and I was on an island, untouchable. The silence could smother magic and anger. The stillness could heal all.

Perhaps life wasn't all that bad, anyway. What had I practically lost, after all? It was brutal and cold to think, but I was right back where I was before I had met Edward. Byron and I were soon to be married. He'd support Anna and me, modestly, until she could find a suitable husband. In many ways, my wish had come true: here I was waking up two months earlier. So, what if I'd never dream again of winning the Golden Inkwell? So, what if I'd failed my father?

I poured myself a cup of tea.

There were, of course, drawbacks. The guilt of Edward's father alone was enough to put an asterisk next to any happiness in my future, but I hadn't done anything on purpose. I had been negligent, reckless even, and stupid, but I would have sooner hanged myself than cause his family any harm intentionally.

I was also sick, now. I had already experienced several outbreaks from my magical malady. Each one seemed to increase in its severity. I knew those feelings would surface again.

However, many people experience the negative effects of illness and still manage to get along in a marriage. I would simply need a strategy to manage my attacks, and that was very possible. Besides, as foolish as it sounded, I could not lose faith in Bram. I hoped one day he could find a cure.

I could just imagine Bram knocking on the door one day, Byron answering to find a strange man asking for me. Who wants to know? I'm an old friend. She's never mentioned you.

We'd be married by then, and I'm sure I could assuage his apprehensions. I'd have to find some way. Or maybe I could arrange to meet Bram elsewhere. It'd be wonderful if the two never had to meet. Even if Byron had suspicions, I was confident that my husband would never seek the warmth of a mistress. He worshipped me, and that was something. That was more than many women could say. In fact, maybe one day I could find it in me to divulge to him the great secrets of my misconduct. The thought warmed me more than the teacup in my hands. Could Byron endure even that?

A gentle knock, which sounded like a battering ram in my quiet kitchen, shook me from my musings. Who could be calling at this ungodly hour? What time was it anyway?

"Just a moment," I called.

I checked myself for decency and found a thick, long coat, effectively covering up any hint of my figure before cracking the door. Byron stood on the other side with an enormous basket of baked goods, a beautiful bouquet of roses and goldenrod, and a toothy smile.

"Byron!" I said, opening the door just enough to poke my head through. "What are you doing here so early?"

"It's nearly half past ten," he replied. "Were you still sleeping?"

"Half past ten?" Had I slept in or did time run away with my thoughts? "No, I was just enjoying a quiet morning. I think Anna is still asleep."

"Out with Mr. Rigby until late perhaps?" he asked with a hopeful smile. I tried to smile back. "All the better. That way, I hope to gain the element of surprise." He motioned with basket and flowers, wafting an irresistible sweet, herbaceous scent my way. "I can drop them off if you would like, but I was hoping we could talk."

He looked so innocent standing there. It was a warm and welcome change to the waters I had been sailing so recently, and he was making an effort at reconciling with my sister. How could I have refused him? Besides, I had missed him last night after my encounter with Bram. "Are those from Mrs. Barkers?" I asked, nodding at the basket.

"You think I'd bother bringing them if they weren't?"

I opened the door and ushered him in, finding a smile warming my face. I needed it. I couldn't go on another day like before, hating every moment and blaming myself for everything. For the next hour, at least, I could dive into some baked goods and try to make the most of it. Even if I were a monster, Mrs. Barker's iced buns two mornings in a row was something to be grateful for.

Byron bustled by me and set the treats on the table.

"Can I offer you some tea, Byron?"

"I would be much obliged, my dear."

"The flowers are lovely. I'll have to see about putting them in a vase." I rummaged through the cupboard, trying to find something large enough to hold the generous spread of flowers. There wasn't much. I settled on a clay pot next to the envelope Anna had stashed away a couple of days before. I moved it to one side and noted in passing that nothing was in it.

"I could hardly sleep last night," he said, sitting down at the table. "Please, let me help you." He stood up.

"I can manage just fine," I said, extracting the old, dusty, clay vase from the cupboards. He ushered the bouquet into it with enthusiasm.

"What can I get you? There are honeyed scones, iced buns, biscuits."

"A scone will be fine. Really, this is too much."

"It will never be enough," he said, with a deep breath. I handed him his tea and sat down across from him. He grabbed my hand and smiled at me. He looked so happy, and I did this. Not with my writing, not with my cleverness or ambition. I did this with just me. That was enough for him.

"Byron, how can you forgive me after everything? I was so brutish to you."

"Couples will have domestics," he said, squeezing my hand. "I was not so noble myself, but if you can forgive me, I certainly can forgive you. I already have!"

I scoffed. "Forgive you for what? I overreacted. I'm the one to blame." I fell in love with another man. I mixed myself up in dark magic. I continued the list in my head, things I wondered if I would ever share with him one day.

"Rubbish and nonsense. I interfered with Anna's prospects," he whispered. "But, let's talk about more pleasant things."

"Yes, let's."

"The date of our marriage," he said, raising his eyebrows. I took a sip of my tea. I knew he would be eager to get to this. "I'm sorry I missed you last night. But, I'm glad you got some rest. I was so worried about the state you were in. Now, how does next Friday sound?"

I nearly spat my tea across the room.

"Next Friday?" I sputtered.

"We can have all the arrangements made up. There won't be too many guests, after all. You can invite anyone you like, but I don't have much left in the way of relatives. A cousin here and a sister there, but they live far off, and I'm not sure they'll make the trip."

"Next Friday."

"It's just that—I mean, why should we wait? We've waited so long already."

He was right. What difference did it make if it was next Friday, tomorrow, or in a year? The decision had been made. I would become Mrs. Byron Livingston sooner or later. Commitment was the only means of coming to grips with it, and it changed nothing after all.

I collected myself. "You're right. Why wait? Next Friday it will be."

"Next Friday?" Anna stammered, standing in the doorway, a loose shawl wrapped around her nightgown.

"Anna, you're not decent," I said. She stared at me like a specter.

"Tall words, dear sister," she said. Her eyes still bore the mark of sleep, but her fingers were alertly gripping the door frame, as if she had woken from a nightmare. I had known that this would be hard on her, and I had wanted to break it to her slowly. But, maybe it was for the best that it just came out at once. I was tired of hiding my hand and moving from shadow to shadow.

"Go put something on. We have a guest."

"Did I just hear what I think I did?" she asked, ignoring the drooping shawl baring her shoulder. Her chin jutted out proudly, and her nostrils flared. She embodied a terrifying beauty, the way I had always imagined Boudica might appear to her enemies.

"You did. And, I'd prefer if my sister didn't scandalize my husband," I said, screwing up my courage. "Byron and I are getting married a week from Friday."

She collapsed against the side of the door frame. Byron stood up.

"Anna, I'm so terribly sorry about my behavior the other week. I'm at your disposal to make it right. I hope that you will look to me as a cherished brother. Please, I beg of you; let me make this right."

She turned her head from him to me. Her eyes questioned me relentlessly.

What are you doing?

I'm doing what's right.

Is it right to marry a man while you love another? You just told me about another man.

It wasn't meant to be.

You shouted at me about following your heart and sacrificing.

Anna, it's closed. It's done. This is my life and my decision. I'm sorry.

She regained an icy composure and covered her shoulder again, holding the shawl closed with one hand. She looked the picture of respect. An awesome, practiced shield maiden of respect.

"I wish you both all the happiness in the world," she said with a curtsy. She was lying. I could tell because all sisters can. She was perfectly polite and bitterly cold. Who knew how much her affection for me dried up in that doorway? She evaded my eye contact, looking at Byron or the ground. I doubted Byron would be able to pick up on her fury, but I knew her. I had practically raised her. If this cost her a marriage with Jacob, it would be the deepest betrayal I could commit. Maybe, for now, lying behind a pretty mask was enough. With time, perhaps wounds would heal.

"Where will you hold the wedding?" she asked Byron.

"The church in Milford Square," he said, shooting me a warm look. I swallowed hard. That was the church where my parents proclaimed their vows. I nodded to him and closed my eyes. I could still feel Anna breathing deeply from across the room.

"How thoughtful of you, Byron," she said. "We're not overly religious, but I think my dear sister would agree it's considered a sacred place in our family."

"Would you breakfast with us?" he asked.

"I'm afraid I'm going out. If you'll excuse me, I have to do myself up before meeting Jacob at the park."

"I cannot fault you for such a worthy excuse. Don't let us hold you back."

She curtsied again and retreated to the back room, closing the door behind her.

"That went well," said Byron. I sipped my tea.

"Excuse me for one moment," I said, following her to the bedroom. I closed the door to the kitchen behind me. She was hurriedly prepping herself to go out.

"Anna—"

"It's done," she said. "There's nothing to talk about."

"Let me explain."

"Are you going to marry him?" She turned around and faced me.

"Yes, but—"

"Then I wish you all the happiness in the world," she replied, coldly and formally as though she were talking to Byron. I wanted her smile. I wanted to feel her companionship, but she turned her back to me, making it clear our conversation was over. Defeated, I made my way back to the kitchen and tried to pretend nothing was wrong.

I didn't get a chance to talk with Anna again before she bustled past us and went out the door. Byron had been talking my ear off about wedding and honeymoon plans.

"And there's *Langley's Miscellany*," he said.

"What about Langley's?" I asked.

"What do you say we announce the marriage in our next publication?"

"What? You mean between Byron Livingston and Travis Blakely?"

At a certain point, after drained teacups and some dent in the basket of goodies, I prepared myself for the day. Byron had insisted we go for a walk, and I didn't feel like I could refuse him. When I got back to the kitchen, I found a small stack of envelopes in place of the breadbasket on the table.

"What's this?" I asked.

"I've been meaning to show them to you, but we've had so few chances at speaking lately. These are letters from Travis Blakely's many admirers."

I gaped at the pile. Letters from admirers? I was at once flattered and mortified.

"Whatever do they say?" I asked, impulsively grabbing an envelope and tearing it open.

"All sorts of things," he replied. "I hope you don't mind. I took the liberty of reading a few of them."

"'Dear Mr. Blakely,'" I read aloud with a voracious curiosity. "'Your supple tongue and ability to turn a phrase make every one of my days brighter. I eagerly await your next story with anguish and dream that one day I might meet the man who has such a grip over my emotions. Should you ever be on Lallsbury street, I hope you don't hesitate to call...' This woman has some nerve!"

"There's another that insists you must speak with her husband about expressing his feelings more openly," Byron said with a giggle.

There were many letters, and a vain part of me wanted to sit, read, and respond to all of them. Who wouldn't like to sit and read compliments and adoration all day?

"This is a merry surprise. I can't believe you haven't brought it up before now! How will I possibly keep up with it all?" I said, eyeing the pile.

"There's one letter, in particular, that I thought you might afford special attention."

He reached into his vest and produced a crinkled envelope with a sloppily written address sprawled across the front. I hesitated to take it from his extended hand.

I knew exactly what it was. I had written so many of those myself, years before, as a child.

Dear Mister Blakly, I began, noting with affection the misspelling, *My name is Sarah. I reely liked your story about frogs. It made me laf. I asked my mum if I cood have a pet frog, but she sed no. My favorite stories are about the Steely-Eyed Detective. He reminds me that I can be brave, even if there are monsters. One day, I want to be a rider just like you. My mom says if I lissen to my governess, one day I can rite stories, too. I think the world would like a girl rider because I'm just as smart as Tommy and Jo. Please ride back, if you have time, and please don't stop riding stories. I like them. Love, Sarah. P.S. Is the Steely-Eyed Detective married?*

I re-read the letter three times. It was like reading a diary entry from when I was a little girl. My eyes glossed up, and I got a painful knot in my throat. Any semblance of anger inside of me was gone. I just felt gratitude, humility, and a heavy weight of responsibility. Was I in any way worthy of this child's approbation? If she knew what I was...

Byron put his arm around me.

"In spite of your best camouflage, my darling, you're still having quite the effect," he said.

I tried my best not to cry.

Chapter Twenty-Five

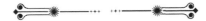

Fit of Violence

Byron and I spent a few more hours together talking about details for the upcoming wedding. We both agreed that there was no need to make a big fuss out of the ceremony. In fact, I was looking forward to having a private affair at the church where my parents got married. The church at Milford Square was a modest chapel with a pair of stained-glass windows. When I was younger, I imagined that my deceased parents could see through the windows to see me when I was there.

It was a foolish idea, and I hadn't attended the church for many years. Still, it was the only place I could imagine getting married. In the off-chance I was right as a younger woman, I wanted my parents to have a view of my husband and me as we embarked into heavenly promises. Or, even if there was no supernatural effect present, I would at least reflect on my own family history as I began a new branch of the tree.

In the early afternoon, I felt cabin fever and insisted we pursue a change of venue. Neither of us had much of a stomach for lunch after all the baked treats, so we opted to head back to Langley's to get back to work on whatever would become the next edition.

As predicted, the snow had melted, and the day was pleasant and sunny, so we opted to walk. On our way there, Byron inquired about my ideas for a next story. I took my time responding. I expected his questioning eventually but still felt unprepared to answer. I satisfied him with some jostle about him working me to death and needing beauty rest as we were getting married next week.

The very idea of getting back into writing was unappetizing at best, but little Sarah's letter to me had set off an orchestra of competing emotions. My guilt over using the pen was overwhelming. All personal effects aside, I cheated at the game. How could I have felt good about winning an award for using magic?

Then again, not only had my stories sold, but they had inspired readers. In particular, they had inspired at least one little girl to dream of making something of herself. Brutus could rail all he wanted on my sensationalist stories, but he would never be able to take away little Sarah's letter to me.

Writing came at a sacrifice. My father taught me that.

If I were to continue writing, maybe it was time to take off the mask, roll up my sleeves, and get into the hard work of it. Fortune had favored me once with a wonderful story, and instead of trusting in my own abilities, I jumped at the chance to seize unearned fame and power, passing off fiction as fact. But, I didn't need the pen. I wrote the Steely-Eyed Detective on my own. I could write others.

Of course, I had all but ruined my Steely-Eyed Detective. My poor Edward. I wondered what he was doing at that very moment. That was a road I could not allow myself to travel.

When we arrived at Langley's, Byron was immediately taken up into the business of explaining the recent cancellation to the other authors. His desk was stacked with messages, and a few of them had made the trip to the office to have it out then and there.

I guiltily squeezed his hand as he took his leave.

"For you, I would endure much more," he replied and made his way into his office.

I made myself comfortable at the little table where I used to peck out my heartfelt stories about window coverings. The worn typewriter sat on the desk in front of me. I traced its metal keys with my fingers, feeling their slick finish.

I could at least try to write something. A letter to Sarah, perhaps. I pulled up the chair and attempted a few mechanical strokes, hearing the satisfying clack of the typeset hitting the ribbon against paper.

Dear Sarah,

It was a start at least.

Thank you for your letter. It is always great to hear that someone reads these stories.

I had to draw the words out like the roots of stubborn weeds.

Don't give up your dream of writing. I agree with you wholeheartedly that the world could use more women writers. In fact, I myself am not exactly what you think. I'm a fraud.

I stared at the last line. I had meant to write, "It wasn't easy for me to begin writing." Instead, the ink on the paper shouted accusations at me. Flashes of fireballs and feverish episodes shot through my head. I winced, and the demon inside of me flared up. How dare I talk about the difficulty of writing. I was a fraud. I was. I was.

I ripped the paper from the typewriter and ripped it up. It was too soon. Perhaps it would always be too soon.

The door swung open, and a familiar face hurried over to where I sat.

"I'll be honest. I did not expect to find you here." Rebecca put both hands on the desk and leaned over the typewriter. "Doug's. Now."

I was so shocked that I could come up with no reason to refuse.

"Rebecca, what a surprise, but I'm just not hungry—"

"We're not going for the food."

She nearly yanked me out the door, hardly giving me a chance to let Byron know that I had to go assist my friend. He nodded to me with a smile. Judging by the exaggerated gesticulations of our political columnist, it looked like he would be busy for quite some time.

We arrived at Doug's after a frantic walk void of small talk and full of silence. Rebecca had a dangerous look about her. I knew she could handle herself, and I knew she was no fool when it came to the ways of the world. I was reminded of the first time I asked her to deliver my stories for me. She saw straight through me and out the door.

We walked into the front hall of Doug's Fish and Chips, and the congenial owner sensed immediately that Rebecca was not here for food. In fact, I suspected that Rebecca had spoken with him prior to my kidnapping.

"The usual place," he said, uncharacteristically professional. Rebecca gave a curt nod before Doug took us past our usual table and into a corner booth with heavy curtains. The booth was dark, lit only with some used tallow candles on the wall. Doug didn't ask if we wanted anything. He just pulled the curtain closed and left us.

Rebecca took off her hat and leveled her eyes across the table at me, shadows dancing darkly on her face.

"We have some things to talk about," she said. She slid a copy of *Langley's Miscellany* across the table. In bold letters sprawled across the front, I read "Banking Scandal Leads to Suicide." I felt cold blood surge through every vein in my body. It was real. It had printed after all.

My fingers twitched.

"Where did you get this? Byron swore to me he recalled them." My voice trembled, and panic swam into my brain, making my head feel heavy. I was quickly losing any sense of gravity.

"He did," she said coolly.

"And yet you have this paper here."

"Our conversation yesterday perturbed me a great a deal, the one where you went on about magic and fog men. Then, I watched you and Edward go into Cooper's office. Then I watched Cooper enter. Edward yelled loudly; a chair hit the floor. He emerged in a fury, and I couldn't even get you to respond to me. You just left, looking like a corpse walking out of a grave. I couldn't let you go like that, but you waved me off. So, I did what any friend should have done in that situation. I followed you."

Followed me. "You just left the station? Was Cooper aware?" I breathed heavily. I couldn't blame her, but my natural instinct was to be enraged that she had taken it upon herself to spy on me. I felt my sickness begin to swell in my stomach like embers with no breath.

"It was practically Cooper's idea."

I breathed through my teeth and lowered my eyes.

"Is this the first time you've followed me?" Mistrust bubbled thickly under my skin. I hardly even knew Rebecca. I'd know her for a matter of weeks. The stress of my failure, of losing Edward and Bram in the course of a day, and the prospect of spending my life in a loveless marriage all muddled together in an overwhelming sense of justice.

"Luella, please, I am your friend," Rebecca said, leaning back in her seat.

"And you told Doug that I was dangerous? Is that it? That's why he's hidden us in this back compartment?"

"He did this, so we could speak in private."

"What are you accusing me of?" She knew. I was convinced she knew. I looked down and saw my hands covered in blood. I let out a startled cry and reached for a napkin to scour it off of my skin. My secret had been discovered. I had to run. I had to silence her. I could not be wrapped up in this. The corners of my vision blurred.

"Doug!" Rebecca cried. I lunged across the table at her, swinging wildly at her face, trying to grope at her wrists, neck, hair anything. She was a threat. She was an enemy, and she had to be silenced.

Two immensely strong hands pulled me back into my seat, and a massive arm wrapped around me so tightly that my arms were pinned against my body.

Doug closed the curtain with his free hand. I seethed in and out, staring down Rebecca, my head thrashing about like a woman possessed. She grabbed a glass of water and threw its contents directly into my face.

The surprise of the cold liquid shocked my senses. It was just enough for reason to stick its foot in the dark doorway before it slammed shut completely, locking out everything but my anger. This was not me.

I needed to suffocate the anger with something else, maybe a hundred other things. I allowed myself to feel horrified at my actions. I allowed myself to feel guilt over Edward's father. I struggled physically against Doug until my muscles gave out, exhausting myself. What was I doing? Rebecca was my friend. I could trust her. She had proven this to me. She cared about me. Could I remember trust?

Before I knew it, I collapsed, limp over Doug's forearm, my senses wiped to nothing, my emotions back to zero, ready to build from the ground up. I blinked my vision back into focus, but I couldn't shake a few floating particles from view. They lingered in the air, appearing almost like some type of floating pathway that stretched out of our compartment and toward the front door. They sparkled in my view, almost like bits of the moon, bits of moon dust. I wondered where a moon dust trail might lead.

Rebecca stared at me with wide eyes. I hadn't noticed before, but her hands were trembling.

"You're not well," she managed to say.

"No. No I'm not," I replied heavily. On a motion from Rebecca, Doug released me and left us again to talk. "I'm so sorry."

"I don't know why I care so much about our friendship," she said.

"Maybe I see myself in you. I don't know. We all need help sometimes. I know something is wrong, and I will be a support for you."

Rebecca's entire countenance blazed with loyalty and love. I could not doubt her words, and they took root in me like an impenetrable truth. I should have allowed her in, fully opened up to her so much earlier. I never understood the value of a true friend before.

"Let's start with this," she said, again indicating the published weekly. "I think they managed to print five copies of the front page before Byron ran into the shop to shut it down. I found this in the bin. Here's my problem. I followed you from the police station to your house to Langley's, in the rain I might add. Then I followed Byron to the printers, where I found this. But, the whole time I followed you, you never once sat down long enough to pen a draft. Can you explain to me when you wrote this story?"

I searched for words, my back against the wall. How could I explain? What would she believe?

"I wrote it the night before," I said. It was time for the truth.

"That's a disturbing confession. You recognize what implications you suggest about yourself? The only way you could have written this the night before is if you knew that Edward's father died that night. How could you have known that."

"I didn't know."

"But you wrote this. Get your story straight because this doesn't sound right. Luella, it sounds like you were involved in his death."

My mouth fell open. She couldn't possibly think what she insinuated.

"You can't think I was involved in murdering Edward's father."

"This front page has details of the crime scene that Cooper never told you. You must have some explanation for this. I am your friend. I know you will be honest with me because I don't want any harm to come to you."

The truth was brimming at my lips. If I could just poke a hole in the dam, I knew it would burst out in torrents.

"Do you remember when I asked you whether you believed in the Fog Man?" I began.

Rebecca nodded.

Chapter Twenty-Six

Rebecca Turner

It took me a long time to explain everything to Rebecca. I wasn't sure if she believed me. She made an effort, but something in her demeanor gave away her inner turmoil, deciding whether her friend had lost her mind or lost her way. She was at least willing to go along with it and hear me out. After all, she could corroborate at least some of my story. She had picked up my trail again the night before as I had made my way to the carnival, where she watched me walk decisively to a specific tent.

In any event, I was either telling the truth, or I had conspired with a carnival worker to kill Edward's father.

I couldn't believe how easy it was for her to follow me without my notice and make a detailed account of my comings and goings. If someone were to follow me with more malicious intentions, I'd be caught completely unawares.

In the end, I explained all about the success of my first story about the Fog Man, about how desperately that pushed me to find new material, and how I was inexplicably drawn to a mysterious magician named Bram. Something about the tent had pushed me to pursue my curiosity of a magical pen.

"I can't believe you never told me about this before," she said, eyes wide. "So, you can write whatever you want with this pen and it just materializes into fact?"

"Well, I'm not supposed to be able to directly change my immediate circumstances with it," I explained. "To most people, I imagine the pen would be a bit worthless. But, as a writer, I've been profiting from the mere occurrence of these events. That's the limit as Bram explained it to me. You can't do something like write about your family member discovering a gold mine."

"So then how did you manage to write a story that resulted in Edward's father's death?"

"I don't know. In fact, I've tried my very best to ensure that I didn't write anything that would result in physical harm to another human being."

"But, it's here clear as crystal," she said, touching the front page of the non-published *Langley's Miscellany*. "You wrote about this suicide."

"I don't remember writing that," I said. I thought back to that feverish night, the rush that came with writing more freely, less guarded, than I'd ever allowed myself before. Bram had told me I had written a simple story about financial scandal, but here were the details of Mr. Thomas' grisly end in black and white. He must have lied to me. How could I not remember what I wrote with my own hand? I shuddered, wondering if deep down maybe I knew something deeper and darker than I could accept. "I've been fooled. Using the pen has made me ill."

"In what way?"

"It's like a magical dependency. The longer I go without using the instrument, or I believe experiencing some type of magic, a rage inside of me builds until it is all but uncontrollable." I winced. "It leads me to do things—"

"Completely outside your character?" Rebecca finished for me. I shirked, ashamed of my outbreak. "Does Bram also have this dependency?"

"I don't know," I said. I hadn't given it much thought before. Bram was involved in who knew what types of magic. Did he also experience withdrawals as I did? How did he manage them?

"But, he knowingly put you at risk by inviting you to use his magical artifact?" she asked. Her tone held a veiled resentment, accentuated by the dancing candlelight.

"It isn't like that," I said, surprised at my own defense of the man I had blamed so ardently before. "There was no way he could have known. He told me he took precautions to protect me."

Rebecca raised one of her eyebrows judiciously. "You have feelings for him."

Sometimes, I hated the way she could see through me. When I spoke with Rebecca, it felt like gazing into a looking glass. Some days, it was flattering, others less so.

"I thought I did," I replied. She let out some mix between a sigh and a scoff before settling her eyes on me in a sisterly pity.

"If only our brain and our heart could learn to be friends," she said, shaking her head. "But, we really need to sort out your taste in men."

"It doesn't matter now," I replied. "Bram is gone, and I marry Byron next week."

"A stupid idea if you ask me."

"How can you say that?"

"With confidence. I could maybe understand if your sister were marrying someone like Byron. But, you and I, we are women with a different backbone than the rest. We can't be satisfied with temporal comforts. There's something deeper at work within us. Did I ever tell you I've been engaged before as well?"

I shook my head. I wasn't surprised. Heavens, just look at the woman. I nearly proposed to her myself.

"It wasn't right. And, I've never regretted walking away. I will marry for love or not at all."

I thought I noticed the slightest flicker of her eyes toward the front of the pub. I had never asked Rebecca about previous courtships or her marital situation. Not only did I consider it rude, but I think I was afraid to discover that my pathway ended at her desk. In many ways, I idolized her, but not as a role model for familial felicity. I choked on her mantra.

"Rebecca, I am marrying for love," I said, "even if it isn't a love for my future husband."

"You're making a mistake. If you're sincere, then run toward Edward, not from him."

"I can't! How can I face him after what I did to him?"

"You've explained it all me well enough, and you insist that you were fooled. I think you were intoxicated, drugged, maybe brainwashed."

"I could have turned back at any time. I could have stopped." My strength was returning, but it was being put to a bitter use. I could feel the tears coming on fast.

"It wasn't your fault. You just wrote something down on a stupid piece of paper!"

"You don't understand," I cried. "The magic is real."

Slap! I heard the sound of skin on skin before the stinging sensation and the blow knocked the tears from my eyes. I rubbed my cheek, numb and warm, and stared at Rebecca in shock.

"Stop this nonsense," she said. Her eyes blazed brightly. "You listen to me. I don't care what you're mixed up in, but I only believe in one kind of magic, and you're trampling all over it. Edward Thomas is a good man who just lost his father in a devastating way. The very least you can do is be a support to him in his time of need. He made your career, and what's more, he made you happy. Is this how you will repay him?"

I was still reeling from her slap and could hardly form a solid counter argument.

"What do you want me to do?"

"He's at the station now. Go to him. Offer your condolences. Leave this foolish engagement with Byron."

"If I don't marry Byron, he will print the story."

"We both know that danger has past. I hardly know Byron, but I know he wouldn't go out of his way to print out-of-date news just to be vindictive."

"I'd still be breaking my word," I protested.

"Then break it," she said. "These are affairs of the heart. They're like manna from heaven: God-sent and impossible to stockpile for later days."

I wanted to hear her. I wanted to run to Edward and press on him to elaborate on the feelings he had shared with me the other day. I wanted to tell him that I was there for him, in whatever way he needed, free of strings, and wholly his.

But, Rebecca didn't know the depth of my sickness or my guilt. I had seen magic. I could not deny its power or its effects. What she considered scribbles on a piece of paper were to me an act as implicating as if I had hung the man myself. I would be cursed to hide it from Edward forever, and because I would hide it, I would always bear the guilt. Because of the guilt, I could never feel comfortable at his side.

At the same time, there was no arguing with Rebecca about his immediate needs. The poor man must have been in the very depths of agony. If there was anything I could do to lessen his pain, I would brave anything to accomplish it. I owed him that. She was right.

"I cannot break my engagement," I said. "But, I can be his friend. Where is he?"

Rebecca did not hide her disappointment or hostility toward my resolve.

"The station," she said curtly.

"At the station?" I gasped. "What's he doing there?"

"He won't stop working," she said.

Chapter Twenty-Seven

Facing Fears

We arrived at the station in the midafternoon. The sun hung low in the late afternoon, shining brightly to say goodbye. I tried to avoid the shadows on my walk to the station, trying to gather at least some warmth from its fading light.

I looked at the dark blue door with its paneled windows and formidable girth. The first time I walked through this door, I was a ball of nerves, a young author embarking on a new journey, throwing the normal convention out the window. The officers felt like strangers then, each more intimidating than the last. Now, I felt like I'd been so wrapped up in the comings and goings of the station that I was practically one of them, albeit one of them with restricted access to just the front hallway and the waiting room outside Cooper's office.

Today, I wasn't just a ball of nerves. I was a complete wreck. The very thought of facing Edward nearly paralyzed me, and without

Rebecca at my side, I'm quite certain I wouldn't have made it even as far as the steps outside.

"Forward, then," Rebecca said, placing an arm around my shoulder. "Let's not freeze to death."

I smiled the best I could. I was grateful to have her with me. She had thoroughly convinced me that it was my duty, rooted in my love for Edward Thomas, that I should go to him in the robes of friendship, but my decision didn't make the deed any easier.

We walked in, feeling a stodgy warm blast of air, a mixture of heat generated from an excessive number of bodies crammed into the building and the radiators going more than they ought to. We walked to the counter, where the clerk didn't bother looking up from his desk.

"Hello. Here to report a missing person?"

"Oh, for heaven's sake, Johnson!" Rebecca chided. "Not every woman is here to report a missing person!"

I bit my lip. For once, I felt like I was missing a person.

"Rebecca, I'm sorry! I didn't see you there," Johnson said, scrambling to straighten himself out. I had never learned this man's name. Now that I knew it, some of the caricature was taken out of him.

"Never mind that," Rebecca went on. "Where is he?"

"Out back with the boys."

"And, how is he?"

"I've never seen him quite like this before," Johnson shook his head sadly. "Poor chap. I don't know how I'd manage what he's going through. Most dreadful thing in the world. It's like losing a father twice over, once in person, once in memory."

His words were enough to ignite a powder keg of guilt inside of me. I knew the pain of losing a father, but he lived on so nobly in my memory. If I had discovered him to be a dishonest crook, could I so continue such a sincere reverence. What had I done to poor Edward? My poor, poor Edward.

"Thank you," Rebecca said, urging me forward behind the counter toward the back of the building.

"Wait, she isn't allowed back there—"

"She's with me."

"She could be with the ruddy Prime Minister—"

"Not another word, Johnson, or so help me!"

This new half of the building was littered with desks pushed in every conceivable nook and cranny. The task force must have been larger than the space. The place was a mess, with papers, sketches, books in every corner, and various articles of clothing draped on each available resemblance of a peg.

On the back wall, I saw an exterior facing door, with a large window on its upper half, through which I noted an open outdoor area. Rebecca led me to this door before turning to me.

"I'm not needed here," she said. I disagreed.

"You're not coming?"

"Edward needs you. I can do nothing for him."

"Where will you be?" I asked, instinctively gripping her hand more tightly than before. She withdrew it.

"Right where I've always been," she said, turning the door handle and ushering me through.

I stepped tentatively onto a railed platform overlooking a large cobblestone courtyard. On its far side, I saw and smelled stabled horses. The courtyard was surrounded by brick walls with a couple of meager, twiggy trees here and there struggling to grow. The fading sun cast everything in sharp contrasts.

In the center of the courtyard, I found Edward stripped down to a blood spackled undershirt, his fists at the ready, facing off against a worse for wear, though much larger, opponent. The big man swung wide, but Edward ducked under his arm and delivered several quick jabs to his rib cage. An audible groan sounded from a few staggered onlookers.

The big man yelled in pain and rounded quickly on Edward, feigning left and delivering a cross with his right, connecting savagely with Edward's jaw, sending spittle flying. Edward staggered back and spit blood onto the ground.

I continued watching for some time as they exchanged blows. Every time Edward took a hit, it sent shockwaves through my heart, down to the heels of my feet, but the fight continued.

Edward dodged a series of quick jabs and tried to counter with a wide punch of his own, but missed, whiffing through air and stumbling from his own thrust. The large man took full advantage, shifting his weight and using Edward's own momentum to meet him with a strong uppercut. Edward staggered back, dazed, trying to shake his senses clear. The big man closed in.

"Stop it! Don't hurt him!" I shouted. I hadn't meant to. The words just came surging out of my mouth. Every face in the courtyard turned toward me, and Edward raised a hand to the big man. I must have been a sufficient surprise to bring him back to his senses. He nodded to his opponent, who clasped his shoulder with those odd, brusque, manly means of affection.

I could hear grumbling nonsense around the courtyard about women spoiling the fun and inquiries as to how I got back there anyway, but Edward made his way over to an old weather-worn table, where he donned his jacket and cleaned himself off with a towel, before crossing the courtyard to me.

"Luella," he said, "what are you doing here?"

He looked terrible, even aside from the bruises and cuts on his face. His eyes looked deep set, framed by dreadful bags hanging under them. His skin was pale, his face disorderly and unshaven, and his gaze lacked its usual luster and shine, drooping instead into tired pits.

"I should be asking you the same question. That man could have killed you."

He coughed out a snort.

"He would never. We spar hard, so we're prepared for what's out there. I'm the only one who can give much of a fight for old Bill." He worked his jaw, testing that it still worked adequately. I winced on his behalf. Merely being around him was enough to make me feel pain and exhaustion. I couldn't imagine what he must be going through.

"Edward." I paused. Discovering Edward fighting another man had startled and distracted me from my fears and hesitations. But, I could not avoid the elephant in the room. Every womanly impulse I possessed reached out to him to lift his spirits somehow. I could not see him pained like this. "I'm so sorry about your father."

He studied something on the ground. "I accept your condolences."

"Please, if there's anything I can do, just tell me."

He breathed in deeply and coughed. I eyed his heaving torso where his lungs worked hard, hidden beneath ribs bruised from the fight.

"I fear I have already prevailed too readily on your hospitality," he said. My hospitality. His words stung, reminding me of how I betrayed him. My writing caused this. All of this.

"Too readily? Don't be ridiculous. Please, tell me how I can help you."

"I must insist you don't trouble yourself."

"Edward, please. I feel helpless seeing you this way."

He grabbed my elbow suddenly and ushered me to a more secluded corner of the courtyard behind the horses. They whinnied but paid us no attention, focusing instead on their dinner troughs.

"Do you insist on torturing me?"

My thoughts flew to my complicity in his misfortune. Had he found me out? How? Perhaps Rebecca wasn't the only one to follow Byron to the printers.

"I can explain," I began.

"It's all crystal clear, Ms. Winthrop. I've apologized for my behavior. I never should have acted so untoward by taking you to lunch the way I did. Please, put yourself in my position now. I didn't take you to lunch because of some passing fancy. I find I can't stop thinking about you, especially now that I've—now that everything has happened the way it has."

"You're not thinking straight."

"My mind is quite sound," he insisted.

"I will do anything I can to help you through this," I stuttered. His words tasted so bitter to me. They were like a dagger in my belly. I could have had him, heart, body, and all, were it not for my continuous ability to ruin everything. I was promised to Byron. I had caused the death of his father. He loved me in spite of one but could not possibly persist upon learning the other.

"Are you not engaged?" he asked, poignantly.

I fought back tears by closing my eyes and nodded. This was for him.

"I'm not sure how your husband would feel about your unrelenting compassion toward me," he said. He looked even more burdened than before, if it was possible. "I wish you quite well. I must ask my leave of you for a time, at least while I find a way to cope with my family's newfound shame."

Ask his leave. So, this would be his coping method. Withdrawal. His decision had not changed my resolve to marry Byron, but it still came like a blow. I had thought it would be some time, if ever, before I could look Edward in the face, but for some reason, knowing that he closed the door and the decision to reopen it was not mine sent winter through my body. The tears came readily. I could not blink them away.

He took my hand and kissed it politely before turning to leave. In response, I gripped his firmly and lifted it to my own lips, kissing it gently, ignoring the gashes and cuts from the fight he had just endured. I did not look at him, only held his hand close to my face and cried on it.

He was too much of a gentleman to ask me to leave Byron. My behavior could not have startled him though. I think he knew that the feelings he had were reciprocated but that something more held me back.

He was so upright, so gallant. As I stood there on the precipice of losing him forever, I allowed myself selfish thoughts. What if he could forgive me? What if Rebecca were right and I could break my word with Byron? I had seen Edward do so many honorable things. He might dismiss my confession as impossible and wouldn't that at least absolve me from the responsibility of disclosing it? We'd be little different than a couple with opposing political opinions, he of one mindset, I of another. A marriage could survive a difference of opinion.

I looked up at him. I saw the invitation there. He could see more to my situation than I let on and wanted me to elaborate. He could not ask it but with his eyes. I could trust him. We could work through anything. We belonged together. My lungs filled with hope, rushing in at a tremendous and powerful speed.

I'll marry for love or not at all. Rebecca's words. Love or convenience. Doug's story from what felt like weeks ago seized my resolve.

"Edward, I have to tell you something—"

"Ms. Winthrop," a voice from across the courtyard interrupted me. I instinctively dropped Edward's hand like I was schoolgirl caught with a boy on break between classes. "Miss, it isn't pretty in this area of the station. Please, let me usher you back to my office."

Sergeant Cooper's commanding tone yanked me back to the reality of our situation.

"I'm sure Lieutenant Thomas has some more training to do," Cooper added. Edward dropped any air of familiarity and snapped to attention. With a curt nod to Cooper and a lingering glance in my direction, he tossed his towel on the table and headed back to the center of the courtyard, where Big Bill stood waiting.

Cooper led me back into the station. I buried my eyes in the ground and tried to recuperate. Edward had cast me off. It felt like my favorite book had been shut and sealed before I could read the ending. Yet, even more importantly, he was experiencing significant pain, and now I could not help him. I heard scattered applause through the door behind us.

"Sergeant," I said, looking for words. "I understand Lieutenant Thomas hasn't stopped working since he learned about his father's death."

"I can't get him to stop," Cooper said gruffly. "But, I don't blame him. It's good for him to be distracted right now."

"I hardly think some extra work will be enough to distract him from such a life shattering tragedy."

"You've never been hit in the face by Big Bill."

"So that's your plan? Beat him senseless so he doesn't have to deal with this? Why not just get him drunk? It's about as noble."

"That comes later." We arrived at his office, passing Rebecca, who pretended to be busy at her typewriter, pausing only long enough to search me for clues on how my conversation had gone. I shook my head toward her before stepping inside the office.

Cooper shut the door behind us. He motioned to a chair, which I took, and sat down formally on the other side of his desk. His frank, know-it-all demeanor felt surreal and had me perturbed.

"Don't you think he should be at home with his family?" I asked, doing my best to bore into Cooper's experienced, wrinkly eyes. I ruminated over my bad fortune that I had neither inherited my mother's good looks nor her fierce stare.

"The police force is his family, or so he's told us. But, you bring up a great point. Ms. Winthrop, I'd like to talk to you about his family, actually."

"I don't know his family," I said, bluntly.

"Yes, that's what I find so interesting," he said. He picked up the baton on his desk and started picking at the end of it, giving off an air of nonchalance. "When I broke the news to Edward about his father, you were quite affected."

"It came as quite a shock," I replied. It was the honest truth.

"Yes, it was. Though, I'd never seen you quite so shaken up before. At the time, I dismissed it as a natural reaction from a woman's more delicate sensibilities and regretted to have had you in the room. But, as I thought about it, I remembered that you are the great reporter, and shocking news is your line of work, is it not?"

What was he playing at? This was the last place I wanted to be. I'd had enough twists and turns for one day. "It is, but it's not the same when misfortune befalls upon someone you know."

"You just said you didn't know the man."

"Certainly not, but I know Edward, and I couldn't imagine what he was experiencing."

He placed down the baton. "This is where things don't add up for me. I knew your father, and I recognize certain of his characteristics in you, especially that need to come to the rescue, much like you thought you did today when you called Old Bill off of Thomas. Why, might I ask, was this deeply rooted characteristic of yours abandoned upon learning of his father's death? It couldn't be the shocking nature of the news. You're a reporter. You make your living off of news like that. And, you say you don't know the late banker, so it couldn't have been the blow of personal loss either. Then, as I've mentioned, I believe such a reaction as you had to be against your very God-give nature."

He looked at me with his fingers interlocked, investigating me like a bloodhound, scrutinizing every twitch of my facial features. I shifted uneasily. I felt under attack. Rebecca's warning at Doug's crept up behind me, haunting me. That front page may have seemed to implicate me in Mr. Thomas' death, but certainly Cooper hadn't seen that page. How could he have?

"I'm not sure I see your point, Sergeant," I said, trying to push down my frustration and not give off the impression I was hiding something. It was a tough play. I was hiding something.

"My point? Well, you may not have known Luke Thomas, but I did. I'm sure that banking scandals and suicide are always shocking, but I would say this one seems impossible. Luke Thomas was scrupulous and meticulous to the brink of annoyance. He was obsessive about paying his debts and keeping ledgers. And, what's more, he raised a hell of a boy, the one that I think you've developed a significant attachment for. So, Ms. Winthrop, I find any accusation of financial misconduct on his part highly questionable and his sudden hanging to be quite mysterious indeed. Forgive me if I'm looking for leads."

I wasn't sure what to do. I sat there, panicked, searching for some emotion to hold on to, some train of thought to give me balance, but I couldn't find words. I felt my anger build.

Please, not now. Couldn't it wait until I was at home, alone? I couldn't lash out at Cooper, not while he suspected me like this.

"I find your insinuation entirely ungentlemanly," I managed to say, through only partially clenched teeth.

"I'm insinuating nothing," Cooper said. "I'm asking for your help. If you know anything about the circumstances surrounding Luke Thomas' death, I'm urging you to come forward and assist my investigation."

I felt it bubbling deep down in my ribs. He suspected me. He was after me. He was an enemy.

I needed to get out of there. I put a hand on his desk and leaned toward him, dangerously.

"Luke Thomas cooked his own books and took his own life. The only mysterious aspect of any of this is your willful blindness about who you consider your friends. While you're quibbling over nonsense, might I remind you of your duty to his son. Instead of encouraging him to get beaten senseless, maybe you should take some useful and fruitful steps forward to help him deal with this tragedy in a healthy manner. Until then, even if I knew something about his father's death, I wouldn't talk to you if you paid me."

I stood up quickly and turned to leave.

"Ms. Winthrop, don't think you can avoid this. If you know something, I will get it from you. Some things here aren't adding up."

"How would you know?" I asked, one hand on the doorknob. "If you knew how to add, maybe you would be more than a ruddy miserable police sergeant."

I stormed out with only a nod to Rebecca and didn't stop until I reached my own front door.

Chapter Twenty-Eight

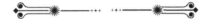

Lost

I made my way down an unfamiliar cobbled street in a strange area of town. It was unusually warm for the new, soft layer of snow covering the ground, and I couldn't exactly remember where I was headed. I thought, vaguely, that I was in the vicinity of where the carnival had been set up near the river. Remembering it gave me a chill.

I should have been heading back to Byron. After all, I hadn't explained how long I was going to be gone, and who knew what terrible drudgery he had been through when explaining the cancellation to our writers? But, I couldn't go back to him like this. I still felt angry at Cooper's audacity. He should have been helping Edward, not accusing me of things he couldn't understand. The truth was, of course, that I did have something to do with Luke Thomas' death, but I suspected that Cooper wouldn't believe the truth. If I did explain it, he would either lock me in an asylum or disbelieve me and feel doubly confident laying the blame at my feet. Perhaps both.

I was taking this walk, I guessed, to calm those emotions beyond my control. My earlier outbreak at Rebecca had shaken me deeply. How could I trust my own body anymore? She was a close friend, and I had attacked her!

There was so much to fear. These attacks would continue, and I felt helpless against them. I felt Bram's little crimson inkwell tucked tightly in my jacket pocket, safely stoppered. I reached in and took hold of it. It gave me a strange comfort, thinking that somewhere Bram was out there working to find a cure for me.

I looked around. The gas lamps were lit, though it was still daylight. Odd. I was sure the sun would be set by now. What a lonely a street. Not a soul on it and not even the usual litter of discarded newspapers and gazettes. A gentle breeze swept down the avenue, kicking snow up into powdery tendrils and flurries. It licked at my feet.

As I pushed forward, the wind grew stronger, blustering up more and more snow. Soon, entire clouds of it were airborne. It looked almost like a thick fog. I coughed, breathing in dense air, cold and humid. My father stood on the street corner in front of me.

"My darling, there you are. I've been looking for you," he said. He smiled jovially, like he had in my previous dreams, but it had lost some of its effect on me.

"Papa, where have you been?" I asked. "I've needed you. So much has happened."

"I've been trying to get back to you. Your dreams have been filled with other things."

"I haven't been dreaming at all," I protested. I walked right by him, convinced more than ever before that he was just a figment of my imagination and not actually the ghost of my father. He turned and walked with me.

"What is it, my darling? How is your writing going?"

"I'm stopping. I'm not going to write anymore."

"What? Why not?"

"I've hurt too many people."

"But you were close! You're closer than ever. The Golden Inkwell is right in front of you."

I stopped and glared at him.

"Why did you tell me to keep writing?"

"You were made to write. That's why I sacrificed like I did to educate you," he replied with a sorrowful look on his face. That wasn't like him. I threw him a pair of scrutinizing eyebrows.

"You what?" I asked. My father had never admitted what he had done for me. I overheard him arguing with my mother about it.

"I could have spent that money on medicine," he persisted. "Instead I spent it on you."

Something was wrong. He hadn't been like this in my other dreams. My father wasn't manipulative.

"You aren't real," I said resignedly. The realization dawned on me eerily.

"I thought we were avoiding that question."

"I'm dreaming. You're just a conjuring of my memory, mixed with my current perspective."

"Luella, don't think that way. We were close to achieving something great."

His personality was too wishy washy. My father had been constant, filled with love and support, never guilt or insistence. He was too flawed to be my father's ghost, and I didn't have energy for a dream that was anything but an escape.

"I wish you were him, but I can see you're not. I need to wake up now. Where is the exit?" I tried pinching myself hard, but I remained on the corner. I bit my cheek until I tasted blood. I slapped my knuckles against a streetlamp and felt searing pain.

I didn't wake up.

I couldn't escape the dream. The magical energy inside of me stirred up like leaves in a breeze. I had never felt it while unconscious before, but as my frustration grew, the power amplified it. I turned on my father. He grinned maliciously, and the terrifying, blood curdling nightmare venom coursed in my veins. The feeling of panic and helplessness.

"What are you?" I asked.

"Your father," he replied, but I knew he was lying. I tried to breathe. All of these dreams after missing him for so long. Did I imagine it was coincidence that he started to appear in my unconscious thoughts so soon after I encountered magic for the first time.

"The fog," I muttered, peering at him anew. Magic camouflaged itself. Bram never told me magic was so blatantly cruel.

His cold laugh echoed before the fog crushed him like a wave on the shore. It enveloped both of us. I could not feel my feet or legs below me. I was buoyed up into a beautiful weightlessness, effortlessly commanding my will against gravity. It was as if I was drowning in soft, cream colored down, but my lungs had adapted to breathe in feathers and my eyes to see through their filaments as clearly as the particles of the air.

In the midst of this peculiar white canvas, I saw a shade, barely distinguishable, in front of me. I could nearly make out a humanoid form, but just as my eyes set to focus on it, the shape changed into something new.

"Let me go!" I shouted, but no answer came in response. Instead, I felt a deep vibration, starting in my feet and making its way up to my head. In the vibrations, I began to piece together some words, not by hearing, but deep in my stomach, where my anger lived.

"What are you! I demand you respond," I cried, giving into the anger. It was better than panic.

"You gave me life," I felt the vibrations communicate. In the white fog, I saw a faint impression of my previous dream and the headline of my accompanying story.

"I beg your pardon?" I couldn't argue with the understanding the entity gave me.

"Summoner, you gave me life. I am yours."

"I just wrote a story. I didn't dream you up. You killed a man, and I reported it. I did what any journalist would do." I couldn't believe I was arguing with a white snow monster.

"What a cruel summoner you are. I've existed through time, but you created me. I've been here since the beginning but have no life without you. I have killed before, and others have found an explanation in every answer but the obvious."

"Magic?" I asked.

"Bid me do. I will obey."

"Don't try to tell me that you're some type of servant," I said, scoffing. I felt as though I was communing with an old friend, almost as comfortable as the back and forth in my own head as I penned my articles.

"Write more stories, and I will make them come to be."

"That's not how this works. I'm a reporter. I describe life events," I insisted.

"Then why did you give voice to the detective's ramblings?" The vibrations flowed through me, more and more persistent. They tried to batter down the wall of reason I'd built up as a defense.

"I'm sure stories like that happen all the time," I said.

"They do, but the world is blind. They stop their ears. The day you went looking for something deeper, I appeared. Do you believe in such extraordinary coincidences?"

"You're aren't making any sense. You can't argue that you exist in spite of time and then prove you exist by means of a linear progression of events!"

"Nor can I even exist, and yet I have killed for you already."

"I did not ask you to kill anybody!"

"You wanted a change in your circumstance, a digression from the plan of things. Do you truly think these deviations come without price?"

"I did not wish harm on anyone!"

"You did not care what would happen to the strangers. The balance is level."

"Bram told me the pen dictated my writing, not the other way around."

"The Meddler is a fool."

"The Meddler?"

"He seeks control. He looks to disrupt and interfere with the natural order of things."

"And what natural order is that?"

"Power can only be yielded by those to whom power submits."

"So, you're power then? And you submit yourself to me?" I was incredulous. I remembered the pen, moving practically of its own accord during my feverish episode.

"Bid me do. I will obey."

"Bram told me to listen for the magic. Why not him?"

"The Meddler is a fool, but he is not without his usefulness."

"And why do you present yourself to me now? You've ruined my life already. Leave me."

"Other forces have prevented our meeting."

"Bram?"

I felt a rushing sensation. The fog around me wound itself into a great agitation, whipping back and forth like it was caught in a cyclone, but I was left at peace. I was the eye of the storm.

"The Meddler is departed. Now there is nothing stopping you."

"Stopping me from what?"

"What you can become. Achieving your desires."

I could not control my thoughts. My heart rushed to Edward. I wanted to be his. I wanted to be his wife.

"If he is your wish, he can be yours."

"How?"

"You know the way."

Lie to him. No. I could not possibly hide the truth that I caused the ruin and downfall of his father. I could not live with myself, knowing and standing beside him.

"No lies. The truth," the vibrations hummed on.

"He wouldn't believe me."

"He can be persuaded."

"And what if he was? The only reason I got mixed up in this in the first place was because I lied to my fiancé about Bram. I went behind his back to spend time with a mysterious man. Scandalous meetings! Lying next to him. Communing intimately! Spending hours getting to know him in a way I never cared to know Byron! This is the truth you think will bring Edward and me closer together?"

"Bid me do. I will obey."

"You cannot force him to love me!"

"Are you so certain?"

"I would know that it was not his own will. I don't want a shadow of a man. I want the real thing. I don't want shortcuts. No more shortcuts!"

"You would never know the difference."

"Would I not?"

I heard a percussive, distant, albeit familiar, sound faintly cutting through the downy fog. It sounded like horse hooves on cobblestone and the clink of the door handles on a cab.

"This meeting weakens."

"Weakens? How?"

"Other forces."

"The Meddler? Bram? Is he still here?"

I jumped up with a start into darkness, my breast heaving to fight for air. I was in my bed, alone. I scrambled to feel the covers, pinching myself. What time was it? I ran to my little window and opened it, allowing the cold air to rush in, revitalizing my senses. I looked out, searching desperately for traces of snow or the white downy fog. Nothing. The night was clear, the ground was wet, but without a flake.

I rushed to my nightstand and opened the drawer, feeling in the darkness and retrieving the small vial of ink Bram left me. It was still there, still stoppered, still full. Deep within me, I felt my magic beating like a heart.

"Anna," I cried instinctively. I needed my sister, needed to tell her everything, just as I had done with Rebecca. She could help me. She loved me as only a sister could. That bond had to be stronger than the magic.

"I only believe in one kind of magic." Rebecca had said so. That magic forged the bond between my sister and me. I hoped.

"Anna!" I cried again, voice trembling, but no response came. I felt blindly on her side of the bed. She wasn't there. I raked my mind, trying to piece together the night's events, but I could not determine how I ended up in my bed at home or account for the previous hours.

Anna was gone. It was the middle of the night. She could be in danger or doing who knew what with Jacob. What a sister I had been! How long did I expect my neglect to accumulate without consequence?

I clambered from the bed and clumsily grabbed a shawl to throw around my shoulder. I checked the kitchen, the bathroom, but there was no sign of her.

I could not lose Anna. I had lost Edward, Bram, I'd even lost any real true relationship with Byron. Not Anna.

I swung open my front door and ran instinctively to Mrs. Crow's flat, banging on it without consideration for the hour.

"Mrs. Crow, please! It's Luella!' I shouted, banging harder.

To my surprise, the door opened quickly, and Mrs. Crow greeted me with a lit candle, dressed in a worn nightgown and a weary expression.

"I was wondering when you would come to my door," she said.

"Please, Mrs. Crow, this is no time for games. Anna's missing. Please, tell me you have seen her."

"I have," she said, holding up a hand.

"When?"

"Right before she left with Jacob. Come inside, dear. I have some tea on." She waved me in sadly and slowly. I followed, put off by Mrs. Crow's tone of voice, as if something inevitable had come about.

I sauntered through the doorway into her flat. It looked similar to my own, except that she had given more attention to cleanliness and less substance in the cupboards. I had made it a point not to visit Mrs. Crow's very often, partly because I didn't want to impose upon her and partly because she could be a bit much to deal with. I noticed, for the first time, a likeness hanging on the wall, drawn in pencil, of a robust looking man in a black suit and top hat.

Mrs. Crow was a widow; this much I knew. She had explained to me several times in the past how her husband had died from street violence. That was before the city had adopted a police force, and a local sheriff's office could not keep up with a surge in crime. She had since spent her life getting by on what she could. They had enough stored away for her to purchase this small lodging, so at the very least, she wasn't expected on by a mortgage, but her life was meager and, I imagined, very lonely. At least she had Mrs. Barker to gossip with.

Still, I now felt a keen desire to connect with her in a way I never had previously. Perhaps I feared that my current path was leading me to her situation. Byron was a good deal older than me, and if I squinted hard enough, I could see a future version of myself living alone, trying to find ways to pass the time.

"Anna left this afternoon," she said, pouring tea from an old battered kettle into a porcelain cup. "Truthfully, I thought she might do something rash like this after I heard about you and Byron getting back on."

"You heard about that?"

"Anna told me the other day."

"Did you and Anna meet often?"

"My dear, did you expect her to just sit here reading while you were off at work and play?"

I accepted the cup presented me and blushed.

"I just—I didn't realize."

"Anna was the closest thing to family as I've had left," Mrs. Crow said, settling into a chair. "Now, I guess I'm stuck with you."

"Stuck with me. What do you mean? Did you two quarrel?" I asked. She put down her teacup.

"Oh, dear, you don't understand. Anna's gone with Jacob," she replied.

Gone with Jacob. Understanding hit me like a punch from old Bill at the police station. I feared that she might do something like this. My distaste for the young man grew. He must have taken advantage of her in her desperate state. It wouldn't be the first time a young rich man tried to abscond with a woman. I massaged my temples. The fallout would be nothing pretty.

"You didn't try to talk her out of it?" I asked, knowing the answer.

"Try talking sense into a young, enamored woman? Is such a thing possible? I believe the last time I tried that, I was banished from your apartment." I winced. "The truth is, we learn these things only after it's too late. Then, we carry the curse of trying to pass down what we know, but the young never have listened to their elders, and they never will. The heart is just too strong. It will do what it wants."

My cup sat on the table in front of me, untouched. I stared at its swirling contents, studying the wisps of steam trailing off its top.

"I just thought he would be different," I said, shrugging my shoulders. "I didn't think he was driven by the same carnal passion that so many men are."

"All men, Luella. Why do think we marry them? It's one of our feeble attempts at keeping them out of trouble. I tried to tell her Jacob wasn't blind, and she was wasting her money with those God forsaken pills she kept going on about."

"What pills?" Even as I asked, I saw the envelope in my memory, how quickly she had swooped it up and hid it in the cupboard, the empty envelope there this morning.

"Luella, you must have been walking through your house blindfolded."

I felt like vomiting. My sister had not been lured away by a rich young gentleman. She had ensnared him.

"An aphrodisiac?" I whispered. "Where did she get them?"

"She wouldn't tell me, at least not specifically. But, after some deduction, I think it was a no-good peddler at that fair that's just packed up across the river. Spanish flies, covered in chocolate, so she told me. If that's not the stupidest idea, I don't know what is. If it were so easy to fix problems of intimacy, do you think so many men would run to mistresses?"

I had been so stupid. I felt weightless, smotheringly weak.

"It's my fault," I said to myself more than to Mrs. Crow. "I told her, if she really loved Jacob, she would sacrifice everything to be with him and let nothing stand in her way."

Mrs. Crow stared at me vacantly.

"And you think those were the magic words that sent her down the wayward path? Luella, I've known you for a long time. I knew you were always book smart, but I didn't know that you could be such a fool. Your sister left with Jacob because she realized that she didn't fit in your life anymore."

"What are you talking about?"

"You're at a crossroads, dear. What will become of Anna when you marry Byron? Do you think she will just happily live downstairs under a head of household she despises?"

My head hurt trying to remember every warning signal, every cry for help I should have recognized.

"Until she and Jacob could be wed, yes."

"And, if Jacob didn't work out?"

"Then we would find another suitable match for her."

"There is no other suitable match," Mrs. Crow said, decisively. "She's a Winthrop. If I know anything about your family, it's that you don't do things the traditional way. While you've been busy being so progressive, you've governed your sister like your grandmother would have. Suitable match, please. She's in love with Jacob just as much as you are with your writing."

"My writing," I echoed. "Anna told you about that, too."

"Yes, though she didn't have to. I read Langley's from time to time, and if Mr. Livingston thinks he can convince me that one of his male reporters can write such a nuanced guide to curtains, then he has another thing coming to him."

Of course, Mrs. Crow knew. The pieces were all there. My life was just a puzzle for those bored enough to take a look. Bram had discovered my pen name. Why not Mrs. Crow?

She made too much sense for me to bear. When did my little sister become so calculating and decisive? I had always just assumed that things with Jacob would work out eventually. But, if they hadn't, living under the roof with the man who started the downfall would be miserable. Was eloping really her best chance to seal her fate with the man she loved?

"My dear Luella," said Mrs. Crow, reaching across the table and taking my wrist gently. "Don't take this too hard. Take it from someone who has lived a good long while. A lot comes out in the laundry. No one is without their demons."

I smiled back at her. If only she knew to whom she was talking. We all had our demons, to be certain. I thought again of the fog and the frightened panic I had woken up to all alone in my bed minutes ago, without the sister that had buoyed me up for so long and in so many ways. Some of us had demons, and some of us had real demons.

"Mrs. Crow, I was wrong to treat you the way I did the last time we spoke. I'm sorry. Please, help me understand what we should do when Anna gets back. I'm sure, if we can act quickly, we can contain some of the damage she's caused to her reputation or at least do something to ensure Jacob does the honorable thing."

"Luella, please, my dear, you're still not hearing me. Anna's gone. She's gone away with Jacob."

Finally, it dawned on me, like the fog clearing at midday.

"She's not coming back," I said, tears welling into my eyes.

"She left this for you," Mrs. Crow said, heading to a drawer and producing a sealed envelope. "She said it explained the best way she knew how."

"Did you read it?" I asked. Mrs. Crow shook her head.

"I'll let you alone now. I think you know the way out when you're done. If you need anything, you have but to call." She set the letter on the table, kissed my head, and made her way out of the kitchen, closing the door behind her.

I stared at Anna's elegant, practiced handwriting, a single word on the envelope's exterior. Luella. My fingers trembled as I opened it.

Dear Luella,

What is there to say, really? You've always been the writer. I never had the intelligence you do, nor the wisdom. But, through our lives together, I've learned to do as you say and not as you do. I hope that I at least have in courage what I lack in my other faculties. I have explained everything I know about your recent activities to Jacob, and upon understanding your mysterious evening disappearances and sudden affection for Byron again, he fears the worst and that scandal is imminent.

I'm sure that Mrs. Crow has divulged my plan to you as well. She always was a bit of a gossip. You'll be happy to know the peddler's love cure I kept in the kitchen cupboard did not work, at least not in the way expected.

I hope that you do not believe me to have just run off with him to be married in secret. He has relatives in the country. We will be staying with them and married soon. I suppose, in a way, I'm getting what you always wanted for me: me married with a family protective of my well-being and reputation.

I wish it hadn't been like this. I wish there had been another way. But, what chance did I have when I lost your confidence? I don't know what you're mixed up in, dear sister, but I'm sure you'll make it through alright. You always do.

If you do manage to break free and clear of everything, with your name intact, I imagine I could convince Jacob to let me come visit you from time to time. I hope, by then, you will see me as a loving sister and your equal. Pray forgive me for not telling you before I left. I knew you would have stopped me. I could not have allowed it. I'm in love with Jacob. He is willing to stick by my side through thick and thin, just as you once did, dear sister.

Isn't love terrible, though? We search so obsessively for the love a family might provide, only to leave a family to have it. I will miss you so terribly. Even writing the words is enough to shake my resolve about all of this, but you told me: sacrifice everything. I have this chance, and I fear to postpone my decision lest it expires before my doubt.

Goodbye, Luella. I will always love you so dearly. I hope you can learn to be happy.

> *With heartfelt gratitude,*
> *Your sister*
> *Anna*

My tears dotted the parchment as I read and reread her note. There was good to be had. I was glad that Jacob's family had chosen to accept the couple, even if it meant them thinking me a scandalous relation.

But, the pain was so real, and it came on in waves.

I felt like doubling over, like curling into a bed and dying. My lungs felt like they had been clamped on by a vice grip. I'd lost her. My sweet baby sister. I had given my whole life to protecting her, and now—my body convulsed.

Even if she did come to visit, things would never be the same. I wouldn't see her smiling. I wouldn't laugh with her over silly jokes or tease with her about idle gossip. I wouldn't feel the warmth of her companionship as we walked to parties or visited Mrs. Barker's bakeshop. I would have no one to share news as it happened. She wouldn't be at my wedding, as I tied the knot with a man I didn't love.

Why had I kept so much from her?

I put my face into my arms, leaned over the table, and wept openly, not for Anna, but for myself. The sobs came, tearing at my insides. My life was nothing more than shattered pieces. I couldn't even run to my father's memory anymore. I had no one.

Mrs. Crow put a hand on my back. I don't know when she came back downstairs, but I lifted my face to see she was crying, too. I embraced her and buried my face into her old, soft shoulder, wishing, pretending she was my mother.

Chapter Twenty-Nine

The Gray-Haired Knight

I woke to the sound of someone knocking frantically on my neighbor's door. It sounded like the steady banging of the bottom side of a fist.

I opened my eyes and lifted my head gingerly. I felt awful. My lower spine was on fire, and I couldn't feel half my face. The other half was iced in drool. I was in my kitchen or at least somewhere that looked my kitchen. The furniture and wallpaper were just a little off. Had Anna changed something?

I sat up and realized I was still sitting at Mrs. Crow's kitchen table. She sat there in the chair across from me, head against her chest, snoring lightly. Anna's letter lay open in front of me. It wasn't a dream. She was still gone.

The light coming through the window made me squint, and there was a distinct musk in the room. The banging continued outside.

"Luella!" I heard a muffled voice accompany my door's deep tissue massage. I looked around haphazardly and checked myself to see if I was dressed. I was still wearing my flannel dress from the day before, dressed the way I had been when I was out in the fog. It was crinkled in deep creases at awkward locations. "Luella!"

"Mrs. Crow?" I croaked, testing my voice. She stirred awake quickly.

"Hands off, sailor!" She woke with a start and looked around, reorienting herself. "What time is it?"

"I don't know."

"Luella, it's Rebecca!" I heard from outside.

"You'd better get the door," Mrs. Crow told me. With both of us conscious, I slid more readily back into reality. I must have fallen asleep at the table sometime last night. Who knew how late I'd been up? I just remembered exhausting pain. This morning, I felt numb. I nodded and opened the door to the outside hallway.

"Rebecca?" I asked, emerging from Mrs. Crow's front door. She turned around with a start. I had never seen her so disheveled. Her hair was a mess of disorganized curls, and I could see a night dress hidden under her heavy coat. "You're hardly dressed. What are you doing here?"

She pushed me back inside Mrs. Crow's apartment assertively and without response. When we were safely inside, she turned around and shut the door.

"I came as soon as I could. Cooper came by my apartment early this morning." She broke off when she eyed Mrs. Crow. "Who is this?"

"This is my neighbor, Mrs. Crow."

"Do you trust her?"

"I do with my life. She can hear whatever you have to say." Rebecca eyed her skeptically.

"She looks like a gossip," she said.

"Luella, should I retire to give you some privacy?" Mrs. Crow asked, exchanging a stern look with my friend from the police station.

"Don't be ridiculous, Mrs. Crow. This is your house."

"I'm afraid we don't have much time," Rebecca insisted, sitting me down. "Cooper asked me for your address."

"What for?" I asked.

"Luella," Rebecca said, leveling her eyes at me with great severity. "He's coming to arrest you."

I couldn't believe what she was saying. I heard the words, and I understood them, but they were like small talk. How do you do?

Would care for some tea? Cooper's coming to arrest you. I was still waking up for heaven's sakes.

"Please, Rebecca, what are you talking about? I haven't even had breakfast yet."

"Don't you understand?" she said, gripping me by the shoulders. "He thinks you're involved in Luke Thomas' murder."

Mrs. Crow began breathing heavily. She held on to a doorframe for support. "Good heavens."

"Murder? Luke Thomas hung himself in a suicide," I said. How could I be mixed up in another man's suicide?

"Cooper's decided the circumstances are peculiar and suspicious, and he's treating the event as foul play. He intends to make you his prime suspect."

"Foul play? But that doesn't make sense."

"Luella, would you just listen to me?" Rebecca shouted. "He means to have you in prison!"

I couldn't doubt her, and the weight of her words finally sank in.

"But, Cooper was a friend of my father's," I stuttered.

"I don't know anything about your father," she replied. "I only know he was asking for your address with the intention of coming here with several officers to arrest you."

"Did you give it to him?" I asked, my heart rate rising, a sick feeling in the pit of my stomach.

"Absolutely not," she said. "But that won't slow him down for long."

I sank back in my chair, feeling like a millstone hung off the back of my neck.

"What do I do? Rebecca, it's as I told you before. I can't say I'm innocent, nor can I say I have any guilt in Mr. Thomas' downfall."

"You are innocent," she insisted. "To think anything else is madness."

"What should I do?" I asked.

"What any sensible woman should do," Mrs. Crow said, inserting herself for the first time in the conversation. "Go to your husband and explain what's going on."

"Byron?" I gaped at her. He was the very last thing on my mind.

"It's too risky," Rebecca said. "You need to pack a bag and leave straightaway."

"To go where?" Mrs. Crow asked. "Luella, you are about to embark into a marriage with this man. He loves you. He will protect you, or he's no man at all. It's time for you to grow up and learn to trust the people who care about you."

"I care about you, and you can't know how Byron will react to the truth," Rebecca said to me.

"That's what marriage is! It's a stream of hurdles you conquer as a team," Mrs. Crow said with renewed vigor. "You have to go Mr. Livingston."

My head swam in dizzying circles. Rebecca had an excellent point. Could I possibly tell the truth to Byron? The whole truth? How would he react? And yet, I could not argue with Mrs. Crow. I had already decided to commit fully to my forthcoming marriage, and if that were true, it meant divulging to him the nature of my distress. I had hoped to do it one day. Now was as good a time as any. Shouldn't I enjoy the benefits that Byron had always promised me with his affection? He had promised me devotion, swore to me his trust and fidelity.

Besides, what other option did I have? I had no other home. If I ran, I would be a fugitive, aimless and wandering. I couldn't chase after Anna. Jacob's family was already saving one Winthrop from scandal. I couldn't risk bringing my mess and shame to her new situation. Besides, I had no idea where she was. I knew about Jacob's family home in the city, but I had no idea where to begin searching outside the city boundaries.

"Rebecca, is there any way you can stall Cooper?" I asked.

"I can try, but he's on the war path. If I start behaving too strangely, I fear he will turn on me, too."

"His own secretary?" I was incredulous, but Rebecca didn't give off the appearance of being overly paranoid.

"I've never seen him like this before. His eyes were so cold this morning. It's like I never knew him at all," she said simply.

"Well, do what you can," I said, rushing across the hall to grab my coat and hat. "I'm going to Langley's."

"Are you sure about this? Think about the risk," Rebecca asked as I locked my door behind me. The question jarred me, and I had to screw up my courage to speak to her honestly.

"What other road can I take?" I said. "I chose Byron in the end, didn't I? It's not just a farce. I made a choice, and it's time for me to act like a good wife."

I stepped out the big, creaky front door, made my way down the steps, and hailed a cab.

* * *

I felt every cobblestone under the cab's wooden wheels as the driver hurried his horses along. It wasn't a far walk to Langley's, and I shaved off a couple of minutes travel time at most, but something inside me whispered that I should save my strength. There was no telling what I might need it for ahead or how taxing it might be to divulge my vulnerabilities to Byron in full. Besides, the cab gave me less opportunity to change my mind.

As the shock wore off, adrenaline slowly took its course. I was furious with Cooper. There could be no greater betrayal than this. He was one of the few people in my life who had known my father, and this was his opinion of me. It disgraced his memory. It disgraced me.

We arrived at the shop quickly, and I paid the driver more than I'm sure he required. What worth is money to a condemned woman?

I ran up the steps and burst through the front door. Byron was in his office talking with someone I didn't recognize. He saw me and waved me over jovially.

"Luella! I'm glad you're here. I have some news. This is Mr. Fairweather. He has the most wonderful idea for a new column: our own report on updates from the world of tennis!" Byron and Mr. Fairweather stood to go through a formal introduction.

"You must be Mr. Livingston's fiancée," he said.

"Byron, I need to speak with you urgently and in private," I said, ignoring Mr. Fairweather's outstretched hand. Byron smiled at me as if I were pulling off some great joke but reconsidered as he studied my face.

"Is everything alright?" he asked. I eyed Mr. Fairweather, and Byron jumped into action.

"Right, Mr. Fairweather, if you will just wait in the—"

"Mr. Livingston is busy for the day. Would you mind coming back tomorrow?" I butted in. The new writer looked awkwardly between my betrothed and me before muttering his assent. He donned his hat, and the moment the front door closed after him, I pushed Byron into his office and shut that door behind us as well.

"What the devil is going on?" Byron asked, leaning against his desk.

"Byron, I need your help," I began. The tears were coming already, but I would not let them sidetrack my intention. "Sergeant Cooper with the Dawnhurst Police Force intends to arrest me."

Byron coughed out a guffaw.

"It's true. His secretary, my friend Rebecca, whom you know as my story courier, rushed over this morning to tell me."

Byron sank into his chair. "Why would he want to arrest you?"

"He believes I was complicit in the murder of the banker, Luke Thomas," I said as calmly as I could.

"Luke Thomas," he tested the name aloud. "The man from your story? The story you begged me to recall." He trailed off, trying to make sense of the new revelations.

"Byron, I need your help, as your betrothed. Luke Thomas committed suicide. Cooper has no right to lock me up."

"Why did you ask me to recall the story?" Byron asked.

"I don't even know Luke Thomas."

"Why is a police sergeant arresting you for his murder?"

I took a deep breath. There was no more avoiding it. I had to start from the beginning, build my explanation brick by brick, so he could understand.

"I'm mixed up in something. I didn't mean to be," I began, staring at his pet bird. "Please, don't judge me too harshly."

I started with the night after the Steely-Eyed Detective story, sparing only the most painful details, but divulging my relationship with Bram, explaining his strange, hypnotic way of speaking and drawing me into his yurt. I told him about the pen, about my fight to understand why I even tried it in the first place. I explained the intoxicating feeling of seeing reality conform to my stories, the luxurious comfort of the accompanying success with the paper. I told him about my writing sessions with Bram and about the crushing weight of expectation that came with each new edition. I told him about the magical dependency triggered by my repeat experiences with the pen.

Having it all out was very cathartic. Byron nodded here and there, urging me forward, and as he listened, I could feel a significant weight come off my shoulders. It was a wonderful feeling, being bonded to the man I would marry, knowing that he cared about me enough to listen and yolk himself to my burdens.

"When I confronted Bram about my illness, I was seduced into writing a final story. I don't know how. I don't even remember writing so many of its details, details I had been careful in every other instance to leave out. When I learned what had happened, I ran here to beg you not to print it."

"So, the magical pen allowed you to know details that would have otherwise been hidden to you about Mr. Thomas' death," Byron said, knitting his eyebrows.

"Yes."

"But, I didn't print the story. Why is Sergeant Cooper so interested in arresting you?"

"After I wrote the stories with Bram, I would go to the police station just to ensure they had, indeed, come to pass. When I went to the station the other morning, news of the suicide broke harshly."

"Why?" Byron asked. "I'm sure the police have dealt with more gruesome stuff than that. Not to say it isn't terrible, but—"

"Because Luke Thomas is the father of the Steely-Eyed Detective," I confessed. Tears bubbled in my throat. I tried to swallow them down.

Byron's eyes went wide. He nodded absentmindedly as if he was finally connecting some dots.

"I was there when they told him, and it affected me because I felt terrible for the man, but also because I felt as though I had caused it to happen."

Byron stood up and walked to the window, studying something outside. He fingered his pipe, the way he often did when deep in thought. The following silence was agonizing. I wanted him to believe me, but I knew what I was asking. It had taken me so long to embrace the truth about the pen, and I had experienced its effects firsthand. As Byron sat there pondering, looking out the window, Rebecca's words pecked at me.

He won't believe you. You need to pack a bag and run.

"My poor, dear Luella," he said, without turning to me. "What is it you would like me to do?"

"Save me, Byron," I begged. I crossed to him, took his hands, and knelt. "Save the woman who would be your wife. Go to Cooper, tell him that his suspicions are unfounded. Provide an alibi if you have to."

Byron looked down at me with weary eyes. I could see that my story had pained him in excruciating ways. It couldn't have been easy for him to hear about my rendezvous with other men. The skylark sang on in its cage, oblivious.

"Byron," I said. "We are getting married next week. Now you know my every secret. I am so sorry for the pain I've caused you. Let's put it behind us. I am yours. Believe me I am yours. Nothing needs to prevent our union and all the happiness that awaits us on the other side."

It was almost true, too. There were still more secrets, secrets about Edward, about my affection for him, but those would never surface. I could never let them surface again.

He helped me up to my feet and kissed my cheek gently.

"Leave everything to me," he said, glassy-eyed and broken-voiced. "I will take care of this."

"Oh, Byron. How could I ever deserve you? You are a saint. I will spend my entire life repaying you for your charity time and time again. What shall I do? Tell me and I will obey."

"You run home for now and just wait for my word," he said, grabbing his coat and heading out the door to fix my problems for the second time in twenty-four hours. Knights didn't always wear armor. Some had gray temples and a mean way with a typewriter.

"Very well, I'll wait for you there," I said.

Right before he vanished out the front door, he turned back to me. The front lobby and work area of Langley's stretched between us, our little haven from the world.

"I love you, Luella," he said. I looked at the floor.

"I'll never know why, but I am so grateful for it."

He smiled weakly and headed out the door.

Chapter Thirty

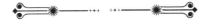

Et tu, Byron

I paced back and forth in my kitchen, trying my best not to think about Byron and Cooper. Part of me thought it was a fool's hope, but the other half believed there was much Byron could do to dissuade Cooper's intent. He could vouch for my character. He could call on a gentlemanly code that men seem to have with one another. He could lie and provide an alibi, saying we were together the night of Mr. Thomas' death. I had to have faith in Byron's resourcefulness. He was my only hope.

He could come up with something. He had already, so many times, come to my rescue. How could I ever forget the chance he took on me as a writer or when he asked for my hand, in spite of my advanced age, a charming characteristic of mine that would have who-knows-what effect on our ability to bear children? All he had ever asked from me was my returned devotion, and I had withheld it from him with firm resolve. If anyone had ever loved me, surely it was this man. Time had taught me I could trust his adoration. Mrs. Crow had been right.

I wrung my hands, turning again to look out my window. I was a ball of nerves, continually reminding myself to draw strength in my union with my betrothed. Nerves yes, but they were nerves like watching someone attempt a daring feat. I was confident he could accomplish the task and reveled in his attempt, even if my breath caught in my throat.

I heard a gentle knock on the door. Was it time already? Had he made it back so soon?

I rushed to the door and swung it open.

"Any news?" asked Mrs. Crow. She was dressed in her Sunday best and clutched a beautiful violet purse.

"Oh, Mrs. Crow," I said, letting out a big breath. "I thought you might be Byron. But, you're all dressed up. Are you going somewhere?"

She blushed but held her head up a little higher. For the first time, I saw the beauty of her younger years, borne with a polished grace and hidden beneath the effects of age.

"I didn't know how else to show my support," she explained. The thought touched me. It was a useless effort, after all. Mrs. Crow's appearance would make no difference in my desired outcome, yet the gesture bolstered my nerve the same. At the very least, I had a courageous, radiant, and wise woman by my side. That had to count for something.

"Thank you," I replied. "Look at us worrying like this. It's quite out of hand now, isn't it?"

"Out of our hands, yes," she said. We waited, stewing in the awkward silence. I offered her some tea, and we made very little conversation.

"I apologize I don't have any more to offer," I said, lifting the cloth on our breadbasket to find stale crumbs. "Anna usually picks up something from Mrs. Barker's, but I guess she didn't before she left." I laughed uncomfortably. Mrs. Crow did her best to reciprocate with a grim smile.

"You haven't told Mrs. Barker about all this, have you?" I asked. I knew it was audacious of me to ask, and I didn't really expect a truthful answer.

"I thought we'd keep this one in the family," Mrs. Crow responded.

Bam. Bam. Bam.

Pounding on the door broke us out of our sparse conversation with a start. With a final squeeze of the hands, I walked to the door and opened it.

Rebecca flew past me like a thunderbolt. She had changed out of her nightgown into walking clothes, but she still bore signs of little sleep. Before I knew it, she had a large sack on the table and was unpacking worn pieces of men's clothing.

"Rebecca—"

"Put this on, quickly," she said, shoving a pair of trousers in my face.

"Don't be ridiculous," I objected.

"Luella, do not interrupt. We have very little time. Cooper is on his way here right now. You need to disguise yourself and leave through the back of the building."

Byron had failed then. My old warhorse couldn't get it done.

"You're wrong," I protested. I wanted to reject what she said. "Byron is going to the station to speak on my behalf. He should be speaking with Cooper right now."

"Byron betrayed you."

I felt the floor give out beneath me.

"You're lying."

"I heard it myself through Cooper's door. He told the Sergeant you have lost your senses and recommended your incarceration in an asylum."

The dizzying nausea. The spinning room. The swelling anger. My familiar demon warming the bellows inside of me.

"Don't slip away from me!" Rebecca said, grabbing hold of my shoulders. "Don't let this beat you. Not like at Doug's. You need to focus now and feel later."

I looked at her, feeling so helpless, but there in her eyes blazed energy and loyalty. Her face was close. I could not see anything else. I could hear nothing save the creaking of the building under the winter sun and horses' hooves outside. Rebecca's eyes went wide. She dashed to the window and craned her eyes to see down the street.

"Put on these clothes, now!" Her voice left no room for negotiation.

"Mrs. Crow, you led Luella astray," Rebecca said.

"I'm a stupid old woman," Mrs. Crow said. I glanced at her between donning pant legs. Her youthful vitality from before was gone without a trace. She gaped out the window stupidly, tears streaming down her face. I recognized the sagging of her shoulders. I, too, knew the bitter sting of guilt.

"There's time for that later," my friend continued. "You have a chance to make up for it now. Go to the front door and follow instructions when you're there."

Mrs. Crow's mouth fell open, but she swallowed her questions and left out the door. Rebecca threw more clothes at me. A workman's shirt. A waistcoat. A long coat. A top hat. I did my best to keep up.

"Now this," Rebecca said, handing me a fake mustache.

"Really, this is too much," I muttered, fumbling to change out of my skirts and pull the shirt over me.

"You've impersonated a man for years on paper. Are you going to shrink now that it's time to test your mettle?"

"I'll never change in time. They'll be bursting through the door any minute."

"Not if Doug has anything to do with it," Rebecca said, holding open the vest.

"Doug?" I gasped. Suddenly, outside, I heard muffled yells.

"I'm not moving at all until Luella Winthrop comes out here and returns my love!" Doug's booming voice shouted. I nearly froze on the spot.

"What is he talking about?" I whispered.

"Stop asking questions and move!" Rebecca hissed.

"I don't care who you are. You could be ruddy Queen Victoria. I know my heart, and it wants that woman." He was positively roaring.

"Get out of the way, man, in the name of the law!" That was Sergeant Cooper. I'd recognize him anywhere.

"Luella! There you are!"

"Oh, Scott!" I heard Mrs. Crow's crackling voice cry back dramatically in a heavy Yorkshire accent. "How can you show your face after what you did to me?"

"Now follow me," Rebecca whispered. I looked like a stock broker when it was all done. I caught the briefest of glances in the looking glass as I moved past it. I made a terrible man. I didn't think my mustache would fool anybody, let alone a police sergeant.

She cracked the door open, and we crept into the hallway, closing it silently behind us. Through the cracked front door, I could see Doug's massive form blocking entrance to the building.

"Forgive me, Luella!" Doug recited.

"How can I?" Mrs. Crow replied.

We tiptoed up the stairs and on to the second floor.

"They'll see us straightaway up here if they enter the building," I whispered.

"Move aside, man!" Cooper barked outside. "This is not Luella Winthrop!"

"You've been lying to me about your name?" Doug gasped in fake abhorrence.

"It's true, Scott. I'm sorry. Me name's Ruby."

"And you have the nerve to ask me for an apology!"

"Move!" Cooper shouted. Then a great scuffling of feet and commotion followed.

Rebecca beckoned me to the back wall, where a large window looked over a single-story building and courtyard below.

"You're mad," I whispered, but before I could protest with a substitute plan, she had opened the window and hopped out, sidling down the back by means of a pipe and woody climbing vines. I felt significantly more agile in the borrowed trousers, and if Rebecca could do it, so could I. I sidled out the window, grabbed hold of the pipe, and lowered myself to the ground with great effort. We were out of the building now, but arguably closer to Cooper and his officers.

Through the window above us, I could hear the police shout between each other.

"There's nothin' here, sir!"

"Just some skirts, still warm."

"A kettle is still on heat, too!"

Rebecca put her arm in mine, as if she were my wife or relative.

"Walk that direction," she said, pointing away from my apartment toward some alleyways between the buildings behind my building. I obeyed, my heart pounding. I tried to control my breathing, but the excitement, the exertion from climbing down the building, and our rapid pace soon had me out of breath.

"Take a right," Rebecca said.

"Rebecca," I said, "what have you done? If they see you with me—"

"They won't. A right, now."

The shouts had grown fainter, but I heard the sound of horses' hooves on the road coming in our direction.

"They're coming," I whispered.

"Take a left," she insisted. It was madness. I followed her instructions, but as I turned down the side road she indicated, I could hear horses' hooves getting louder. It sounded like we were heading right toward them. The brick buildings around me felt like they were caving in, the cobblestones kicked up at my feet. I could see our path ahead down a narrow alleyway. It looked like the alleyway from my dream about the fog all that time ago. We walked faster, but I saw a police officer atop his workhorse cross the opening in front of us.

Rebecca saw it and cursed under her breath. I started trying service doors in the alleyway as we saw a police wagon roll by. They would undoubtedly see us before long.

I tried a handle. Locked. I tried another. Locked again. We tried door after door to no success, and we were fast running out of alleyway.

Ahead of us, a policeman walked across the alley's opening and turned to look directly our way. Rebecca instinctively hid her face under her bonnet. I nonchalantly tried to turn us around to walk back the way we came.

"Oy! You there!" the copper called. I pretended not to hear, maintaining a brisk but unhurried pace, but I heard his footsteps start down the alleyway toward us, pumping faster.

My pulse quickened again, adrenaline surging through me. The alleyway was suffocating. Everywhere I looked was brick and mortar. They would soon fall and crush me, a tidal wave of reality.

"Excuse me, sir!" the officer called again.

I ignored him still. We were almost to the opening where we had entered. At least then we'd have an opportunity to make a break for it and hide.

The thought perished with the view of two more officers talking to each other near the outside of the opening. We were trapped.

I scanned the walls for a side street or an open window, but I could find nothing, just more locked doors. If I attempted any of them, it would give us away immediately.

Suddenly, one of the doors burst open, and I was absolutely astounded to see Mr. Barker walk out with a large bag of moldy bread. We were just on the other side of the bakery! How had I not noticed? I was familiar with this area. I had walked the streets on the other side of the building so many times. Mr. Barker gave me a curt nod, but I made my way through the door without a word.

"Hey, what do you think you're—" he started. I ripped off my fake mustache, shielded from the officer's view on the other side of the open door.

"Mr. Barker, it's Luella," I said, holding a finger to my lips. He dropped the bag of bread in surprise.

"Luella?" He gaped.

"I'm very sorry about this. I'll explain later." I closed the door and locked it, sealing him outside. He started banging on it immediately and demanded to be let in. Mrs. Barker was hard at work on her butcher's block kneading a large pile of dough. She toweled off her hands and made her way toward us.

"I'm coming! Don't need to be in such a fuss, George." She nearly bumped into us, letting out a stifled scream, surprised at the appearance of a strange looking couple in the back of her bakery instead of her husband. But, she recognized me in a moment.

"Luella, why in heaven's name are you dressed like that?" she asked.

"Ask Mrs. Crow. She can explain everything."

We bounded out the front door on to a police-free street. We ran across and slipped into another alleyway, hiding behind a tower of wooden crates. We held our breath and watched as the officer burst out the bakery door and turned left and right searching the street. After some deliberation, he headed north.

I bent over and tried to catch my breath, but Rebecca pushed me on.

"We can't stay here," she said, grabbing me by the wrist and pulling me upright. I watched as she led me down the alley, poked her head out to examine a new street, and then hurried us along, ever the happy couple. "Put your mustache back on," she said. I tried to acquiesce, but the adhesive was failing. I held it up with my hand.

My mind raced, trying to discover where, if anywhere in Dawnhurst, would be safe for me. I figured I would have to get to the east side at least, where I knew so many little places I could hide away. But then, the police force might know the east side even better than I did. There had to be somewhere on the west. Perhaps over by the clock tower, or I had heard that some churches allow a type of sanctuary. The thought of going to my parents' wedding altar in my shame made me taste bile.

We meandered through side streets and lesser traveled roads until we were close to the west bank of the river, looking out onto a large open square, bordered by large trees and the riverfront on one side and large, waterfront residential apartment buildings on the other. The square was alive with morning traffic, including fishmongers hawking wares, ferry captains directing the loading or unloading of their vessels, a grocer's stand trying to unload the last of his fall wares, and a few of the city's police force. Whether these officers were part of the womanhunt, it was impossible to say.

Rebecca pulled me under one of the trees and took my hands.

"I've arranged for your travel out of the city," she said. "There's a stage coach just on the other side of the square to take you to the country."

Out of the city! I'd never considered it. I'd never been out of the city before. This was my home, my father's home.

"You're not coming?"

"It would raise suspicion, and Cooper doesn't know I've helped you escape. I will be fine here. It's better that you go on alone."

"What will I do?" I couldn't show her that leaving the city made me almost as afraid as facing the police.

"Start a new life. Lie low. You may want to live by a new identity for a while," she suggested.

"How can I ever thank you?" I asked. I felt naked, ridiculous dressed as a man, and completely indebted to my friend for it.

"Don't get caught."

"Rebecca," I searched for words. There were so many questions I wanted to ask her, but one rose like a clamor to my lips louder than any other. "Why?"

She hesitated, ready to push me forward, but my reticence dragged an answer from her.

"You remind me of my sister."

"You never told me you have a sister."

"I don't anymore," she smiled sadly. My heart reeled with the recent loss of my own sister.

"What happened to her?"

"One day perhaps I'll tell you, when you can afford to think less of me. Now go. Walk to the stagecoach there on the south side next to the flower cart, get in, and hit the ceiling in the carriage twice."

I didn't understand, but it was clear that was all she was prepared to tell me, and time was not on our side. She hugged me once and gave me a deep, lingering look. Her eyes were filled with encouragement and love bridled by the affected street smarts older siblings hold out having. Then she turned and disappeared around a corner.

I looked across the square, where a stagecoach lie in wait to take me away from Dawnhurst-on-Severn for the first time. I had failed the city. I had failed my father, the man who took it upon himself to look after all who knew him, who had paid for my education with his own health. I'm sorry, father.

I took a deep breath. Rebecca had gotten me this far. I could go the rest.

I stepped into the square, doing my best to look casual while still keeping a watchful eye on the officers chatting near a chestnut roaster. I felt out of place and awkward. I looked ridiculous in these clothes. I couldn't walk like a man. How does a man walk?

Halfway there. I choked down my relief. It wasn't time to celebrate yet.

A fish vendor shouted at me. I gave a polite nod back, not hearing the words coming out of his mouth. I could see the coach now. It must have cost Rebecca a good portion of her weekly income. Four horses stood in front, bridled to each other. The driver sat cross-legged atop it, reading a newspaper.

I dodged around a group of men coiling ropes and hoisting heavy wooden boxes. I was almost to the coach. I was almost free. I turned to see the police officers. They hadn't moved. I smiled with relief. I had a straight shot now, hidden safely behind the grocer's stand. The police wouldn't see me now. I could start a new life. Perhaps one day I could even reunite with Anna, once I'd re-established myself. I was used to living under a fake name. I could work in a mill or as a seamstress. I could put writing away, put it all behind me.

The coach shone bright with renewal, beckoning to a longing inside of me I never knew was there. I could be done with the constant, hard competition of the Dawnhurst print industry. I could love a quiet life.

I put a foot on the step of the carriage when a hand grabbed my elbow forcibly. I looked down in terror at a police glove.

"Mr. Blakely, you do make a funny looking man."

Edward Thomas, dressed in full uniform, pushed me into the carriage, following right after me.

Chapter Thirty-One

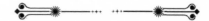

The Steely-Eyed Detective

I sat in the carriage across from Edward, feeling very afraid and very stupid. Sweat clung to me in uncomfortable places. I tried hard to steady my breathing. There was no telling what Cooper had told him or what he believed.

He studied me calmly, but his features betrayed the confusion at work behind his practiced demeanor. This was the face, I was sure, that had unraveled so many criminals under questioning. I wished he would say something, yell or scream at me, hit me if he had to. I felt the weight of his father's tragedy suffocate me, like our carriage was running out of air. The silence, heavy as a millstone, stretched on for what felt like hours, but my heart rate did not slow.

"Do you have anything you want to tell me?" he finally asked. Couldn't he have just arrested me? The question told all. Cooper must have clued him into his suspicions about my involvement in his father's death. There was little I could do now to explain; I was sure of it. If only I had confessed everything to him before he had heard an alternate version of the story from someone else.

"You wouldn't believe any of it," I said, peeling off my stupid, false mustache. I was even disguised. The guilty run, so they say. Perhaps the guiltiest run in costume. I loosened the tie around my neck and buried my eyes in my own lap. Looking at him was so painful. He must think me the wretch of the earth.

I felt his hand on my chin, firmly lifting my face toward his.

"Try me."

"What did Cooper tell you?" I asked, the shame building. I couldn't stop inventing details that the old sergeant must have fabricated in order to secure my arrest or thinking about the atrocious things I would rather go through than explain that I inadvertently killed Edward's father.

"Nothing of consequence. Just that the beautiful woman that has been inhabiting my thoughts for months is likely involved in my father's financial scandal and subsequent suicide." He said it so nonchalantly that I almost missed the grimace between words. Yes, probing a little deeper under the surface, it wasn't hard to see his significant stress and deep pain. His jaw clenched in what I assumed was an attempt to curb his emotions.

"I can't imagine what you must think," I choked out.

"I think that Cooper's accusations were absolutely ridiculous," he said. "I was ready to dismiss them entirely, until I heard what Rebecca had to say."

"You spoke with Rebecca?" A painful lump caught in my throat. My mind was arrested by a bizarre, slow panic. Had Rebecca betrayed my confidence and revealed to Edward what I had so adamantly decided to hide from him?

"I did. She sounded even crazier than Cooper," he said. "And now, I don't know what to believe. I would have sworn that it was impossible that you had anything to do with my father's death. But, two of my closest colleagues have approached me, unprovoked, either to accuse or excuse you. So, forgive my abrupt manner of speaking, but do you have anything you wish to tell me?"

"I wanted to tell you so badly," I said, warm tears pooling in my eyes. I was wondering when they were going to surface. Crying had become a daily reality. "You have to believe me. I had no malicious intent toward your father. I've never wanted to hurt you in any way.

You must know that."

"You don't deny your involvement then?" he asked with wide eyes.

"Had I been in my faculties, or otherwise in control of my senses, I could deny it in full conscience."

"And yet?"

I searched for reasoning, an excuse, anything that could help make him understand. But, there was nothing available to me. I had played my hand so strategically, with such devious gamesmanship that I now found myself where all cons and tricksters end up. I was adrift, with no defenses, destined to weather whatever storm assailed me. I couldn't lie to Edward if I wanted to. Not only would it break my heart, but he had me out by two witnesses.

I was a fugitive disguised as a man, escaping from the law, skulking away like a sneaking fox, now caught by the tail and hung out for inspection. My hands trembled.

Edward grabbed and steadied them.

"I don't understand," he said. "You have entrusted me with your other secrets, with friendship even. Was it all a means of getting to my father?"

"I didn't even know who your father was until you told me at our lunch."

"Then what the devil is going on?" He looked desperate, confused. "Please, Luella. I've lost my father inexplicably and without warning. He was accused of a crime that was leagues beside his character, and I'm left with no answers. The way you're evading my questions leads me to no other conclusion save that you were somehow implicated in this rotten business. Whose story is true? Rebecca's or the Sergeant's?"

I mustered my courage. If I were to lose everything, I could at least decide now to maintain my integrity. What was the point of hiding it? I took off the oversized coat Rebecca had provided and pulled off the vest as well, leaving me intimately vulnerable in just a work shirt. I wanted Edward to hear this from Luella Winthrop. I knelt in front of him awkwardly in the small space and looked up into his face in supplication.

"Rebecca's," I said. "Though I don't know what details she included. Cooper's suspicion that I was an accomplice to a murder, or otherwise participated in the financial scandal that ruined your father, could not be further from the truth. The honest truth, which you may believe or not, is that I tangled with forces beyond my understanding and inadvertently, though not without culpability, set off a chain of events that ruined an honest and good man. I am so sorry."

"I don't understand. Forces beyond your control?"

"Magic. I met a man in a carnival, and he taught me to use magic."

"You mean to say that magic killed my father?"

I hung my head and nodded. Edward's face flushed. He leaned back in his seat and released my hands, looking out the small window of the carriage at the square outside with its handful of police officers. I tried to follow his gaze. I wouldn't fight. They could take me quietly.

Absent-mindedly, he fiddled with a ring on his finger, taking it off and putting it on. His jaw was clenched tight. I stayed on my knees, darting my gaze to the seat, the floor, his boots, anywhere but into his face.

I think what hurt the most was knowing that it all could have been different, that instead of arresting me, he might have married me, if I had just the courage to leave Byron and the humility to stay away from Bram.

Without warning, Edward lifted his arm and delivered two sharp blows to the roof of the carriage.

"Hiyah!" I heard the driver cry accompanied by the whip of the reigns. The coach jolted forward, and I watched the world outside pass by like sheets off a printing press. The police in the square shrunk and soon vanished from view, obscured by buildings. I felt the bumps of the road reverberate up through my knees, gravity pulling my torso awkwardly this way and that.

"You knew the signal for Rebecca's driver," I wondered aloud.

"My driver," he said. He continued to stare out the window. "This is my carriage after all."

"Your carriage? What are you talking about? Where are we going?"

"We're leaving the city. I'm taking you to my home in the country, a day's ride away."

"I've never left the city," I stammered, watching as we passed streets I knew so well. These streets used to feel so safe and familiar to me. Now, I feared someone would see me in the passing window and signal Cooper. "Why would you take me there?"

"I need to get you away from Cooper," he said. "He is convinced that you have acted with my father's competitors in a plot for financial gain. I cannot dissuade him from the idea. He says that I've been blinded by—well, by everything going on."

I wiped my eyes, blinked blankly, and clumsily retook my seat across from him. Edward was rescuing me. After everything, he was rescuing me.

"I've sent a message ahead to my mother," he continued. "She is expecting us there."

"Edward," I whispered.

"We can stay there for as long as needed to sort everything out."

"Edward."

"I think it's time I took a break from police work, anyway. At least until everything with my father is settled."

"Edward."

He exhaled loudly and finally turned his head to look at me. "What is it?"

"Do you believe me?"

He chewed on his thoughts before sharing them. "I don't believe Cooper. And, I don't believe you could be a criminal. I could very well be blind, as the Sergeant said, but I can think of nothing more contrary to nature than a vision of you scheming and colluding to ruin or kill Luke Thomas."

"I will explain anything you ask to the best of my ability," I replied.

"There will be plenty of time for that when we're both in a better state of mind. For now, I'm trying to satisfy myself with what you said, that you've never harbored any malicious intention toward my father."

I kissed the palms of his hands and let my tears run. I squeezed them in mine and felt regret overcome me, regret for every choice I'd ever made that had separated me from him. There, in that moving carriage, he did not reciprocate any of my affections, but he did not pull his hands away from me.

"I'm so sorry," I said. "I've lost control of everything." I wrung my hands incessantly. I felt so restless, uneasy. I looked out the window to distract myself from crying again. We were in a part of the city now that was unfamiliar to me, on the far north side. Soon, we would be past its most outer buildings, into agricultural land, and then off to a new, foreign world. I watched the world I'd known my entire life disappear, clattering along the cobbles.

"I heard that you were to be married next week," Edward said tenderly.

I coughed out a laugh in spite of the painful knot in my throat. I couldn't help it. The thought now was so absurd it couldn't be believed.

"We had the church scheduled," I said. "I guess the wedding is off." I hadn't thought about Byron. Rebecca had forbidden it. It was time to act, not to feel. Time to act. Her words had given me the strength to ward off the terrible anger inside of me. I clung to them still. Thinking of Byron kicked up the embers.

"I hope not to offend any feelings you may have toward your fiancé if I can offer you my support," he said.

"Rebecca said he recommended me for an asylum." Time to act, not to feel.

"Forgive me, but a man who treats his wife-to-be that way can, in my opinion, hardly deserve her."

I laughed again, darkly. I couldn't believe what I was hearing.

"He was more than I deserved."

"A man like that? He measures very low on my ledger."

"Even so. After hearing my explanation, is an asylum not unreasonable?" I asked. My emotions swelled, and I fought to push them down and shut them up. I was afraid to unstopper whatever foul brew was concocting inside of me in response to Byron's betrayal.

Edward scrutinized me, trying to decipher my words and fit them into the great puzzle before him. He shook his head.

"I'm afraid we were unable to collect your things," he said. "I'm not certain we'll be able to retrieve them anytime soon, either. Cooper will certainly have your flat watched in case you return."

This wasn't excellent news, considering my only outfit was the men's clothes on my back, but what could I feel but gratitude at being snatched out of the hunter's snare? Did I have the sense to grab anything during our flight? I couldn't remember.

I patted my pockets and discovered, with great relief, a crumpled version of Anna's letter.

"What is that?" Edward nodded his head to the paper.

"It's from my sister, Anna," I said. "She has just gone off to stay with her fiancé's family in the country." I clutched the paper desperately, trying to feel my sister's presence through it. In many ways, I was glad she hadn't been around for what just happened.

"Congratulations," he replied. "You must be very happy for her."

I nodded, choking back fresh emotion. Time to act.

I patted my other pockets and, to my surprise, felt a strange lump in my right trouser pocket. I reached inside and pulled out a small crimson inkwell.

The sight of it sent a jolt of electricity through me. I stared out the window to hide the feelings on my face. I couldn't identify the emotion. Fear? Panic?

We were out of the city now. I craned my head to catch a final glimpse of the familiar clock tower before it faded away. The sound of the wheels on cobblestones had softened to the crunch of gravel roads then to the muffled sound of earth. Green and yellow patched meadows, preparing themselves for winter dormancy, spread out before us like a dream, spotted with occasional ponds and great willow trees. We passed a fieldstone wall, and everything that I had known was behind me. Unbidden memories of my father flashed through my mind. This had been his home and his resting place. He married my mother here. He spent his life here, and I had made a mess of his city.

I'd make it right somehow, Papa. The Golden Inkwell was out of the question, but at the very least, I'd clear our name and go home. I just needed time.

We rounded a large bend, and I was ambushed by a final panoramic view of my home from across a river. It shrunk smaller and smaller until we entered a wood. Then, it vanished from my view entirely, replaced with dappled shade and wild nature. Shafts of light stole through the trees, and the wood stretched out before me, staggeringly exponential until the very edge of my vision and beyond. One might vanish among those trees and never come out again. One might become a tree themselves if they didn't have their heads about them.

At some point, my adrenaline dumped off. Exhaustion, exertion, and the gentle rocking of the carriage lulled me to a heavy, dreamless sleep.

Chapter Thirty-Two

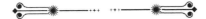

Fernmount

I woke to the sight of Edward, peacefully looking out the carriage window, an angel in uniform. He had unbuttoned his jacket and rested his face on his hand, which I noted still had the scrapes from his sparring match with Big Bill yesterday.

We were now navigating hills covered by vast lawns and fading heather. I blinked and rubbed my eyes. I had read about places like these in my favorite stories, but I had never had the opportunity to see them in person. My whole life was wrapped up in work and toil. I inherited that life when my parents passed. Even as a governess, I was never taken along on holiday.

"How long was I asleep?"

"Several hours," Edward said. "You had quite the morning."

I stretched my limbs under my clothes, remembering that I was dressed in trousers and shirt still. "Where are we?"

"Near Dursley. By now, I think it's safe to say we haven't been followed. I imagine you could use a stop for some refreshment."

"Thank you," I said, my stomach growling. I couldn't remember the last time I ate. There was nothing that morning, and the evening before had been eclipsed by my episode at the station and the following events. Did I eat anything at Doug's the day before?

"We'll see what we can do about some clothes as well. Nothing raises suspicion like a traveling woman dressed as a man."

I blushed and nodded. "Of course, I'm all a mess."

"On the contrary. You are quite becoming," he said. "That's not to say—I mean—I think only of your comfort."

"Of course."

The conversation lapsed, and we sat quietly as the carriage made its way into Dursley. Edward made some clumsy inquiries about size and style of clothes I might prefer. To his relief, I asked for a piece of paper and pencil, leaving specific instructions for whatever shop keep waited on him, then waited for him in the carriage, trying to remember the last time I had purchased a new dress, tailored to my size. I hoped that I would fit into whatever Edward brought back. I couldn't recall the last time I wrote down my size for someone.

Before long, he returned with a very sensible skirt, a jacket, and a blouse only moderately decorated with frill. He passed the parcel into the carriage and waited for me outside while I changed. I breathed a sigh of relief when the buttons closed comfortably. The whole situation felt less alien to me now that I was back in a more familiar set of clothes.

I tucked my sister's letter and Bram's inkwell into an attractive leather wallet (an accessory I certainly had not expected Edward to see to) and exited the carriage and presented myself. Edward approved with a blushing nod. He discreetly put another large box on top of the coach before leading me down the quaint road we were on, lined with planter boxes filled with flowering chrysanthemums. Scattered local residents milled about the street, wrapped in warm, albeit courser, material than one might see in Dawnhurst. They smiled at us warmly. The afternoon sun still hung brightly above the tree line.

"What was that package?" I asked.

"I'll explain later," he replied. "Here we are. We shouldn't stay long, but it's my turn to surprise you with a restaurant." He led me into a local tavern, The Walnut Hearth, and we dined on a humble but delicious vegetable pie and salted pork. We spoke carefully, with just a few staggered sentences here and there, mostly about the logistics of the escape or possible strategies of keeping me safely away from Cooper's jurisdiction.

"The police aren't a unified national force," he explained. "In fact, there is a great sense of rivalry between certain cities. If we can convince my local force of your innocence, perhaps even at the scorn of Sergeant Cooper, I think we could get them to support your cause with their indifference."

"And how might we do that?" My plate had been devoured, devoid even of any crumbs. Now, with some food in my belly, I was feeling more and more like myself. I could think more clearly and more easily committed to Rebecca's advice to put my emotion on hold.

"If a member of Cooper's police force were to suggest that the case had no merit," Edward said grimly. I winced.

"You mean if you put your reputation on the line for me," I said. He downed the rest of his mug.

"If my father really died by magic, then I'd be doing old Cooper a favor, now wouldn't I? Without hard facts, he'd be eaten alive in court. It's best that he cools down and lets the investigation reveal that there is no evidence supporting your conviction."

"Still, it's a little bit risky, isn't it?" I asked. I winced as I thought of the only incriminating evidence there was, an unprinted edition of Langley's and an embittered witness testifying I begged him not to print it. "Instead of just hiding me away discreetly, we gamble by getting another local police force involved, hoping they see our side of things."

"It is risky, but I'm confident we can get them to side with us," he said firmly. I took a deep breath and sighed. I had to trust him. He hadn't yet let me down.

Of course, neither had Byron, until he did. Now that my energy back, the angry energy inside of me had woken up as well. Byron's name triggered something. I swallowed hard and tried to fight it.

"I trust you," I said, clenching a hand under the table to stop my twitching fingers. I looked at Edward. His face was resolute and dedicated. He looked back at me, and his gray eyes locked with mine. My heart warmed my whole body. I felt the budding anger dissipate, replaced by something else, something lovely.

"We should probably resume our travels," Edward said. I nodded, and the moment was over. I couldn't let myself get carried away. Edward had just lost his father. I had just escaped arrest and lost all contact with my sister. I pushed away from the table, and we made our exit back to the carriage.

We swept out of the city, the driver making a more furious pace than before, eager to achieve our destination before nightfall. The food had made me drowsy, and the rocking of the carriage over gravel and soft earth almost overcame me. I slipped into a weird half-sleep. Edward kept to himself, reviewing some papers by the light coming through the window. The white noise outside settled in heavily, and the occasional whip of the driver sounded like a violent violation of the atmosphere.

Soon, we crested a large hill and a large, wild looking vista spilled across my view. Untamed woods stretched across the earth in amorphous patterns, surrounding a little hamlet on the shore of a lake. The sun was retreating quickly behind a shallow hill on the horizon, but it reflected brilliantly off the lake's surface. I had never seen such a picturesque expanse.

"Quite a view," Edward said, noting my admiration.

"What is this place?"

"That is Houndstone Town." He pointed casually at the hamlet. "It's the only town on Greenlake there. Beyond it just a ways, we'll see Fernmount House, my not so ancestral home."

"You grew up here?"

He nodded tersely without looking at me. I couldn't tell if he was pleased to see it or not. I wondered what memories laid in wait for him here. To me, it looked like a poem, but I remembered what he had said a long time ago about his father wishing he had taken up the family profession. Perhaps to him, the town was a prison. A delightful, picturesque, beautiful prison where he was rich and powerful.

"Did your parents live apart?" I asked as gently as I could. "It's just that I realize your father worked in town."

"My father was a banker. He used to spend considerable time working away from his family." A shade passed over his brow. "After finding a measure of success with his profession, he devoted more time to the upkeep of Fernmount and his other hobbies, spending a week here and there in the city only when certain affairs required his attention."

"Other hobbies?" I asked.

"Whatever it is rich men do with their time. I'm not sure he knew what his hobbies were either. I suspect they weren't hobbies at all, but a means of connecting himself with a certain social layer of society. It was a means of working on his career while staying at home, with my mother believing he was just happy to live a quiet life." He shook his head.

"You disapprove," I surmised.

"He spent his life earning and multiplying his money. Now he's gone. I guess we will see if his accounts can settle his debts to my mother." I must have looked confused because he went on to clarify. "When my father's business began to prosper, he purchased Fernmount. I was just a child, but my mother told me he purchased it from a noble family who had lost everything. They didn't want to sell, but my father bought them out at a price they couldn't refuse."

"Did you always live in Houndstone?"

"My father grew up in Hillborough. Houndstone and Fernmount were a dream for him. Something he worked for relentlessly. I always considered his time away from my mother and me a lot like the house we lived in. The family didn't want to sell it, but he bought it anyway. Neglect is very expensive."

The setting sun cast dense shadows across his face, outlining the bruises and cuts from his sparring at the station. Occasionally, he would twitch or touch his face gingerly with his fingers. The carriage came to the bottom of the hill swiftly. We took a fork to the right and traveled through country until the sun had dipped below the horizon and darkness descended slow and steady.

I'll never forget the first time I saw Fernmount House. Six-foot walls surrounded the border of the property, disappearing into dark foliage. Beyond, partially visible through an elaborate iron gate, a large stately mansion made of stone and brick stood over a beautiful courtyard, crisscrossed with holly and boxwood hedges and white gravel paths. Rows of lit, dressed windows dotted across the facade of the estate, divided by a large set of double doors recessed in a sweeping archway entry. Stone sculptures guarded the entryway on either side, a dog and a lion made after what I predicted was a Celtic fashion. I couldn't help but marvel as the carriage made its way through the iron gate and into the courtyard.

"Welcome to Fernmount," Edward said. My breath caught in my throat.

Several dressed servants stood outside as we rolled to a stop. Edward swung the door open and hopped out, before offering me a hand to help me down. As I stepped out of the carriage, I saw a woman dressed in a beautiful black gown made of silk, her hair pulled back into a braided bun. This could only be Edward's mother. Selfish thoughts immediately flooded my mind. I was embarrassed of my modest clothes in an instant. What would this woman think of me? How could I make her like me?

She lifted her hand in the air, and Edward left me to kiss it with a deep bow. She nodded once before her face began to break. She pulled Edward into an embrace.

"Edward, I wish so badly that a more joyous occasion brought you here," she said in a weak voice. He pulled back from the embrace but held her by the shoulders affectionately.

"It is good to see you, mother. I pray you got my letter."

"Of course," she said, again assuming her formal etiquette. "Is this the girl?"

She turned her gaze on me, and I realized I had absolutely no idea how to behave. I tried to remember something about curtseying and performed one as earnestly and deeply as I could.

"I am so very sorry for your loss, Mrs.—er—Lady Thomas." I tried to sound sincere, but my sudden cognizance that I didn't even know what to call her made me sound like a brown-nosing oaf. Why hadn't Edward explained more to me? Why hadn't I asked? I had never imagined that Lieutenant Thomas would have come from such wealth. He had mentioned his father was a successful banker, but this? I was completely unprepared.

She nodded curtly to me, without bothering to correct—or clarify— which title I should have used to address her. I could have kicked Edward in the shin for not providing me with any details.

"Edward has told me that you are quite the writer," she said with a stone-like expression. I could not read any emotion, positive or negative, to indicate how she felt about the stumbling idiot her son had brought home. I was suddenly struck with fear about what Edward may have already revealed to her.

"That is kind of him," I said warily.

"It sounds like a perilous job," she continued. "You write under a pen name?"

"I do," I confessed.

"Edward said a recent story of yours has earned you some notoriety."

I nodded. It didn't seem like she knew the specifics. That was something at least.

"Well, you are welcome here," she said with a terse glance at her son. He buried his eyes in the ground. "I regret that the house will be in mourning during your stay. Tragedy has fallen on us."

I didn't know what to say. I tried my best to look supplicant.

"Rose will show you to your rooms. I'm sure you'd like to freshen up." She raised an eyebrow and looked me over on the last words "freshen up." "Don't you have any bags?"

"Unfortunately, she had to make a quick exit, and her bags could not be retrieved at present," Edward said. "She has only this." He grabbed the package he had bought earlier from the carriage. "I'll carry it up to her rooms for her."

"Very well," Mrs. or Lady Thomas said. Her face and posture were the picture of politeness, but something emanated from her that put me on edge. She had to be suspicious of my motive and my background; any good mother would be. She had just lost her husband of many years, and her son brought home a woman she'd never heard of before. As she excused herself, I couldn't shake a cold, snubbed feeling. I don't think Edward's mother liked me or that I was here this week of all weeks. This intuition spoiled any feeling of surprise that came upon learning that Edward's mystery parcel was for me. I followed Rose into the house, Edward toting the package at my side. She led us through tapestried hallways and deep mahogany woodwork framing marbled floors.

"I'm sorry about my mother," Edward said quietly. "You can imagine she isn't quite herself."

"Of course," I replied. "Still, I may like to know what you told her about my situation."

He slackened his pace a step and lowered his voice more so to escape Rose's earshot.

"Nothing about magic," he said. "My mother is deeply superstitious. She thinks magic is very real and very dark. If she heard that you had some connection with it—" He stopped himself here. I imagined he was struggling to finish the sentence in his head. I wasn't sure I wanted to know what he came up with.

This was not great news. I had really been hoping that she was a no-nonsense, the earth is solid all the way through, type of person. That way, even if the truth about my accusation came out, she would at least consider any magical involvement hogwash.

I shook my head. Even without the magic, that unpublished edition of Langley's haunted me. I had planned to lock it safely away behind my marriage with Byron. Now, there was no telling what Byron would do. I had never known him to be spiteful, but his betrayal had caught me flat-footed. I had never really known him at all.

"Very well. We will have to keep the mysterious details of my magical experience under lock and key. From her at least. To you, I will explain everything and anything, if you would like."

He carried the parcel in silence. An occasional gas lamp illuminated his ruminating features. Given the age of the house, I was surprised that gas lamps had been installed already. Edward's father must have been enterprising. I had read that young money was always eager to innovate in ways the old families never liked.

"Would you like me to explain anything?" I prodded after another moment of quiet. I needed Edward to trust me. I needed to open up to him. There was a whole part of me he didn't know, and I regretted not telling him before. I wouldn't make that mistake again. I needed him to know me completely.

"Here you are, miss," Rose said, opening the door to a richly furnished bedroom. I turned to Edward, awaiting a response. He looked uncomfortably at the floor.

"We will be having dinner shortly. You may want to change," he said, handing the parcel to Rose. He turned and retreated down the hallway, leaving me with nothing to do but follow Rose into the room.

The room was carpeted with a beautiful and bright rug, under a carved four poster bed, accompanied by intricate end tables and muslin curtains on tall windows. On the wall was a beautiful oil painting of a ship at harbor. Its attendants prepared it to embark on the sea. I had never dreamed of staying in such a lavish room.

Rose unpacked the parcel on the bed and produced a decadent green dress and crinoline. The silk sleeves were designed to drape off the shoulder, to accentuate the thin, velvet-paneled bodice. It was gorgeous. I eyed the fit dubiously. Were those the measurements I had given him?

"How will I fit in that?" I wondered aloud.

"Not to worry, miss. I can help you into your corset. I've helped Lady Thomas countless times, and you look to have a good shape about you."

So, it was Lady Thomas. I wondered how they managed to procure a title. I assumed Luke Thomas had bought one with the house.

"Thank you, Rose," I said. My sister had always been the fashion conscious between us. "I confess I haven't worn a corset much before."

"Oh," Rose said, a little bit troubled. "I'm afraid it's an acquired taste, miss. I'll make it as loose as I can this time around."

"Thank you."

"Would you like me to draw up a bath for you as well? I imagine you'd like one after such a long journey."

I blushed. "Oh, that's not necessary. I can draw up my own bath."

"Your own, miss?" She looked concerned.

"Well, I just mean I don't wish to trouble you," I said. I hadn't expected her reaction.

"I appreciate your concern, but I'm a maid of the house. I'm here to help." She performed a practiced curtsy.

"Of course," I said, regretting I'd mentioned anything.

"Bid me do, I will obey."

Her words hit me like a hammer to the chest.

"What did you say?"

"Bid me do, I will obey," she stared at me expectantly. "I'm at your disposal. Shall I draw the bath?"

Bid me do, I will obey. My mind raced back to my dream about the fog man. Or had it been a dream? The downy fog. The floating feeling. The sudden exit. Instinctively, I reached for the wallet hanging around my wrist and felt the inkwell through the fabric. It was still there next to Anna's letter.

"A bath would be fine," I replied, without looking at Rose again.

Chapter Thirty-Three

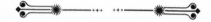

Mrs. Lady Thomas

I followed Rose through the hallways of Fernmount toward the dining room. I tried to be as graceful as I could, the green gown rustling between tapestries and portraits of what I assumed were Thomas family members or else family members of the previous owners of the house. All of the eyes in the portraits seemed to follow me, peering at me with scrutinizing expressions, each of them asking silently one to another what the city rat was doing in their home dressed like an imposter, as if she dared to belong.

I passed bedrooms, a front room, a study, each with a warm fire blazing to fight against the winter heat, but I still felt cold air on my bare shoulders and the back of my neck, giving me goosebumps. Or did the goosebumps come from the unshakeable feeling that I had not truly escaped the evil that faced me? Cooper, yes. The magic, no.

Rose's earlier utterance haunted me, the echo of the downy fog being, a letter from the space between reality and fantasy. Bid me do. It was such a peculiar syntax. Was it possible that it could have been a coincidence? I shuddered to believe there were more forces at work in Fernmount than I wanted to believe.

We turned into the lounge, where Edward waited for me, looking at odds in a smart bow tie to compliment the boxing wounds on his face. He stood next to a warm fire in a carved, stone hearth, staring into the flames. Rose curtsied and gave me an encouraging look before vacating the room. Edward turned toward me, an expression of longing chasing out his vacant stare.

"Luella—Ms. Winthrop," he said, "you look stunning." He looked embarrassed. I had never seen him embarrassed before. I found it endearing. I felt the misgivings over my appearance begin to melt away the more he looked at me.

"Thank you. You clean up quite well yourself. I've never worn anything so elegant in my life," I confessed. Or daring, for that matter. I had been self-conscious of the way I filled out the gown he had chosen for me. I had never considered myself a true beauty, always relying more on my ability to turn a phrase and make men feel comfortable around me.

In fact, I had used a frumpy appearance as a measuring stick in the past. My father had taught me that a man who spent too much attention on outward beauty wasn't worthy of my affection, anyway. But now, I hoped so badly that he found me pretty. If my beauty was ever worth anything, let it be tonight.

"It looks like it was made for you," he said. I blushed before accepting the drink he offered in a crystal glass. "They have held dinner for us."

"Thank you," I repeated, unsure of what else to say. There were a thousand questions I wanted to ask him and a thousand answers I wanted to explain to him, but I couldn't find the words to start.

"I'm sorry that I had to bring you here under such difficult conditions. It's not how I would have liked to introduce you to my home life." He looked pained and uncomfortable. I wanted to apologize as well, but for what? I was the woman that got his father killed. I had already said the word sorry what felt like a hundred times, each one sounding more hollow than the last.

"How are you managing with everything?" I asked as delicately as I could. He scoffed.

"As well as can be expected, I suppose. I may still be in shock. I don't know. None of it seems real. I'm half-expecting my father to join us for dinner in a matter of minutes. It's difficult to fathom that—well, that he's gone."

"Is there anything I can do?" I asked. He looked at me with the same feeling of longing I sensed from him when I entered the room. My question felt pre-drafted, formulaic, but I held my breath, hoping for an answer.

"You have already been such a support to me," he replied.

"A support?" I couldn't believe what he was saying. He held up his hand to stop my reply.

"I know. I know, but even in spite of it. I don't know why or how, but just being around you gives me strength." I moved closer to him and took his hand. The generous fire gave me a warm feeling all over.

"My presence is the least I can offer you."

He leaned toward me, and suddenly, we were very close. He looked down into my face and I up into his beautiful grey eyes, allowing myself to give in to them. They were like two magnets, pulling me closer, closing the space between us, space that I had considered insurmountable. If I were to kiss him, would it ease the pain he felt? I would give him a thousand kisses if it were true. I forgot how to breathe. The fire danced on his eyes like glossy fireballs.

Fireballs.

Images of that night in Bram's yurt came flashing back to me in fragmented order. I could almost see myself in the tent, at that rickety table, penning the story that would kill Edward's father. I could almost see myself writing feverishly, recklessly, playing God.

I could not let myself kiss this man.

I pulled back and turned to study the flames. They licked up at the air in random and reliable flickers. The flames held nothing for me but a reminder of the kiss I just ran from and the indelible memories of Bram. Toss a paper in the fire, watch the magic happen. Wasn't that the way of it? My past lived in a frame of stupidity. It hung in my mind like a bad painting. I recoiled from the flames and searched for something, anything, else to talk about.

"This is a beautiful rug," I said. Sometimes, I disgust myself.

"Are you alright?" Edward asked.

I wasn't alright, but I couldn't complain or unburden myself to him. I couldn't imagine what dark feelings swirled around him. Unburdening myself now while he dealt with that would be so selfish. I'd have thought that he'd feel more settled by asking about the details of my magical folly, but I could not press those details on him. To do so would risk ever repaying him for the countless charities he had bestowed on me. If only he would change his mind and the painful memories that held me prisoner could illuminate him with the knowledge he needed to grieve for his father.

"Do you have anything you want to ask me, Edward?" I said, scrutinizing the hammered metalwork on an old bookcase.

"Ask you?"

"I don't mean to press the issue." I turned but did not look him in the face. "I just thought that maybe I could offer you some degree of closure."

He drank from his glass deeply before gripping the edge of a writing desk near the sofa. I waited for him to speak, trying my best to urge him onward with my expression. He looked at the back of his hand, intently. One side of him was illuminated by dancing firelight, the other by the faint glow of gas lamps from the hall.

"Luella, I—"

"The two of you haven't exhausted your conversation topics already, have you?" Lady Thomas' humming, alto voice cut through the room. She strode forward in her sweeping black gown. "After such a long ride, I mean. Edward, would you pour your mother a glass as well?"

We both instinctively jerked backwards, not for the first time, as if we were two children caught in the larder. Edward sulked over to the bar and poured his mother something from an expensive looking bottle. I busied myself studying an elaborate globe.

"Edward," Lady Thomas said under her breath, "I'm so glad you're here. Since news got out, I can't tell you how many of your father's acquaintances have sent me letters or stopped by to offer condolences. It's exhausting, and I can hardly keep up with it all. It'd be one thing if they were family friends, but I'm talking about men I spent my marriage despising. You know who I mean. All of those brutish personalities that kept your father from me. Now they're trying to cozy up like we've been friends all along."

I noticed Edward's broad shoulders slump a little lower as he handed his mother a glass.

"Well, I'm here now, mother. I'll see what I can do to manage the brunt of the condolences," he said.

"Fortunately, the full story didn't get out into the papers," she went on. I couldn't help but feel like this last comment was directed at me.

"As far as everyone else knows, your father suffered an unfortunate accident. An accident! It's ridiculous."

One of the servants, a tall gangly man I recognized from the front courtyard, entered the room and gave us all a curt bow.

"The dining room can receive you now," he said.

Lady Thomas nodded her approval and swept out of the room, leaving her unfinished glass with the servant. Edward finished what remained in his own glass before putting it down on the table and extending an arm to invite me through the door. I curtsied and followed his mother, regretting that I could not continue my conversation alone with Edward. I did not look forward to dinner with her. I couldn't help but feel this woman was harboring an increasing dislike toward me. All the same, I found myself in the dining room, looking at the end of a long table, built for twelve, dressed for three. The room, like the rest of the house, had been updated with gas lighting, but lit candelabras stood on the table, adding ambience and a sense of intimacy. Ornate mirrors hung on the wall, reflecting the light in eternal patterns.

Their servant pulled out a chair for me, and I found myself sitting directly across from Lady Thomas.

"Mother, why don't you sit here at the head of the table?" Edward said.

"Don't be ridiculous. My son, you've inherited the estate. It's your household and your table."

"It's a little early to be talking about inheritances, don't you think?"

"Not at all, if that's what it will take to get you to come home and live with me."

"I don't want to discuss this now, mother." There was no mistaking the tension between the two Thomases. I was instantly defensive over Edward, but I couldn't deny that she was asking questions to which I also wanted an answer. He had taken me out of the city to his home, but I had assumed that his plan was to go back to work at the force. Now, after seeing what he really was giving up to be there, and the state of his inheritance and widowed mother, I wondered whether the Steely-Eyed Detective might be hanging up his hat.

The first course arrived, a soup made of potatoes, cream, and a rich cheese. Edward and I ate in silence while Lady Thomas prattled on about how difficult it was to keep the estate up these months prior to winter or how agricultural and textile productions in town were experiencing a significant low. To hear her speak, even the trees in the area needed some serious "doing up." How one might "do up" a tree escaped my simple-minded city-dweller's mind.

Edward ate his meal stoically. I did my best to look polite and gracious but felt almost incapable of appeasing his mother. It didn't take much for me to understand that I was her son's guest, not hers, and while Edward was quietly brooding, I couldn't do much but try to emulate the etiquette I had read about in books and novels. I tried desperately to remember the research I had done to write my boring articles for Langley's but to no avail.

When we had finished a beautifully roasted duck and the plates had been cleared away, Edward's mother got on to the real business.

"Now, humor your dear mother. I know you're tired from your traveling, but we really have to address the memorial. It's coming in a few days."

"What memorial?" Edward asked, breaking his silence and folding his arms.

"It's customary for a family to grieve and bury its lost members."

"You can't intend to have a funeral."

"I most certainly intend that."

"He hung himself," Edward went on.

"His acquaintances don't know that," Lady Thomas said through pursed lips. "We have to keep up our appearances."

"They will in a few days. Mother, these things have a way of getting out."

"They'd better not. You don't trust your own fellow officers?"

"Even in the tightest groups, scandals like this seep through the cracks. If we grieve the man like he died honorably, we'll look like we've been taken in and draw attention to a disgraceful death." Edward leaned forward now, both hands on the table. I could nearly see his pulse starting on his neck.

"Your father was a well-known and respected individual. If we don't hold a service, we'll all but confirm his distasteful end." She choked on the last words, as if she couldn't yet decide whether her husband's suicide was a betrayal or a tragedy. "Enough. I'm holding a service, and you will attend. It's time that you get on with a serious plan for your life."

"Our first dinner together, and you're already throwing this at me. You are being uncivil toward our guest," he said with deeply furrowed brows. I was suddenly quite conscious of how my hands were positioned. How was I supposed to respond to that comment?

"You can't bring a woman home to shield you from the reality of our situation. I wouldn't care if we had a hundred guests; it's time for you to step up. If you won't do it, I'll do it for you. Your father's acquaintances will be attending the memorial, as well as other families who mean to pay their respects, many with beautiful daughters."

I nearly choked on my wine. Edward's face flushed a deep red, and I buried my eyes in the lace table runner, silently counting the number of threads in its cross-stitched pattern of rabbits.

"Good heavens, mum. Would you give me even a few hours or a night's sleep before you've married me off?" He pushed his chair out aggressively and walked out of the room, leaving me with the most formidable woman I'd ever met in my life. My stern neighbor, Mrs. Crow, seemed like a turtledove in comparison.

I looked after him, wondering whether I might not just follow him right out. His mother stared at me with an expression that showed plainly her belief that I was the reason her son was not eager to marry anyone else. Her inquisitorial gaze made my blood boil and filled my chest with unbridled excitement at the same time. She was meddlesome and controlling, and Edward had been through enough. But, she accused me of a monopoly on her son's affection, and the very fact she accused me of it gave me a shred of hope that it was true. Maddening flattery.

"Edward always has been a gentleman," she said. "Especially as he grew up and became friendlier with his young female acquaintances, even if they did try to persuade him to behave ungentlemanly." She let words drip off her tongue like venom. I didn't need a lesson in etiquette to know she was trying to make me jealous.

Fool of a woman. Who cared what Edward had done before meeting me? What a peculiar tactic, a noble lady trying to convince a girl from the east side that her son was morally unworthy of marriage. Still, while the substance of her strategy fell harmless, the attempt stung me adequately for her purpose. I felt my anger rising. It wasn't proportionate to her comments, but I was tempted to dive in. It would feel so good just to let go. I knew this had been building, that I had repressed it for days. I had been plugging the top of a volcano, and its rumblings gave me sweet, devilish power.

"He always played the gentleman with me as well, even if our relationship made my former fiancé uncomfortable," I replied nastily. Let her digest that. Let her think on her son's behavior while working in the city. Her slack lips betrayed the slightest twitch, letting me know my fletchlett had hit its mark. I hoped it hurt.

No. This wasn't like me. A charitable and deep-feeling part of my heart chimed in. This woman had just lost her husband, whom she loved despite the distance between them. I couldn't imagine her current pain. How could I add to it like this? I would not be a grotesque monster. I would not open that dark door. Was it not enough to take her husband; must I also take her son? I clenched my core and my fists. I needed to fight the rancor.

"You're no beauty," she responded, directly. "You are, of course, invited to the memorial. It should be quite illuminating. You'll see what caliber of women you're up against."

Her words were like a battering ram. Each one weakened my resolve. The volcano took back over and brewed nasty thoughts. How dare she insult me to my face? I didn't care who she was. I looked down at the table, trying to control my breathing. My eye caught a fine, silver spoon. It was the perfect size to hurt but leave no lasting damage. Why not prove her right and show her what caliber woman she'd dined with?

What was I thinking? My thoughts flashed to my father, the lessons he'd taught me as a girl. Defuse with kindness. Respond to aggression with love. Give a fixing only to those who deserved it. She was a grieving widow. I would not give into another episode again. I could not. If I were to be angry, let me be angry at the fog and its monster. Let me be angry with the magic that corrupted the memory of my father. I would not allow it to corrupt anything more. I pushed my fingernails into the palm of my hand. I wouldn't give in.

But, she was a grieving widow that stood in open defiance to what could be certain happiness. Not a spoon, there were other ways.

She smirked at me, sizing me up like a lioness and trying her best to make it apparent that any future I might have with Edward would be plagued by her every sabotage.

Bid me do, I will obey. My thoughts flashed to the crimson inkwell, and scenes of traceless interference played in my imagination. The fog monster had been so confident that it could change my life, bring to pass my desires without anyone else being the wiser.

What might this woman look like on a sick bed?

This wasn't me.

"I'm very sorry for your loss, Lady Thomas," I said, boring a hole in the table with my eyes.

She stood and walked slowly, dangerously across the room. I

couldn't breathe well. The corset was suffocating.

"Go home," she said. "You don't deserve my son."

Maybe it was the boldness in her voice, or because she had given voice to the inner critic I knew to be true, but I lost the battle. The dark door inside of me swung wide open.

Critics are evil monsters.

I stormed out of the room.

Chapter Thirty-Four

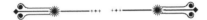

Two Dormant Trees

I practically sprinted to my room, trying to outrun Lady Thomas' accusations and my own venomous thoughts. There was so much anger, and its thick roots took hold inside of me. An evil plan formed from within, not from my own mind, but from somewhere else.

The ink inside of Bram's gift was magical. I was certain of that, though he had never told me so. I was also convinced that, in my last meeting with the fog monster, I had grown more powerful than Bram ever was. He may have understood more about magic, but I had a working relationship with some type of magical entity, an entity that wanted me as a partner in bringing out more magic. There was a portal inside my heart to that effect, and letting the illness take over, giving into it was the key.

My idea was plain and simple, albeit malicious and maniacal. I would use the ink to write the end of Lady Thomas' story. The fog creature would effect my wishes. It couldn't be simpler. With her out of the way, I had a straighter path to Edward.

I reached the door to my bedroom but could not bring myself to push it open. Once I walked inside, the inkwell waited. This door alone separated me from a twisted, evil design.

Open the door. Open it and bid me do.

But, I was afraid of being alone, afraid of what might happen to me. I felt the anger swelling in ways I never had before. It was worse even than when I lashed out at Rebecca.

My insides churned like a forge. I clenched my fists as tightly as I could and hugged my torso, trying to restrain the feelings. I was becoming a monster. I could not take the life of Edward's remaining parent.

He would never know. It could seem so natural. The desire was overwhelming. I collapsed against the closed door. I hated the world. It never gave me anything. I worked and scraped, grit and hay pennies under my fingernails to crawl my way to a semblance of respectability. This world deserved nothing from me. It had stolen my father. It had stolen my mother. They didn't deserve it.

But, Edward didn't deserve the evils the world gave either.

I sunk to my knees, exhausted. Perhaps I could just die here, on this floor, fighting the dark.

Then, I felt a cold breeze call to me from down the hall. A door or window was open somewhere. The air chilled my bare shoulders, giving me goosebumps all the way down my spine. The air felt fresh and real. I wanted to seek it out, escape the musty perfume of the indoors, and breathe cold freedom. The smell of nature and the crisp night worked like smelling salts.

A sapling of strength trickled into my feet. I found the will to get up.

I didn't have to do this. I could close that portal.

One slow step at a time, I made it down the hallway to my right. A set of different portraits stared at me from their canvas addresses. Next to them were oil landscapes. They felt more real in the cold breeze than they did in the warm, fire-lit lounge. In front of me, I could almost see a trail of particles in the air leading down the hall. They flickered and sparkled like moon dust. As I inched forward, the particles filled me and made war against the dark magic.

My name is Luella Winthrop. My father loved me. He loved me enough to trade his life for my future.

I followed the trail of particles, craving clarity, craving the sweet relief of a clean conscience. Somehow, I knew this trail led to redemption. At the end of the trail was potential and meaning.

The fog creature had never replicated my father in my dreams. Yes, I saw his image, but in no dream had his spirit been as present as it was in these particles of magic, floating in the air.

I pushed down the hallway and around the corner, where I found lightly billowing drapes framing an open set of glass double doors wrought in wood and iron. Beyond it lay a large balcony with potted trees already dormant for the winter. The trail of particles led out, past the balcony, into the night air. It led me on.

But, next to the trail, between the dormant trees, Edward stood gripping the railing and looking out at the winter sky.

He looked so troubled. My heart went out to him. The trail faded from view like spots after looking directly into a gas light.

I thought about the sharp, bright-eyed detective I met only a couple of months ago. He seemed so different now. Older, maybe. A part of me didn't want to disturb him. I felt I had caused enough damage, wreaked enough chaos in his life already. But, I could not resist the urge to help him. If there was anything I could do, I wanted to make myself available to help him. Besides, I could not shake the hope that he might help me as well.

I walked on to the balcony and stood by his side, looking out at the stars as well. I had never seen so many before. A sight like that was enough to remind that God was plausible, perhaps even probable.

"Please excuse my mother," he said. "She is under significant stress." His plea shot pangs of guilt into my heart. I had not excused her. I had almost assaulted her with cutlery.

"Perhaps we are all a little tired," I suggested with a sigh. He looked at me and started taking off his jacket. "Please don't trouble yourself. I'm actually enjoying the air." He hesitated before easing his jacket over his shoulders again. It was true though. The crisp winter air was having a positive effect on my mood.

"Then, I must not allow you to remain out for too long."

I nodded.

"I should apologize for my own behavior as well," he added. "I brought you here knowing full well that this reunion was not likely to be a happy one."

"You're both grieving your father."

He turned back to the night sky. "I guess all roads lead me back there, don't they?"

"It gets a little easier with time." I thought about my own father. Easier wasn't exactly the right word. It never felt easier, but I certainly became better at carrying it. Here I was, more than a decade later, and I still missed him so much. I carried him with me everywhere.

"You lost your father?"

"When I was quite young. But, I still remember him, and I hear him sometimes, when I can quiet my thoughts. He was a good man." Good was an understatement. My father had opened the world to me with that singular gift. Now, even the poorest in Dawnhurst learned to read. But, he lived in a different world. He was an outlier. I can only imagine the looks the governess got as she made her way to our house in the east side the few times a week she came.

"How did he die?"

"Fever," I said, looking down from the stars and into the dark forests over the walls of the estate. "Like so many others. I often wonder if there wasn't more we could have done." I shivered.

"It is natural to wonder as much," Edward said. "I've been wondering the same since Cooper broke the news. Could I have prevented it?"

"But, you couldn't have," I explained, putting a hand on his arm. He stared at it.

"According to you."

He still didn't understand. Perhaps he didn't believe me. I shut my eyes tightly, rueful of the pain I had already caused him, conscious of all the turmoil unanswered questions can bring.

"Edward, there was nothing you could have done to prevent this," I insisted.

"I'm a detective, aren't I?" he asked. "Weren't you the reporter that wrote up the story of the Steely-Eyed Detective and the Fog Man? I saw the fog kill a man. I lived through it, and I did nothing to investigate it. I just treated it like a common theft."

"What could you have done? You're not a wizard."

"I don't know. Something at least." He turned his body to face me in the dark. "It was my negligence that caused my father's death. You ask me what I could have done? I could have noticed a pattern of strange happenings reported by the woman I let into my heart. I turned a blind eye when I should have pressed you on it."

I could not tell with what energy he looked on me. Was he angry? Was he finally ready to blame me for all that happened?

"You can ask now. I will tell you anything you want to know," I said. The cold was constricting my lungs. Between the temperature and the corset Rose had fastened for me, breathing did not come easily. She had said this was as loose as she could fix it. I had a fleeting thought about all the noble ladies of the past who mistook the side effects of their gowns for romantic butterflies.

"It's all too late, now. No good can come of any of it."

"You could find closure. You could recognize that it was completely out of your hands. Please, Edward, ask me something. Let me help you."

He turned away and paced to the other side of the balcony, where he stood, motionless and quiet for another spell, before turning back to me. The dark obscured his features, making it even more difficult for me to read him.

"Don't tempt me," he said, his voice low.

"Tempt you? I'm only trying to ease your pain." And my own. I needed him as a full partner to fight my own battles.

"It's just that—I mean the problem is, I love you, Luella."

His words knocked whatever breath was left out of my lungs in one fell exhale. Edward Thomas loved me. In spite of everything. I wanted to believe him. My heart flew to him. My head spun. But, this couldn't be right. He was affected by his father's death. His judgment was cloudy. He was drunk on the wine from dinner. He was angry at his mother. Anything. There must be some reason he was lying to me, to himself.

"Edward—"

"Can you imagine what it must be like to hear the woman you love is tangled in the questionable death of your own father? It's tearing me apart."

Finally, he was speaking plainly to me, and what a bittersweet brew he offered. His words stung like poisoned barbs, but at least it was not a veiled patchwork I had to try to see through. It was too much to feel all at once. The confession of his love and how much that pained him. I had nothing to offer him, nothing but myself, and there was only one way to give it to him.

"Let me explain everything to you. It will help you understand."

"I can't hear it," he said, his voice breaking. "Oh, I want to so badly. I want to know all about you. I'd love nothing more than to hear any detail that would let me further acquit you of this wrong in my mind. Not to mention the joy I would feel knowing the degree of trust we shared. The very fact that you are willing to explain it all fills me with hope."

I remained silent, waiting, dreading what came next.

"But—I can't hear it. I can't tempt myself with the bitterness or jealousy. The details of your experience with that man from the carnival, with my father's death, they could be enough to overcome me altogether. What unhuman passion might seize me? I could chase after that man with an idea to kill him. Or, worse, what if some detail unfolded that put in my way a stumbling block too much for my human capacity to forgive? Don't you see? I want to love you. I want the details to come out slowly, over the course of a lifetime, one little piece at a time, digestible, beatable, with you beside me."

I felt an enormous lump in my throat. He wanted me to hurt him for a lifetime, so that he could give me all of himself. I had not experienced such pure love since my father's passing. I had dreamed of falling in love since I was a little girl, since that hole formed in me, but I never could have understood it until this moment. Love wasn't opening parcels at Christmas. Love was this, two wounded souls together, aboard a ship in a storm, mending the sails as best they knew how.

"What are you saying?" I asked, blinking away tears that came out unnaturally hot against my now frigid cheeks. He walked closer to me and scooped me into his arms. My heart hammered against my chest. He looked down at me, and he was close enough now for me to make out his big, pleading eyes in painstaking detail.

"I want you beside me, forever. I don't want to take all of this alone, running the estate and rebuilding after my father. I don't want to face a day of this without you, and I know you think that your mistakes killed my father, and maybe they did, but I know you could not have done so intentionally. I want you to bear me up while I go through this and marry me afterwards."

The stars above me shook. Tears flowed down my face and dipped on to my collarbones, creating chilly little riverbeds on my skin.

"You can't mean it," I stammered.

"I'm quite sure I do."

He kissed me then, chasing out any feeling of cold on my shoulders or lingering anger in my breast. I felt the warmth spread across my chest, in my fingers, on my neck, and in every part of me. I felt everything crashing down at my feet, all doubts, fears, or resistance. I was swept up into this beautiful paradise. I walked into the vision, and I could see myself happy there, on a beautiful hilltop overlooking the lake, my head resting on Edward's shoulder, serene and peaceful.

We pulled apart, and I looked up into his eyes again, breathing lightly, afraid I would wake up.

I didn't say anything, but he rested his forehead on mine.

"Please forgive me," he said. "Technically, I think you're still engaged."

"Don't remind me," I said.

"Then you aren't still loyal to Mr. Livingston?" he asked, his eyebrows raised hopefully.

I shook my head. I was still processing the betrayal Byron had rendered me, but I was confident that portion of my life had concluded. Edward tightened his grip on my waist, belaying his excitement.

"And do you have a response for me?"

I wanted to say yes. I didn't have words to express how much I wanted the life he had proposed. I wanted to stay with him, become his wife, run the estate, even deal with his mother, but I couldn't.

"I hope you can determine my answer by my actions," I said. I was evading a response. What was wrong with me? My heart still raced being so close to him, absorbing the scent of him, feeling his warmth.

"You do have a way with words," he said amidst a boyish grin. "My sweet Luella, it feels so good to smile again, at least for a moment."

I touched the cuts on his face tenderly and kissed him again. Let him smile. Let me forget the looming horizon for a moment.

I had never seen him so vulnerable. There was something touching about the simplicity of this brief reprieve from his grief. To Byron, I had often felt like a trophy, a trophy he was delighted to have, but a trophy nonetheless. Edward made me feel like fresh water. But, I could not be open with him while he was in such a tender state. For tonight, at least, it would have to be enough to bask in his kisses and get a small taste of what a simpler life would have been.

We stood there on the balcony for a long time. After a while, I consented to accept his jacket to protect me from the cold, but before long, the safe comfort of his arms reminded me of how tired I felt. The excitement of that morning and the long journey to Fernmount had taken a toll on me. As much as I wanted the moment to last, I fought to keep my eyes open. Still, my time with Edward had accomplished a miracle. I no longer feared an outbreak tonight. I would be safe from myself until the morning.

Edward escorted me back to my room, where Rose waited for me.

After a heartfelt goodnight, he left me in her able hands. She helped me out of my evening dress and into a nightgown. I fell asleep amid conflicting emotions and thoughts about inkwells.

Chapter Thirty-Five

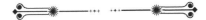

Skylark

I woke early the next morning after a tumultuous sleep. I had tossed and turned most of the night, trying to make sense of rich detectives, grieving widows, and magical hallucinations. The early dawn light filtered through the blinds. I lay on my side, staring at the crimson inkwell sitting on the nightstand.

Had I really almost used it to do Edward's family more harm?

I wanted to dream again of the downy fog monster to ask it my burning question. I wasn't sure if my last encounter with it had been real, but Rose's recital of its peculiar way of communicating had me on edge. Then last night, as I fell asleep, its words came back to me, words like a dark poison. Could I trust Edward's confession of love, or had it been affected by magic? The monster had promised that I would not be able to tell the difference. I wanted answers. I wanted clarity. I wanted to know if I could accept Edward's proposal.

Instead, I had dreamed of my real father and mother. We were at a small park in the city, enjoying some bread and cheese my mother had packed for lunch. It was a calm spring day. I ran among the rushes and laughed when I found butterflies and chased small birds. My father clapped his hands and kissed my mother. It felt like a memory more than a dream. As a result, I woke before the dawn and laid in bed thinking about him. His memory lived on in me through the lessons he taught me. On this particular morning, I tried my best to piece together things he had said so long ago about love. I wished so badly that he were still here.

When I thought of my father, though, I sadly felt more confident in my decision not to accept Edward's proposal outright.

First, he was in no state to make a decision like that. He had just fought with his mother, recently lost his father, and had decided to violate the law by harboring the fugitive his entire station pursued. I simply could not trust his faculties at present. I would feel like I was taking advantage of him in a time of weakness.

Second, the inkwell made me mistrust whether Edward had even exercised his own free will when confessing his feelings toward me or if they even were his own true feelings. I thought about the peculiar attractions I had felt toward Bram, how that first night he had so easily lured me into his yurt. Those feelings confused me even now. Had he cast some type of enchantment over me? Who knew what he had in that chest of his? The meddler. That's what the downy fog monster had called him. That monster had a mind of its own. Had it cast some similar enchantment on Edward as it had hinted to me?

I could never live and happily love him if I knew, deep down, there was a chance I was living a farce. I couldn't bear knowing that first I killed his father then bewitched him. What would I become?

But, there was something even deeper than magic that kept me from Edward.

I took a deep breath and pulled my blanket off me. It was still early, and the room was very cold. Through the curtains, the early light of dawn was creeping through the window. I pulled them back and looked out at the dreamland that surrounded Fernmount. A heavy fog settled on the meadows and forests around, painting everything in light, muted colors. It was like a painting. I wanted to live it. Out there, somewhere, lay the end of that trail of magical particles I saw last night, and what a wonderful trail it was. Simply following in its path had been enough to dispel the darkness in me. It led me to Edward and beckoned me even beyond. I wanted to see if I could find it again.

I found a thick robe and wrapped myself up in it before putting on some shoes and sneaking out the door. There was no sign of Rose. She must have still been sleeping or attending to some other need of the house. Perhaps she was preparing Lady Thomas' wardrobe.

I made my way through the house. Everything was quiet. Somewhere, I imagined the servants should be stirring and preparing for the day, at least preparing dinner, but I did not encounter a soul. I found a door near the back of the house. It was less elaborate and heavy than the front door, perhaps a servants' entrance. I slipped through and walked across a small courtyard, breathing in the fresh, crisp air. It shocked my lungs. I hoped it would shock my mind as well. The courtyard gravel crunched beneath my feet as I cleared the gate and strode into the meadow. The grass had yellowed, but there hadn't yet been a heavy snowfall. It stood tall but parted easily as I explored the fog. Soon, it obscured the view behind me, and I could see maybe fifty meters in any direction. One side trees, the other meadow.

The last time I had felt like this had been something like a dream. That encounter had brought nothing but questions. Now, I sought clarity. I sought the road to peace. I squinted my eyes, trying to find moon dust in the air.

A few months ago, my life had been so normal. So many terrible things had happened since. But then again, some good had come of it. Perhaps I never would have found the courage to leave Byron, and I knew now that marrying him may have been the biggest mistake of my life. Anna, too, had come away from my mistakes with a secured prospect with Jacob. It was easy to get carried away justifying regret with silver linings.

I reached out my hands and brushed the plants around me, breathing in another crisp lungful of air and smelling nature. It smelled so different than Dawnhurst. It smelled more like home, somehow. Like my father. The air was peaceful. I felt like I could spend every morning in this spot. If I married Edward, I would make it a ritual, maybe even ride out with a book and think. What a wonderful life it would be.

But, I couldn't stay here. No. I wished the field and the morning sun could have changed my mind, but something quiet, so unlike the voice of the magical anger inside of me, spurred me on and solidified my decision. I did not know what lay ahead, but I was sure of something. Whatever had saved me from the darkness last night led past Edward, not to him.

Even if my balcony date with Edward had been nothing short of a fairy tale. Even if his eyes were warm and his kiss gentle. Even if I had felt so safe in his arms. It's so easy to pine after the roads we pass as destiny whisks us along. This beautiful glimpse of a new life felt like the beginning of a whole different story, one that I hoped to read one day. But, for the time being, Fernmount was not my final destination.

I felt like a woman looking over her burned down home the morning after a fire. I had spent my whole life trying to make something of my education. My father had sacrificed for it, and I owed him a debt, but the fog creature had it wrong. My father didn't care if I won the Golden Inkwell. He didn't care if I became a writer at all.

Perhaps he just wanted to show me that my potential to achieve wonderful things had no limit. I had learned to read and write, not to win prestige for our family name, but to become something more than I could be before, to inspire others to reach for the same.

Fame and recognition was not the goal; it was an obstacle.

At the end of that trail lay the woman my father wanted me to become. That was a woman who could deserve an Edward Thomas. That was a woman who could deserve an Anna Winthrop.

Or was it Anna Rigby by now?

The gentle sound of horses' hooves on the soft earth stirred me from my musings. I looked around for a place to hide. I wasn't eager to make my first acquaintance with the servants or someone from a nearby town while wearing my nightgown and robe, but there was nowhere to go. The grass wasn't even long enough to hide me if I had laid down.

I didn't have long to rue my lot, though. Through the mist, I saw Edward's gallant figure on horseback. I breathed a sigh of relief before remembering the news I would have to give him. Maybe I would have preferred running into someone from town after all.

He slowed to a trot before stopping ten meters from me and dismounting. Apparently, he had an itch to get out this morning as well. Under his riding coat was a hastily donned shirt, untucked over his trousers and boots.

"This is a surprise," he said while he got down.

"I'm afraid I'm a bit of a dreamer," I replied. "The picturesque setting you've brought me to has me feeling like a little girl reading her first novel."

He smiled. "For Fernmount's flaws, I never can resist the morning, before the world has woken up, even if it is a little cold."

I nodded and folded my arms. Neither of us spoke, and both of us made random eye contact before recommitting to a thorough examination of the woods or the grass below us. When we did speak, we both went at once, then stopped again.

"Please, you first," Edward said. I shook my head. I knew my words weren't going to be welcome to him. I wanted to savor his affection for as long as I could.

"Very well, then," he continued. "I wanted to apologize to you about last night. My behavior at dinner was unsupportable. I hope you don't believe that I often quarrel with my mother that way."

"Of course not," I said. Though, secretly, I would hardly blame him if he did.

"Second, I hope that I didn't take advantage of you while you were in a vulnerable state. I'm only now registering that your day must have been the epitome of shock. I can't imagine what it must be like to leave your home at the drop of a hat and under such turbulent circumstances. I fear the kisses I stole from you were unjustly gained."

I wanted to tell him the only thing that was unjust about his kiss was that it hadn't happened weeks ago and lasted much longer.

"I also pray that you don't think I said what I did last night because of my own troubled mind. I wish I could have told you sooner. I lacked courage, and I found it easier to postpone, perhaps indefinitely, considering I believed you to be engaged."

"You have so many regrets for a man who claims to be in love," I said with a sad smile.

"I think I'm discovering that love is regret. It's regret for every imperfection and missed opportunity."

I walked closer to him and took his hands.

"You do have a way with words."

He laughed, a scoff, but the warmth from his hands radiated through me. This wasn't going to be easy.

"Edward, I'm afraid I have a regret of my own." I felt his hands go limp.

"Please, Luella," he stuttered. "If this has to do with my father, respect the wishes I expressed last night."

I put my hand to his face. "You told me you wanted the truth piece by piece over a lifetime. Accept this first piece as a promise that more will follow." He looked puzzled and, for the first time since I'd met him, afraid. I put my forehead to his, like we'd done the night before.

"I can't stay here."

He exhaled forcefully before taking in quick breaths, as if he was going to say something and stopped himself several times. Finally, he stepped back.

"Is it my mother?"

"No, though I wouldn't be surprised if she were happy to see me leave. And it's not you either. You are the man I've dreamed of since I was a little girl. You regret not sharing your feelings with me earlier. Well, I regret any choice I ever made to separate us. Because of those choices I made, I have to separate from you now."

"I don't understand," he said.

"I don't expect you to." I searched for words. He didn't want to know everything, but it was time for at least one truth to come out. "I'm not well."

"We can send for a doctor," he said quickly, desperately.

"There's no doctor that can help. It's one of the byproducts of that horrible magic. It's like some type of parasite. I constantly fight a feeling of rage, something that was never there before. At times, it becomes too strong for me, and I lash out in terrible episodes. Rebecca can confirm this."

"What kind of episodes?"

"It's like I've lost complete control. I—well, once I attacked Rebecca."

"Good heavens." He let go of my hands. Why that? He didn't have to draw away from me in disgust.

"Forgive me, Edward," I willed myself on, "but similar feelings nearly surfaced last night after you left the dining room table."

His mouth hung open, and he searched the air around me, as if he were inspecting my aura. I wondered what he saw, what combinations and fears his mind concocted.

"Is there no cure?" he asked.

"None that I know of. But, Bram, the man Rebecca mentioned from the carnival, has promised me he will find one." At the mention of Bram's name, Edward turned around and rubbed down his horse's neck. I jolted forward, positioning myself between him and the animal, trying to force him to stay with me until he heard it all. "He has studied these things for many years, and he believes he can find something." I placed my hand on his forearm.

"I need to find him, so I can assist his efforts before the malady takes me. It's getting worse all the time."

He turned and walked several paces from me before turning around with a grimace.

"So, you have to leave me in order to be with this other man," he surmised.

"I need to be cured, so I can be yours. Completely yours," I said. "I can't have this hanging over me. You deserve better than that, and I want to give more to you." I walked after him. I grabbed his reluctant hands and fought my way into his eyeline.

"How long will it take?" he asked.

"I have no way of knowing. A month? A year?"

"How can I believe this?"

"One piece at a time," I said. He hung his head, the weight of his own words pulling him down, but I felt his hands slowly find their strength again. "Edward, please. Trust me."

He kissed my hand awkwardly before letting go and stepping formally backward.

"So begins our journey, then." His smile was so sad, I wanted to kiss it off his face forever. I stepped toward him. He stepped backward. "If it's as you say, it's time for action."

Now it was my turn to hang my head. What did I expect? Perhaps I was just tired of people telling me what I tried so hard to ignore. I nodded. When I looked back up at him, I saw the man I met months ago. Detective Edward Thomas. Fearless. Strong-willed. Powerful. Inspiring.

Seeing him there, strong in his vulnerability, standing beside his horse, shrouded in mist, made me feel for the first time in a long, long time that I wasn't alone. With him behind me, I felt hope that we could conquer this. That we would conquer this.

"What do you need from me?" he asked.

An hour later, he was leading a horse, packed with clothing and supplies, to the edge of the property.

"I wish you would reconsider," he said. He had spent the past hour trying to convince me to let him come along. We had run back to the house, quietly, to prepare everything. He found Rose, but no one else knew a thing about my departure, the mysterious woman that came to Fernmount for a night.

"I insist that it is unwise," I responded. I was dressed now like a common woman from the nearby village, a loose, hanging white dress, cinched at the waist, a long coat. My sister would have cringed, turning her nose up at the aesthetic style, but Rose had been kind enough to lend it to me. I had promised her I would return it in one piece. As wonderful as the gown from the night before was, I felt much more at home like this. We'd also scrounged up a large hooded cape, better to hide my face.

"I disagree."

"Please, don't tempt me," I said. It was hard enough to be the strong-willed naysayer. If he pressed it, I would give in. I was filled with fear for the road ahead. I was a city girl in foreign territory, trying to unravel a mystery larger than I could understand. But, his mother needed him, and after my near outbreak the night before and my unchristian animosity toward her, I couldn't deprive her of her son's strength and support.

We arrived at the end of the dirt road we'd been walking. Clouds overhead blanketed the sky, filling the air with the warmth of a brewing storm. Behind us, on the hill above, Fernmount stood like a beacon, inviting me back. It was the most beautiful place I had ever been, the place where I had received the best news of my life. I would come back. I would return this dress to Rose. I would spend my life dedicated to Edward's happiness. This was just the first step on that journey.

"Your mother needs you. You need to be here for your father's memorial."

He nodded grimly and handed me the reigns.

"Stay to the road. Don't travel at night. There's a man in the village named William who is a dear friend of mine. He will harbor you. Take a fake name. Cooper will still be searching for you."

He grabbed me by the shoulders and looked into my eyes intensely.

"Be smart and safe. Come home to me," he concluded.

I did my best to nod, the weight of farewell crashing down with the reality of the situation. I could be brave like him. I could at least try.

We embraced then. I squeezed him so hard, hard enough to make it last for however long we'd be apart. Letting go was the end, and I wasn't ready. I could not have possibly prepared myself for a goodbye.

I wasn't sure how much time passed before he pulled away. He helped me onto my horse and gave it a slap. I turned my head backward to watch as long as I dared. The tears came now, quiet, peaceful, and inevitable. Edward stood on the road, a sentinel, a fixture of the house. I would return to this.

When he had grown smaller, and I could no longer distinguish him from the other features of the landscape, I looked ahead at the road to come. I could see the sun cresting over the hilly horizon. I heard the birds and breathed in the world. A skylark passed overhead. The world called its great challenge to me in every blade of grass. I was finally ready to respond honestly, and faintly, ever so faintly, I saw the magical particles on the trail ahead of me. I was headed toward my father.

I was only on the road a half-hour before I heard a horse behind me at full gallop.

"I'm sorry, but this is ridiculous," Edward said, pulling up beside me. "My mother will have to manage."

Thank you for reading The Crimson Inkwell

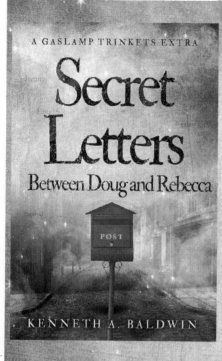

Thanks for reading.

If you enjoyed the book, please don't hesitate to leave a review to let others know.

Made in the USA
San Bernardino, CA
20 May 2019